For PLEASURE or WORSE

KARISSA KINWORD

Cover artist: Ink and Laurel

Editor: On The Same Page Editing

Formatter: Grace Elena Formatting

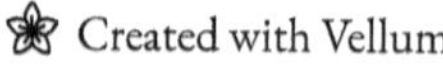 Created with Vellum

For Pauly and Jo-Ann, I hope wherever you are you're reading to one another

playlist

Jackie and Wilson - Hozier
Lost In The Light - Bahamas
Photo ID - Remi Wolf, Dominic Fike
Paint The Town Red - Doja Cat
Seven - Jung Kook, Latto
Never Be Like You - Flume, kai
Dark Red - Steve Lacy
Wild Ones - Bahari
Sure Thing - Miguel
Kiss Me - Sixpence None the Richer
My Type - Saint Motel
Talk Too Much - COIN
Mess Is Mine - Vance Joy
Northern Attitude - Noah Kahan, Hozier
High - Stephen Sanchez
Bathroom - Montell Fish
Devil Eyes - Hippie Sabotage
Pink Rover - Scene Queen

In My Mind - Dynoro, Gigi D'Agostino
Funny Thing - Thundercat
OXOX - Dutch Melrose, Lost Boy
Feels Like (La La La) - Repiet, Julia Kleijn
Silver Lining - Mt. Joy
Sweater Weather - The Neighbourhood
Hostage - Billie Eilish
Meet Me in the Hallway - Harry Styles
Daddy Issues - The Neighbourhood, Syd
Interlude: I'm Not Angry Anymore - Paramore
Turning Page - Sleeping At Last
Only - RYX
Soaked - Shy Smith
Lose Control - Teddy Swims
Home - Good Neighbours
Music Sounds Better With You - Stardust, Benjamin Diamond,
Alan Braxe, Thomas Bangalter
Fake ID (Coke & Rum Remix) - Riton, Kah-Lo, GEE LEE
Turn off the Lights - Chris Lake, Alexis Roberts
Boyz N Da Club - Shermanology
Pump It Up - Endor
Grip - Baby Tate
Pretty Boy - The Neighbourhood
The Best Part - anamē, gardenstate, Bien
Hard Times - Paramore
MILLION DOLLAR BABY (VHS) - Tommy Richman
BIRDS OF A FEATHER - Billie Eilish
Bellyache - Billie Eilish
Boys - Lizzo
Misses - Dominic Fike
Bulletproof - La Roux, GAMPER & DADONI
RIZZ - AYYBO
Out of My League - Fitz and The Tantrums
10:35 - Tiësto, Tate McRae

chapter one

Natalia

I WAS USED to seeing my fiancé twisted into many revealing and appealing positions. Both of his ankles tied to the metal slats of our bedframe by my old sorority ribbons. Or with lean muscles and corded thighs flexed, one leg up on the mattress to find that perfect angle. Sometimes with his knees spread so far apart in a squat one might ask how his perineum wasn't also doing the splits.

Mateo Duran was the love of my life, my future husband, and the only man I'd ever unironically shouted at to "put a baby in me." Which, for me, meant just as much commitment as the two-carat rock I intentionally left off my finger anytime the two of us were filming sex. Too rough, too much gyrating, too many fluids. We took our safety precautions very seriously.

Today, my brutishly handsome, freckle speckled Special Forces veteran of a man—all two hundred pounds of honed, Florida sun-kissed skin and perfectly shaggy salt-waved hair—was on hands and knees in front of me. His cute, dimpled, boyish asscheeks pinched together so tightly I couldn't even swipe a credit card through the crack.

I had the upper hand. Not only physically—because the plum purple strap-on wagging like a limp noodle and attached to my waist was not going in *my* secret garden this go-around—but mentally as well, because he couldn't see my face as I curled my lips into my teeth and stifled the urge to make yet another joke about the amount of lube Matty brought home in preparation for our regularly scheduled content night.

Just like any other job, Mondays were the beginning of *Mat & Nat's* work week. There was a whiteboard above the computer desk in the corner of the bedroom with sticky notes and user-names. Mateo color-coordinated the calendar: yellow for ideas, orange for things we hadn't tried before, purple for my solo film schedule, blue for his. Green meant someone was paying very handsomely for whatever was on the docket. Red was code for *'film this now, time is ticking.'* Sometimes the colors would over-lap; often the list of requests from our Monday night stream would get so long Mateo would break out a ruler and separate the whiteboard into columns.

Tuesdays were theme night, roleplay. The usual, predictable doctor/patient, rodeo rider/ cowgirl, school teacher/naughty little student. Wednesdays I was the director for my better half, and Thursdays Mateo put on a ridiculous fedora that he insisted made him feel like Tarantino and stood behind the camera for me. Saturdays were reserved for our kinkier crowd—all the bells and whistles and belts and leather were pulled out of a tote under the bed. Sundays were for the Lord, of course. We watched the porn back instead of making it.

But on Fridays we filmed. Tonight's sticky note was triple-tiered: green, red, and orange.

"These have to come apart at some point." I rubbed my palms down Mateo's tailbone and tried to coax his whiter shade of cheeks apart with gentle circles.

"Just...give me a minute, Tally." He reached across the mattress and popped the cap off a near empty bottle of lubricant. "Are we sure this is the right angle? I feel like we might need an adjustment on the lights. It's too yellow; the hue is throwing me off."

Our display screen mimicked us as we turned our heads

slightly to peer into it. Mateo's gold cross dangled from around his neck, glinting in the staged lighting. His naturally tanned Italian skin and chest tattoo glowed under the layer of oil and dew drops of water I misted out of a spray bottle onto his naked body minutes prior. One of our tripods was at the side of the bed, both of us filling the horizontal frame; another was front and center to catch every hanging jaw and eye-rolling second of the cam video we were commissioned to produce by *mommyhole91*.

"This lighting makes your eyes pop, though. It brings out all those burnt orange notes. Too bright and we both get washed out." The lube bottle squelched on its last slimy legs as I emptied it over my faux cock. "I'll do some color correction during editing. Don't worry about it now."

Mateo's fingers sunk into the white duvet and the veins in his forearms bulged thicker. "Maybe being on my back would look better." He adjusted himself, flopping over, so negatively turned on that his dick could be mistaken for a ballpark hot dog stuck to some chewing gum.

I glanced back into the display, my black lace push-up bra and criss-cross harness giving me a wicked power trip, and made an unimpressed sound. "To be honest, this is more submissive than the doggy."

"I'm *not* submissive," Mateo pouted.

"You're *not*," I agreed. "You are a trusting, giving, all encompassing, pleasure seeking, euphoric sexual partner. One who is so kindly fulfilling his woman's erotic dream of pegging her Dom and claiming all of his body as he has claimed hers."

Mateo sat up, our noses brushing. "Wait, that's seriously your erotic dream?"

"No. It's *mommyhole91*'s. They were very detailed in this prompt."

He huffed, throwing himself back into the pillows. A bit of lube dripped off my purple friend and landed on his fleshy one and he flinched. "How much money is this person paying us again?"

I tangled my fingers in the cold metal chain lying on his collarbone and tugged him up by it until his ear met my lips. "Ten."

Mateo's eyes widened, a forced, delighted shiver rippling across his shoulders and lighting a spark underneath him as he promptly flipped back over onto all fours. "Do they want me to bark?"

There's my business partner.

"That pays for all those orchid centerpieces for the cocktail hour," I murmured, leaving tiny kisses on the tail of his spine as my long dark hair hung down and tickled him.

"God, I love when you talk dirty to me."

"Extended open bar," I added.

"Fuck's sake, Tally, I'm hard as a rock right now."

I reached between his legs and tugged experimentally. "Fully stocked bathroom toiletries, with the classy mints and the name brand over-the-counter migraine meds."

"Sweetheart, if you don't stick that Barney dildo in my ass right now I'll do it myself."

I bit his butt playfully and gave it a lazy swat. Tension worked itself out of Mateo's shoulder blades, those big wings of muscle opening up ever so slightly across his back. "If I knew wedding talk could get you going I'd have started sooner."

"It's not the wedding talk, it's the smile on my future wife's face as she spends all our money on lobster crostini and an ice sculpture in the middle of June in Key West."

June. We had six months to plan and execute the most extravagant wedding my mind could muster. The kind of wedding everyone expected from a Russo girl. I'd been planning it in secret in diaries, with scissors and glue from magazine cutouts, and on private Pinterest boards since I was old enough to binge-watch *Say Yes to the Dress.*

My family all had some very strong opinions about our relationship and the pace at which Mateo and I decided to get hitched. Not that anyone had outright said it, but if the phone call to my mother after our Christmas engagement gave any inclination, I'd say "*how pregnant are you?*" doesn't equal an exuberant congratulations.

Not pregnant at all, by the way. Were it any other couple I might understand the hesitation, but Mateo and I were *different*. We *did things* differently. Not just the lube and the sex toys and the getting naked on camera aspect of things, either. From the moment we met last fall my life felt like I had hopped in the passenger seat of a fire red muscle car and stepped on the gas pedal on a never-ending straightaway.

I was a bored, overworked, uninspired *bank teller* when I met Mateo. I'd been doing cam work on the side in secret for years and finally experiencing an ounce of the financial freedom that I needed to feel like I wasn't *entirely* the family disappointment.

My parents wanted me to go to Johns Hopkins—I settled for the other side of the country at Colorado State. They wanted me to study medicine—I majored in art studies. They wanted me to marry an age-appropriate businessman with a trust fund and connections—I climbed the thirty-five-year-old Delta Force veteran with a mouth like a sailor and family construction roots in the Bronx like I was a monkey and he was a fucking banana tree.

We were technically still on our first date, because we hadn't spent a full day apart in over a year. Although against Mateo's nagging, I had kept my apartment across town in Coconut Creek as a buffer of independence...and subliminally to keep my parents from having another reason to give me grief about the path I'd chosen to pursue in life. But when the first of January rolled around, I decided not to renew my lease and instead packed all of my belongings into the bed of Mateo's truck and moved officially into his house where I'd been unofficially living anyway.

This wedding had to be perfect. It had to be everything my parents would expect from my sisters and *more*. So that I could truly show them that I didn't need to be a doctor, or a lawyer, or a multi-million-dollar real estate agent in Florida to afford the finer things in life. I didn't even have to leave the comfort of my own bedroom.

The deep red ambiance lights around us shifted to a regal purple. "We only have six months to throw this thing. We need to focus."

"Is that not a lot?" Mateo wiggled beneath me, his hips inclining slightly back.

"It's laughable," I sputtered. "I already have pressure on me with Mom and the girls. If the dress doesn't fit like a glove and my lips aren't swollen with filler it's going to be an issue."

"I'll swell your lips naturally."

I rolled my eyes and squeezed a generous amount of Astroglide onto my fingertips. "Spread 'em, Captain."

Mateo grunted, not impressed that I used his call sign against him in such a compromising position—and finally let me ease a slender finger in between.

"Well, I mean, how much is there really to do?"

Fucking *men*. The mental list of wedding planning items that hammered me in the back of my head all day, every day, materialized.

"The dress fitting is tomorrow. Mom, Camilla, Isabella and Mia are all clearing their schedules to meet me there. I'm sure that's not a coincidence at all. They're probably dying to critique in true Russo fashion, which means I'll be lucky to walk out of there with a shred of my dignity left."

"Your sisters aren't that bad." Mateo's voice shot up an octave as the pad of my finger absentmindedly traced his tight ring of muscle.

"It's telling how you left my mom out of that."

"Mother-in-laws are supposed to be the Devil, and I'm well equipped to handle a crazy mother hen. I'm a first-born Italian son; we are doted on and coddled and spoiled in a way that no other man in the world would ever have the pleasure of understanding. Sistine Russo might be a tough egg to crack, but I'm gonna split her open."

"I'm going to vomit."

"Anyway, the dress."

"And catering for the venue. We have to try the food and the cakes and—"

"And you're complaining?"

"Have you forgotten who has the bottle of lube and the cock strap on right now?"

"No, ma'am, I have not."

"The catering," I continued. "Then the florist. The invitations have to be sent soon, which means the accommodations have to be ironed out for the hotel because this is a destination wedding for your entire family. We need bridesmaids gowns and tuxedos for the groomsmen too."

"The boys can wear their dress blues."

"Ew."

"Ew? Four decorated veterans and my wife is saying no to showing us off?"

"Four decorated veterans and *Angelo*," I reminded him. "What the fuck is your brother supposed to show up in? His tool belt and that bright orange T-shirt with the permanent pit stains?"

"He might just do that anyway."

I groaned. That was a battle for another day, much like most of the next six months were going to be. Mateo and I were spoiled to death in our little palm tree bubble up until now. Other people didn't have any kind of sway or hindrance in our relationship; the majority of them probably thought it was one of those flings that would cool down to flickering coals and the wind would completely blow out with time.

I'd never even met his parents.

Not in person, anyway. Over FaceTime. We were friends on social media. His mom was the kind of woman who left stickers as comments on every photo of us together while mine was the kind who pretended she didn't see them at all.

"You of all people should appreciate the value of uniformity," I said.

"Fine." His voice had returned to normal, though I still had a very curious appendage tapping around between us. "Tuxedos, flowers, invitations, and I'll try all the cakes you want me to try. Don't worry about your mom and your sisters. If I need to come down to the dress shop myself and stand in the corner with my nose to the drywall I will. So there's no funny business."

"You're sweet when you want to be."

"I'm just picking and choosing my battles right now, baby."

The camera blinked across the room at the two of us still doing more talking than working. A curl of Mateo's hair had fallen perfectly in front of his forehead and I reached down to tousle a few more of those auburn brown locks into choreographed disarray. The "sweat" had dried and I spritzed him with the spray bottle again like he was a misbehaving cat.

"I never thought I'd say this, but can you fuck me already?" Matty sighed. "My back is starting to hurt on my hands and knees like this."

"You should really start coming with me to yoga." I adjusted myself behind him nonchalantly, lifting the purple silicone to rest on the base of his tailbone. "Lengthen your spine a bit. You're so tense right here."

"I could not imagine why."

I paused. "Are you sure you're comfortable doing this?"

"Just a little nervous," he admitted.

Orange sticky note—things we hadn't done before. Mateo and I shared something that transcended intimacy, especially when it came to our cam work. It wasn't just necessary, it was crucial. We got so many requests per week in so many different shapes and sizes, some more enticing than others, some downright ridiculous and immediately disregarded. The price tag on this one made the two of us sit down and discuss it like we were at a high-level business meeting. We sat at either head of our dining room table and presented one another with the job. I usually shuffled around a stack of printed how-to manuals; before and aftercare prep; my ideas for costume, lighting, editing, and sound design; and a very large pros and cons list that Mateo always took a marker to and added to the pros: *I get to have sex with you.*

I also ran the financial side of it—ironic, considering I wanted nothing more than to escape my bank job. Payments, funds, investments, taxes, et cetera. The boring albeit necessary side of any business. My complaints couldn't extend any further though, because in our day-to-day lives Mateo ran TechOps from the ground up and never asked me to lift a finger. That business was his baby, and this business was mine. He was happy to play side-kick, trophy, ornament, and fucktoy if I asked him to.

"You do have the hottest ass I've ever seen on a man," I encour-aged. "The back dimples are aesthetically perfect."

"I don't want to be aesthetic. I want to be tough and rugged. And covered in dirt, but not dirty. Like I might get under a car or something and fuck around with the engine every once in a while, but maybe also read a book for pleasure on a lazy afternoon."

I looked down at his little pink hole and did that stifled, mouth-curling-in-on-itself laugh again. "You definitely have the ass hair for it."

"You're one to talk."

My jaw popped open. "Okay, that's enough lip out of you, Cinderella. Cameras are rolling. Smile big."

My finger dared to breach him, and as if divine intervention, the telltale sound of our kitchen cabinets slamming shut down the hallway ripped our attention toward the door. We waited cautiously, both entirely sure we weren't hearing things but also eagerly hoping it was a freak occurrence. Our cellphones were across the room.

"Cup probably fell," Mateo reasoned. "A mouse."

Another cabinet hammered shut, followed by a fainter noise.

"Did the mouse open the faucet, too?" I let loose a hard breath. The metronome of my heart picked up behind my ribs and sent a cool wave down my body.

Normally the noise wouldn't have stirred any kind of panic. We were used to an extra body milling around the house day and night. We'd actually learned to completely tune it out. Mateo's best friend, Frankie, lived two doors down in his own bedroom up until two weeks ago when he'd up and shipped off to Colorado with *my* best friend. The two of them fell head over heels for each other over Christmas and left us official empty nesters.

It wasn't Frankie getting himself a glass of water and a snack from the fridge at 9 p.m. but there was someone, *something*, milling freely about the kitchen.

"All right. Stay put, Natalia." Mateo had exited submission and entered the side of himself I rarely got a glimpse of, but marveled at when I did. The retired veteran half. The no funny business, all work no play, lethal and militant, sharp as a knife side. He climbed quietly off the edge of the bed and grabbed his boxer briefs from the floor, pulling them on.

The closet door across the room squeaked open on its hinges and unveiled a heavy safe I thought about so seldomly I often forgot it was even there. A keypad beeped beneath his steady fingers and the door dislodged before he reached inside and pulled out a blocky, black handgun.

"Oh my god." I gasped. "Not the rifle."

Mateo's eyes flickered to me, a pain that wasn't physical stricken across his face. "We will talk about whatever the fuck it is you just called this later. But seriously, Tally, lock yourself in the room. Do not answer the door for anyone but me. I'll knock twice, jingle the doorknob, then knock again."

"Can't you just say, like, 'hey babe, it's me'?"

He racked the gun back and stepped in front of the bedroom door. "Can't you just, like, listen to me for two minutes?"

"What if I hear something bad?"

"Call the cops."

He left me alone on the bed as the door clicked shut quietly behind him.

Fuck. *Fuck.* I shot over and squashed my ear to the wood, attempting to listen over the thump of my pulse in my eardrums. It was silent on the other end which was just as terrifying because it allowed my mind to race and the anxiety to take over. This was a nice neighborhood. No one ever had their house broken into. There was sweet, old little Gino living next door with his tomato plants and the Corleys across the street with their kids. We had potlucks, and joint garage sales, and a block party on the Fourth of July like it was *The Sandlot*.

What if he got ambushed? What if there was someone out there with a sleeper dart waiting to shoot it into his neck and drag him away by his underarms? What if I was standing here waiting to hear a knock and my fiancé, my future husband, the father of my unborn kids needed my help and he couldn't call out for it?

"Fuck me, fuck me, fuck me, fuck me, FUCK—" I chanted, rounding the bed and scrambling in the nightstand drawer until I came up with a cold, metal pocketknife. I tried to whip it open as I'd seen Mateo do a thousand times, but my fingers weren't quite strong enough and so I wrestled it with two hands until the sharp tip of the knife finally dislodged.

Instead of letting myself deliberate any further I slipped out of the bedroom and into the hallway. Listening be damned. Mateo's shadow was plastered to the hardwood farther down at the edge of the wall, and I crept in behind him, wielding the little knife and ready to take on whatever lay waiting on the other side of the divide.

More cabinets opened and closed and voices murmured in the quiet. Mateo rolled his shoulders back. "Cops have been called," he announced. "I'm armed."

Instead of waiting for a reply he turned the corner and barreled into the kitchen, faster than I could follow without tripping over myself. The light inside flipped on and two intertwining screams rang out, followed by Mateo's own bellow of shock, which triggered my fight or flight. I came around the corner screaming like a wild banshee and waving my knife beside him.

"Don't shoot!" A short, plump woman stood in the center of the room with her hands in the air. "For Christ's sake, Mateo David Duran! Giving me a fucking heart attack!"

Time froze. I could see the dawn of realization crest Mateo's face, softening his eyebrows, widening his eyes, flaring his nostrils. His mouth dipped from a straight line into an open frown.

"Mom?!" Mateo shouted back, dropping his weapon immediately to his side. My head followed him on a swivel to the other person in the room, the uncanny resemblance of an older, grayer Mateo staring back at us. "Dad?!"

"Mom?!" I yelled at Mateo. "Dad?!"

And then all three of them turned to look at me. My chest rising and falling in a chaotic rhythm, hands shaking with the pocketknife still suspended between us. And a bright purple strap-on dildo dripping lube between my legs and onto the floor.

chapter two

Mateo

IT WAS the worst night of my life. Undoubtedly. Worse than the night I got so drunk taking swigs out of a bottle of Goldschläger before senior prom that I threw up peppermint and a McChicken all over the limo. It was worse than in the Army when I got stuck in the forest for three consecutive rainy days and my boots soaked through to the socks on day one. It was worse than my girlfriend's dad catching her blowing me behind the backyard shed when we were sixteen.

Because at least then my conservative Christian father didn't think I casually took it up the ass on a quiet night in. He didn't have to see the woman I was going to marry standing in the middle of our kitchen in the laciest bra she owned with an artificial, veiny dick hanging limp off her hips. And when she turned, squealing, and beelined back down the hallway, I didn't have to share the full moon view of her ass with the woman who gave birth to me.

I was surprised Tally even showed her face again, joining us in silence around the kitchen island five minutes later under the brightest fucking light we could have possibly installed. There was no hiding the red under her eyes that continued across the bridge of her nose and splashed across her permanently blushed cheeks. The black eyeliner she had been wearing was scrubbed clean, her hair up in a bun. The biggest, thickest, sweatsuit of an outfit she owned covered her head to toe.

I had to give it to Natalia, if it were John and Sistine Russo in our kitchen I'd have packed my bags and left out the back door never to be seen again. But if anyone could recover from what just happened it was my Tally. She was braver than I was. Stronger than me, smarter and more unyielding. Even when she thought she wasn't.

It occurred to me as she slid onto the barstool beside me facing Mom and Dad that this was their first official meeting. After a year of phone calls and promises to come up to New York for a visit as soon as we could, all the putting it off came back to fuck me in the ass harder than Tally was ever going to.

This is what you get, Mateo. Defy your mother long enough and she just shows up unannounced, eighteen hours from home and rummaging through the kitchen cabinets for an acid reducer. *Fuck's sake.* Mom's thin lips were pressed into a line, the crease between my father's eyebrows deep and worried, worse than the rest of the wrinkles that had grown into his face with age.

"So," she squeaked. "What a story for the grandkids, am I right?"

Anxiety crawled like a spider up my spine and to the base of my skull, exploding like fireworks and touching every single limb on the way back down. I laughed weakly and tried to scratch the itchy feeling off my neck.

There was a twitch of, dare I say, *amusement* from across the table. My parents exchanged looks and I stiffened in my chair, waiting for the expected berating. The one I'd have surely gotten if this were anything like getting in trouble growing up. Angelo and I would sit next to each other on the couch with our chins to our chests, trying our very best not to fidget or speak, knowing our bikes were getting taken away. Saturday cartoons were out of the question. We were going to be stuck clothes pinning Mom's wet underwear to the line outside to dry, and Dad was definitely —*definitely*—volunteering us for altar duty at church.

But that wasn't what happened at all. In fact, the sound of a low, smoky chuckle made me think I was imagining things. I'd already descended to the pit; the underlord was mocking me. My father didn't *laugh* like that. The most you'd ever get out of him was a huff, or a gurgle, or something like there was inflammation in his chest that he was trying to suppress by clearing his throat. The only thing my father thought was funny was that one specific pop culture XM radio show that had inexplicably not been canceled yet.

"Not sure how many grandkids we'll be getting that way," he offered with a bite.

What is fucking happening?

The tips of my ears reddened while three of the most important people in my life started laughing together. My body didn't know what to do; I was still teetering on the edge of a panic attack and that rush of cortisol hadn't evened out yet. Tally reached over, reading my stress, and massaged my thigh thoughtfully, then worked up my back to my neck and gave it a gentle squeeze, taking away the tension in increments.

"I'm so sorry we didn't hear you at the door," she said. "We don't get a lot of guests here this late, as you can probably tell." Tally glanced pointedly at the firearm beside me on the table and I pushed it farther away.

"Yeah, what *are* you doing here, exactly?" I found the courage to finally ask.

My mother, Anna, stood from her stool and resumed what I assumed she was doing in the dark like the Hamburglar, opening cabinets and pulling a glass down. "We wanted to surprise you."

My knuckles had turned white from all the fist clenching. "Well, surprise!"

"The front door was locked, so we came around the back and tried the slider. And whaddya know?"

"I *know* that's called breaking and entering."

"That doesn't apply to mothers. Or the Bronx."

Natalia's lips curled into a small smile. My parents were the polar opposite of what she was used to. I had been around the Russos a handful of times, brief dinners at their immaculate Palm Park mansion, enduring topical conversations about the weather and the stock market that I knew next to nothing about but faked it well enough. The plans we had with them were weeks in the making, more than likely jotted down on a calendar like an appointment and subject to rescheduling at a moment's notice.

John Russo was an anesthesiologist, Sistine a nutritionist and self-proclaimed guru. The kind that went on podcasts and answered questions live on social media about the negative effects of random household staples on your spiritual health. They had four perfect daughters and sent all but one of them to expensive private colleges that set them up for success in lucrative career fields. That all but one was the best thing that had ever come out of that family. Bat shit crazy, the black sheep, and so beautiful most of the time I didn't know what to do with her.

The last time we'd seen Natalia's parents I was asking her father for permission to marry her and I couldn't tell if he thought I was joking or was all too happy to have someone take on the burden. "All my luck to you," John had said. "You're going to need it."

Then there were the Durans, a working-class, blue-collar family from the moment Enzo Duran stepped off the boat in 1914 on Ellis Island and started slinging building material. My father, his father, and his before him. I was the only one who joined the military when I turned eighteen and left the business to my younger, less-inspired brother and hadn't heard the end of it since.

"We're glad you're here," Tally said. "It's about time I met the family. I mean, we're getting married! This was so overdue."

"When is your return flight?" I asked.

A sharp slap disguised as a caress came down on my shoulder. "Mateo needs to know how much time he has to show you all our little city has to offer."

I actually needed to know how much time I had to hide how

utterly insane my family was from my future wife so that she didn't call off our wedding before it even happened. I could handle Mom and Dad in small, concentrated doses, with guidelines and set plans, a heads-up at the very least. When those things didn't exist, shit like my mother and father catching me in my underwear about to get pegged started happening.

"We didn't book one," Dad said.

My mother found her way to the refrigerator and popped the door open, glancing inside. "Mateo, someone really might have robbed you. There's nothing in this fridge."

"What do you mean, you didn't book one?" I addressed my father.

"We do a lot of takeout," Tally answered Mom. "But we always try to cook on Sunday!"

The door to the refrigerator closed slowly. "We'll just have to run to the store, then. Keep some staples in the house. Italian bread, tomatoes, cold cuts for sandwiches. You waste a lot of money not making him lunch for work."

"I haven't bought lunch in thirty years," Dad boasted.

Natalia had never made a man a sandwich in her life and she wasn't about to start.

"We're getting away from my question," I cut in. "Let's focus on the important things here. Like what prompted this spontaneous, one-way ticket to Florida, and where you're staying."

We would run in circles all night long with the small talk and my parents wouldn't think twice about it. But it was late, the kitchen was turning into a sauna, there was a catch coming I knew would knock the wind out of me, and the only place I could stand being jerked around was in the bedroom.

"We came to spend time with you and get to know Natalia before the wedding," Mom finally said. "She's a part of the family now; we ought to know our new daughter, don't you agree? Your father retired, so we figured we could spend the next six months down here for the winter like the rest of the retirees and help with planning in whatever way we can."

A distinct feeling hit me, like heartburn mixed with the stomach pain that accompanies getting halfway through your coffee and realizing if you don't get to a bathroom in two minutes you're going to be a grown adult who just shit their pants. The kind where you need a minute, where sweat starts to accumulate on your temples despite being in an air-conditioned house.

"When you called last week and told us Frankie moved out to Colorado, we decided to take the leap and buy the plane tickets. You finally had an extra room, and you're always telling us the offer is on the table to come for a visit." My father pointed this out as if updating them on my life during our weekly phone call was me summoning them to the beach.

I'd told my parents off-handedly a hundred times that they had an open invitation, knowing full well that they would never leave New York, especially not without a place to stay. It was etiquette, pure obligation. Did I think they'd ever show up unannounced and use that invite against me? Never in a million years.

"If that's not a problem..." Dad added after sensing my hesitation. "We could always find one of those rentals, if it is."

The saturating guilt was settling like cement in my stomach. I was either the worst son in the world, or I was putting Natalia in a position she wasn't prepared for and neither of us would survive. I lost no matter what.

My attention swept to her and I could see the cogs turning in my fiancée's tiny little head. Her lips thinned, the thinking finger came up to rest on her chin, and she glimpsed innocently in my direction, a shrug living on the edge of her shoulder. I knew that look; it was her deciding to be the hero. A muscle in my jaw tensed and my head started a slow, involuntary shake back and forth.

"Natalia, can I talk to you for a kinute?"

Our fingers linked and her dangling feet plopped to the floor as I whisked her off the chair. We made it halfway down the hallway and out of sight before I nudged her into the wall and closed her in with my hands on either side of her head.

"What's wrong?" she asked.

Oh, my naive, do-gooding, hospitable princess. The worst part of this was that I wished I could welcome my parents with open arms. It would have been so much easier than trying to explain to her that my parents were better experienced from afar and that's why I'd kept them there.

"You weren't about to do what I think you were just about to do...were you?" Her lips twisted into a pout and I tucked a strand of dark hair behind her ear.

"What was I about to do that you think I was about to do?"

"You know exactly what you were about to do that *I know* you know you were about to do."

"Well if you know what I know"—she stuck a pointy finger in the dip at the center of my chest—"then we know the thing I was about to do is kind, and helpful, and *the least* we could do for your parents if they're going to be here for six months."

Fuck she was cute, and good-willed, and had a terrible relationship with her own family that made the prospect of entertaining mine seem like a walk in the park. What she didn't know —but should have been glaringly obvious after the last thirty minutes—was that my family had no boundaries. There was not a statue of couth erected in the Duran house. I wanted to protect her as much as humanly possible.

"Right, well, if you know what *I know*, then you'd know that offering to let my parents live in the room across the hall from us for six months is equivalent to castration. Do you want to castrate me, Tally? Do you want to take a sharp knife to the seam of my jewels before I can get you pregnant?"

Her eyes narrowed. "You can't fuck me with your mother in the house?"

"I can fuck you anytime, anywhere, anyway I please, sweetheart. But if my mother's big girl bloomers get tangled in the dryer with my T-shirts, my dick will probably turn into a gummy worm."

"I don't think that them staying here could get any worse than what happened when they showed up."

She was probably right, but I knew in my gut that if it could, it very well would. And considering our line of work, the chances immediately doubled. "Why test it?" I shrugged.

"You're hardly home anyway, and the cam business takes up most of my time. If I'm not filming and editing, I'm usually bored or shopping. So look at this as an opportunity for me to bond with your parents, Matty. They're part of you, and I want to know every part. I promise to be a perfect host; it'll barely even feel like they're here."

I laughed. She seemed to believe that allowing Anna and David Duran free rein of our house for months was going to be like taking care of a pair of elderly, self-sufficient cats. Cats that disappear outside for a few days at a time and you don't worry about it because eventually they'll show back up meowing at the front door in the middle of the night.

"I could really use the help with wedding planning while you're overbooked at work because Frankie is gone," she continued. "Plus, it saves them from renting a place. Your mom will get to spend time with her baby boy, and you can take your dad out golfing, drive him around downtown, introduce him to the neighbors..."

My hand scrubbed disparagingly down my face over day-old stubble. It was sharp and graying through the once reddish-brown beard from my twenties. The gesture reminded me I was a thirty-five-year-old man afraid to establish any type of boundaries with my parents because I hadn't needed to since I left home for the military almost two decades ago. I would rather avoid them than invite them to stay at the house because that's where I was most comfortable. An arm's length away from the overbearing and intrusive love-bombing. Here, I could just call home every week and get an update on which bars Angelo got banned from for being drunk and disorderly again.

My aversion to my parents wasn't fair to Natalia. She deserved to know the family she was marrying into. The good, the bad, and the ugly. I wasn't sure if Mom and Dad would be a better fit than her own parents, but I did know that she'd been given a sour hand there, and not allowing her the chance to feel a sense of belonging with the Durans was nothing more than me being selfish. I didn't want to overwhelm her, but it was me who was really worried about being overwhelmed.

I leaned down and kissed her forehead. "If I agree to this, we need to establish some ground rules."

"You're the boss." She knew I'd love hearing those words slip through her lips.

"First of all, we need a safe word. And not the sexy kind. The complete and utter opposite of the sexy kind. This is one for if and when either of us needs out, and needs out fast."

"Simple enough." She nodded. "Coconut."

"Coconut? You got nothing else? Nothing more original?"

"Palm tree."

"Seriously?" I parried.

She deadpanned, "Rigid purple fucking dildo."

"Fine, coconut it is."

Tally lifted a small, victorious fist. "What else?"

"If you're dead set on this, we need to be extra careful *working from home*." I raised an eyebrow. "I'm still trying to figure out how you talked us out of this first one, but we don't have room for second or third offenses. My parents are old school, Tal. It'll send them to an early grave."

"Pick up a deadbolt for the bedroom door and hide the cork-boards in the closet. Got it." She tugged her bottom lip between her teeth and looked up at me with wide eyes. "Anything else?"

"Yes." I pulled her closer by her chin, talking against her lips. "We have to prioritize our relationship. You don't get it yet, but this is about to be a full one-eighty from what we're used to. There's a reason I left New York and didn't go back. I need my girl with me, on the same page, every step of the way. Understand?"

Tally pressed up on her tiptoes and took my mouth with hers. Her eyelashes fluttered against my cheek and I deepened the kiss, tangling my hand in the hair at the base of her neck.

"I vow to follow all your rules, Mr. Duran," she said.

"Then it looks like we have ourselves a shitshow, Mrs. Duran." I smiled. "Hope you brought your pooper-scooper."

chapter three

Mateo

15 months ago

FOUR. That's how many times I'd peeked around the cubicle wall at the girl sitting behind the front desk of the bank in as many minutes. Her head was still down, fingers working the keyboard in front of her, and a long strand of dark-brown hair caressed the side of her face outside of a slicked-back ponytail.

Natalia Russo.

I'd gone against my own rules to find out that name. It was easy enough to poke around in the system at the credit union where my company was installing security to pull her information. Usually a work photo wouldn't do a person justice, but hers? Damn near black hair, dark irises that could melt you, high cheekbones and faint blush, a few buttons open on her white blouse—she looked like magic from the moment my eyes caught a glimpse. Still did, while avoiding me. Or trying her hardest to.

The pen in my hand tapped anxiously against the desk.

"Why don't you just go and talk to her, Cap?" my best friend and business partner, Frankie, suggested from the rolling office chair beside me. He hadn't looked up from the desktop he was fiddling with, writing code into an open text box and wearing that hat I'd told him a dozen times looked unprofessional.

The bank was slow this afternoon. Barely audible Jim Croce crooned in the background, fluorescent bulbs burned down onto the white tile floors, and a man darted back and forth across the puke green throw rugs with one of those silent vacuum cleaners. I jammed my tongue in my cheek and craned my neck to look around the makeshift wall again. Still there. Still pretending I wasn't.

"I made a move, Pike," I said. "I put that sticky note right in the center of her screen. She's either seen it or she's writing emails with an obstructed view and pretending she didn't."

"Why are you waiting for her to text you when she's sitting ten feet away?" Pike ran a finger across his top lip and continued typing. "We're going to have to pass her walking out the front door. Or are you going to ignore her like you're in high school again?"

I flicked the back of his ear, earning a frustrated grunt. "Type, monkey."

This wasn't like chatting up a girl at the bar after a few drinks and sparring with the jukebox. I couldn't just go *talk to her*. I wasn't an ugly guy, but some dim lighting and a beer blanket never hurt anybody. I could use that extra confidence at the moment.

"She's probably nervous, too," Pike added, as if reading my mind.

"I'm not nervous. I just don't want to come on too strong. She can't leave if she's not interested and I waltz over and back her into a corner." I scratched at the base of my neck, pulling at the tufts of overgrown hair. Then, just in case, sunk my nose into the crease of my armpit for a perfunctory sniff.

Frankie jammed a key finitely, then twisted in his chair to face me. "But you're aware of that, unlike most other guys. So use that expertly honed intuition and retract yourself if you feel like she'd rather stick a fork in her eye than speak to you."

"I'm not that bad," I reasoned. "Do you see that girl? She's dealt with the worst of us. Trust me."

He slapped his hands down on his knees. "If it were me, I'd just go talk to her. Ask her if she liked her coffee this morning."

The coffee I left on her desk before she arrived, with a note and my number, leaving the ball in her court. Of course she liked it, because I'd fished her empty cup out of the break room garbage the day before to take a photo of the order sticker.

That wasn't weird, I kept telling myself. What would have been weird was if I tasted the coffee before dropping it off at her work station. The garbage thing was smart.

"Oh, fuck off. If it were you, you'd run home with your tail between your legs and jerk off about it for three days."

"Screw you, man." He tried and failed to keep a straight face, reclipping paperwork into a three-ring binder and shutting it with a soft thwap. "You know what, whatever. Wait for her to text you, don't fucking wait, I don't care. But the job is done here, so it's now or never. I'm going home now to jerk off about something, I guess. Are you coming?"

"You want me to come jerk off with you?"

Pike's patience with me was next level but he had his limits. He pressed the button on the console and the computer powered down like a jet cooling its engines. Then he was out of the desk chair and shouldering past me and into the lobby of the bank. I spun with him, pinching the bridge of my nose. We were done with the installation, and if I walked out that door with Pike I'd pretty much never have the chance to talk to her organically again. He was making my decision for me.

Natalia looked up for the first time, watched him traipse by with the binder under his arm and the car keys swinging around his fingers, and glanced in my direction. We locked eyes for a long second before hers shot back down to her screen.

That small gesture was a glimmer of hope, the tiniest opening of an invitation. I weighed the options quickly, deciding not to hit my pillow later asking myself what-ifs. Swiping my phone off the desk, I slid it into my back pocket and hustled in Frankie's direction, catching him before he pushed out the door. "Be out in a few minutes," I told him. I tilted my head toward the front desk and he smirked back, saluting me with two fingers to his forehead.

But then Pike looked past me. "He's a good guy, I promise. You make him nervous, so you have an advantage anyway." I turned and Natalia was watching us again, a shadow of a smirk lifting her lips.

"Yeah, yeah, see ya, Pike." I cleared my throat. "Hey, I heard if you use your left hand it actually feels like someone else is doing the job," I hissed under my breath.

His laughter trailed off as the glass doors waved open and thud shut behind me, leaving me and her mostly alone. A shy, albeit smug grin lit up Natalia Russo's face.

"Do I make you nervous?" she asked quietly. Something pinched the inside of my chest, hearing her voice for the first time. Soft yet deep, it matched her dark hair and the shade of her lipstick. It felt familiar in the way that déjà vu does, like maybe I'd heard it in a dream before, and forced me to imagine all the other alluring pieces of her there were to uncover.

"Most pretty things do." I shrugged, blasé. "Probably because I was never allowed around the china plates as a kid. But I'm learning to be gentler."

Her nose scrunched in the most adorable way, all of her features coming together and kissing at the center of her face. Then she slid the keyboard in front of her to the side, propping her arms on the desk. "Gentle is boring."

That was a whisper tossed into the loaded space between us. My eyebrows knitted together and then relaxed. Either she was flirting with me or I was deeply confused and now mistakenly aroused. Her pupils danced forward and back; the ring around them was a brown like toffee. "Now that I see you up close I guess it makes sense. There's something in those eyes that makes me think you like getting in a little bit of trouble."

On cue her eyelashes met the topmost part of her lids and it felt like she was telling me to look right through her. To find a secret hidden somewhere. "Thank you for the coffee," she said. I hadn't been able to stop staring and she knew it too, because I felt the teasing sureness in her next words before she even said them. "Little cold once I got here though, if I'm being honest."

God, I loved a brat. She was more and more my type by the second. And I liked that I'd made her comfortable enough to take a playful shot at me. It made me more confident in my gutsy reply.

"You know, it's really good right out of bed first thing in the morning."

Her blinks slowed, and my smile followed hers, all the way to my ears. We were both enjoying whatever this little thing was. She wouldn't be entertaining it if she wasn't interested.

"You're inviting me over for a slumber party?"

"I was just buying you a coffee, sweetheart. You're the one talking about slumber parties."

She laughed then. It was so quiet and short-lived and she closed her hand over her mouth like she'd get in trouble for it. But that sound was even more perfect than her voice, bubbling up to a higher pitch before tapering off. Whoever made her self-conscious of that laugh was a son of a bitch because I was yearning to hear it again.

Natalia's face returned to neutral and she shot a glance behind her, to the rooms where her coworkers sat. A guy in his mid-twenties with a thin tie and a too-tight dress shirt watched us curiously, with a crooked nametag on that said "Andy." Her expression soured and I stared at him until he turned back around. Yeah, I'd say Natalia Russo fucking hated her job. She pulled her cardigan across her chest and folded her arms.

"Am I going to get you in trouble?"

"Possibly," she said. "But I don't really care. Let them fire me." Her long, French-tipped nails tugged at a loose thread on her sleeve.

"Who needs a job anyway?" I shrugged.

There was a little caddy with a pair of scissors on her desk. I reached for them slowly, asking for permission and curling the fingers of my other hand toward her arm. She lifted it hesitantly, curiously, and watched me snip the yarn.

"Aren't I a little young for you?"

"I don't know. You haven't told me how old you are yet."

"Twenty-five."

I blew out a breath and counted the lights on the ceiling. "How's your relationship with your father?"

"Terrible."

"Then I think we'll be just fine."

Her tongue darted out, painting her bottom lip, and I leaned my body farther over the counter. I didn't want to whisper but I wanted our conversation to be just that. Ours. She was thinking about every last reason this could be a bad idea, and I knew so because I had all the same tells. Her eye contact had waned, her hands fidgeting and anxiously picking; even her breathing was coming quicker. Not quite panicking yet, but weighing the pros and cons of something that could lead to it. I made *her* nervous. I backed up again.

She tapped her fingernails against each other. "Why don't women your own age like you?"

"I travel a lot."

"Is that a money brag?"

"You couldn't pay people to go to the places I've been." My neck craned over the ledge of the counter, catching a glimpse of something blue and crumpled inside the small garbage at Natalia's feet. "Did you throw my phone number away?"

She kicked the tiny basket farther beneath her desk. "Yes."

"I thought this was going well."

"Customer service is my specialty..." She squinted, reading the name embroidered across the chest of my work shirt. "Mateo."

"Duran," I added. "What do you think of that name?"

"What do I think of your name?" she said with a laugh. Like it was the most ridiculous question she'd ever heard. More so than the hundred she got a day sitting behind this desk clicking buttons and counting change. She pulled her keyboard back in front of her and started jostling the mouse to wake the screen, alluding to work. For all anyone could tell I was there opening a new account. Not trying to get the bank teller in my bed.

"Yeah. I figured it might be yours one day. So I wanted to make sure you liked it."

"Wow, that was something." She snorted. Natalia had the most perfect full lips, and I would die just to see her teeth sink into the bottom one. At the very least I amused her; she tolerated the way I was coming on, terrible pick-up lines and all. It made me keep trying.

"That was an honest question."

She rested the end of her pen between her teeth. She was fucking calling my attention to her mouth; I wasn't imagining things. "Duran is a good name, but...Mateo doesn't exactly roll off the tongue."

"You can call me whatever you want," I offered. "Whatever makes your tongue happy."

I remembered Pike for the first time since I stopped to talk to Natalia and glanced at the door. It was a bright and warm late October day in South Florida, not a cloud in the sky, but the tints on the windows of the bank made the entire room feel gray. It was the kind of job where clocking out at the end of the day felt like being let out of prison.

"Look." She sighed, dropping the pen. "I think you're attractive, and I appreciate the coffee and conversation, but I don't know anything about you, and..." A pause. "I am not the type of girl to do relationships. My life is...complicated."

I rubbed at the hair along my jaw. Usually, I was pretty off the cuff. I could hold a conversation with anyone, talk myself out of anything. I was trained in crisis prevention and de-escalation in the special forces of the United States military; it was literally part of my day-to-day to be the guy who knew exactly what to say. But for some reason this five-foot nothing bank secretary with the pencil skirt and the little attitude that turned me on more than it should have had me stumped.

"You want to know about me?" I asked. "Okay, I'm thirty-four. I was born in the Bronx and I have a younger brother named Angelo, so if you think my name is bad, get a load of that one. When I was eighteen I enlisted in the Army. My parents fucking hated me for it for years, maybe they still do, but we don't talk about it. I drink on occasion, mostly to relax, but sometimes not. I've never done any hard drugs, never even smoked weed, and after spending fifteen years in the military that's basically unheard of. My favorite movie is *Dirty Dancing*, and I can't watch horror. I actually had nightmares so bad as a kid I peed the bed until I was twelve."

Natalia was shaking her head but her straight white teeth curved into a smile.

"I started this business two years ago with that jerk outside waiting for me to make a move on you. We live together. His name is Frankie, but our buddies we served with and I all call him Pike. He and I are kind of a package deal, so if you've got any friends..." I trailed off suggestively. "And I love a challenge. Our job is done, so if you tell me no today, I'll find another reason to come back in here again tomorrow. And not because I can't take no for an answer"—I leaned forward, close enough to notice her eyes had some flecks of yellow—"but because if I'm reading this right, I don't think you want me to."

Natalia tucked the strand of her hair hanging in front of her face behind her ear and I imagined a moment where I might be able to do it for her.

"Am I reading this right, Miss Russo?"

Her neck tilted. "I'm not a cheap date."

"I've got money."

"And I'm terrible at expressing my feelings."

"I'm a great listener."

"Sometimes I just want to sit in silence, or read a book, or stare at the ceiling and not talk to anyone."

"I bet you're gorgeous to look at from across the room while you do."

A curious, fiery light flared in her eyes. She relaxed backward into her desk chair, the thin plastic creaking softly. "I'll drive you crazy."

"God, I hope so."

The bell on the front door jingled and the sunlight from outside brandished a sliver on the floor as a woman walked in and formed a line behind me. That was it, that was my verbal vomit attempt at convincing this woman to give me a chance. I alluded to marrying her and then told her I was a bedwetter. To save the shred of my dignity that was still left, I stood up straight and took a step back, gesturing with an arm for the woman behind me to take my place with Natalia.

"Think about it," I said. "And if you ever decide to call me, I'd love to take you on that date."

She glanced toward the floor, my guess at the garbage can and the neon Post-it note with my number scribbled on it. "I'll think about it."

I nodded. With that, I turned on my heels, shouldering outside into the daylight and the busy parking lot. Our installation was over; there was no reason for me to ever walk through those doors again unless I decided to open a new bank account as an excuse to show up looking for her weekly. The fact that thought even crossed my mind was alarming, and I pushed a shaky hand through the front of my hair, slicking it back.

The thing about me was that I *did* get nervous. I overthought everything, but I was damn good at keeping a cap on it. For the first time in my life, that wavered. All I could think about was how badly I'd just fucked up, how she'd laugh about it to her girlfriends, how she was probably already in a relationship, or had a roster of men at her disposal. My anxiety had me glued to the sidewalk, knees locking into place as I contemplated turning back to ask her to forget it ever happened for the sake of us both.

Frankie was sitting in the driver's seat of the truck across the parking lot watching me with an eyebrow lifted. You know what, I would just blame him. It was his bright idea to go talk to her. I was always going to let her make the decision, leave my number, hope for the best. Now it was all fucked.

I took two aggressive steps in his direction, about to point a finger before my cellphone started ringing in my pocket. I put it to my ear without a second thought. "Hello?"

"I thought about it." Her voice was slightly higher pitched, filtered through the receiver, but I knew it all the same. I twisted back toward the bank, looking through the window at the girl there with the phone to her ear, a coiled wire strung down to her desk. "And I'm not busy Friday night." I watched her lips move, confirming she was indeed saying what I was hearing.

"No? Okay. Me either."

"Okay," she said softly, trailed by a hum of a laugh.

chapter four

Natalia

MATEO OFFERED Frankie's old room to his parents. His best friend and ex-roommate hadn't owned much, or taken much, of anything when he left for Colorado to pursue *my* best friend and ex-roommate. The spare bedroom was fully furnished, emptied, and relatively clean. Minus the bedsheets I ripped off and replaced with new ones and the bedside drawer that had an impressive pack of condoms in there, half-empty.

I would have left them, but something told me the Durans weren't too worried about conception at their age, and Mateo might have a heart attack if he heard his parents boning across the hall. He should know better than anyone else that kinkiness is hereditary. His dad probably liked nipple stimulation just as much as he did.

Anna was awake bright and early in the morning, milling around the kitchen again like it was a pastime, familiarizing herself. The cabinets, pots and pans, the silverware drawer, the coffee mugs, the dishwashing detergent under the sink. Then she found a bottle of antibacterial spray and paper towels and spent a good fifteen minutes wiping down every flat surface in the room, removing the stains from our stainless-steel fridge, scrubbing the stovetop with a sponge that needed immediate replacement after she was done with it. I couldn't tell if she was passive aggressively showing me how to sanitize or genuinely happy to help.

My mom had never picked up a rag to clean something in the entire twenty-six years I'd been alive. We had people for that. Our family kitchen was surgical-core. Everything was white and silver, shiny, sterile, untouched. The chandeliers never got dusty, the floors never needed a mop, the food was always meticulously stocked with choices that were organic, free-range, or encouraged proper gut health like Jamie Lee Curtis was hiding in the fucking fridge waiting to jump out and sell it to me.

My sisters and I weren't allowed to have any of those sugary cereals or sodas when we were kids. No artificial coloring—*especially* not red dye—no enriched flour, no corn syrup, nothing that looked like it was made to taste good or bring happiness. Our meals were portioned, we had set times we ate them, and there was a little bell at the top of the pantry door that alerted everyone if we ever dared try to open it without supervision.

So naturally, whenever I could get my hands on something I was *barred* from having, I did. Sneaking juice boxes on playdates, chips and cupcakes with all that extra grocery store frosting at birthday parties, Bomb Pops at the beach on the Fourth of July.

As I got older, that harmless rebellion extended into everything else. Whatever was a hard no became a *watch me*. I wasn't allowed to have a boyfriend, period. Never mind a boyfriend who came over and hung out watching movies and eating popcorn together on the couch. So the shaded stairwells of the private school I went to became the ideal spot to go to second base with a guy. I couldn't wear makeup, so every dollar of allowance I got went to drugstore lipsticks and colorful eyeliner, sparkly eyeshadow, and way too bright blush I put on in the bathroom before homeroom. I stole all the clear alcohol out of the bar cabinets and drank it out of plastic water bottles, told Mom and Dad I was sleeping at a friend's house when I was most definitely in a basement I shouldn't have been near FAU, and—I smoked weed. I smoked it and I enjoyed it, and I found creative ways to keep it in my bedroom at home that included Altoids containers and dryer sheets.

What was most ironic about the strict rules in our house was that my parents never paid enough attention to enforce them. Dad was always at the hospital or on call, and Mom was always shut away in her office, or on a business trip, or out to lunch with a client. They were one way on paper and the exact opposite in practice. By the time I was a senior in high school I saw my parents so little I think I was practically begging for their attention with the things I did. I wanted to get in trouble. I wanted to be yelled at and told to go to my room. I wanted them to *notice* their youngest daughter while Cami was being accepted into medical school and Bella was making waves at Yale and Mia was just finishing her third straight semester at college with a perfect GPA. I was the last Russo girl still living at home and it felt like, for my parents, the nest was already empty.

When it came time, I filled out one college application across the country at Colorado State, and my life was entirely my own once that acceptance letter came in the mail. My last act of defiance got me put on my parents' permanent shit list, accosted with the burden of my own student loans, and the satisfaction of reminding my mother every time I saw her that I was taking full advantage of the natural, holistic, and beneficial qualities of marijuana, just like she'd want me to.

I met Ophelia at Colorado State and learned that platonic soulmates were real, and sometimes they came in the form of squirrely and meticulous education majors with too much time and too many highlighters on their hands. If there was anyone in the world that could rationalize the fact that I'd invited my mother-in-law to watch me try on wedding gowns after meeting her once, it was Phee.

Anna and I breezed down the road in my bright yellow Wrangler with the top down. A perfectly sunny, cloudless day to compliment it, our hair whipping in the wind. One of my very favorite things to do, but taking one short glance over to the passenger seat, I couldn't tell if Mateo's mother was having so much fun her face was paralyzed with it, or if there was a bug that had flown down her throat and she was afraid to swallow.

"I'm so glad you and David decided to stay with us," I said, turning down the radio.

"What?" she shouted.

"I said I'm so glad that you and Mr. Duran are staying with us!"

The thrum of the engine wasn't doing me any favors. Anna's bob was shoulder length and coarse and there was a strand of it stuck to her periwinkle pink lipstick that I longed to reach out and pick free. She clung to her pocketbook sitting in her lap like a second seatbelt. Note to self: Driving with the top down was an acquired taste, one that might have gone better with a ponytail or a hat.

"Me too, sweetie," she eventually answered.

"Angelo should try to come down for a visit soon, get the whole family together at least once before the wedding," I suggested.

"That boy is a busy bee, just works and works. Running the whole business alone is hard for him without Mateo's help."

Her tone was sharp enough to give my head a tilt. One thing I knew about Matty was that he never intended on putting up sheetrock and drywall for a living. Not only did Mateo earn himself the leadership position of his special forces unit, he came home and started an incredibly successful business that had nothing to do with the avenue of construction.

"Mateo is so busy, too," I reminded her. "He lost his business partner when Frankie moved, so now he's taking on that workload until he has the time to find another cybersecurity expert. It's been a lot of long days for him. He's exhausted when he comes home."

"I'm sure Angelo would love to sit in the air conditioning all day," she said. "A chair and a desk, tap-tapping on the keyboard, long lunch breaks, flirting with the bank receptionist." She wiggled her eyebrows. "But of course we're proud of them both. They're very special in their own ways."

"Of course," I parroted, focusing on the gray blacktop and the yellow lines on the road.

My fingernails dug into the soft cushion of my leopard steering wheel cover and I leaned a little heavier onto the gas pedal. If there was contention between Mateo and Angelo it was bleeding into the entire family dynamic. Not to mention Mateo had asked Frankie to be his best man, and I was pretty sure that news hadn't made its waves yet.

I slowed to a stop at the dress boutique, surprised to find my mother's Range Rover already parked and empty. Out of habit, I pulled out a compact mirror from my bag to check that my makeup wasn't creased, and took a comb to my untamed hair. I reapplied a layer of lip gloss, wrestled my push-up bra into a flattering shape in the white A-line sundress I wore, and took the most staggeringly deep breath I could before joining my future mother-in-law at the front door, hoping that her skin was as thick as her accent. I knew no matter what I said or did, the short, stout woman was about to get unabashedly judged and implicitly ignored by my mom and each of my sisters for the next two hours. Mateo had to worry less about me not wanting to join his extended family and more about his own mother warning him off the mess that was mine.

Sistine was tapping on her watch when we walked inside, next to my twin sisters, Mia and Isabella—all three dressed in different variations of white. It's a rule not to wear white to a wedding, but there had to be some type of handbook somewhere that said wearing white to *any* wedding affiliated function was reserved for the bride unless implicitly stated otherwise.

Even better, it seemed a rack of stark white, floofy, bedazzled dresses had been put together by my mother on my behalf. My style was less razzle-dazzle and more muted, crème, lightweight— something that drapes off your body and accentuates your curves. Mom wanted a cake topper that blinded you with how many cheap rhinestones were sewn into the bodice, and was so heavy it'd take out a startled child on the dance floor with the ass train.

"Mom," I greeted her. We both extended our arms out as if to hug but never got close enough to actually touch. My mother, sisters, and I all shared the same short, hereditary frames, thin nose, and dark hair. But Mom had taken to dyeing hers blonde despite the roots popping through with vigor within a week.

"Talia," she said warmly, looking me up and down. "I got started without you. Couldn't help myself."

"Story of your life," I said back with equal affection. Anna was in the shadow behind me and I stepped aside to include her in her blue paisley blouse. It was like introducing a Real Housewife to Barefoot Contessa. "This is Mateo's mom, Anna. She and her husband are visiting from New York for a few months to help with the wedding."

"Sistine." My mother held out a limp wrist, her lips pinched into a smile. "I hope you're enjoying the weather. New York is so dirty and cold this time of year. John and I prefer a late May in the Hamptons when we find the time."

I turned away before she could catch me rolling my eyes and moved the attention to my twin sisters standing by. If not for Isabella's chic, professional, lawyer bob that looked immaculate paired with a pantsuit, she and Mia were nearly impossible to tell apart. Mia had more flare, a small nose stud, and several piercings in her ears. She wore her eyeliner winged and was partial to a leather jacket, but knew exactly when to dial it back. The two of them were equally uptight and obtuse. Bella was as blunt as a baseball bat, Mia would bite your head off, and neither could ever admit they were wrong, especially not when it came to each other.

"Mia," I said, making a flighty introduction. "And Isabella. Older sisters. Mia sells houses, Isabella sues people. I still can hardly tell them apart so don't worry if you forget."

"I see there's a trend in names," Anna noted.

"And you haven't even been graced with Camilla yet." I plopped onto the cream cabriole beside Bella and patted the cushion to invite Anna to join me. "I'm glad you all cleared your schedules."

"We wouldn't miss it, honey," Mom announced. "This is a milestone in a mother's life, wedding dress shopping! I can't believe it."

"How funny that your youngest is the first one down the aisle," Anna said. "I've been begging my son for a daughter-in-law for years. I was convinced he would never settle."

"I thought I'd have more time," Mom commented. "Mateo has so much more life experience than Natalia. He's—what, again? Thirty-nine?"

"Thirty-five," I mumbled.

"I know you said you're not pregnant, but it doesn't hurt to ask one more time."

My cheeks flamed as she took a long look at my torso as if she could see through it. "No, Mom, I'm not pregnant."

"Six months to plan a wedding *is* going to make people assume," Bella said. "Gossip, at the very least. I'll just come straight out and say it, I'm concerned with how you're affording a wedding in the Keys on a bank teller's income. No offense to the hubby, but I didn't realize tech support was reeling in the cash."

Tech support. Somehow both my eyeballs twitched at the same time. If only I could pull up Mat and Nat's most recent royalty statement and hold it out for them to gawk at, just once. Apparently everyone was so *worried* about me, my lack of life experience, and lack of funds. I guess it shouldn't have surprised me that they still saw me as the same aimless, rebellious kid I was in high school.

My family was still under the impression that I worked at the bank. That was my cover for what I really did with my nine-to-five hours during the week. It was safe. There wasn't any danger one of them would show up looking for me, and I couldn't exactly tell them I was unemployed without heavy questioning. But now Anna thought I had a job at the bank as well and I'd backed myself into a corner.

"Mateo does *very* well for himself," I bit out, panicking. "So much that I cut my hours back at work."

"Go off, feminist icon." Mia picked some invisible lint from her skirt.

"There's something to be said about a woman with her own independence though." Mom crossed one long, tan leg over the other.

I shrugged. "Then say it."

"It's about security, Talia. God forbid this doesn't all work out for you, because you've become entirely dependent on Mateo to keep you off the street."

Keeping our content creating a secret was never an issue, because no one ever asked. No one ever cared. But having to grin and bear it knowing how independent I truly was made me bitter. I could see where Mom's worry came from, but there was also something so disingenuous about only caring when there was a ring on my finger.

Before I could say something I'd regret, a lovely young woman with a measuring tape around her neck and a pin cushion fastened to her wrist spawned at the edge of the viewing floor.

Her blond bob wiggled as she took in everyone on the couch until she had to focus more intently on differentiating the sea of white between us four Russo women. "Good afternoon everyone, I'm May." She waved with both hands. "Who is my bride?"

I stood up to shake May's hand. "That's me."

"Let me steal you away for a few minutes and get you in a gown. Don't get too emotional out here, ladies, but there are tissues on the tables if you need them!"

Despite having a dress picked out already, I tried on whatever fugly, ridiculous thing was hanging on the mystery rack to placate my mother for half an hour. That way when I finally put on the gown I'd had shipped to the store specifically, I could sell the fact that it was pure coincidence.

I was shuffled into a room and stripped down, every limb shoved into a jungle of tulle and ribbon, bodice cinched like a medieval corset. I took one look at my reflection, at the ballgown of my nightmares that needed nothing more than a pair of elbow-length white gloves to turn me into Mia Thermopolis, and blanched.

There was no way I could *move*, let alone dance in it. It would take me more time to get in and out of a limousine without ripping the fabric on the door hinges than it would to say our vows. Never mind the heat of Key West in June and the gymnastics it would take just to go to the bathroom. I would have to wear a diaper to my wedding. I would have to voluntarily *pee* myself at my wedding.

Mia and Bella's faces screwed into narrow amusement the moment I emerged from the dressing room. Making matters worse, I tripped over the ledge of the circular pedestal in front of the mirror *twice* before Anna and the dress consultant leaped to my rescue to lift the twenty pounds of material around my knees.

"You look like a princess," Mom said.

"I look like you just cut the rubber bands from around my arms and neck and took me out of my cardboard box."

"I think I actually did have a Barbie with a dress like that." Mia pointed at me. "And she left Ken at the altar and went and scissored her other Barbie friend in the backseat of her convertible."

My saucer eyes swept to Mateo's mother apologetically.

"It is a beautiful dress," Anna said, unperturbed.

"But it's not *the* dress," I replied. "It's too big, too heavy, too..."

"Preteen wet dream," Bella finished. "Nobody wants to fuck you in that."

It was like watching a trainwreck happen in slow motion. Mateo's mom was getting the full Russo treatment from top to bottom. There was nothing I could do to keep my mother's misplaced opinions and my sisters' unfiltered commentary from colliding and starting a fire.

"My son would do you in a chicken suit covered in grease,

honey," Anna shot back to the shock of absolutely everyone. My jaw unhinged and Mia's eyes glimmered in satisfaction. "Everyone knows you can't choose the first dress you try on. Let's see another."

"Agreed." My mother clapped twice. "The winner is in there somewhere, Talia, you just need an open mind. What about something with a train?"

My eyes flickered to hers in the mirror. "I don't want a train."

"A train is classy," she argued. "Just like the veil."

"I'm not wearing a veil either."

"Next you'll say you don't want your father to walk you down the aisle!" She threw up her hands.

"Trains get stepped on, dragged through the mud, and end up looking filthy and tattered halfway through the night. Then all anyone is doing is pointing and whispering about how dirty the dress is, and how hard it's going to be to dry clean like I'd ever wear it again."

"You could get it preserved," May suggested. "Put it in a beautiful box, frame it in a closet so that you can look at it whenever you want!"

"So every time I walk into my closet I think the Corpse Bride is there to murder me until I flip on the lights?"

"Trains are kind of out, she's right," Bella agreed. "But the veil is still doable."

"A veil is an old, outdated, and ridiculous symbol of the patriarchy." I crossed my arms over my jeweled bodice. "So men knew they were getting a pure, modest, *virgin* wife—who, let's be honest back in those days, was probably the ripe age of thirteen."

"The theatrics with you, Natalia." Mom sighed.

The bell on top of the entry door jingled to life as it opened and another tall, perfectly put-together brunette walked in silhouetted by a beam of mid-afternoon sunlight. Like the angels had held her by her arms and flown her directly from the pediatric ICU to the bridal salon on a cloud.

"So sorry I'm late." Camilla rounded the couch and kissed my mom in that la bise way. "I got stuck in a surgery and then caught up with some of my kids on the recovery floor. Next thing you know I'm reading one book to them, and then another—it's impossible to pry myself away." She glanced up and noticed Anna for the first time stuffed into the corner beside Isabella. "Hi. You guys wouldn't happen to have any tea here, would you? Or water with lemon will do, but sparkling, if possible."

"Cami, this is Anna, Mateo's mother." I cleared my throat loudly. "I didn't think you were going to make it."

"Of course. Wouldn't miss it. It's not every day your sister gets married for the first time." She walked over, pinched the material of my dress between her fingers, and circled me assessingly.

"It takes a special occasion nowadays to get all my girls in the same room," Mom added. "I can't even remember the last—"

"That random day last June," I fired back. "Dad hired the private chef and we took the boat off the coast for a few hours, but he got so belligerently drunk he threw the cold, dead swordfish that we were meant to eat back into the ocean to 'be with its family.' Then we watched a shiver of sharks enjoy our thousand-dollar dinner."

"Sounds special to me." Mia popped an almond from the bowl on the coffee table into her mouth.

Cami finished her silent judgment of the dress and stepped back. "The train is atrocious. It will be a nightmare in the sand, the neckline does nothing for your boobs, and the embellishments look like I won them out of a claw machine."

"I was going to say the same thing," Mom agreed.

My skin bristled. "But you just said—"

I stopped myself and sucked in a long, deep breath. A mounting ire idled in that dark space behind my eyes at the center of my forehead, willing all the intrusive thoughts I was having—like sending the side table with the tissues on it careening into the mirror—to the recesses of my mind. Because if the side table went, the potted plant beside it was next. And then there was no stopping me from filling my hands with dirt and running down the length of the salon tainting every hanging dress in sight. While I was at it, I would probably end up hooting like a gorilla and tearing my own dress off my body until all that was left was me standing there sweating and gyrating in my tightest pair of Spanx with my nipples out.

"That's settled then," I breathed out instead. "Be right back."

The next several trips in and out of the dressing room were as productive as the first. I tried organza and tulle, chiffon, lace, high neckline, long sleeve, cap sleeve, and strapless, with a combo of every single one of those things in A-line, empire, and sheath. All met with resounding, underwhelming reactions from everyone but Anna, who was happy enough to simply be there.

My expectations leading into the day had been too high. The minute that all of my sisters decided to come together for this I should have known it would have nothing to do with celebrating me and more with sticking their fingers into the process. Making sure that even though I was getting married and settling down, I was still just Natalia. I wasn't the doctor, the lawyer, or the real estate mogul. They reminded me without having to say a word.

Ophelia would know exactly what to say but she was thousands of miles away in Colorado. Probably still lying in bed with Frankie on a lazy Saturday morning, spooning each other and giggling and saying "I love you" over and over again in a borderline baby voice, because that's the shit you do when you first fall in love with someone.

My fingers hovered over her contact in my phone. She would answer, she always did. No matter what time of the day, even if it was during her work week or on a holiday. Hell, she even picked up the phone once in the middle of a pap smear. She had shifted her whole schedule to make it to all of our upcoming wedding events, and stayed up late after grading papers to research places for a bachelorette party on the Las Vegas Strip. Ophelia had compiled lists of florists and caterers and local graphic designers that I should consider for invitations, and made spreadsheets with all of this information neatly accessible in a joint document titled "THE BEST DAY OF OUR LIVES" that she updated daily.

All of this and she wasn't even officially my maid of honor. I hadn't chosen one between my sisters and Ophelia and the expectations lingering there. The right thing to do was to choose a Russo and interchange who got the maid of honor spot at each of our weddings. I could pick Mia, and then Mia could choose Bella, Bella could have Cami, and then Cami could reluctantly ask me like it was the sisterhood of the traveling bridesmaid. Or, I could have all three of them and they could split the responsibility, split the speech, split the torture of having to say and do nice things for me for the next six months.

I could also have nothing and no one. Mateo and I could elope at the courthouse and cancel the entire thing right here and now and I would get *no* complaint from him, that's for damn sure. As excited as he was to get married, he was not expecting the amount of work that went into making a wedding a reality.

The option tickled me momentarily. How freeing that lack of planning would be. No appointments, fittings, or tastings. No decision making, or inevitably pissing people off. God, it was an appetizing thought. But I couldn't live with myself if I regretted it.

Bothering Phee didn't feel right, and I knew she was already beating herself up for not being here for this. I shoved my phone back in my bag as May returned with an armful of new and heinous dresses for me to try on.

"Actually," I stopped her. "I did have one dress in mind that I had shipped to this store to try on. I'd like to see that one."

It was my dream gown. Delicate and trimmed with lace, with enough shimmer that it attracted your attention but had nothing close to a jewel sewn into the chest. The fishtail accentuated every last well-earned curve on my body, hugged my hips, cinched my waist, and put the girls on their pedestal with the most perfect sweetheart neckline. There was a flare at the knee so I could still dance, and spaghetti straps so I didn't have to worry about adjusting it all night. To top it all off, like fate, the bite of the zipper clasping together as I looked on in the mirror confirmed that it fit like a goddamn glove. No extensive alterations necessary.

All of the emotions came whirring in at once, choking me up and catching my breath. I'd tried on twenty other dresses and felt nothing but stress for the moment I'd been looking forward to since I was a little girl. But now I was that little girl again. I was so overwhelmed I started to cry.

May took on a misty sheen of her own. "I think we've found the winner."

I stepped out of the dressing room with a bundle of bunched tissues clutched in my fist and a full, genuine smile lifting my cheeks, expecting that every single eye in the bridal salon would be dancing toward me.

That wasn't what I found.

The couch was empty save for Anna, who, in her defense, lit up like a firework as soon as she saw me standing there. My eyebrows pinched together and a gutting disappointment that I couldn't hide stabbed at the center of my chest. My heart went from a frantic thump to an uneven stutter.

"Absolutely breathtaking, Natalia," Anna beamed. "Mateo will lose his mind if he sees you in that."

"Where is everyone?"

A pang of guilt washed across her face and her eyes cut toward her shoulder. My mom and the twins were behind her, occupied by none other than Camilla staring at herself in another mirror, *wearing a wedding dress.*

The hurt sliced through me like a hot knife, draining every ounce of excitement from my body. I deflated instantly. It was the most humiliating, demoralizing moment of my life, but it wasn't far from expected.

"Oh, honey." Anna laid a warm palm on my shoulder and gave it a squeeze. The best I could manage was a flat smile before the dejection turned into rage and the tint of the room blurred to red like a video game alerting its player that shit was about to go fucking down.

My feet carried me like I was possessed across the room. "What the fuck are you doing, Cam?"

Finally the attention I'd anticipated was totally on me, but I was way past that. It was too late, too raw. There wasn't a praise on the planet that would undo what had been done.

"Holy shit, Talia, that dress is amazing," Mia buzzed. She was smiling, fucking *smiling*. As if there wasn't a problem in the world. My eyes narrowed into slits. Bella and Mom tried to circle me encouragingly and I stuck my hands out, keeping them at arm's length.

"Take that off," I said bluntly, glowering at Camilla in the reflection of the mirror. My tone struck a chord because she sobered in the wake of it and stepped down from the platform. "You're supposed to be here for *me*."

"We are, sweetie," Mom piped up. "It's harmless fun. All eyes back on you now, promise."

A scoff rocketed out of me. The nerve of her to try and brush this off after seeing how clearly it took the wind out of my sails, as if I was the perpetual little sister and there was nothing to be upset over. I was in my dream dress waiting for the reaction that every single bride deserves from her family and instead I was hit with total duplicity. I could never get this moment back.

"You're not even getting married," I spat.

"She's not even in a relationship." Mia threw fuel on the fire, staving off a thrown elbow from Bella.

"You're not even in a relationship," I repeated more sternly. "How did this seem like a good idea to you? To *all* of you?"

"You're making it something it's not, Talia." Cami said it so nonchalantly it sounded like a joke. *Oh Camilla, you're so silly. What a funny thing to gaslight your sister about.* But I knew from the disheartened look on Anna's face, and the fact that she'd stepped away from the conversation and let it play out as a family dispute, that I wasn't crazy.

"It is something to me," I shot back. My voice cracked and betrayed me. "One day you'll get married, however far in the future that may be, to whatever rich dickhead you decide to tolerate for the rest of your life, and then you can try on dresses and you won't hear a peep out of me."

Camilla's face fell into a scowl.

"Let's not bicker, girls," Mom said. "It's a little misunderstanding."

"Yes," Camilla agreed. "It's only a dress. We've watched you put on about fifty already and you've hated every single one of them. No need to be a bitch."

It didn't matter how rough and tumble it got. By next week we'd all be back to the same old antics, fiasco swept under the rug and forgotten like it never even happened until it happened again. We didn't hold grudges in our family, we just pretended our problems didn't exist. With that being said, it didn't occur to me at all how nail in the coffin it might sound when I stepped up to my eldest sister and said, "I'm fine with being a bitch, because you already have being an insufferable cunt in the bag."

You could have heard a train pin dropping in that bridal salon. I might as well have kicked a baby.

"Fucking hell, Talia," Mia purred. "You're just throwing around the 'C' word like it's nothing."

My eyes rolled. "It's not even that serious. It's Australian."

"*Robert Irwin* is Australian," Bella said. "Robert Irwin does not say 'cunt'."

"Do you honestly think Robert Irwin hasn't called one of those crocodiles a cunt before?"

"This is classic Natalia," Cami interrupted. "I just think if you're expecting us to throw showers and plan parties and take time off from our very *real* jobs," she said pointedly, "the absolute least you could do is not take everything so personally."

My expectations were so astronomically low for my sisters' participation in wedding planning but this was next level. If playing a part in the happiest day of my life came with a guilt trip and an obligation to kiss their asses for the rest of eternity I would rather staple my lips to a fucking telephone pole. I didn't need any of them to help me. I didn't need their half-assed showers or unorganized parties. I most definitely didn't need them to, God forbid, sacrifice a day of work for me, either.

"It's a good thing you don't have to worry about any of that," I decided on a whim. "Because Ophelia is my maid of honor."

My stomach was twisting in an uncomfortable knot, flipping over and over on itself. I was going to have to debrief Mateo and hope he could convince his mom that I only saw my family on the rarest occasion, and there was more to me than swear words and phallic paraphernalia. Though at the moment, I wasn't sure of that fact myself.

The silence from my sisters and mom that followed my announcement spoke all the unsaid words I could already hear. There I was again, being the rebellious, defiant, black sheep Russo. Nothing was ever going to change.

I turned to May, glued to the wall by sheer panic and disbelief. "I'll take this dress, please. And I'm paying cash."

chapter five

Natalia

14 months ago

MY BEDROOM WAS A DISASTER. Which wasn't saying much, because my apartment was always kind of a disaster. It was an organized mess. I knew where everything was, but to someone else it might look like I was a hoarder who wore the same socks over and over again because I couldn't tell which laundry was clean or dirty. Some nights I slept under unfolded clothes, and other nights I moved said unfolded clothes to what I liked to call "the chair" in the corner of the bedroom. "The chair" also doubled as my sleep paralysis demon whenever I dozed off for an afternoon nap.

Up until a few days ago the mess wasn't an issue. There was no one coming upstairs into my apartment to see it. My parents never stopped by because they never left Palm Park unless for an extravagant vacation, and my sisters couldn't be arsed to meet me out for a drink, let alone have a sleepover. Now, the very real potential of a very real man, with cute little dimples and shiny brown hair, who filled out a shirt like a mannequin and smelled like what a candle company would call "driftwood", was minutes away from my door.

This first date sent me into full-on crisis mode earlier in the day. I spent half of it ripping apart my closet and pairing skirts with tops and shoes with belts, and then decided to hell with it and ran to the outlets to pick out something completely new to wear. I had no idea where we were going; he hadn't even hinted when I asked. All Mateo said was he'd pick me up at seven.

I posed in the standing mirror, opting to keep it safe in trendy sneakers and my favorite jeans, a lilac figure-hugging tank and layered gold jewelry from my ears to my fingers. The Neighbourhood played while I fluffed the roots of my hair, applied a clear glossy lip balm, and checked the time on my phone.

Any minute.

I fought the urge to tidy up a bit, only closing a few drawers and kicking a lonely heel under the bed. Because I was not going to sleep with him. Not tonight. I didn't want to fuck this up. I didn't want him to think that was all I was good for, or that he didn't need to try with me, or that he could add me to his roster because a girl who gave it up so easily couldn't possibly be *the one*. He was an older guy, more experienced; the last thing I wanted was to not be taken seriously.

My phone lit up with a call. Mateo didn't text; the straightforward confidence was so disarming it made my stomach flip.

"Hello?"

"Ready for me?"

Fuck.

"Mm-hmm," I said sheepishly.

"Good, I was getting bored of doing circles around the block so I didn't freak you out by showing up too early."

My heart tripped over itself. I moved toward the window and opened the curtain. A black pickup truck was sitting at the curb below and I could see Mateo through the windshield with his phone to his ear, one hand gripping the steering wheel.

"I'll be right down."

The call disconnected and I spun on my heel, taking one long look around the bedroom with my hands on my hips before I shoved every last thing I owned into the closet.

Just in case.

Mateo was waiting for me on the curb, very cool in dark-black jeans, a Henley, and a sandy corduroy jacket on top. I noticed the Catholic cross chain he wore around his neck when we first met. I wasn't religious, my family never went to church, but they liked to preach about the values it instilled anyway. Like they were too busy to visit God at home, but they'd send a Christmas card.

Mateo pulled me in for a hug immediately, one of those half hugs that felt professional instead of intimate, and dropped a coy greeting kiss on my cheek that was more skin than lips. He held me out by my hand at arm's length so he could freely let his eyes roam down my body.

"All right, give it a spin." He twirled me slowly and I ducked under our outstretched arms, flattered and giggly. I came to a stop facing him and he ran a hand down his face and grinned. "God, you are something."

My cheeks flamed and I instinctively looked to the concrete, kicking at the loose black mulch windswept onto the sidewalk.

"Really, Natalia. You're making me nervous again."

"I doubt I'm making you nervous if you're telling me I'm making you nervous." Mateo opened his passenger door and helped me up into the dark interior of the cab.

"I become brutally honest when I'm nervous. It just flows out of me like there's no filter there. You'll see. I've already done it twice tonight."

"I think it's charming," I said.

Mateo grinned and walked around the car. The engine purred and the mumblings of a song on the radio played as he stepped up on his side and closed us in. He was so much bigger beside me in such a confined space, so broad in the driver's seat, his smell concentrated. It took everything in me not to let my eyes flutter shut and breathe him in.

Instead of putting the truck in drive he turned toward me and my chest tightened.

"How was your day?"

I blinked. "My day?"

A corner of his lips parted into a sideways, amused smile. "Well, I already know how mine went."

He was asking about my day? I was used to dinner with one-sided small talk and a lousy go between the sheets before I saw myself out the door. To which I would then call Ophelia and we would trade horror stories from our somehow identical dating scenes despite her being across the country in Colorado. It was becoming a competition at this point.

"Yours was probably way more interesting than mine," I deflected. *Yeah right.* Three hours of my day were spent with a tentacle the size of my forearm suction cupped to the refrigerator in my kitchen. "Just...work," I answered.

For the first time, "work" gave me a hot, itchy feeling at the back of my neck. Because I knew if anything were to go anywhere with a guy, the extremely prominent and promiscuous side of my life would have to be revealed. I couldn't quite gauge yet what Mateo might think of it, but the possibility of rejection unnerved me already.

His smirk remained despite my dry answer.

"I'll loosen you up, Natalia Russo."

I wrung my hands in my lap and allowed a shy smile. "So, where are you taking me?"

Mateo's hand disappeared, digging into the pocket of his jeans and pulling out several rectangular pieces of cardstock. He read through what was scribbled on them, sorting them quickly. "Let's find out."

I laughed, bubbly and girlish, a sound that felt very childlike, or maybe youthful and distant because I hadn't heard it in so long. "I'm intrigued."

"It was too hard for me to narrow it down, and I didn't want to pick something you didn't like. So I figured if I put down a bunch of different options, and then had you blindly choose from them, you couldn't blame me for a shitty date choice. Plus it's a little spontaneous and fun, so..." he trailed off, shuffling the cards. "It's a little weird though, now that I'm saying it out loud."

"It's perfect." I stopped him from tucking the cards away. "I love that."

"Yeah?"

"Come on, then."

He fanned a few cards face down in front of me and I plucked one from under his thumb.

"I hope it's the couple's ashiatsu massages," Mateo joked.

"Why pay someone to walk on you when I'll do it for free?"

"I didn't know that was an option." Mateo playfully grabbed at the paper in my hand. "Give that back, I need to do some modifications."

I held it close to my chest and flipped it over, two words scribed on it in that universally manly all caps style of handwriting.

"Roller skating."

"Roller skating," Mateo repeated with a touch of disbelief.

"Yeah." I laughed, though my cheeks burned beneath the blush I was wearing. "Did you forget you wrote this?"

"Not at all," he said, straightening in his seat. "Have you ever roller skated?"

I paled. "No."

Mateo's tongue perused the inside of his cheek, gaze ping-ponging between my eyes then down to my mouth so briefly I wouldn't have never noticed if I wasn't so attuned to everything he did.

"It'll be great," he said abruptly. "Seatbelt, please."

* * *

THE ONE ROLLER rink in the area was old and oval-shaped, from the outside as well as in. There was a long handicap ramp and vertical beige vinyl siding with a sign outside hanging by a thin thread, the letters off-kilter and dimly lit.

High Roller. Or, H----oller.

Inside, the carpet was the kind of black that had turned gray over time, smooshed into a thinner, matted material by shoes and skates. It smelled like dust and burnt popcorn, a little bit like stale piss and mothballs.

Despite it, the glossy wooden rink in the center of the place was packed with people. Friday night dance-skate was in full swing, and a neon light show dotted and waved across the walls and floor.

I found a sticky plastic bench to sit on while Mateo rented the ugliest tan and orange wheeled skates for us to wear. Across from me three teenage boys were fighting over the joystick on a claw machine. Another stood at the side of the glass box coaching his friends in the direction of an iPad that I'm certain was glued to the base of the thing.

"This place is a shit hole." Mateo dropped the pairs of skates on the ground in front of me.

"How is it that no one has given it an update since 1986?" I laughed.

"I don't even think they've hired anyone new since '86," he said, nodding at the old man behind the skates counter. "Guy smells like rotting leather."

I kicked off my sneakers and tucked them under the bench. Before I could reach down, Mateo sank to a knee and grabbed my ankle, bringing my foot to rest on his thigh. My skin prickled to attention, and a swallow got stuck halfway down my throat. I'd been so deprived I was losing my mind over the muscle in his quad that I could feel through the thin layer of my sock.

God, his legs. He was stretching that denim to its limit, tight across his lap, but I wasn't looking... No, I was definitely not looking.

"I'm...I'm probably going to embarrass myself out there," I said to fill the silence as Mateo guided my heel gently into the skate. He pressed his thumb into the toes, testing the size, like a parent to a child with new shoes, and when he must've been satisfied, he started on the laces.

"That's okay." He smiled. "Embarrassment is a state of mind. I'll be with you every step of the way."

His fingers made quick work of the thin brown strings, weaving them all the way up and around the back of the skate once before giving me a double knot. We swapped ankles. This time, his thumb crept higher under the seam of my jeans, rubbing against skin. It was so inconsequential, he probably hadn't even realized he'd done it, and yet I was pleading silently that he'd planned that secret touch and knew exactly the effect it would have on me.

He laced the other skate up just as fast, twisting it into a knot that cinched at my ankle and giving me two pats of approval. "You're nice and tight."

My mouth twitched and Mateo caught it.

"And cheeky," he added.

"I'm trying to be good," I admitted. "First impressions and all."

"Don't be good," he said. "Be yourself."

"All right." I nodded. "I wasn't going to say anything but you probably caught chlamydia from that carpet."

"That's all right. I like the view from down here."

My lips parted and warmth settled low in my stomach. "Who's cheeky now?"

He clambered to his feet again, rubbing dust off his jeans and clapping it from his hands. "I can tell that you and I are just scratching the surface."

The rink itself was surrounded by four-foot walls, little slats of empty space to enter and exit back onto the safety of the rug. I hobbled from our bench to the wall a few feet away, one skate in front of the other, and swiveled back around. Mateo was still sitting on the bench with his skates tied, his hands clasped and elbows on his knees.

"Coming?"

"I have a secret." He scratched the back of his neck.

"Oh?"

"Yeah, it's nothing cool. It's actually more of a confession than a secret. But depending on how the rest of tonight goes, it might be a secret for us."

"That's quite the burden to bear. It better be good."

"Now"—he lifted his finger to no one, conducting his own dialogue like I'd noticed he often did—"you have to promise me, okay? That this stays close to your chest."

"God, the suspense is killing me."

Mateo took a long breath, filling his cheeks with air and blowing it out. "I don't know how to roller skate."

A short laugh burst out of me. His expression remained flat and I recouped. "Wait, what?"

"Never been."

"Mateo." I was still catching up to reality. "Why did you put that on the cards?"

He shrugged. "What were the odds of you actually choosing that one out of all of them?"

"Pretty fair," I said. "As good as anything else. You could have told me to pick a new one!"

"I could have." He stood slowly, wobbly knees quaking beneath his stocky build. I reached a hand out for balance and Mateo grabbed it. "But that wasn't the game. It was you pick the date and we do it, not you pick the date and I approve it."

That was a very hot way to put it. Mateo was more aware of himself than any other guy I'd dated. I liked that he was honest, and blunt, and somewhat abrupt; it was invigorating to be kept on my feet. He made me laugh without trying to. I glanced toward the rink, busy circles of people leaving a breeze as they flew past. "We have to try. You didn't get me all booted up for nothing."

"Oh, we're going." The toes of our skates clacked together. "I'll be the first man to take you roller skating even if it kills me." At that, he tugged me to the cusp of the rink, timid like jumping into a swimming pool for the first time. Our fingers interlaced and we leapt off the rug together.

And immediately ate shit.

Like, a theatrical amount of shit eating. Arms pinwheeling, legs swept out from under both of us, four skates pointed at the ceiling. But we never let go of each other's hand.

A low groan rumbled out of his chest. "Holy fuck, I think I did just die." Slowly he sat up, bringing my limp, windless body with him as I was too busy shaking with laughter. There was nothing that could have prepared me for that. "Are you okay?"

Skaters swerved around us like we weren't even there. "I think I broke my ass."

"That would be a tragedy," he said, miraculously getting back to his feet and extending a hand to hoist me up. This time we were more careful, smaller baby steps instead of the very optimistic stride the first time. I bent my knees and glided along beside him until it was like I was a sidecar holding on by a shaky hand.

"There we go, just needed some adjustment time. It's all about assessing and adapting."

"Do you approach everything like a video game map?"

"Everything in life can be navigated," he said. "I've been doing it for fifteen years. It's like second nature now. Another reason I didn't veto the date card you pulled. I figured if there was a will there was a way. I'd figure it out."

"Look at you now, *Roll Bounce*."

"If they put on a little disco I'll start doing spins." Mateo moved as if he was going to twirl us in a circle and I squealed in protest. His skates flared out and he did a balancing act of running in place to stay upright. "Maybe not quite yet."

"Save it for next time."

"Next time?" Mateo raised a brow and smirked. "Am I impressing you enough with this to get a next time already?"

I'd exposed myself. I wanted a next time, of course. I wanted a third time and a fourth to get to know him, and that scared me. Knowing him more meant letting him know me more.

"I'm optimistic," I said. "The night is young."

"So I will take you roller skating," he started, "and then wine and dine you at that glorious concession stand with a stale pretzel and a Coke the size of your head."

"Oooh, this is really stacking up." A laugh floated out of me.

"Then I'm going to take you over to those sticky, disgusting arcade games and win you enough coins for a bamboo finger trap of your choice, and we're going to forget that I'm in my mid-thirties and pretend we're meeting for the first time as nineteen-year-olds, and this is the first day of the rest of our lives."

My cheeks were starting to hurt. "God, I was such a bitch when I was nineteen. You probably wouldn't have liked me."

"I would have followed you around like a fucking puppy on a leash."

"Shut up." I nudged him playfully.

"On the other hand, you wouldn't have given me a second look at nineteen," he said. "Scrawny kid with buzzed hair, fresh face, little Bronx accent. I'm glad we're meeting now."

"I was going through a rebellious phase," I mentioned. "I wanted out of my parents' house more than anything. They couldn't stand that I was going to a state school instead of a private college. So when I left in August I only ever came back for long holiday breaks. Even stayed in Colorado for most of the summer with my best friend and lived with her."

"We have that in common." Mateo had picked up our pace and went from stomping along to actually coasting.

"Family is a bit of a sore subject for me," I said candidly. "They're the only thing in the world that has the power to hurt me worse than anything but I can't stop loving."

"Because it feels like you're the one who's wrong for it." He nodded. "Like, how dare you not love something that you came from."

I breathed out a squeak of relief. "Yeah. Exactly."

His thumb grazed back and forth lightly across mine, and that simple touch woke up my nerves all the way to my shoulder.

"Why are we having such a deep conversation?" I cut the swallowing silence in half. "This is our first date. We're supposed to be talking about stuff like our careers and our favorite TV shows."

"I already know what you do." He chuckled.

My stomach hollowed. "You do?"

Mateo tilted his head, confused. It took me a second to remember that he'd met me at the bank, and to him, I was still a normal, average, unassuming woman who sits behind a desk all day.

"Oh, fuck. Right, you do."

"Did you hit your head when we fell?"

No, I was just paranoid that you knew I was a sex worker and this entire date was a farce and a ploy to sleep with me after watching me perform online. I was careful, but my biggest fear was being recognized and pursued in real life, and I didn't know if I'd ever shake it.

"Tell me something less deep," I blurted.

"I don't think I'm capable of having regular conversations with you. I'm either sharing too much, or worrying about sharing too much and then doing it anyway. Like now. I'm doing it right now."

"Tell me about your childhood pets," I suggested.

"I had a one-eyed schnauzer named Peppy. He was the ugliest dog I'd ever seen. My brother found him under a shed looking like he'd been run over by a car and when he got home my mother thought he'd grabbed a rat off the street."

"A rat that big?"

"Oh, pretty girl, you've never been in a New York City subway have you?"

I twisted my lips into a shy smile. Hearing him call me something so endearing so nonchalantly was nothing like what I was used to. It rolled off his tongue, like he was the only man on earth who could say that and get away with it.

"What else do you have for me?" Mateo poked.

"Where were you when you found out Michael Jackson died?"

"Afghanistan."

I choked up a laugh. "Oh. That sucks."

"I had to sob quietly in the barracks." He sighed. "Listen to 'Billie Jean' on repeat on my iPod and pretend like everything was okay. Like MJ hadn't hee'd his last hee."

I crackled with laughter. My bottom lip was worn raw by my teeth and the constant clenching to tamper down a smile. "I was at little league softball practice," I countered. "Also sobbing because my dreams of going to Neverland were crushed forever."

Mateo bellowed out a hearty, rumbling laugh. His light brown eyes twinkled beneath the neon stripe of light, his teeth beaming even brighter and straighter than before. "I think you might have dodged a bullet there."

"I was in crisis for weeks, watching all of his music videos on repeat on MTV. I started wearing a fedora."

"Natalia." He said my name like a sweet warning. It spread something cool and lingering through my body, and gave me the kind of chills that made my hair stand on edge and my bones vibrate in anticipation for what was next. I was hanging there by a thread to hear it again.

"You know, no one ever calls me Natalia, really. My dad. But mostly in a scolding way. It's nice to hear it said with a smile."

It healed something small. A stitch into a wound.

"Does anyone call you Tally?"

"Tally?" I hummed. "No."

He hesitated. "Well, what if I did?"

I'd bite. I thought the name over and over again in my head and it felt foreign and a bit silly, but also like a new identity. A person I was only with Mateo. "I'm not sure." I shrugged. "Test it out."

He cleared his throat as we rounded the curved end of the oval rink. Skating had become involuntary. "I think you are absolutely breathtaking, Tally."

A seed planted in my heart and started budding.

"Sounds all right," I lied, my face giving it away.

"Okay." He smirked. "How about, 'You are smart, and deep, and funny, Tally.'"

He let go of my hand and slid it across my lower back, inching us closer together.

"I am?" I couldn't take a compliment for the life of me. I felt averse to it, undeserving, even if what he was saying was true. I didn't know what to do with it.

Mateo's tongue drew across his bottom lip, and my throat went dry. "I'm going to do that honesty thing again with you now."

"Okay," I said quietly. I was scared of how much more honesty he had in him. Because I knew what I would be doing if I were honest with myself at this moment and it wasn't anything *near* innocent.

"I am trying so hard to be respectful, Tally," he drawled. That low sweep of an accent curved around me. "So hard to be a good boy, you know? You are easy to forget my manners around, and I don't want to lose my gentleman card on a first date."

No one around us had a clue, not a damn idea that heat was sinking low in my belly and my legs felt an instability that had nothing to do with the skates. The music was drowned out by the pounding of my pulse in my ears as my senses gravitated in the direction of the man in front of me.

"Well for...let's say *research*, so I can confirm or deny"—I found my courage—"what would you say if you weren't trying to be so respectful?"

A muscle in his jaw rippled; yellow-brown eyes darkened to umber. He pulled me closer again, impossibly closer, feathering his fingers against my hip, and the tip of his nose dipped into my hair so his mouth sat just behind my ear. God, everything in my body was thrumming.

"Tally, for every good, pure, adoring thought I've had about you since you walked your tight little ass outside and sat in my car tonight, I've had another just as wicked and ten times more raw.

Because I can tell you you're beautiful all night, but you know that about yourself, don't you?"

He looked at me. My mouth had parted silently; my eyes had drooped. He pinched my jaw between his fingers and made me nod back in agreement. His touch lingered.

"But, Tally," he whispered. "I want to tell you how beautiful you are with your mouth full." Those same fingers swept across my bottom lip and a sigh fell out of me. "You have such pretty fucking lips," he added. "So pretty that if I was being disrespectful I might even think about kissing them."

"But you're definitely not." My gaze flitted to his plush mouth, the stubble of hair framing it so perfectly. "Being disrespectful."

"I couldn't." He leaned in. His breath fanned across my mouth and it was pure warmth and mint. "I wouldn't want to screw this up."

I let my eyes close.

And then I caught an edge. Or he caught an edge. Or both of us leaned too far in one direction at the same time and my skate dipped behind his. Either way, we were on our feet one moment, the next in a tangle of flopping limbs on the cold, hard wooden floor for the second time in one night.

Mateo groaned, holding his side. I stared up at the perforated ceiling tiles like they were the stars in the sky. "This is what I get for being disrespectful. It's all my dead relatives keeping me in check."

I laughed. I laughed, and laughed, and went willingly into his arms when he picked me up off the floor and dragged me off the rink.

* * *

IT WAS past ten when he walked me to the door of my apartment. The air had a bite to it. Early November coolness washed over us like the dim overhead light that cast a white circle onto the concrete.

That almost kiss had lingered for the entire drive home. It was like an unanswered question. A blinking cursor begging us to finish the sentence. In my head he was backing me into a wall and claiming me, but in reality, Mateo's hands were resting comfortably in his pockets while I scraped at an invisible line in the sidewalk with my shoe.

"Do you—"

"This was—"

We spoke over one another.

"No, you—" I started.

"Go ahead," Mateo offered, putting a hand out as if letting me have the floor.

"I had a lot of fun with you."

His smile widened, and he looked up at the sky, clearly thinking about something. It gave me a chance to admire how handsome he was in another light, the sharp angles of his chin still so prominent when basked in darkness, his full lips, the freckles on his neck that brought my eyes down to the dips in his collarbone.

"Do you ever howl at the moon?"

I blinked up into his soft stare. "Howl at the moon?"

"Yeah, like tonight. It's a full moon. It kind of makes me feel like a kid again, hearing all those myths about wolves and the moon. I would pretend I was a wolf sometimes with my brother, because that was a very cool, manly thing to be." He was pacing in a small line. "What I'm trying to get at here is that the moon reminded me of being a kid just now, and how things were really simple and fun, and how there wasn't so much stress back then. Or even if there was, we could still pretend we were wolves and howl at the moon and that stuff disappeared for a little while. That's how the last few hours have felt for me, at least. Like being a kid again."

That seed that was planted in my heart earlier was growing a stem, I could feel it stretching itself out in my chest. He thought nothing he said was making sense but it did perfectly. He was describing healing. I didn't know everything about the man in front of me—in fact, I knew next to nothing—but I wanted to. I wanted to know what he needed healing from, too.

I didn't think about it. I just took a long balancing breath, and howled.

There was no one else outside, but a light switched on a few buildings down, and I swore I saw a rogue curtain rustle in a window. Mateo's eyes widened, and a shocked, almost saccharine grin spread across his face.

My breath tapered out and I sighed. "You're right, that felt good."

He brushed his palm down his face. "Yeah? Fuck it."

Mateo howled louder than I had, his neck stretching toward the full bright moon. It tinged him in blue and he looked even more dazzling than ever. Everything about this date was entirely unexpected. It was an unsolvable puzzle. It was new and fun and made me wish it would never end. I wanted to keep opening doors with Mateo. I wanted to keep guessing what was next.

"Look at where my honesty has gotten us now," he finished, laughing. He took a step toward me, leaving little more than a finger of space between us. His body heat radiated through my thin top, and I wondered without looking down if my even thinner bralette was exposing something different.

"Can it be my turn to be honest?" I asked.

His throat bobbed as he swallowed. Another inch closer now, pressing our hips together. "Of course."

"I wasn't going to sleep with you tonight."

"I wasn't expecting anything."

"But if I kiss you, and send you on your way, it's just going to be me and my vibrator upstairs for the rest of the night."

"Fuck's sake," he sighed out, pressing his palms against the front door on either side of my head.

"Wishing it was you being very, very disrespectful instead."

He tucked a fallen strand of hair behind my ear. "Well, what are we going to do about that, Tally?"

I turned and unlocked the entryway, falling into my small foyer that led up a flight of stairs. I didn't look back but I left the door open as I climbed slowly to the second floor with my lungs and my heart in my throat. There was a very strong possibility that I'd just blown it. Coming on too hard, too strong, overconfident. I'd have to live with it whether I liked it or not.

I'd almost reached the top step when the door slammed shut behind me, stopping me in my tracks. Followed by Mateo's footsteps trailing me upstairs.

chapter six

Natalia

"IT WAS A FUCKING DISASTER, PHEE." I pinched my phone between my shoulder and my ear. "J.T. and Janet Jackson level catastrophic. I might as well have ripped my top off and saved myself the embarrassment."

"I doubt it was as bad as you're making it seem." Ophelia's soft voice crackled on the other end. "It's always worse after the fight, because you keep thinking about all the things you could have said and done in the moment. When you take a shower, especially. I have full disagreements with my shampoo bottles."

"I called Camilla a cunt in front of my future mother-in-law."

A beat of silence passed. "Well, that word is so much less taboo now."

"That's what I said! Like, I'm sorry you haven't caught up yet, no need to make me feel like a Victorian woman with her ankles out."

"It's a small hiccup," she said. "You got your dress, and it's perfect. Camilla will get over it."

"This is why I need you here. You're the only one who gets me. I'm not ready for the next six months of doing damage control. And after the other day, good luck trying to get my sisters to be complicit in anything that has to do with this wedding.

They're actively campaigning against me now that none of them get to wave the maid of honor flag around."

"You know I love you," Ophelia reminded me. "I am very okay with being the secret unofficial maid of honor if it's going to ruffle feathers. I don't need the label."

"No, you *deserve* the label."

"So Frankie and I are public enemy number one at the Duran wedding," she noted. "Got it."

"For being two of the most delightful and giving people on the planet. Whom we love and cherish so much we couldn't imagine it any other way." I put Ophelia on speaker phone to free my hands and gave the esthetician beside me a silent thumbs-up. "You are so welcome for him, by the way. Not everyone gets to live out their real-life Hallmark Christmas dreams."

"Thank you," she said. "For not only inspiring orgasms all over the internet, but also all over the bedroom in my apartment. And the kitchen, and the shower, and the linen closet, interestingly enough."

"I want to know the details."

"You really don't."

"Please," I pressed. "Sex biz over here is taking everything out of me. Mateo works late every night now that Frankie's gone, and I'm pulling double time between the sheets. Do you understand how boring playing DJ on the downstairs turntable gets when the vault of daydreams runs dry? I can only picture Winston Duke naked so many times."

"Playing DJ on the what?" Ophelia laughed.

"Masturbating, Phee. I am sick and tired of masturbating ten feet down the hall from Mateo's mother, because that is *all* I can think about when I'm doing it. Indulge me. Does Frankie hold your hand when he goes down on you? Does he wash your hair all slow and clumsy-like when you're in the shower? Does he put a towel down on the bed? God, please say yes."

Phee sucked in a deep breath. "What if...I tell you he puts the towel in the dryer first?"

"Oh, shut the fuck *up*," I yelped, followed by a low hiss as a strip of wax was ripped from between my legs.

"Where are you right now?" she asked. I focused on the dim ceiling lights above me, balancing my phone on my chest and butterflying my knees apart. "Are you getting your pussy waxed while you're on the phone with me?"

"How do you know that?" I looked up as if Ophelia's bright blue eyes would be watching me from across the room. Another hot dollop of wax hit my skin and I tensed.

"I have your location on," she said. "Duh."

"Duh," I repeated. "I have a very specific client this afternoon who requests a borderline hairless cat. I make him settle for Bermuda Triangle. Mateo isn't a fan of hardwood floors and neither am I."

"Have you ever seen a guy clean-shaven down there?"

"Atrocious," I commented.

"Agreed," she said. "I call those men Pinocchios. And the rug burn on your nose is *not* worth it."

My esthetician let out a humored grunt before ripping another long strip of wax off me. "Some of us have a gag reflex." I released the breath I'd been holding in anticipation of the pain. "Not *me*. But some of us."

"So what's the deal with the client?" Ophelia asked.

"He's a loner with internet access. We chat once a month for a few hours, and I make a couple thousand dollars talking about the weather with my tits out while he jerks off."

"That's it?"

"That's it." I shrugged. "It's almost Valentine's Day, I'm going to be drowning in company-keeping for the next two weeks. Then the personalized requests. Do you know that people gift their significant others videos of Mateo and I boning?"

"Doesn't surprise me," she said. "It's like Build-A-Bear for porn."

"Exactly," I sang. "Why can't you be my real sister? Or my mom? You basically already are like my mom. I never would have passed that Excel lecture sophomore year without you writing my assignment schedule out on our whiteboard. I'll call you Mommy any day if it means I'll feel like less of an idiot to my own family."

"You are *not* an idiot. You are a beautiful, smart, badass businesswoman with more heart and work ethic than anyone I've ever met. And you're going to be married to the male version of yourself in six short months."

I took a deep, reprieving breath. "Hopefully I'll just fly under the radar for the most part so I can plan this wedding between disappointed phone calls and obligatory events."

"Don't overstress, Frankie and I are handling everything we can. The Vegas stay is secured, everyone's been informed—"

"What did my sisters say?"

"Well." A nervous little laugh escaped her. "They didn't exactly answer the group chat. *But*, I know they received the message because I was sent money for...'*Natalia's final fuck*'." She paused. "And I'm putting together all the scheduling and reservations for that weekend, so it's going to be epic and I hope you remember none of it."

"That makes two of us." My wax specialist sat back and motioned for me to flip around. "Gotta go, I need to spread my cheeks for the butthole strips."

"They surprisingly hurt the least," Ophelia said. "Have fun with your lonely rich guy, and then drink some wine in the bathtub and add some really expensive linens to your registry. So your sisters can buy the sheets you make more money than them getting fucked in."

"That is exactly the pep talk I needed." A happy hum warmed my chest. "Thank you, love you more."

"Love you more."

chapter seven

Natalia

14 months ago

OUR FINGERS WERE LAZILY INTERTWINED as I unlocked the beige door to my apartment, shouldering the latch that often stuck in the humidity. I'd left the ceiling fan turning and a waft of cold air hit us. I breathed out a sigh of relief but my pulse hammered in my ears. I hadn't brought a man into my apartment in months, and even then I was just scratching an itch. This *was* scratching an itch—a very irritated, persistent, violently growing itch named Mateo Duran, because if I went to bed tonight without knowing what his mouth felt like on my body I might never sleep.

The brassy bulb hanging over the table buzzed to life as I flipped the light switch and dropped my keys on the kitchen island. Mateo shrugged off his jacket and draped it over the arm of the couch while I tried to discreetly swipe a pile of mail into the corner of the counter, as if he cared. As if we could think about anything other than the massive weight of the elephant in the room. I quite literally invited him upstairs to have sex, but now I was so nervous I couldn't even look him in the eye. It hurt to swallow, and I knew a patch of red was starting to form right at the base of my collarbone like it always did when I couldn't rope my emotions.

"Do you want a drink?"

"No." He shook his head. "I think that liter of soda at the roller rink was enough." For the first time I glanced up and though his words were light-hearted, his hazel eyes had darkened to coal. He had both hands in his pockets, studying me as he stepped closer. His tongue swept across his lips.

My back hit the counter and I braced my hands on it. He was so close now I could see the threads weaving over one another on his black shirt, and the subtle tease of his cologne invaded my space. I wanted to run my nose across the vein on his neck and breathe it in. Every nerve low in my belly was tying itself in a knot in anticipation. But this is what I did—*sex*. Sex was second nature to me. I knew how to entice a man, intrigue him, put on a show, exude confidence. I did it regularly. But for some reason, with Mateo standing in front of me, I forgot everything. I wanted him so badly it froze me in place.

Mateo's eyes fell to my mouth and he spoke slowly, sending a flutter straight through me. "Tell me again, what happens if I kiss you right now?" His sweet voice was low and deep. There was something cutting about how naturally he went from playful to dominant.

"I think I might kiss you back." I was as breathy as he was heady.

His lip twitched and our thighs brushed. "Then I might get a little handsy, fair warning. Because I have been dying to touch you in a way we won't come back from."

Chills pebbled up my arms and my core tightened. I tilted my chin up and he braced one of his arms against the counter, his much larger hand landing beside mine and partially caging me in.

"As long as I have your permission, Tally."

I let my eyes close and my lips part, his nose brushed against my cheek so briefly, and then soft lips fell over mine. He kissed me like I might fall apart if he wasn't careful. Like he might scare me away but needed to do it anyway, and I momentarily forgot my promise to kiss him back because I was so lost in that pillowy caress, how our lips moved perfectly against one another and how the hair on his lip brushed me so sensually that I sighed.

He pulled away timidly, waiting. Honeyed eyes flitting back and forth between my glazed ones. Mateo wanted me to take the lead, and I tasted what little wetness he had left on my mouth like it was water in a drought and slid my fingers through the hair at the nape of his neck, tugging him back to me.

That was like opening a gate. Suddenly, we weren't moving slowly or cautiously anymore. Mateo's lips crashed into mine and our tongues lashed against one another in a way that confirmed the sexual frustration wasn't one-sided. My entire body reacted in a wave of tingling shocks, from my head down my spine, gathering at my core in a flood of heat and desperation that I welcomed. Mateo wrapped his arms around my lower back, pulling me to him, his large warm hands sliding up and down. I felt fragile in his strong hold and without thinking, I lifted my hips, pushing up slightly onto my toes. Immediately, both of his hands slid under my ass and lifted my legs to latch around his waist.

My head fell back and he kissed my exposed neck, tasting me as he worked his way up and sunk his teeth into the lobe of my ear. The noise that came out of me made him huff out a short, deep laugh.

"I want more where that came from," he said. "Tell me what I have to do to hear you like that in my ear for the rest of the night."

Mateo took a step forward and planted me on the counter, pressing his entire body between my legs at the perfect height to feel that hard resistance between us at the zipper of his pants. I pulled his shirt over his head and dropped it to the floor. At the center of his chest was a tattoo of a family crest that spread over tight muscle and dark hair. His happy trail ran in a line down his torso, patching over his belly button and tucking itself into the waistline of his jeans. I traced my fingers over fine lines, touching everywhere there was ink. Mateo's breathing toppled over itself, every swallow cording his throat as if my timid graze were too much. Goosebumps fanned across his arms and chest.

"Do you have any tattoos I should know about?" he asked.

His erection had grown impossible to ignore and I didn't try to hide the fact that I was looking, my gaze filling in the blanks. Very large, veiny blanks that I prayed my optimism wasn't over-compensating for. "If you can find them, you can see them," I said.

Mateo ran a hand up my thigh, to the hem of my shirt, and lifted it swiftly over my head. He didn't pause before closing the distance and winding his hands behind my back to unclip my lacy black bralette. It dropped onto my lap and the cool air puckered my already sensitive nipples.

Mateo's eyes dropped, hooding almost entirely before clamping shut. He bit down on his knuckle in glorious, welcomed agony. "Fuck. *Fuck.*"

I dragged his rough hands to my breasts to coach him into squeezing and playing with me. To my satisfaction and on his own accord, Mateo dipped down to take one in his mouth, sucking on my nipple. My eyes lulled into the back of my head.

"Bedroom," I called out. "Second door on the right."

"Yes ma'am."

Thank God I'd thrown my entire life in my closet before our date. I was so predictable, I couldn't even fool myself. I slid to the carpeted floor, kicking out of my shoes. Mateo's hands went to the button on my jeans, and mine flung to his in the same pattern —through the hole, zipper down, my fingers breaching his waistband and pulling it off until he stood in only tight black boxer briefs.

I let him wrench my jeans by the belt loops toward the floor, and my stomach flipped in figure eights when he dropped to his knees to help me step out of them. His gentleness was something I never expected, and I couldn't ignore the way having such a masculine, rough-edged man kneeling before me set me on fire.

His fingers wrapped around my knees and his mouth met my thigh, kissing, licking, moving upward as my legs threatened to give out. He lifted one, hooking it over his shoulder and putting my entire sex inches from his face. I steadied myself with my hands in his long hair, gripping hard enough to unfurl a noise from deep in his chest. The vibration of it sent a pulse straight to my clit. "I told you I liked the view from down here."

"The view from up here is monumentally underrated." I tossed my head back at the first feeling of his warm mouth over the thin material of my panties. I was wet and writhing, canting myself toward his lips to feel it again. He hummed, licking me over my thong and taking the strip of material between his teeth to drag it to the side, exposing me.

"I'm going to eat your pussy, Tally. Until your knees give out and you're nothing but a puddle for me to carry to that bed."

"Please." My knees nearly buckled then and there. His head got lost between my thighs and his tongue parted my core in one aggressive lap that I swore I'd remember the feeling of for the rest of my life. Pass after pass it became harder to breathe or stay quiet; I lost myself in the pleasure of Mateo going down on me. He was thorough and practiced, a quality I might raise an eyebrow at if I were in a stable state of mind, but in the throes of it I was silently thanking all the women who may have come before me to train this man well.

His tongue circled my clit languidly, rotating between flicking and sucking, making it impossible to tell where the slick of his spit ended and my drenched arousal began. A very familiar feeling I'd only ever replicated with a vibrating toy started in my pelvis, spreading like warm water to my thighs. My body keeled in on itself, limbs going numb and worthless and I dug my nails into the back of his neck to keep myself upright.

"Fuck, you're good," I managed.

"If the taste of you gets me this fucking hard I'm a goner when you let me inside."

He licked a spot that made my eyes flutter shut and I pressed his head harder against it, moving him where I needed the friction. My hips met his mouth and I bucked on his tongue until my legs started shaking and his promise came to fruition. A broken, begging noise squeaked out of me and his fingers tightened around my thighs.

"Ride my face until you come on it," he groaned. "Please. I need it, Tal, I need you to."

He needed me to.

Nothing pipelined an orgasm like a desperate man pleading for it. My stomach tightened, pleasure reaching a peak as my jaw went slack. He curled one thick finger inside of me, taking me by surprise, and the rush of my climax slammed violently to a brink in three short strokes. I came so hard my vision blurred and my brain and body seemingly disconnected at the wire because when I reentered a stable plane of existence, I realized I had *soaked* him. My thighs, his cheeks—the shining evidence of my earth-shattering orgasm was even dripping down his neck. I went from boiling over the edge to ice queen in seconds.

"Oh my god," I panicked, slipping my knee off his shoulder.

"Oh...my god," Mateo repeated.

His breath was coming in uneven bursts, eyes blown wide and dark as fucking obsidian. He licked his lips and I started wiping his face with my hands which did nothing but coat us both more. "I'm so sorry."

"Sorry?" He tugged my hand away from his face and pulled me closer. "You're seriously apologizing for that? God, what kind of morons have you been with? That was the hottest fucking thing that's ever happened to me, Natalia."

A nervous laugh bubbled from my throat; it was the only reaction I could find beyond utter disbelief. Looking down, his cock was pitching his briefs so aggressively I could see the entire outline of it. "Are you serious? I just..."

"Squirted on my face. And I want you to do it again." He stood, taking me with him to the bed. I fell flush against the sheets and he pushed his briefs down his legs, his erection springing free and full. "And again," he said, moving to my panties and ushering them off. "And again." He spread my knees apart, folding his body into the space left open and settling his shaft against the apex of my thighs.

Mateo's mouth and his strong, warm body slid against mine. His pulse drummed against my chest more fiercely with every lock of our lips, and every tangle of our tongues brought me closer and closer to another peak. I thought that this type of undeniable, devastating chemistry only existed in my dreams. It was more than lust—we *meshed*. We enjoyed one another, connected on a personal level that made it easy to be here doing this with him after one measly date. Everything between the two of us clicked like a latch into place.

I reached to my bedside drawer blindly, rustling around for a tiny box and a foiled condom then pressed it into the palm of his hand.

Mateo paused.

"I haven't had to use those in months," I rushed out. "I haven't been with anyone. I'm clean."

He shook his head, rubbing the head of his cock more deliberately against my already soft and begging entrance. "You're my hero right now."

"I am?"

"I didn't have one. I thought I was fucked."

"Not fucked," I said sarcastically.

He laughed. "Not fucked."

I took the condom from him, opening it without ever breaking his eye contact. The room blurred around us and the air became thicker, like everything except the two of us was dripping in a melting pot. My fingers curled around his shaft and I pumped, smoothing a bead of precum over the tip with my thumb. Mateo started kissing me again as I rolled the condom down and guided him back between my legs.

"How do you want me?" he asked tersely. My brows furrowed; I didn't think that would be an option. It was new territory to have a partner who didn't think he knew what I wanted without working for it.

"I don't think I've ever been asked that question," I said honestly. My pussy was thrumming for him, every cursory graze of his tip driving me crazy.

"Well that's not how it's going to go with me." He grabbed his cock, stroking it. "I don't see the point in playing guessing games, Tally. I want to make you come. I want to make it hard to shake me once I leave here in the morning. I want you crawling back for more, blowing up my phone, zoning out in the middle of the day at the bank replaying the way I fuck you. So tell me exactly how you like it."

If I didn't know any better I would swear I was burning alive. He was making damn sure I'd be touching myself to the thought of him for the foreseeable future with his words alone.

I rolled us over, pushing his shoulders into the mattress and straddling his hips. "In the morning, huh? You're very confident."

"Don't act like you aren't dripping for me," he dished back. His fingers dug into my hips on either side and he rocked me harder back and forth. My nerves multiplied, the coarse hair at his base rubbing my clit until I was climbing to a peak again in no time at all. "Talk to me, angel. Tell me what I'm doing right."

Praise. Mateo was a praise guy. Of course he was. He worked so hard for it, too. My teeth sunk into my lip and a hum of pleasure rattled my chest as he jerked his hips upward and poked at my budding nerves. "Your tongue is incredible," I said. "I've never come that fast in my life."

"Let me do it with my cock."

In a swift motion I seated his tip at my entrance and slid down until the stretch of his shaft stole the breath from my lungs. I had to stop and adjust to it. My stomach tightened all the way through my core and my walls gripped around him. Mateo threw his head back, the glorious veins in his neck straining against his tan skin. His groan of satisfaction spurred me on and I brought my hips up and back down, swallowing him fully.

"Christ, you're a tight fucking fit," he swore. "Open up for me, baby."

A strangled moan rushed out of me and I bounced in his lap, using his chest as an anchor to hold me up. His hands flew to my ass and the blunt tips of his fingers dug into my soft skin so hard I knew I would be finding the marks in the mirror later that night. "Keep talking."

Something wicked flashed in his dark eyes. "Is that what you like, Tally? Someone in your ear talking you through it?"

"Fuck." I nodded. "Yes."

His chest rumbled, and he sighed through gritted teeth watching the place where our bodies connected through the heavy lids of his eyes. I wished I could lick his sounds right out of his mouth. I didn't want him to talk me through it, I wanted him to *goad* me with it. I wanted to be taunted to the edge of degradation until I was a flush, heaping mess and then brought back to life at the precipice of an orgasm. I'd never been confident enough to say that.

Mateo pulled me down to his chest and slid his mouth over the shell of my ear. His hips pistoned upward, spearing into me and making me whiny and breathless. "You look so pretty getting fucked. So perfect with your tight little cunt wrapped around a cock like mine."

Heat flamed up the side of my neck. "I was desperate for it," I murmured.

A hoarse chuckle sifted out of him and his thrusts came faster. His chest was hot with sweat underneath mine and I dug my hands into the pillow on either side of his head, fisting it tightly. "Desperation suits you, baby. You take me so fucking well."

Each snap of his hips made it harder to breathe, let alone speak, but I needed to. "I like it rough," I stammered. "I like to be a plaything in bed. I want to be yours."

Mateo groaned deeply, muffling his sigh of pleasure against my skin. "You're saying you want me to use you, Tally?" His lips opened around the pulse in my neck and kissed languidly. "You want to be treated like a princess, and fucked like a slut?"

That's all I wanted. Fuck, how was this man so perfect? I nodded frantically, sliding my hips back and forth and creating a friction that made it impossible to focus on anything but the foreboding rapture between my legs. A wanton sigh slipped out of me. "Please, Matty."

Mateo planted his feet and hugged me to his body, jerking his hips upward. The room filled with a cacophony of slaps and grunts of satisfaction and he shoved my hips down against his, meeting me with each thrust, until I was crying out in ecstasy and holding onto the hair at the nape of his neck, coming apart right alongside him. I could listen to him losing himself until the world crashed down around us. He was completely unafraid, unabashed, unashamed. I threw all caution to the wind as the pulse of my climax burst through me, claiming every last sound from my throat. Mateo tensed and shook with a final thrust before emptying himself in spasms until his body went slack and mine went limp on top of him.

It took several minutes to recover. His gentle fingers brushed up my sides and down my spine, and I lifted onto my forearms to rest on his chest. The most perfect sweat-coiled strand of hair had fallen over his forehead. He was still inside of me.

"Wow," he finally said.

A grin blossomed across my face and more warmth stained my cheeks. "Wow."

Mateo swept a lock of hair behind my ear and left his large palm there against my face. I could have fallen asleep just like that. "The slut thing," he mentioned. "Is there more to that?"

I rushed out a laugh. "Yeah, sorry. I was really in the moment, and it kind of just came out. Little tense for a first date."

"I told you I didn't want to waste any time." His thumb traced my temple. "It turned me on, too. For what it's worth."

Talking about sex after the act was awkward and embarrassing. I was two completely different people in and out of the bedroom and some of the things I was capable of when I was horny were shocking, even to me. Like telling Mateo to use me like a plaything while riding him into the sun.

"I have some particular tastes, I guess. Degradation, for one. Which I know takes a lot out of a partner, so I totally understand if you never want to do that again." I paused, kicking myself. "Not that I'm assuming having sex with you will become a regular thing."

"You know I'm yours now, right?" His wandering fingers stopped at my ass and took a handful. He twitched inside me. "I'm claimed."

"Don't tell me you're a virgin."

"You marked your territory like a dog when you squirted on me, and now I'm yours, Tally. I don't make the rules."

"It sounds exactly like you're the one making the rules." I laughed, aimlessly tracing the lines of his lips. They were swollen and kissed to hell and I leaned down and kissed him again. "I wasn't expecting this."

"I'm glad you called me."

I steered clear of relationships because of my line of work. It was always easier to hook up with men when the need got too pressing and then move along. Less of a mess, less prying, no fear of disappointing someone or being judged.

I didn't need a companion.

I had Ophelia, or my family, or my clients if desperation ran deep, but I never let myself believe I might be lonely without someone else. I was perfectly fine alone.

But for some reason being *alone* with Mateo was what I found myself wanting. I wasn't done with him, no matter how much I knew I should be. No matter how selfish it was to keep seeing him and pushing this hope along. But it was just sex, fun, and a date. We weren't committing to each other for life here. I didn't owe him anything unless there was the possibility of something *more*.

More felt like a rock sinking to the bottom of my stomach the longer I lay there on his perfectly hard chest, staring into his golden-brown eyes.

I fell to his side, stretching my limbs while Mateo sat up and tugged the condom off, tying it and tossing it into the garbage can beside my nightstand.

"I think there's three left," I said enthusiastically.

A bright smile crested across his face and he dropped back onto the pillow beside me. The lights were on, and we were fully naked and relaxed like two people who'd been together a decade already. I felt like I'd know this man just as long in not only my heart but my soul.

"You don't have any tattoos," Mateo said matter-of-factly. There was a graft of amusement in his gravelly voice.

I tugged my lip between my teeth. "No, I don't."

chapter eight

Mateo

I HAD an *inkling* of how badly Frankie was going to fuck me by up and leaving Florida with Ophelia. Logistically, letting my co-owner and only employee quit without a proper two-week notice was going to leave me in the doghouse as far as my clients and my sanity were concerned no matter what. And no, I wouldn't have had it any other way. As a matter of fact, in the end, I had been the one to kick him in the ass and drive him to the airport to go chasing her onto her flight—and I would do it a thousand times over. That didn't mean in the back of my mind I didn't know how much backwork and scrambling was going to be needed to replace him.

Pike and I as partners were a well-oiled machine. We'd been that way since Delta. I called the shots and he was the driver—or the pilot in our case. TechOps was more of the same. I did the clerical shit, marketed the business, talked my talk, and then showed up with Pike and he operated the mechanics.

I'd spent two weeks interviewing potential replacements for him and gotten a revolving door of newly graduated frat boys with not a dollop of cybersecurity experience or eagerness to learn a new skill. I had no problem training someone—software was software—but I would never let fresh meat go out on their own and risk tainting the name I built without proper guidance. I was proud of the things I'd accomplished in life. The military, Tech-Ops, our cam business, Natalia. But what I couldn't train was *uninspired, unwilling,* or *unmotivated.*

The radio in my car mumbled a rock song as I idled in the parking lot on my first and only break of the day. Losing track of time at work meant lonely meals at three in the afternoon and calling Frankie to fill that void with complaints.

"They're a bunch of do-nothings, Pike." I balanced my phone on the dashboard and unzipped the lunchbox on my lap. The first thing I noticed was the napkin folded at the top and covered in Sharpie. *Made with love, from your momma xo.*

"You gotta hire someone," Pike said. "Pick the one you dislike the least."

I quickly crumpled the love note napkin in a ball and tossed it in my center console. "The one I dislike the least has a fucking mullet. It's 2024, and the kid looks like he's gonna break out in a dance number with his buddies on the top of his high school bleachers.

"What's wrong with that?"

"It's about integrity." I opened a food container filled with short stalks of celery, all lathered through the middle with peanut butter and dotted with raisins. I closed the container. "What other rash and unintelligent decisions are you making when you already have a mullet?"

"What other choice do you have?"

My head dropped back against the headrest with a thud. "I had two interviews, a new client consultation, and three installations already today. My mother has called me twice to tell me she found eggplant on sale, the second time because she forgot she told me the first time. Last night I fucked Tally wearing a tail and covered in blue paint that stained my balls on top of all that, oh yeah, we're planning a fucking wedding!"

"I want to know *less* things about you."

"Too bad." I dug into a plastic sandwich baggie and pulled out one corner of a ham and cheese that had been cut in four. I shoved the entire piece into my mouth. "You're my best man. It's par for the course."

"I meant to tell you, I *adore* these cute little groomsmen boxes you sent us."

"Fuck off, you know I had nothing to do with that." Tally wouldn't take no for an answer. Even when I explained that men don't need the same fanfare and a group text with a date and a time would do just fine to get my four groomsmen to the altar when they needed to be there. She took the liberty upon herself anyway, and I'm too smart a man to fight her.

"Particularly the 'I couldn't tie the knot without you' tie. Very punny, man."

Jesus fucking Christ.

"Tally is very creative. I agree. The girls got the same ritzy bedazzled bullshit with hair ties and wine glasses."

"Nah, this has you written all over it," Frankie said. "The rest of the guys loved it, Cap. Don't worry."

"Right, I'm sure they're not all dying to hold it over my head for the rest of my life, too. When you guys get married, you'll see. And I'm going to be the first fucker in the group text to say I told you so."

"Hold that thought."

"No, come on. I'm trying to enjoy my lunch here—"

The line cut out and I sighed at the screen. I ate one more quarter of a sandwich before a message came in from Frankie to all my groomsmen. Angelo, Tyler—aka, Echo—and his brother Sam, who we called Wink.

PIKE

I just wanted to thank Cap for these tastefully put-together groomsmen gifts, and say I will be there to tie your knot anytime, brother.

ME

You're a dickhead

WINK

I'm pouring one of these little nibs of alcohol out for you to mourn the loss of your sack

PIKE

I personally will be drinking all the tiny bottles of alcohol

ECHO

There's shit inside this box? I've been using it as a Squatty Potty.

ME

Fuck every single one of you, from the bottom of my heart

ANGELO

I haven't checked the mail since Mom and Dad left. What am I looking for?

ME

You should probably check the mail before USPS sends someone to the house for a wellness check

PIKE

There's beef jerky and Jameson in it

WINK

Mine had a handwritten love letter with a lipstick kiss

ME

In your fucking dreams

ECHO

Don't get testy, Cap, it's very thoughtful and not at all homoerotic to send your friends presents. Also am I the only one who got a vibrating cock ring?

ME

Tally put a lot of time into those and I'm gonna tell her you fucks are making fun of them

PIKE

We love Tally

ECHO

Tally is the best

WINK

An angel

ANGELO

What they said

I tossed my phone in the passenger seat and stared out the windshield. A sprinkle of rain began dotting the glass and leaving lazy rivulets of water behind despite blue skies.

Tally and I got engaged over Christmas and it was like it set a ticking time bomb for the inevitable conversation with my brother. The one where I told him that my best man was actually Pike. To be fair it wasn't only him I was being a pussy about relaying that information to. I was more terrified of my mother's reaction.

Angelo's response was a toss-up. He could either care too much or not at all, and I wasn't proud to say I had no clue which side of that coin was going to hit the pavement.

I came back home from deployment after four years on and off in the Middle East and the punky kid who was always snooping around my bedroom and sneaking into parties on my coattails had gone from a well-intentioned nuisance to a full-on public disturbance. Drinking, smoking, stealing my parents' car and totaling it when he forgot to put the parking brake on and it rolled into the fucking Hudson. His actions were inconsequential, because like he always said, he wasn't going to college anyway, and Dad couldn't fire his own kid.

Nobody ever expected him to be better. There was a part of me that thought my decision to go into the military cemented my brother's fate. Mom and Dad were forced to let me go, so they were holding on to Angelo for dear life. Anything he did was naught compared to me leaving and starting a life in a new place where they weren't a part of it twenty-four-seven. I was the one who got the guilt trips and the sad phone calls, the *when are you coming to visit's* and the *you wouldn't even recognize us anymore's.*

He and I had grown apart, and I was worried that choosing him as a best man out of obligation to my parents was a recipe for disaster. The Angelo I knew wasn't responsible enough for the task, and his inability to step up to the plate didn't only affect me, it affected Tally and our entire wedding, too.

There was no use putting it off. I picked my phone back up off the seat and called my brother. The line rang twice before he answered.

"Ayo."

"Hey brother, get you at a bad time?" I could hear the click of a lighter and a drag of breath, almost see the bright red burn at the end of a Marlboro. A terrible habit that he couldn't seem to kick even twelve years later and after my mother begged him to. Eventually she gave up trying.

"Almost done for the day on a jobsite."

"Are you ever gonna quit those?"

"It's this or drinking myself to death." There was a smile in his voice.

"You're sober?"

"No." He coughed out a laugh. "Fuck no."

"How's business?"

Angelo was quiet for long enough that I pulled the phone away from my ear to make sure the call was still connected.

"Something wrong, Matty?" he eventually asked.

"Why do you say that?"

"Well, you're calling me. You don't ever call me. And it's the middle of a work day. Let me guess, Mom and Dad finally got to you. How far are you from the ledge right now? Do I need to call someone?"

It was my turn to laugh. "How'd you know?"

"Between us, these last couple weeks have been the most peaceful of my entire life. I hope they don't come back."

"It's the constant hovering. Dad walks around here in his underwear in the morning and I have to keep Natalia in the bedroom until the coast is clear to save her the torment. That's what I'm working with. Like we're guests in our own home."

"I stay in the basement. Unless I smell food."

"I know it was always like this, but it's like quitting something cold turkey and then diving right back in with no warm-up."

Angelo was walking outside; the familiar sound of beeping cars and distant city sirens followed his heavy steps. "They haven't changed. You have."

My throat contracted around some invisible rock as I swallowed the urge to hang up the phone. "Hey, listen. The real reason I called was because I haven't had a chance to talk to you about the wedding. This is important, so just hear me out. You know that you and Frankie are both my brothers. He and I spent a lot of time together in Delta, and we've been through some shit I couldn't even explain to someone who's never been there. Then we were living together until a month ago, so we're as close as it gets. You're my blood, you're everything to me, but I figured with the time commitment and the distance, plus you being busy with Duran & Son, it would be a lot more on your plate. Frankie's girlfriend is the maid of honor, too, so they can do all this dumb wedding shit together and you wouldn't need to get caught up in that if he's the best man."

Angelo took another drag of his cigarette. "Take a fucking breath, Matty. You're making me light-headed."

"I don't want there to be any bad blood," I stressed. "It's not like that."

"It is, though. He's your best friend, and a hell of a guy. I love Frankie; everyone loves Frankie. How could you not? Believe me, I get it."

"You do?"

"You're making the right choice."

Guilt flushed over me, head to toe. My fingers tightened around my cellphone. He was supposed to be giving me a hard time. I had prepared my body for a fight. Now all this energy was whizzing in a circle with no outlet and the stress I'd anticipated was humming beside it.

"Are you sure you're not sober?" I asked.

"I still live in the basement of my parents' house in the Bronx."

"Good point. I just thought this conversation was going to go differently," I admitted. "You're very relaxed in comparison."

"I don't know the first thing about weddings, and I'm terrible at public speaking. To be honest, being the best man sounds like a nightmare," he said. "Don't feel bad about it, Matty. I'm just happy you finally called. I missed your girly voice."

I might have changed, but Angelo was exactly the same. Where maturity was concerned at least. He loved cracking a joke at my expense, or whenever the conversation got too serious. "I'm sorry it took so long." I paused. "Love you, man."

"Love you, too." Angelo sniffed. "Yeah, all right."

"I'll talk to you soon."

"Later."

Mom and Dad couldn't hold this against me if Angelo wasn't upset about it, even though they might try. I could rest easier knowing I had one less thing on my plate after that phone call. That didn't mean putting my brother in a house full of Russos in Vegas was going to be easy, but it did mean he wasn't coming into it with a chip on his shoulder.

More pressingly now was TechOps. If Tally saw me crack under the pressure of keeping it afloat by myself she would drop everything to help me, and I couldn't let that happen. She had too much to deal with, and I didn't need to add to that. I needed to be her anchor right now. That wouldn't work if I had to worry about training a newbie to pick up Pike's work and prove that I could trust them. Being a perfectionist was a blessing and a curse, and if I was going to end up doing all the work anyway, I might as well just do it by myself.

It would be my little secret. My burden to bear.

chapter nine

Natalia

THE DOOR to our bedroom closed and I glanced up from the blue light of my laptop to Mateo tiptoeing toward the mattress. He reached behind his head and tugged the collar of his shirt up and over, gold chain dropping down onto his naked chest, then shimmied out of his sweatpants and rubbed his hands together giddily before diving beneath the covers beside me.

He was getting home at nine o'clock most nights now, because what was usually the work of two people at TechOps had been allocated to him alone. I had no reason to be resentful, but the afterhours doing security installation was cutting into what little time we had to work on the cam business side of things.

"Parents asleep?" I asked.

Mateo pulled the white duvet all the way up to his chin. "I'm getting the cold shoulder from both of them. Which means they called Angelo and got a straight answer about the wedding."

Luckily, the weekend had arrived, so I wasn't going to be alone to mediate that while Matty was at work all day. Although if they were anything like my parents, this would all blow over in a long sleep. "I thought you said your brother was totally blasé about it?"

"He's not the one who has to tell my nonna, or my aunts and

uncles. That's the problem. Everyone expected Angelo so it makes the family look bad that it isn't."

"I didn't realize so many other people would care." Although I understood it to a degree.

Mateo rolled over on his side toward me, flinging his forearm over my lap between my stomach and the keyboard. "Working?"

"We're way behind." Our list of neglected cam requests was piling up. Not only had we thrown what was already scheduled on the back burner to adjust to our new house guests, our regular content had slowed down and subscribers were getting antsy. Our overall creator ranking had plummeted an entire percent in just five days.

After my sisters let it slip that I was "working at the bank" in front of Anna, I had to find a place to be three days a week during normal business hours as an alibi. Those few days away from my equipment and editing software set me back substantially. I couldn't post content that wasn't edited, and I couldn't edit content that wasn't filmed. There was always our emergency bank of scrap porn from chopped-up footage that I could salvage into something, but I saved that for true emergencies.

"We missed theme night," I said.

"That's all right, we haven't missed one of those in months. What was the theme anyway?"

"Blue alien anal."

Mateo's head lifted off the pillow. "That won the vote again?"

"By seventy-four percent."

"Huh," he hummed, resting his head again. "Yeah, that'll upset some people."

"But it's okay," I assured him, moving my cursor around again and reorganizing a few cells in the spreadsheet. "Because we can just move the Scottish virgin roleplay to your solo slot on Wednesday and combine the brother's best friend request with our bondage demonstration on Saturday."

"Lucinda is going to give you grief about pulling my Wednesday."

I tapped the keys aggressively. "Lucinda can spend a day scrolling your greatest hits playlist, because seriously, who would you rather answer to? The monster fucker community or one lady in Bumfuck, Ohio?"

"Fine," he complied, tugging me closer to him. "But that blue paint better wash off this time, Tally. I can't go into work like that again."

"Speaking of work..." I slammed my laptop closed and put it on the nightstand. "This whole thing is making me think I'd be better off with a regular, normal, report-to-the-office job again. I wouldn't have to case our house like there's an intruder every time I need to sit down and film, and my parents would get off my case about the bank."

"I know you're joking." He rested his head on my stomach again, this time nibbling on the strings of my sweatpants. "It was really adorable though."

"I am not." My fingers dipped into his hair. "Think of how much easier life would be if we were a normal suburban couple." Normal like Frankie and O, or Mateo's parents. Never having to worry about subsidizing our time into film windows or keeping a questionable closet of costumes at the ready all the time. At least that was easy enough to talk our way out of.

Mateo's nose crinkled. "You're spoiled, and hate authority, and you deleted the alarm clock on your phone because you think time is an illusion."

"I didn't delete it," I argued. "I banished it to the app graveyard, right next to GarageBand, Compass, and Fitness."

"Regardless, you're not switching up your day job because it would be *easier*, Tal. You work so hard at the content, and it shows in the following. We've made a name here. There's no going back now."

Mat and Nat was my crown jewel. He was right; if all of a sudden we just fell off the face of the earth, people would definitely notice. Not to mention the wedding we were planning in all of its overwhelming extravagance was reliant on the money we pooled in monthly from our subscribers. Mateo's salary paid for the house, the truck, the taxes, insurance. It was a perfect, legitimate front, but my sisters were right to question where all this extra cash was coming from.

"Did you ever think it would get to this point?" I asked. "When you first decided to film with me, the audience was a quarter of the size it is now. I wasn't prepared for it to grow like this, and you never really got a choice. You just got pushed in blind."

Mateo's five o'clock shadow tickled my stomach and he squeezed my hips tightly. "I do wonder how many strangers on the internet have seen my junk, and sometimes I worry about being recognized, but it's different. It's not like I can get fired. The only woman I care about impressing is underneath me, and I would have done anything you asked me to do if it meant you were mine, Tally Duran."

Tally Duran. God I love that fucking name.

"I'm not your wife yet, lover boy."

Mateo's head tilted thoughtfully and he climbed up my body, settling over me and brushing his nose against mine. Our eyes met beneath thick lashes, and the sweet smell of his skin caressed my senses. It ignited a very distinct memory of our first meeting and how he smelled like heaven even from two feet away. "Every part of you belongs to me. Right?"

My chest expanded but got stuck beneath his heavy body and our hearts thudded against each other. "Of course."

"So it doesn't matter whether we're ink on paper or I carve my name into your pretty little ass." Mateo lifted my left hand and I wiggled my fingers, the low light catching on the engagement ring there. "Mine," he said definitively. "Mine in every timeline. Every universe. I've already married you in another life, and I'll do it again in six months, so I'll call you wife because that's the truth."

Heat danced across my cheeks, and I admired the lips those words had just come from. My thumbs rested on his cheeks and dipped into his dimples. "How are you both the most foul-mouthed yet deeply romantic man I've ever met?"

"You bring everything out of me. What can I say?"

I kissed him softly. His large frame above me blocked out the light of the room. "What are we going to do about your parents? I need them to like me, Matty, it's my only chance at a normal functioning family. It hasn't even been a month yet and we're already in the doghouse."

Mateo cleared his throat. "I'll think of something. Play my mom at her own game."

"You're seriously going to try to out-petty your own mother?"

"I'm not going to try, baby. I'm going to *do*."

I pushed at his chest until he flopped back over on the bed next to me. We both stared up at the yellow glow of the ceiling light together and a thought crossed my mind. A poorly executed but well-intentioned thought. "I'll cook dinner for them. Nothing says I love you like Italian food."

Mateo hummed and linked his fingers together on his sternum. "No promises that it will work, but it definitely wouldn't hurt."

"We can do this. After your parents are placated, I might need some support to patch things up with my sisters, too. Think of all this as the first real test of the rest of our lives. You and me versus the world."

"It's always you and me versus the world," Mateo echoed. Not only did I need those words from him in that moment of stressful uncertainty, I believed every last syllable. If anyone in this universe would stand beside me through whatever life could and *would* throw at us—it was Mateo.

chapter ten

Natalia

13 months ago

THIS WAS the moment I'd been dreading for over a month now. Every single time I got comfortable, or felt happy, the needling understanding that this conversation with Mateo was inevitable would drag me back down and taint it.

There was a wing special at the local sports bar where he met me after work, and the music was so loud I couldn't even hear myself think. This restaurant felt less intimidating than waiting until he was back at my apartment to talk, and also gave him an out if he needed it. I curled into myself, rubbing the chills off my arms as the beer I ordered sat untouched in front of me, bubbles dancing from the butt of the glass into the foam rimming the top.

We hadn't left each other's sides since Mateo took me out on that first date to the roller rink. We were playing musical houses between my bed in Coconut Creek and Mateo's much larger one in his house in Pompano. During the day he'd leave me under the covers to go off to work with Frankie, and I'd hobble to the bank, counting down the hours until I was back in his arms. Even then, we never stopped texting. I had a toiletry bag sitting on the vanity of his bathroom, his clothes were on my floor, and my jewelry had taken up residence on his nightstand next to his watches. I had never eaten so much takeout in my entire life.

There was no hope in keeping this relationship casual. The only one who was even trying was me, and try as I might, the way I felt around Mateo was indescribable and addictive. I couldn't leave his side without crawling back on my hands and knees.

Which was the real issue.

The sex work was suffering. My clients were wondering where the fuck I'd gone, my servers were dwindling in subscriptions by the hour, and content had come to a screeching, ghostly halt with no explanation. Because how could I be naked on a livestream in my apartment if I was reverse cowgirl on a veteran down the road?

Beyond that it felt...morally gray. Unfaithful in a way that didn't even make sense. It wasn't as if Mateo and I were exclusive. We hadn't discussed it; he hadn't asked me to commit to him, nor would I expect that despite spending every waking hour together for the last month. I knew his favorite color, songs, and foods; he was afraid of heights, played baseball in high school, and broke his arm in fifth grade when he ran his bike through a crosswalk and got sideswiped by a taxi. He had twenty-seven first cousins and five of them were named Anthony.

But I couldn't quit my business for a man. Not one I'd just met. I couldn't keep it a secret from him either. I was way too invested in my career and I'd worked my ass off to bring an ethical, empowering, high-quality porn experience to my audience. It was really starting to pay off and bud into something I was deeply proud of.

My eyes darted from a pie chart of indecipherable sports stats on ESPN to Mateo sitting across from me licking hot sauce from the end of a chicken wing. A spot of it was left in the dimple on his cheek and I reached over, wiping it off. He grabbed his napkin and patted down the rest of his face. "You're awfully quiet over there. Everything okay?"

Everything was not okay. My nerves braided around each other, tightening until even my throat stiffened. Rehearsing something to say would have been a helpful idea in hindsight, but winging things was much more my style, no pun intended. "Yup."

He was fully reading me now, dragging his eyes down my face and raising a brow. "You've barely even touched your food."

"Big lunch."

"Oh yeah, what did you have?"

I swallowed. "A sandwich."

"From where?"

"What's with the twenty questions?"

Mateo smirked. "Fibber."

I ignored him, picking up my beer for the first time and taking a generous few gulps. Which definitely piqued his attention. A worried crease formed between his eyebrows and Mateo swiped his hand down his chin, smoothing the hairs. Hairs I wondered if I'd ever feel on the insides of my thighs again after this.

Two plates of bar food marinated the air between us as we stared at each other and I could all but see the way my cheeks were blazing, panic rising as I searched hopelessly for the courage to say *something*, anything. Find a middle ground between us, a commonality to gracefully connect to the bomb I needed to drop.

There was no normal way to go about telling the man you're seeing that you see other men by the thousands—virtually.

Mateo tilted his head. "Should I be worried?"

"Do you watch porn?" I rushed out.

Nailed it, Nat.

His eyes widened and he shifted awkwardly in his seat, thinking hard about his answer. "I..." Mateo shrugged indifferently. "I've dabbled."

At least he was being honest. All men watched porn. They might say they don't, or that it's against their beliefs, that they've *never really been into it*, or the absolute bullshit morality story that they can't stand the way women in the industry are taken advantage of—but they're fucking liars.

"How do you feel about the women in those videos?"

"Like, during the viewing of the video?" He pressed his fingers to the table. "Or are we talking in general?"

I almost laughed. "As a concept. Women who do pornography."

He slowly picked up a chicken wing again, using it like a conductor's baton. "I guess I always wonder what would make someone want to do that. But I don't live under a fucking rock, and financially it's a career that pays more than we can really fathom. So from a business perspective I'd say those women know exactly what they're worth."

"Right." The column of my throat constricted.

"If the porn is a dealbreaker I can quit it cold turkey. I'm more than satisfied in that department, Tal. You'll never have to say it twice."

"No, that's not it," I garbled out. It was hard to make eye contact with him, I couldn't bear it. "It's more complicated than that."

Mateo sat forward, grabbing my hand across the table. "Look, I know this has been nonstop since we met, and it's usually bad news to give your all to someone right off the bat. But I can't stop myself from doing that with you. I've never had this type of connection with someone so quickly. I feel like we *know* each other, Natalia. Like we fit in all the weirdest possible ways. I enjoy talking to you, and being around you, sitting in silence with you, waiting for you to get to my house at the end of the day, waking up with your head on my chest. Fuck, I know, I'm rambling." He sighed. "If you need to slow down, I can do that. If you want to see each other less during the week, take a few days to do our own thing, whatever makes you more comfortable with seeing me, I'll do it."

"I don't want to do that." I shook my head. I really didn't. I wanted this to stay exactly the same, the endless first date, giving my all to someone who felt the same way toward me. I wanted to be with Mateo Duran. "I like what we're doing now."

"Me too." He let out a deep breath, wiping an invisible bead of sweat from his forehead. "I thought for a minute you were going to tell me you wanted to see other people." He took a bite of his chicken wing.

"Mateo, I do porn."

The chicken wing came sputtering back up.

Fucking hell, Natalia.

I winced, handing him a napkin across the table. Mateo was usually so easy to read—he wore all of his emotions on his sleeve or on his face—but this time his expression was a slate so blank I felt the emptiness of it like a spear to the chest. I couldn't tell if he was going to erupt in anger or leave in silence. I'd never felt more ashamed of my life than in that moment because for a split second, I realized the path I chose might have cost me the man I was meant for, and I wanted to take it all back. I wanted to be me for him, not for me.

"I have a really successful page where I post pre-recorded videos and livestream. I also have personal clients who pay me for requests to do specific things. I've been supporting myself since I graduated college entirely on the money I make as a sex worker, and I enjoy it. I love creating and filming and being my own boss. It might sound stupid but it feels powerful in a way. The bank job...well, I fucking hate working at the bank, you know that. But I keep it to use as a cover story for my family, or whoever else must know, and for insurance, the technical shit, what have you."

His lips parted, but he didn't say anything.

"I don't date because, well, I can't imagine that having this conversation gets easier, but you're the first person I've ever cared enough about to have it with. You're the first man I've ever told this to—the first person, actually. No one knows except for you. Not even my best friend, and that's saying something. When you started talking to me in the bank and brought me that coffee, my hesitation wasn't because I wasn't interested in you, I was *definitely* interested," I stressed. "I knew that I was going to fall for you, because you were charming, and direct, and confident, and I was already thinking about kissing you before you walked away, so

I was trying to protect myself from the inevitable heartbreak. I haven't worked since that first night we spent together. It didn't feel right and I was trying to let what happened between us make my decision for me, and now it has. I know how selfish it was not to say anything right away, to let you feel the way you do about me and then rip it all out from underneath you. And I'm sorry, I'm so fucking sorry. I would never blame you for wanting to walk away. I just needed to tell you this before we got any more involved."

Silence. More deafening, soul-crushing silence, and I wanted to fucking kick myself for getting even a dollop of hope up for this going differently than I had expected it would. Mateo opened his mouth to say something and then let it fall closed without a word and that window with a silver lining slammed closed with it. A piece of me cracked and shattered.

"Okay." I nodded, gathering myself to save the humiliation. I tucked my phone into my bag and pulled out my wallet to cover the food on the table. My hands were shaking, and I couldn't stand being in my own skin or looking at him when I could feel all my insecurities coming to life while he remained quiet.

When I stood from the sticky leather booth, Mateo's hand shot out to wrap around my wrist and my breath caught on a gasp. I finally looked up and tears sprang to my eyes. My heart was beating hard against my ribs. I'd already given in to the fallout and didn't know what to do with myself now.

He swallowed, and guided me back down to my seat without letting go of my arm. The pads of his fingers were tight against my pulse. "Will you tell me more about it?"

"I'll tell you anything." Honesty was the least I could give him. He deserved to know all the details so I wouldn't hold back.

"Do you do it with other men?" Mateo asked quietly and directly. "Make...content like that with them?"

"No," I said. "I don't have physical relationships with anyone. It's purely parasocial. I've never filmed with a partner before. This all started in my dorm the summer after graduation. I stuck around to finish a ridiculous unpaid internship and needed the money. I didn't want to ask my parents to help me, and my major was working in cameras and film media. I had the equipment, and the expertise, and...I was alone, and single. It's always just been me and the camera."

He wrung his fingers around each other, working through something in his head. "Would you?"

"Would I...?"

"Film with a partner."

I struggled for the right words. because he'd asked me that question as if he was imagining dating me while I made porn with other men. I would never commit to that. Never want to. If I ever decided to start bringing other people into my work, having a boyfriend on the side would be out of the question. There were too many emotional variables. Not to mention the health screenings and regular tests to stay physically protected.

"That's something that would require an intense level of trust for me," I told him. "I wouldn't invite just anyone into such an intimate, personal moment, or give them power over me that wasn't deeply discussed and consented to. It's more than just fucking on camera."

"What about with me?"

All the blood in my body slowed to a crawl. My pulse thumped in the side of my neck, trying to acclimate. I was still so far into my head that part of it was telling me to run, but the rest of me was an inferno, and he was stoking the flames. My voice was low and doubtful. "Is that something you would want to do?"

"I want you, Tally. There's a lot of things I would do if that was the result. Don't you get that yet? I'll have to warm up to it, and get over the preconceptions, but I think I owe us that much. Throwing this away can't be the right thing to do. You work in that bank for a reason; I *met* you there for a reason. Maybe it's something to do with this, I don't know." He chuckled. "I'm not much of a romantic."

"This is romantic," I confirmed with a blithe smile, trapping his hand holding my wrist. It was also egregiously sexy that Mateo was secure enough in himself that my work wasn't an immediate dealbreaker. He might change his mind, but for the time being, I was holding on to his willingness to make us work with everything I had. "You don't have to do this, you know. You don't have to pretend to be okay with it. I'm giving you an out."

"Stop trying to get rid of me, Natalia. It's not going to work."

My lips twisted upward into a smile that I tried to hide behind the rim of my beer as I brought it to my mouth. "All right, I'll stop."

"Will you show me?" He finally let go of my wrist to dig back into his plate of wings. The pressure that had been building in my chest that entire time released in one deep breath. His nonchalance caught me off guard.

Show him the most secret, intimate, vulnerable part of me? The woman I was on camera was not the same one sitting across from him. She couldn't be. But if this was going to work, I needed to let Mateo in completely. No secrets, no lies. "Okay," I said softly.

"And to be clear about what I said before, watching *you* do porn isn't the same as watching porn, is it?"

My cheeks budded crimson. "I think you get a hall pass for this one."

"I can't believe you tried to convince me this was something negative."

Maybe this could work, I thought. Maybe I had finally, actually met my match in Mateo. I didn't want to get my hopes up too soon, but all signs pointed to the promise that I had.

chapter eleven

Mateo

THERE WERE a few things in life that made me nostalgic. The smell of fresh wood shavings off a hot circular saw. Cigarette smoke and candied pecans in the summertime, a revved engine and the sweet scent of gasoline idling in a muscle car. Garlic and onions crackling on a stove.

Mom spent every Sunday when I was growing up bent over the gas burners in the kitchen. When she cooked, the entire neighborhood knew it. Every window in the house was open to offset the heat of the oven, and the sound of news playing on the radio whistled through the windscreens.

Just like we knew when the streetlights turned on it was time to ride our bikes home, when the dishes started clinking together and Dad hobbled off the couch toward the dining room, it was time to eat.

For my family, food was most definitely a way to the heart, and Natalia's idea to get back in my parents' good graces with a bowl of spaghetti and a bottle of wine was better than any other option I'd come up with.

Tally was pulling pots and pans from the cabinets when I stepped into the kitchen. She'd tied her long dark hair up into a big knot on the top of her head and was wearing an apron I didn't even know we owned. A perfect pair of leggings hugged her ass, the sleeves of an oversized sweater were pushed up to her elbows, and she slid across the floor in a pair of fluffy slippers that swallowed up her feet. It was my favorite thing I'd ever seen. Like both my worlds colliding into one, that Sunday afternoon nostalgia and the girl I was going to spend the rest of my life with rewriting those same memories in our own font. Something about it felt like a snapshot into the future I'd envisioned with Natalia from the moment I first saw her. I couldn't think of anything I wanted more.

She melted into the curve of my body as I stepped behind her and closed my arms around her waist. We swayed back and forth in front of the counter and I breathed the subtle, flowery scent of her in. "You have never looked hotter than you do right now."

Tally's head turned toward me, a kittenish smile playing on the corner of her mouth. "I haven't even showered."

"I'm so serious, all this"—I tugged her hair and pulled on the neckline of her apron—"it's doing something to me."

"I'm ready to be a stay-at-home house wife whenever you are," she said, gesturing to her comfy clothes. "This is the dream. Rotating from one pair of yoga pants into another slightly different pair of yoga pants."

"Call me old school, but I think this is your calling."

"You think so until you taste my cooking, and then you'll be begging me to leave dinner to the professionals."

"You're a natural," I assured her. "How hard can it be? Three ingredients: meat, sauce, pasta."

"That's easy to say when your mother never made you cook a day in your life."

"I have cooked the most delicious MREs anyone has ever eaten."

She deadpanned, "You microwaved dehydrated cat food?"

"It counts."

Tally shuffled out of my arms and stacked a few blue boxes of pasta on top of one another on the counter, then took our largest pot over to the sink and started filling it with water. My mom appeared in the archway to the kitchen as soon as she heard the burner click on and a flame spark to life on the stove, like a cat reacting to the jingle of a bell.

"Need any help cooking, honey?"

Tally shook her head. "Absolutely not. You just sit back and relax."

Mom didn't look at me. Instead, she pulled a stool out from underneath the breakfast bar and watched disparagingly as Tally moved around the room from fridge to counter and back again, shaking with the need to stick her fingers in a can of Tuttorosso.

The sliding glass door opened from the backyard and my father stepped into the house in nothing but a pair of board shorts and a fanny pack barely visible below his beer gut. In the couple weeks since my parents had arrived his skin had gone from cream to leather after spending hours outside. He crossed the living room, whistling to himself, and started pressing buttons on the wall thermostat.

"Jesus Christ, Dad, you want to put some fucking clothes on?"

He ignored me as he squinted at the small display screen and turned the air conditioning down several notches.

We were used to the temperature being set at a comfortable seventy-two degrees, but lately waking up in the mornings the wood floors were too cold to walk around on with bare feet and I'd had to take my robe out of retirement in the closet. I checked the thermostat when my father refocused his attention on finding a bottle of cabernet from the wine rack nearby, and noticed he'd reset the system to keep the house at a cool sixty-seven.

Little changes like that had started piling up around the house in seemingly inconsequential ways and making our perfectly controlled living situation more aggravatingly intolerable. Like the furniture being moved so that the recliner sat more to the left, easier for my father to see the television while he watched baseball. The mugs in the cabinet had all been shifted down a shelf to accommodate Mom's five-foot frame. The hallway bathroom now had plastic storage draped over the back of the door full of pill bottles and toiletries that rattled whenever you opened it. Small, innocuous, bemoaning things I had to give up so I didn't look insane.

I made a show of punching the keypad back to a livable number and my dad's jaw twitched as he ground his teeth together.

"Mateo, grab another glass for your mom, please." Tally flung open a drawer in the kitchen and quickly tossed a bottle opener to me as the water in the pot on the stove started bubbling. I stuck a tongue in my cheek and carried a pair of tall wine glasses to the table, stabbing a cork into the burgundy wine and twisting it open reluctantly, only for my mother to swivel in the opposite direction, right in time to see Natalia crack the long pasta in half over the pot and let it fall in.

A sound of agony tumbled out of my mother and her hand settled over her chest like a knife had just gone through it. I didn't know anything about cooking, but I knew snapping raw spaghetti like the spine of a book was sacrilegious.

My mother meandered off the barstool and migrated next to Natalia, so I shuffled closer too, leaning on the countertop beside her, feeling protective and equally on guard. I was stressing myself out waiting for a problem to arise. External conflict, I could do. Emotional disputes made my skin prickle with something between a sweat and an itch, and my family brought it on in spades. Natalia's shoulders tensed to her ears and she quickly covered the boiling pasta.

"Ma, you're smothering her," I said harshly. My mother's light eyes cut to mine and a swallow lodged in my throat.

"I'm fine. Just taking it one step at a time." Tally let out a nervous laugh, but her neck was blooming in red patches beneath her sweater. "I've actually never cooked for a crowd before, if you couldn't tell." She hip-checked me out of her way then and began rooting around in the low cabinet I had been standing in front of, pulling a large frying pan out and swatting off some residual dust with her sleeve.

I clapped my cold hand over the back of her neck to give her some relief and support. "You're doing great." My control was slipping, though. I could try to mitigate calmly, but there was nothing that could get my mother to sit the fuck down and let Tally cook besides physically removing her from the kitchen. She was overwhelming to govern on a normal day, but on top of that was the egregious silent treatment.

What did they want me to do? Apologize for Angelo? Get on my knees and beg for a second chance at being a perfect son? Demote Pike back to a groomsman? Unfortunately I knew the answer, and it was all of the above.

Natalia pulled a tray of pre-rolled, store-bought meatballs from the fridge and Mom croaked. A literal frog-worthy bellow. All because they weren't made from scratch with the tears of a thousand ancestral Italian women and a recipe handwritten on a piece of decaying paper shoved into the back of a junk drawer somewhere.

"You okay, Ma?" I dared her to say something. "They look just like yours."

A retort was on the tip of her tongue, but instead she bit it so hard she probably drew blood. She turned away from me and sat back down at the end of the table farthest from the stove with a sulk twisting her face that set me off.

"Angelo isn't ignoring me. I don't know why you still are," I said, shrugging. "He's totally fine with not being the best man, and that should be enough for you, too. Nobody's even going to notice, if that's what you're so worried about."

Natalia started slowly placing the meatballs evenly apart from each other on the sizzling pan, and the television clicked on in the living room with a playoff football game screaming. A dull thud started spreading across my temples, different than a normal headache, though. I could pick apart every sound in the room. The arms on my watch ticking, Tally's slippers shuffling across the tile, my mother gnawing on the inside of her cheek to spite me, the pattering of my quickened pulse. Everything hit me at once.

Mom pulled her pocketbook across the counter toward her and started rummaging through it, adding to the noise, until she found what she was looking for. She unfurled a piece of paper the length of a drugstore receipt.

"I put together a list of addresses that need invitations to the wedding, Natalia."

Tal jolted at her name and the metal tongs she was holding dropped into the pan. She quickly wiped her palms on a towel hanging off the oven handle and turned around smiling. "That's great, thank you, Anna. So helpful."

A few family members from New York made sense to ask about. I sure as hell didn't know their addresses off the top of my head, but a list that folded over on itself didn't sit well with me at all. I plucked it out of my mother's hand and turned it over.

"I'll have to see how many extra invitations I set aside." Tally left the stove to come peek over my shoulder, and her sharp nails tightened around my arm. "By chance are any of these the same household?"

My blood pressure spiked rolling down the list of names. "Who the hell are all these people? Mr. Thomson, my high school principal? The Osmonds from church? Darren and Steve who cut your grass? The last time I saw half these people was at my confirmation in the seventh fucking grade, Mom. I have no obligation to them. They don't know me anymore, and they sure as fuck don't know Tally. They're not coming."

"There are so many people back home who can't wait to see you two married," my mother said to Natalia, in a guilt-tripping, sing-songy way. My fiancée smiled sympathetically, and that manipulation pissed me off even more. She was too good of a person, and she was easy to exploit because Mom knew that Tally wanted to impress her. She also knew from the dress fitting that her relationship with Sistine was rocky at best, and that she'd be eager to please as a consolation.

Looking toward the living room for some support, I found my father still standing three feet in front of the television completely nonplussed and holding his glass of wine on his belly like a shelf. Muscles on both sides of my jaw clenched and relaxed over and over again, and the dull headache I had was now piercing, spreading to the base of my neck, like knuckles knocking against a door.

"We'll make it work," Tally said enthusiastically. She took the paper delicately out of my hand before I could crumple it into a ball and throw it. "Maybe we can make some compromises. That way everyone is happy."

I admired her faith in my mother to comply. What I knew, and the reason I was getting so worked up about it, was that Anna Duran didn't compromise. It'd been that way my whole life. Part of the contention in our family was my unwillingness as a teenager to let her get her way. When I left for the Army against her every beg and plead it was like metaphorically putting a stake through her heart.

"Don't bother," I said. "After the first five it's like reading off the phone book."

Natalia spread the list out in front of my mom anyway, running her dainty finger down the blue ink. Neighbor of twenty years and their adult daughter I used to run through the sprinkler with, the deli owner down the block who gave me my first job, my high school baseball coach and his wife, my orthodontist. People who had vague impacts on my childhood, and the last shred of connection I still had to the Bronx that my mother was trying so hard to keep relevant. I slid open a drawer on the island and pulled out a pen, then went down the list crossing names off finitely.

My mom tried to tug the paper back across the counter in her direction but I swiped it out of her hand. She reached over and grabbed a corner and pulled; I smacked my large palm down over the center. She held firm to the top of the looseleaf and added two sets of fingers, and this time when she pulled, it ripped the paper in a jagged pattern. My barber's name got split in half.

"Oh look at that, Benny got cut," I said sharply.

"Mateo..." Tally murmured. I was pleased with myself for standing my ground until her attention darted to my mother, sitting there with her eyes puffy and watery, a faint quiver on her lips.

My shoulders dropped and all the fiery adrenaline hit me square in the gut. "Oh come on," I said. "It's just a list, Ma. It's not a fucking big deal."

Her mouth twisted, and she crossed her arms over her chest. Her refusal to speak to me, especially now, only amplified the overstimulation I was feeling. It made me irate. If she couldn't be an adult about this I wasn't going to be forced to be one either.

"You're trying to guilt-trip me, Mom, and it's not going to work. I refuse to let you play the victim here." I jabbed my finger into the table and realized it was shaking. My entire body was. Like I'd gone into some kind of manual overdrive and I had no control over it. Then my breath caught, but my pulse continued thudding and thudding until a cold sweat licked up my neck. I paused and tried to regather myself but failed, voice shaking. "You've done this my whole life, all right? Made me feel like shit for making my own choices and not yours. And I let you give me the cold shoulder for the weekend about Angelo, but I'm putting my foot down here."

The tightening feeling in my chest got worse. I was holding onto air that I physically couldn't expel, my body rejecting my attempt to stand up for myself. I was well aware that something foreign and unexpected was happening to me and there was nothing I could do about it but try to fight back as my vision clouded, and my head grew heavy.

"I'm not a bad son," I forced out. I didn't even know why I said it. I didn't believe that I was, but the silence from my mother was making me feel like I needed to fill in the gaps. "Dad, come on, help me out here."

My breaths went from miles apart to shuttling in and out. I was begging for air. The harder it was to find some, the harder I tried until I was hyperventilating. And the more aware I was that I was hyperventilating, the harder it was to stop.

"Coconut," I struggled out. "Coconut."

There was a hand immediately at the nape of my neck, and it took a second for me to realize it was a concerned Tally comforting me while the room started to spin.

"Matty? What's happening?" My body turned toward Tally's voice before my brain did. It was like looking down a tunnel at her. "Baby, come sit down."

I found a chair and dropped into it, and then Natalia was in front of me on her knees, holding my face and telling me to focus on her. Her sweet, worried eyes and heat-stricken cheeks. The rogue baby hairs that stuck out of her bun and fell onto her forehead. I counted her eyelashes.

"Oh my god, David!" my mother's panicked voice rang out. "David! He's having a heart attack!"

I held up my hand, my right ear ringing, and I rolled my neck back and forth like that might stop it.

My father sprang into my peripheral with beady, brown eyes boring into mine. "What do you mean? Call 911!" he yelled.

"He's not making any sense. He's talking about coconuts!" My mom rushed me, putting a cold hand to my forehead. She was hysterical. "Oh my god, I gave him a fucking heart attack! Is your face numb? Are your arms numb? Oh God, please Lord."

"Give him some space!" Natalia shouted back. She ran her sharp nails down my jaw and mimicked slower breathing. "Keep focusing on me. Do what I do."

"I'm calling 911," my dad announced.

"Don't!" Natalia and I cried in unison.

My mother crowded me again, invading the little bubble between Tally and me while my father paced in the background asking questions I couldn't hear anymore. I closed my eyes and winced away from the noise.

"Anna, I say this with all the respect in the world—I need you to back the hell up." Tally's stern, commanding tone slowed me down on impact. One of my eyes peeled open to see my mom taking reluctant steps backward, leaving me alone with my fiancée. Her hands trailed up my legs, my sides and arms, and settled at my collarbone. One palm resting over my heart as it returned to a more stable beat. "Hey. Are you here with me?"

"I'm here," I assured her. "I'm sorry."

Tally shook her head. "Don't apologize to me. I'm sorry I didn't see it happening sooner. You said the safe word."

I was so grateful for her, maybe more so at that moment than ever, knowing that my mother's approval meant so much to her and she was still willing to raise her voice and stand up for me when I needed it. The room around me edged back into focus again and I stood from the chair, pulling her into my chest. "I love you."

My parents crept toward me again, treading carefully this time.

"Are you okay, Mateo?" Mom asked. "You scared us."

"Near death is what it takes for you to talk to me again?" I joked, tugging her into my other side. "I'm okay, just don't ask me to invite the mailman to my wedding. You've been warned."

She sighed away an argument.

My dad stood with his hands on his hips. "Does that happen a lot?"

"Never," I said. "Must have been a freak thing." That was the easy answer. The one I would give rather than field questions I didn't have an explanation to, because it *had* happened to me before—in smaller, less catastrophic ways. If I worked myself up about existential things late at night, or if I thought too hard about some of the shit that went down in Delta. Sometimes panic crept in and made it hard to breathe, but I'd learned to bring myself back to a neutral state without any help. This time was different; it was like those smaller moments on steroids.

Natalia rubbed my back, her fingertips trailing up and down

my spine and bringing me all the way to the ground, steadying me.

"What was that about coconuts?" Mom's eyebrows pinched together.

A small chuckle burst out of me and I was about to make a ridiculous excuse, but my nose twitched first, catching a whiff of something charred. They all noticed the same thing I did simultaneously. The room was hazy, and the stove was crackling ferociously as we all turned and took in the very burnt, rock-solid meatballs in the frying pan alongside a full pot of overcooked pasta. Things had an affinity to being burnt to a crisp in this house.

We ordered takeout, and ate in silence.

chapter twelve

Natalia

THERE WAS no use talking to Mateo about the panic attack. After the smoke had cleared he moved on from it like it had never even happened. He wrote it off as a mix of dehydration and pent-up frustration with his parents, years in the making. I knew what had conspired in the kitchen was something totally different.

That's why my instinct to protect him made me lash out. I wasn't proud of shouting at his mom, but Mateo was my person, and something was hurting him, and I wanted it to stop. It was a normal psychological reaction. I wouldn't have cared if it was Jesus Christ himself, all I wanted to do was cover him with a shield and keep everyone else out.

Unfortunately, the entire ordeal had made things in the house more awkward. Yes, Anna was back to speaking to Mateo, more so out of fear for her son's health than anything, but I'd begun sensing a bit of jealousy as well after she was pushed aside. Though technically that meant the task I had set out to do had been done. Just in a more traumatic, round the block, burnt meatball way than originally intended.

Still, it was like walking on eggshells between everyone. I thought wedding planning would be a fun way to bond with Mateo's mom, but after the disagreement over invitations I didn't even want to bring up the details anymore. She didn't seem too interested in it anyway, which was especially confusing after using that as a reason to visit in the first place.

There was no time to agonize over that though; I had my own family to deal with. Isabella had texted me a place and time to meet her for coffee and considering the fate of my wedding party lay within a confined time, I really had no choice but to answer the call. I left my house pretending I was on my way to work at the bank and instead met Isabella inside a cozy modern roastery in Coconut Creek. The bright interior was designed in light wood and earth tones, and artwork decorated the walls with tasteful splashes of color. A few people sat working on laptops at the bar counter and sun drenched the front of the store through the big open windows.

Bella looked as beautiful as always with her short hair curled close to her ears, designer earrings, a matching tennis bracelet, and a few dainty chains layered around her neck. Gold. Always gold. She was wearing a light-pink blazer and a white turtleneck sweater. Meaning she was either done for the day, or on her way to make someone's life an absolute living hell in the courtroom. She was infamous for bringing grown men withering to their knees in front of the judge.

I plopped down in the wooden seat across from her that was two inches lower than I expected it to be, and the chair whined gracelessly beneath me.

"Coffee?" Bella asked.

"I'm good. One of those chocolate eclairs might entice me though."

She pursed her lips, probably fighting back a comment about the calories. "I'll buy."

"Are you sucking up to me? Or is this an apology? You can say the words, you know. I'll help." I traced my mouth with my finger. "I'm—sorry."

Bella crossed her arms over her chest. "You know that a Russo doesn't apologize. We just move on. The eclair is the truce."

"That is called a toxic relationship," I pointed out. "Just

because it's how we grew up doesn't mean we need to continue it as adults. I'd much rather forget the entire portion of my childhood where Dad apologized by buying me a new Chia Pet every time he missed a school concert, or ran over my bike backing the car into the garage. I had, like, seventy-two Chia Pets."

"You did have a lot of Chia Pets." Bella pushed her tortoiseshell reading glasses into her hair like a headband. It was both stylish and effortless.

"I don't want your pity eclair, Bells. I want to have a normal relationship with my sisters. Plural. Because the parent ship has sailed."

"That's not true." She tilted her head ruefully. "Mom is just as fucked up as we are. Think about the generation before her that put all those ideas in her head in the first place. It's not us, it's men. I work in a field absolutely dominated by the most narcissistic assholes on this planet, so I can vouch."

Even so, my mother was a brilliant woman. There was nothing she couldn't do if she wanted it badly enough; she was an extremely career-focused and calculated entrepreneur. She *knew* right from wrong. It was her inability to admit her wrongs that infuriated me. She was too vain to protect us from the things kids should never have to endure growing up. Her own misaligned, volatile parenting included. My parents loved each other in a checks and balances kind of way. My dad provided the check, and my mom balanced the duties of motherhood by pushing them off onto a nanny for twelve years.

"If she stood up for me, maybe just one time, I could have sympathy. At this point in my life I don't feel responsible for another grown woman's feelings being hurt. I love her, but she is a witchy woman."

"She's terrible at articulating herself, and you're the baby of the family, so you always take things way too personally. Fact of the matter is that we don't want you making any rash decisions, just as much as you don't want any pushback. We do care, Talia. You're not Donnie Darko."

"God, just get me the eclair," I grumbled. "I'll be rehashing this conversation in my nightmares later."

Isabella reached over the table, in one of the most foreign gestures I'd ever seen, and closed her hand over mine.

We did not touch. We barely hugged. I could count on one hand the number of times I'd ever embraced any of my sisters just for the heck of it, and the last was my grandfather's funeral five years ago.

"What are you doing?" I asked, closing my fingers into a pinched little claw. "Did someone die? Is that why you asked me to come here?"

Bella's eyes rolled and she returned her hand to her side of the table. "Didn't you just go on this whole rant about healthy relationships and undoing familial trauma? You can't even hold my hand."

"Well, that's because it's weird," I volleyed. "We look like lesbians. You look like a lesbian in that outfit, and I look like your sad, alt younger girlfriend who calls you Mommy."

"Oh, for fuck's sake." Bella reached into her pocket, leaning back on her chair and pulling out a tube of Chapstick to apply.

"Baby steps," I suggested. "You know what would really prove to me that you, Mia, and Cami actually care? Answering Ophelia's text messages about Vegas. She is way too nice and non-confrontational. You can walk all over me but my best friend is where I draw the line."

Bella sucked in a breath that blew up her cheeks and then let it out dramatically. "Fine. We will comply with Ophelia and her Excel spreadsheet."

"Thank you." Finally, getting somewhere. A tiny weight lifted off my shoulders and took flight into the metal rafters above us.

"But does she really need our underwear sizes?"

That question did not even faze me. It registered in a very neutral area of my brain as just a matter of fact, because I wouldn't have expected anything less. Phee and her crafty ideas never ceased to amaze me. If I'd done everything else in life wrong, at least I got Ophelia right. She was my invisible string.

"What's the worst that could happen?" I shrugged. "You get a brand-new pair of underwear?"

"Right," Bella conceded. "So the world keeps spinning, and we will work on communication and answer Ophelia's texts. And emails, and invitation to the Google calendar, and the collaboration on the Pinterest board. Now can I actually do my job, as your sister and lawyer?"

I sat back in my chair, crossing a leg over my knee. "Was I arrested for something I don't know about?"

Bella leaned down to her bag on the floor and plucked a thin binder out of it, settling it on the table between us. It resembled a menu you'd get at a swanky restaurant, stocky paper with tiny bindings and even tinier letters when she flipped it open.

"Don't ever tell me I don't love you," she said. "Consider this a wedding present, because I'm doing it pro bono."

My eyebrows knitted together as I pulled the binder closer and stared down at the professionally formatted legal paperwork. Isabella had tabbed important clauses and highlighted keywords in the text, but the only thing that stuck out to me was the bold and underlined words at the top of the page. PRENUPTIAL AGREEMENT.

She couldn't have been serious. A slew of colorful words rose to the top of my throat with what stung like bile and it took everything in me not to swipe the book off the table like a miscreant cat.

"Uh, thanks." I slid it back in her direction. "But no thanks."

The milk steamer across the room hissed as the barista worked a metal cup underneath it and I buried my attention in the people moving around the cafe. If I didn't look at it, it would simply cease to exist. My sister reared the binder back in my direction like a petulant child.

"What do you mean, *no thanks*?"

My deep brown eyes met her more hazel ones. "I mean, we aren't doing a prenup. I don't need it."

"You and Mateo both decided that?" A pen had materialized between her fingers. At the ready to take notes, or lecture, or stab me. Preferably stab me.

"No, we never talked about it," I said. "But we don't need a divorce contract. That's fucked up, don't you think? It's like dooming us from the start."

Mateo and I had never had the conversation, but I knew my fiancé. If one of us were worried about the possibility of calling it quits, we never would have gotten engaged in the first place. Agreements like this were for people with asset management and money tied up in stocks, second homes to account for. That was not us. Apart from the success of the cam page, we were extraordinarily regular people. To me, a prenup was like admitting we weren't positive about one another. That while things might be great now, there could be a day I didn't love him anymore, and that just wasn't fucking possible.

"That is the most childish way to perceive this, Natalia." Bella nearly scoffed. "This isn't a loyalty test. This is protecting each other in a worst-case scenario. I see it day in and day out. Couples who thought the sun shone out of each other's assholes fighting over canned beans in the pantry. Men caught wanking off to a twenty-year-old on OnlyFans while their wife bathes their children resentfully in the bathroom. Things change, people evolve, life happens."

I crossed my arms over my chest and sank my teeth into my tongue. *Mateo wouldn't do that*, I thought. My skin bristled but I swallowed down a sour retort. "Matty and I aren't like that."

She nodded sympathetically. "I know you're not. And this is not me trying to say I think you're going to have a failed marriage. But think about Mateo." Bella's pen hovered over a paragraph of words. "He is the breadwinner, he owns a business, he has assets from the military, benefits, money, et cetera. This is to say, if you two ever needed to go your separate ways, his business still belongs to him. If nothing else this is *showing* how much you love him. Willing to lose your main source of income over a divorce if it comes to it."

I could have screamed. *I* was the breadwinner. *I* owned a business. *I* was not helpless, or dependent on anyone to take care of me. *I* took care of myself. But like always my mouth remained shut. Prioritizing keeping my personal life to myself because it was the one thing I had that no one else could take from me. It was my and Mateo's secret to share. Frankie and Ophelia were the only two people we trusted with it.

A deep, long, annoyed breath let out through my nostrils. "So this is me agreeing not to claim any stake in his company in the event of a divorce."

"Part of it." Bella tapped on a highlighted passage. "This also keeps your inheritance safe, like any money from Mom and Dad. It defaults debt back onto the person with the debt, and details protocols if—God forbid—one of you kicks the bucket."

My knuckles rapped on my wooden chair. If I had to pick and choose my battles, letting Bella explain a bullet-pointed legalese to me was the least I could do, regardless of what I was going to do with the information afterward. She went on and on, scribbling into the margins upside down, stripping each sentence into something understandable, and after the final sentence, she flipped the binder closed and pushed it toward me again.

"This is just a draft. I'll need you and Mateo to sit down and go over your assets together, compile an itemized list of what you want to keep separate, and then we can go from there."

I wouldn't be doing any of those things, but I put on my brave face and smiled as I said, "Thanks for giving me the rundown. I'll talk to him."

Bella checked the time on her cellphone and dropped it back into her bag, then rooted around for her keys. "I have to get back to the office, but seriously, Talia, don't shove that thing into the back of a closet as soon as you get home and forget it exists."

That was exactly what I was going to do.

"I have to go to the florist and design the flower arrangements for the wedding anyway."

"Did you talk to Mom?" she asked, standing from the chair as it scraped across the floor. "Dad's birthday dinner is coming up."

Right. My father's sixtieth birthday. A night of listening to the same stories about the good ol' days at Harvard and then watching him drink gin and tonics until he falls asleep on one of the pool loungers. Even more exciting now that my in-laws were invited there to bear witness to it.

"Anna is already permanently scarred from that dress fitting. I can only imagine what the Durans are going to think of us after a night with John Russo."

"It'll strengthen your bond." Bella trotted toward the exit, her expensive heels striking the floor with each step as I followed. "You couldn't hide us forever, Tals. Mateo is part of the family now."

I couldn't hide him from them, but I could protect him from them. I'd been doing it, and I would keep doing it for as long as I needed to. Until my parents stopped treating me like a child, and my sisters started seeing me as an equal. So that I didn't have to make excuses for them every step of the way. Being with Mateo taught me how love *should* feel, how a healthy relationship works, and what I would never settle for. The two of us were going to break our generational curses together.

That prenup could go fuck itself.

chapter thirteen

Natalia

PRETENDING I had a job was harder than keeping my real one a secret. I was planning the wedding entirely from the driver's seat of my car on most days, relying on retail therapy and drive-thru meals to keep me company. If it weren't for the fear of getting caught and arrested for public indecency I might have also started filming content from the front seat, too.

Our client base declined every time we missed a regularly scheduled posting day. Even when Mateo came home early enough to make some quick magic, we were pigeonholed into short, uninspired bursts of coitus by the looming presence down the hall. I missed my apartment bedroom and the makeshift studio Matty and I used to film most of our sex in when Frankie was still living in Florida. Back when things were easy and I could orgasm as loud as I wanted to whether it was six at night or nine in the morning.

Five o'clock rolled around and I made my way back to the house after yet another grueling day of bumming Wi-Fi from the local library to field important vendor phone calls and emails. In the last week I'd finalized the floral arrangements, sticking to the classic white rose theme that was elegant, but ultimately boring, and mailed the invitations, which were equally sophisticated and forgettable. I had to remind myself several times that black tie was everything I ever wanted for my wedding day, because the more I agonized over the details, the more I realized the dream had more to do with proving my parents wrong than color schemes.

The house was quiet inside. I dropped my bag on the entry table and kicked my shoes into the small coat closet by the front door. The Durans were usually milling around the living room but the television was off and the kitchen was empty. Eventually I heard a hushed conversation happening behind the open crack in the guest room door. Anna was folding laundry into piles on the bed, and David was sitting near the headboard. I would have walked away had I not heard my name mumbled in the conversation.

"She means well," Anna was saying. "But I have to worry, or what kind of mother would I be? He's choosing his friends over his family, he's barely eating, and he's having panic attacks."

"Times are different, Anna," David answered. "Women aren't traditional anymore, they're independent. They have full-time jobs just like their husbands, and when they have kids they put them in daycare. It's how the world is going."

"There's nothing wrong with that." Anna's voice dipped lower, but not low enough that I couldn't hear it. "It might make sense if they had a baby, but...she's *here*, most of the time. All I'm saying is that Mateo goes to work all day until late at night. The least he should expect is a hot meal when he gets home at the end of it."

"But he loves her," David reasoned. "That's enough sometimes. Maybe when all this honeymooning wears off and reality sets in he'll smarten up and tell her what he needs."

"He's head over heels," Anna said. "And she's young and has to learn a thing or two before beauty gets boring."

My chest felt caged in, lungs swelling against iron bars. I wanted to crawl inside my own skin and hide. Part of me was ready to burst out of the shadows and confront what I'd heard, but most of me collapsed in on myself, regressing back to that young, insecure teenager being scolded by her parents for having no motivation or redeeming qualities. This was worse than that, because all I'd ever tried to do was make Mateo's parents like me, and they still somehow came to the same conclusion.

What if they were right? Being a partner to someone was more than taking up their space, and sooner or later Mateo was going to realize that I wasn't the type of woman you'd want as a wife. I wasn't a homemaker. I couldn't even blame the staff of chefs and maids that I grew up with for it. I never learned because I didn't have to. It was pure laziness. I was exactly what Anna and David were saying I was, and now I wasn't sure if Mateo felt the same and chose to ignore it all this time because I was loyal and good at the one thing every man wants. Sex.

That's what I got for eavesdropping. Before I could hear anything more, I carefully tiptoed away, folding my lips over my teeth and biding a few extra seconds to get into our bedroom, close the door, and sink to the wood to let myself cry.

* * *

AS A DISTRACTION, I made myself busy doing the pre-production work for our Valentine's Day shoot. It was the loneliest, horniest holiday of the year, and if it went anything like our previous together, it would also be our most lucrative. We had requests pouring in for video gifts and personalized Hard-O-Grams, as I had named them, and a poll for the livestream showed the current vote for sex position of choice was the pretzel dip. Classic.

I didn't leave my bubble of sorrow until I heard the front door open long after dinnertime and Mateo's voice greeting his mom and dad. My insecurities were irritated like a rash I kept on scratching, and every time I looked in the mirror I was more and more unsure that the man I was going to marry was even attracted to me anymore. I'd become too comfortable, I couldn't cook a roast or iron a dress shirt without leaving it worse than it began, and like his mom said, once the novelty of a wife with a shallow G-spot wore off, eventually I would be useless.

The door to the small laundry room was cracked when I crept down the hall and I ducked my head inside to see Mateo tugging his work polo over his head and tossing it into a half-full washer. The movement tousled his hair, and it fell so perfectly across his forehead and in wispy strands in front of his eyes I leaned against the frame to admire it for a second as he filled the machine with detergent and turned it on.

He noticed me staring and a smile curled his lips. "Hi, angel."

"Hi," I hummed back. He tugged his white undershirt from his jeans and unfastened his belt before pulling it entirely out of the loops and setting it aside. "Can I help?"

I didn't wait for an answer before slipping into the room, nudging the white door closed behind me and twisting the lock. Mateo's eyebrow lifted at the sound of the soft click. "Are we hiding from something, Natalia?"

"Maybe," I answered coyly. The rumbling washer swished to life as I wedged myself in the space between it and Mateo. My breasts pressed into the bottom of his ribs, spilling over the low neckline of my tank top. I looked up at him but he was already looking down, gaze hooded, focused where I expected him to be, and then those yellow-brown eyes found mine and *need* rushed violently between my legs.

Both sides of his jaw twitched, and his throat corded on a swallow as I trailed my long fingertips across the rough denim on his thighs, up to the hem of his undershirt, and slipped them beneath. His stomach pulled taut under my touch, and I drew circles in the light-brown hair that swirled around his belly button and down toward his waist.

"There's nothing suspicious about doing laundry together with the door locked," he reasoned. "Perfectly normal."

"The dryer broke," I joked, tugging open his pants button then bouncing onto my tiptoes to reach the exposed skin at his collarbone, lashing my tongue against his neck.

"Goddammit, woman," he said gruffly, his fingers looped into the band of my jeans. "You know my mother's thirty feet away."

"I distinctly remember you saying you could fuck me anytime, anywhere, any way you please."

"I didn't say I wouldn't. But you can't keep your mouth shut when I'm inside you, Tally. I'm not sure you want everyone hearing you while you cry on my cock."

My face flamed, the hint of degradation sending me far away from any rational decision making. He *knew* what those words would do to me. "I'll be quiet," I promised, taking the lobe of his ear between my teeth and biting down lightly. The soft groan it pulled out of his chest surprised us both.

"What is this about?" Mateo lifted me to sit atop the washing machine and wrenched my knees apart. When he stepped between my legs our noses were nearly brushing. "Something got you all hot and bothered while I was at work? Tell me."

I hid my face as his vein-swathed hands rubbed up and down my legs, squeezing gently at the juncture of my hips, and setting my nerves on edge. "It's not that."

"Don't lie. I'll get it out of you *my way* if you do."

Most of Mateo's threats did the opposite of the intended effect. My blood raced at the thought of a punishment, his hands around my neck, a red ass, edging, withholding. I could turn myself on just imagining it, but he was doing all the work himself.

"I'm not." His touch climbed up my body and tangled in the hair at the nape of my neck. I let my head fall to the side ever so slightly and Matty's gentle lips grazed the spot where my pulse hammered just below my ear. "I was working."

"So I was right."

"I was thinking about you and how stressed you've been." I slid the zipper of his pants down. "I don't take care of you enough."

Mateo's eyes flitted to the closed door as I peeled the band of his boxer briefs away from his body and slid my hand into them, coiling my fingers around a hot, hard shaft. His hips jarred into it, asking for more while I tugged slowly.

"Fucking Christ, Tal, you're more than taking care of me."

He wrenched the low neckline of my top down, uncovering my budding, sensitive breasts and with my free hand I lowered his head, guiding his mouth to suck on them, one after the other. His cock beaded with precum under my fingertips.

"Doesn't this bother you?" I gestured to the washing machine.

"I have no complaints about fucking you on the washer. In fact I'm thinking about turning you around and bending you over it."

"No, not that. Does it bother you that you had to do your own laundry? That the washer was full when you got home?"

His head lifted, nose meeting the curve of my cheek. "What?"

"Or do you ever wish I had dinner plated for you in the kitchen when you walked through the door?"

"I mean, I wouldn't *dislike* that."

"So you're disappointed that it's not something I do often." I kissed him, dipping my tongue into his mouth and swirling it against his.

"I didn't say that," he mumbled against my lips.

Mateo jerked my pants down my hips, my skin prickling against the cold metal of the washer and I managed to kick out of one leg, leaving the jeans and my panties dangling on an ankle. "Do you think I'm lazy?" I asked. "Am I a spoiled brat?"

"Yes," he answered half-heartedly, focused on the space between my legs and where it met his tented boxers. With another quick look at the closed door he put his palm out in front of my chin. "Spit."

"Yes?"

"Spit." His eyes were all pupils.

"Mateo, this is serious."

"You want to know if I think you're spoiled, when this is the third time I've asked you to spit and I still haven't spanked your ass for not listening yet? Yes, Natalia, you are fucking spoiled. I spoil you, I pamper you, and I am a patient man with you when all I want to do is break you because I can't turn that part of me off completely." He squeezed my cheeks together, puckering my mouth. "Now do what you're told, brat. Or I'll leave you in this laundry room with your pussy dripping and an empty hole where my cock should be filling it."

My mind looped. I had come into this laundry room to seduce my fiancé as a twisted way of reminding myself he was irrevocably in love with me, desired me, needed me, and that all these insecurities were baseless. All I'd managed to get was half-naked on the top of a washing machine; confirm that I was indeed useless, spoiled, and lazy; and transfer every ounce of control to Mateo in a split second. Now I wasn't just sad and horny, I was also spitting into a hand like a—

"*Good little slut*," Mateo purred. "I knew you had it in you." He shimmied his pants and boxers down enough for his cock to spring free between us and rubbed my spit down the shaft and over the head while my core fluttered in waiting.

Was this self-sabotage? My fingernails dug into the soft cotton of his T-shirt as Mateo pushed closer, notching himself inside me, even sinking in that tiny amount that had my eyes pinching closed and a dulcet whimper trickling out of me. I almost gave in—I *nearly* let go and let myself get lost in this little raunchy moment hidden behind our laundry room door with the spin cycle bustling beneath me. But I would have never gotten over it if I did.

"I just want to be enough for you," I blurted. "I want to know you're going to love me if all I can cook is a freezer pizza and scrambled eggs. Or if I forget to switch the wet laundry over to the dryer for a day and it starts to stink. And if I don't leave the house for three days and waste away in the bedroom buried in work unshowered in your sweatpants."

His dick was at least two inches inside me and came to a dead, pulsing stop as Matty refocused. Like he'd been drunk and splashed with ice cold water. My breathing galloped, juxtaposed between the feeling of us connected and the intensity of his stare. He didn't pull out.

"Where is this coming from, baby?"

"It's been on my mind."

"Natalia."

"Really."

He slid out and thrust back into the same spot and my entire body shuddered. "What do you think I did before you?"

I absentmindedly played with the long, soft hair at the nape of his neck. "Waited for me to show up."

His hum of approval accompanied another push of his hips deeper inside me. My legs parted to accommodate the space he took up between them. "I am a grown fucking man, Tally. I can feed myself, I can wash my own clothes, and I know you don't want to hear this, but I can even fuck myself. Now, it'd never compare to this"—he enunciated that point with another thrust, bottoming out as my head dropped backwards—"but you are not my keeper. You're my partner."

A whine of satisfaction shot out of me as he picked up a steadier rhythm, and Mateo glared in warning. I dug my face into the crook of his neck, picking up all the subdued notes of his aftershave still lingering from the morning. He somehow smelled even better after a long day than freshly showered. "You know how much I want your mom's blessing."

"Shhh." Mateo shook his head.

"Did you just shush me?"

"Did you just bring up my mother while I'm inside you?"

I couldn't stop thinking about his mother. She was the catalyst to this entire thing. "We're multitasking."

Behind the closed door a dust bunny had gathered in matted lint and shed hair and I frowned at how long I'd probably gone without noticing it, and how I would likely never gaze around a room again without thinking about how dirty I'd let it get. The corner of the ceiling was cobwebbed, the decorative circular mirror hanging over the hamper in the corner was smudged, and the light from the window hit it perfectly at this time of the day. When I blinked out of my self-reflecting daze and returned my focus to Mateo, he was already staring back at me.

"What did she say?"

My chin fell. "No, it's nothing. I'm just feeling shitty about dinner again."

"That wasn't even your fault, that was *my* fault. If I hadn't gone off the deep end everyone would have eaten your amazing dinner and there wouldn't even be a doubt in your mind." His fingers guided my head back up, but I still didn't meet his eyes. "You're not telling me something."

I bit the inside of my cheek, gesturing to my bare boobs and our lewd bodies. "Can we just...get back to this? This is something I know I'm great at."

Matty butted our foreheads together, invading my space. "Look at me, Tally." It only took a glance for him to make my walls come crumbling down. He looked at me like the thoughts were written in my irises. "I know you."

"I know." I sighed.

"So?"

"The last thing I want to do is cause more of a rift between you and your parents," I said reluctantly. "It's not important."

"If it's important to you it's important to me. Let me guess, she said something passive aggressive about housework? Went on a tangent about what she does for my dad?"

"It wasn't exactly passive."

Mateo's brows jumped. "You're kidding."

"I wasn't supposed to hear them talking. I came home this afternoon and they were whispering in the bedroom. Well, as much of a whisper as your mom can manage."

"Which is a normal speaking voice," Mateo said.

"Right, and it wasn't that bad, it just got me thinking. That I'm young, and you were attracted to me based on appearance first, and that probably makes it easy to overlook the things you wouldn't otherwise. But I won't always have great tits, and my skin will definitely wrinkle. Plus I've pulled no less than five gray hairs out of my head in the last month. So when that all starts to happen, I also can't cook like your mom, and I don't pack you lunch every day like your mom, or fold the laundry the same way as your mom, or with nearly enough frequency as her."

"Then it's a damn good thing I don't want to marry my fucking mom." He pinched the bridge of his nose until the skin turned purple. "You're not giving me any credit at all here, Tally. Do you think all you are to me is a warm body? Maybe the issue is actually your confidence in me as a husband and nothing to do with what someone might have said about the dirty dishes. Do you think I'd stop loving you over that?"

"Well, that's pretty selfish." I crossed my arms. "You were begging me to tell you what's bothering me, even though I felt self-conscious about it because I *know* it's dumb. I was vulnerable, looking for some reassurance, and you've gone and made it about you."

"It's not *making it about me*, it *is* about me. If you think that if you gain a few pounds and grow a few stretch marks I'm going to start looking around at how good of a job you're doing with your 'wifely duties', that is a direct reflection of how you view our relationship."

"That's not what I meant," I countered, frustrated.

"Then explain it to me, Natalia."

"Don't call me *Natalia* when we're arguing. You're not my father."

Mateo's head tilted and the corner of his lip tugged upward. "Well now that's opening up a whole other can of worms."

"That!" I yelped. "*That* is what I'm trying to say."

He squinted. "I'm not seeing the point." It'd been several minutes since we addressed that our bodies were still very much connected, and I was mildly impressed he hadn't gone entirely limp noodle in the midst.

"Would you still love me if I was a worm?"

"For fuck's sake..." Mateo rolled his neck and his Adam's apple bobbed.

"Answer the question," I pressed.

"That's like fucking bestiality."

My jaw unhinged. "Oh...my...*god*, Mateo. What am I, the Alaskan fucking bullworm?"

"No, that's obviously not—" he backtracked, shaking his head.

"Your first thought was, 'How am I gonna fuck that worm? Where's the worm hole?'"

He ran a hand across his mouth, concealing a laugh. "You are unhinged."

"No, now that I think about it, I'm so glad you answered the way you did, because I was right. That was your only concern. Not my personality, or my character, or all the memories we have together. Sex is the most important thing to a man. If it came down to it, you wouldn't love me if I was a worm because you couldn't fuck me if I was a worm."

"I would try," Mateo said.

"What the fuck?"

"I would try to love you! I would try to love you, if you were a worm. I would carry you around in a little plastic sandwich baggie of dirt or something. I'd become the town psycho walking around talking to my worm bag and calling it my wife."

"I'd definitely suffocate and die that way."

Mateo scrubbed his palm down his chin and massaged his jaw. "So how do I win, Tally? What do you want me to say to you right now? This is all about you being insecure. I reassure you day in and day out about how much I love you, how beautiful you are, how deeply I care about you, and today that isn't enough for some reason. I want you to feel confident in our relationship no matter what outside force gnaws at you. I *need* it actually, because I'm going to marry you and marrying you isn't casual to me. So tell me, please. Tell me if I'm not doing enough."

Guilt rocked through me. Mateo was more than enough; he

treated me how every woman dreamed of being treated. I couldn't help but fall back into bad habits no matter how good it got with him because I was conditioned my entire life to think I wasn't enough. I was deathly afraid of Mateo realizing one day that I wasn't either. Worse, the novelty of having a sex-working significant other would wear off for him, or his parents would find out and convince him I was the biggest mistake of his life. Their reaction would be no different than my own parents, that no self-respecting woman would ever take her clothes off for money. And maybe they were right. Maybe my respect for myself laid in other people's respect for me.

Before I could say anything the door handle to the laundry room started jarring violently and every single hair on my body stood up like lightning had struck.

"Mateo, are you in there?" Anna bellowed, jingling the handle again despite it being locked, like an impatient toddler outside a parked car.

Matty fumbled from inside me and tugged the neck of my tank top up over my tits again, scrambling just as quickly to tuck himself away and zip his jeans closed. Our eyes were wide and frantic, and my skin turned a glorious freshly sunburned shade as I jumped down off the washing machine and hopped gracelessly on one leg to put my pants back on. It was a mess of hushing and pitter-patter; my heel slammed into the metal appliance and Mateo cleared his throat entirely too loudly to try to mask it.

"Mateo?" Anna's voice was closer, like she was pressed against the door and sniffing it.

"Just a sec!" he answered.

"What are you doing in there?"

"Um." He looked at me. "Laundry?"

Unhappy with that reply the door handle jiggled again, more aggressively.

"Fuck, she's gonna know," I whispered. I'd barely gotten over the embarrassment of the dildo debacle and now we were getting caught in pound town again.

"She won't." Mateo paced in front of me. "Will she?"

"We're in here with the door locked. What else could we be doing?"

"Is that Natalia?" Anna murmured through the wood.

Mateo ran a hand through his hair. "Yeah she—she got stuck in the dryer. I was helping her get out."

My eyebrows creased and my jaw dropped open. "Stuck in the dryer?" I mouthed. Anna was never going to believe that, and the cliché would haunt me.

"Well, is she okay?" Anna's voice hinted at genuine concern. "Need help? I can get a stick of butter; it'll loosen her right up."

"How big does your mother think I am?" I mumbled sharply and Mateo's palm came down over my lips.

"Don't worry, she slipped right out of there like nothing when I got her a little wet."

The bastard had the audacity to wink at me before unlocking the door and swinging it open, dismissing us, his mother, our conversation, and the ever-nagging feeling that sooner or later this was all going to feel like shaking a bottle of soda and opening the cap for it to blow up.

chapter fourteen

I WANTED to pull my hair out. I was close to it, sitting at the reception desk of a new law office in Coconut Creek with an Excel spreadsheet of backwork, pages of firewall breaks and detected malware staring back at me. The building was dark, nothing but the blue light from the desktop keeping me awake for yet another late night working after hours. Most places preferred that I came when the work day was over so I didn't disrupt employees or force shutdowns on programs. That led to a lot of lonely dinners and load buffering while I stared at my watch.

Working alone was taking its toll on me, but I was too proud to admit it. I had dug myself too deep into a hole to come back. Every time Natalia asked me if I hired a new assistant yet, I gave her the same spiel about the employment market being thin, and waiting for the right candidate to come around. Our Valentine's content had taken a back burner, the live stream cut short by half an hour when I was late coming home, and though I knew she was unhappy with it, she didn't press me too hard.

That was weeks ago.

I knew from my nightly recaps that Natalia was spending every waking minute she wasn't working on planning the wedding. The catering was set, the room block was full, our photographer had been prepped, the suits were ready to be picked up by all the groomsmen at their earliest convenience, and our flights to Vegas were booked. I was grateful Tally had a handle on all of those things because I was silently losing my mind juggling the work of two at TechOps, and pretending having my parents as roommates wasn't dramatically weighing on my mental resilience.

Plus, the anxiety was getting worse. That episode I'd had in the kitchen only set off a chain reaction and made me more panicked that things like that were going to become normal for me. I was worried about loud noises and tight spaces, too many people, tension. Things I was once so good at controlling. Being the point person was my literal job in the military, the reason I was "The Captain" to all my brothers, and now I couldn't even handle small pressures. Years of war and trauma were catching up to me quickly and the effects were leaking through and affecting my civilian life.

I needed to relearn myself again in some capacity. My brain was wired for Delta; those thoughts don't just dissipate. The need for control was valiant when I was in the service, but allowing myself off the hook now, even three years later, wasn't coming easy enough.

Bothering Natalia with it wasn't an option either. I knew how stressed she was in her own life, with her own family. It would be selfish of me. At the end of the day, I was a grown man. I could deal with whatever mental shit I had going on myself. I could learn to stand up to my parents, and I could handle my business myself just like Tally was handling hers.

My phone lit up on cue with a text from Natalia, asking how the install was going and if she could expect me home soon. It was a Friday night, a live stream night. The loading bar on the desktop was only blinking halfway, which meant at the least I had another half hour sitting there waiting for it. There was no way I was making it home in time for the scheduled stream in ten minutes.

Instead of texting back, I hit the call button and pressed the phone to my ear.

"Let me guess," she jeered. "You're stuck at work again?"

A sigh rippled out of me. "I'm sorry. This law firm has several layers of security for file protection and I had to code and test every single one of them."

"Our female audience has dropped off the face of the earth on Friday nights with you going into hiding. I did an analysis last week and the subscriber percentage was skewed by eighty-three percent in favor of both of us on camera together."

"You had a loyal following before me," I reminded her.

"I work so much better with my partner, though."

My teeth ground together and I leaned back in the computer chair, rubbing a guilty wrinkle from the space between my brows. "I promise I'll be there next week for it. I'll clear my schedule to make sure."

"You could always hire someone to take a load off your shoulders," she goaded.

I changed the subject quickly, pouring my attention into impatiently tapping the keyboard as if it might make the software load faster. "What are you wearing tonight?"

Sheets ruffled around in the background of the call. Tally was likely lying on our bed in a matching lingerie set waiting for the chat server to fill and the top of the hour to roll around. Without me physically there, she would be limited to using her fingers, or taking out a toy as a treat. "That's privileged information," she said.

"You act like I can't hop on the stream as a viewer and see it for myself."

She pulled in a breath but went otherwise quiet on the line. I struck a nerve. A glorious, exhibitionist nerve. My stomach tensed and a spark of intrigue jolted my cock against my zipper. There was an external CCTV security system on the outside of the building, but as far as I could tell from looking around the office space, there were no cameras on the inside. I slid my personal laptop out of my bag and opened it on the desk in front of me.

"You'd like that, wouldn't you?" I said. "Knowing I was watching on the other end while you touched yourself."

The hum of her voice crackled to life. "I thought you were working."

"I have some time to kill." I opened my browser and quickly found our page. I wasn't home to play my part but that didn't mean I couldn't still do it from across town. My mind was already made up, and the pressure below my waist wasn't going anywhere any time soon. "Don't hang up the phone," I told her.

"I have to go on in a minute," she trilled, a gust of disappointment weaving through her words. "I can't stay and talk."

"I don't want you to talk. I want you to listen," I explained. "I want to hear all the breathy little noises you make in my ear while I tell you exactly the kind of thoughts I have about you while I'm working late, and I'm all alone."

"Like what?" she asked quietly.

My palm slid down to readjust the growing bulge in my pants, but the contact only made the ache more prevalent. I kicked away from the desk, stretching my legs in the chair. "Put your earbuds in."

Our mattress squeaked underneath her, and a bedside drawer opened and shut as she followed my direction. My pulse was hammering as I stared at the blank video screen, wondering what she looked like on the other end, wishing I could peel whatever barely-there piece of lace she was wearing off by my teeth and make her choke on it while I slammed into her.

Fuck, I couldn't be thinking things like that. I was at work, I needed to remain professional, and jerking off behind the reception desk to live porn on a job was the least professional thing I could think of. Besides, I would rather treat it like foreplay, and take the pent up frustration from this back home to Tally afterward.

Her voice returned to the line, clearer and softer. "Can you hear me?"

"Start the stream, Natalia."

She made a noise that might have wanted to be a word, but got lost on the way. I was well aware it was too early to go live, because there were still subs spilling into the chat window, and starting before the scheduled time might piss a few late arrivals off. I needed to see her body react to everything I said, though. "Be a good girl and get on that camera for me."

A few seconds passed feeling like my chest might explode from anticipation, and then the computer screen lit up and Natalia was there in the video feed, perched on our familiar bed and wearing my favorite red bra and panties, looking straight into my soul.

"Fuck." A growl rumbled from deep in my chest. "So fucking pretty, baby." She had wireless earbuds in her ears that were hidden beneath the curtain of her long dark hair, but I knew they were there because a blush crept up her chest and blossomed over her cheeks. "Now do me a favor and stay nice and quiet, Tal. Try your hardest to keep that mouth shut. Don't say a word while you do what I tell you. This is our little secret, right?"

She nodded, her top teeth sinking into her bottom lip. The pulse previously hammering in my ears shot straight down to my cock and I palmed it again, looking for some relief and finding less and less of it the longer I gazed at my fiancée.

"God, I want your mouth around me right now," I said. "That's what I think about when I'm working late and I'm so fucking hard that I can't focus on anything else. Your pretty eyes looking up at me, and my hands in your hair while I shove my cock down your throat until you choke on it."

Tally's chest rose and fell faster and a breathy moan drifted out of her. I was stiff and swollen and there was precum gathering against the fabric of my briefs that made it hard not to move my hips looking for friction.

"Take your top off and let me see you." Tally reached behind her to the clasp and her bra came loose; her tits dropped out in a way that made my eyes roll back. She was so devastatingly hot it would have brought me crumbling to my knees if I wasn't already sitting. "Play with your nipples, baby. Roll your fingers over them."

The rush from watching her trail her sharp fingernails across her chest to tug and circle the taut buds made it hard to breathe. A sigh rolled off her parted lips and graced my ears, and her head lolled back to expose her neck and her collarbones. The lighting was perfect. She was so smooth and delicate, and absolutely mesmerizing. My dick twitched against my palm and I groaned in approval.

"That's it, sweetheart. Now pretend it's just us, and spread your legs open for me. I'm going crazy wondering what that pussy must feel like right now. Are you wet, angel?"

"Yes," she cried out.

My jaw clenched. "Oh, Tal, what did I tell you about keeping that fucking mouth shut? You're supposed to be my quiet, quivering little slut right now. Since I'm not there to shut you up myself, you're going to need to listen to me."

Her head dipped and she nodded slowly, going from sitting on her calves to her ass, and parting her knees so that I could see the damp lace barely covering the flesh between her legs. She was slick with arousal, positively begging for a smack of my fingers or a lash of my tongue, something to touch her clit and satiate her.

"Slide your panties down your legs," I told her. "Then I want you to put them in your mouth. See if that doesn't teach you how to stay silent." Her eyes widened and a rush of color tickled her skin on the live stream as heat pooled in my abdomen. I worked my wrist faster, bringing a climax within reach, while her thumbs hooked into the band, pushing her thong down and off her ankles. She hesitated for a moment, staring into the screen where she knew I was staring right back. "Now, Natalia."

Her mouth popped open, and she shoved the thin lace between her lips, biting down on it. Every nerve in my lower half was on edge, thrumming in warning and a sweat started at my back while my cock throbbed for the touch I was denying myself.

"How does that desperate little cunt taste?"

Natalia whimpered and her gaze fell to half-mast as her hips jarred forward, searching for something to rub against. The chat window was moving too fast to read, but the audience was loving every second of the show she was putting on. I squeezed my erection as if that might alleviate any of the delicious pain and a hiss pulled through my teeth.

"You're fucking soaked," I said. "Touch your pussy. Show me how badly you wish I was there to take some of that ache away, baby."

Tally speared her fingers through her core, brushing the nerves at her peak in slow circles, and a whine of satisfaction tumbled out around the lace in her mouth. She moved her hips against her hand, and dropped her middle finger down to tease her entrance and plunge inside.

Another garbled *fuck* snuck out of me watching her finger herself. "You look so empty without my cock inside you, Tal. I'm so hard right now wishing I was there putting every inch of me in that tight hole where I belong. I know you'd be a perfect wife and squeeze every drop of cum out of me."

She was nodding again, breathing hard through her nose, her eyes pinched shut and a wrinkle forming between them as her legs threatened to close around her hand. My balls drew tight, and the familiar feeling of near bliss spread through my body. I grunted out a protest. "Keep those fucking legs spread open, Tally. You're driving me so crazy I could come just looking at you right now. *Fuck.*"

Natalia massaged her clit faster. The sounds of her struggling with her mouth gagged and her own euphoria building sent me over the edge. A ripple of pleasure coiled down my spine and made me go completely rigid, legs flexing, my fingers twitched against my shaft practically begging to pull my dick out and tug on it. There was no one around, there was no reason not to let go, and for weeks in our house I'd been holding back. I couldn't. This was as much of a punishment to myself for not being there for the live as it was a reward for the both of us later when I was.

It was pure fucking torture to be watching her writhe on our bed, searching for release without me there to fuck it out of her.

The room spun in a circle and my vision swam, I forced myself to refocus on the live stream. Tally's knees were shaking, her fingers were trembling against her supple clit, she was teetering on the precipice of an orgasm and I couldn't let that happen. She knew the rules.

"Don't you dare fucking come, Natalia." I sat up, pulling the chair closer to the open laptop while she struggled to fight the urge. "I'll take care of you when I get home."

She ripped her hand away from her core and yanked the earbuds out, tossing them on the bed and tugging the red panties out of her mouth. Tally's pupils were still blown and her cheeks fully flushed when she slid off the edge of the bed and ended the live stream.

chapter fifteen

Mateo

13 months ago

NATALIA'S BEDROOM was entirely different than how I'd gotten used to seeing it. Her soft flowery sheets were usually rumpled and unkempt, her bed unmade, the mismatched throw pillows tossed hastily at the headboard—but now it was perfectly tucked with plain white sheets and two pink pillows.

The nightstands were bare, all but a box of tissues and a potted plant in the spot she kept her jewelry and her discarded hair scrunchies when she tugged them out after a long day. The place I would put my watch, or a box of condoms, a glass of water, my phone—all cleared like it was nothing but a prop. Her alarm clock was gone, the photo of her and her best friend from college nowhere to be seen. Even the pesky charging cord that stuck out of the bedframe and that I'd nearly gotten wrapped around my neck in my sleep was unplugged and put away.

It was like there wasn't a trace of her personality left. In front of the camera, at least. Behind the tripod and the ring light all those bright-colored blankets and eclectic wall decorations were tossed on a chair and in the empty space on her desk. One half of the room was one way, what she wanted the world to see, and behind the scenes it was something completely different.

I stuck my hands in the pockets of my jeans while Tally clicked the mouse of her desktop around, pulling up a chat window and a video window. She waved her hand in front of the camera and it echoed on the screen.

"Did you get your test results?"

I plucked a folded sheet of paper I'd gotten from my doctor out of my pocket and handed it to her. "Clean."

She scanned it thoroughly, the corner of her lips curling upward before she spun and filed it in a manila folder in her desk drawer. She handed me her own sheet of paper and I pretended to read it. Natalia was so adorably thorough, I was in love with this side of her and how seriously she took it, and for once in my life sitting back and letting someone else boss me around and take the reins was like fresh air to my lungs. I could trust her the same way I could trust myself.

"I use an IUD for contraception, so we're safe there."

"Tal, if you wanted me to get a vasectomy in order to fuck you raw I'd take myself into the bathroom right now with a pair of scissors."

She put her hands on her hips and blew out an amused gust of breath. The time on my watch read nine forty, and I knew from our extensive talks about this and her scheduling that at ten on Friday nights Natalia did live camera sex by herself for her top-tier subscribing audience. But this week, for the first time ever, "Natasha" would have a male guest.

"Is this really fucking weird for you, too?" She wrung her fingers in circles.

I pulled her computer chair out and sat on it backwards. "What are you talking about? I'm just visiting you at work. This is our bread and butter."

Tally glided over and took my face in her hands. "I know you joke as a coping method, but you don't have to make light of every situation. It's fine if you're having second thoughts. I want to know these things before I take it too far."

"I'm just trying to figure out where you learned how to make a bed that tight. I haven't seen something like that since boot-camp, Tal. Impress me more, please."

She jutted her tongue into her cheek. "I told you this is all very procedural."

"I'm seeing that." I lifted my head and met her for a kiss that turned heated when I sunk my hand into her hair and flicked my tongue through the seam of her lips. It took all my strength not to lay her down on the bed with my weight on top of her. "What's next?"

Tally crossed the bedroom to her closet and rustled through the hangers, turning toward me with two of them pressed to her chest side by side. "Red or black?"

Fuck.

She was holding two equally lacy infinitesimal pieces of lingerie. My stomach flipped and a rush of pressure made itself known in my groin. "Red," I said between clenched teeth. I abandoned the computer chair the second she slipped her shorts down her legs. "But I might rip them in half, so I'd say go with whatever set you like less."

"We have to talk about this." She tried to wrangle me, but I caught her around the waist, then plucked her spaghetti straps from her arms and hooked a finger into the neckline of her tank, tugging it down until her round breasts sprung free. I was admittedly very distracted by the smell of her skin, and the soft way she laughed at everything I did. She was delicate and gorgeous but also passionate and strong. I felt completely inadequate and undeserving of her on my best days, and focusing on anything other than Natalia was debilitating for me. When I wasn't with her I thought about her, and when I was with her, I was obsessing over her. I was entranced, and I knew no one else would understand it. Not Pike, not the boys, not my brother. They'd probably think I was fucking nuts for doing this.

Maybe I was.

"You talk." I took one of Tally's nipples into my mouth and her back arched toward the sensation. "I'm listening, angel."

"This is serious." She pulled my head back up. "Tonight's live stream is relaxed. We feel out the audience for what they might want to see and go with the flow. We can make a game plan if you're more comfortable with that. Or we can start slow and move onto sex as you open up, but I need you to remember that I'm not expecting anything at all from you, Mateo."

Up until that moment I'd been brushing off my nerves as excitement. In my mind it was simple—I was having sex with Natalia like I'd done dozens of times before. I wasn't afraid of the audience. I couldn't see them so I could pretend they weren't even there, but the pressure I felt to perform *for her* outweighed all of that. I was terrified of fucking this up for Tally. To not be good enough, or sexy enough, or well trained enough to make her proud of me. That simple insecurity was tearing me apart. What if she never wanted to work with me as a partner again? What if, after all this, she decided she didn't want me anymore?

The day she told me she was a cam girl, I knew that it wasn't going to change the way I felt about her. She was fucking brilliant, level-headed, careful, and calculated, and she held so much respect for herself that I couldn't help but respect her exactly the same way. Maybe another man might be too jealous for this or too possessive, and there was nothing wrong with that, but I looked at Natalia and I wanted to lift her up on my shoulders and shout at the top of my lungs. I wanted to show her off, wanted other people to look at what was mine and wish with all their might that they'd ever have a chance. She comes home to *me*, sleeps in *my* arms, makes love to *me* and no one else. Never again.

"I'm following your lead." I dropped my forehead to hers. "If I need a break, or I need to stop, I'll tap your ankle."

"I'll do the same," she said. "Let's talk about limits. This will change depending on what we're filming, but for live cam I'm not comfortable with any type of physical degradation. No slapping, hitting, spitting is a hard pass, and if you pee on me I will smoosh your face in it like a dog."

"Understood." I cracked a smile. "I also concur with those."

"Unless we plan it, I don't want to be tied to anything. You can restrain my wrists or ankles with your hands, hair pulling is fine, and light choking is A-OK. Doggy or missionary look better on camera, but I'm not married to either." Tally took a steadying breath. "Do you have anything for me?"

I did have a request. It was selfish, and I'd been thinking about it for days knowing this night was coming after we first discussed the possibility. There were things I was okay with, and things I wanted to keep just for myself given our unique arrangement. If Natalia and I were going to do this, bare all, have sex for an audience, I needed one thing.

"I don't want you to come."

Her eyes widened. "Oh."

"I'm okay with sharing parts of you, Tally. But not that. I want that to belong to me."

Tally thinned her lips and shimmied her tank over her head, leaving her stark naked and tauntingly poised. My eyelids shuddered closed. "I can do that," she said, disappointment seeping off her tongue.

She didn't understand. She thought I was telling her I didn't want to make her come, or that she wasn't allowed to come, like a punishment or something, but that wasn't it. I fully intended to bring this woman to orgasm. Privately.

I grabbed her hip and tugged her body flush against mine, my erection rubbing against the soft skin of her belly. "I think you're mistaking this as me telling you that I'm not going to make you feel good, Tal. I'm going to do my job, make you all warm and limp and satiated, but that's too real for me to give away. Does that make sense?"

"So you want me to...fake it?"

"For the camera. For the people who aren't me."

Her bottom lip folded between her teeth. "Should I make a really obnoxious noise, like a mating call?"

"Naturally." I grinned. "Like you're on another plane of existence."

"Like a ghost?"

I coughed out a laugh. "If there's one person on this planet who could make orgasming like a spirit hot, it would be you, Tal."

She leaned forward, nuzzling her face into my chest. I had already been acutely aware of how naked she was and how warm her body felt but my skin prickled with the need to feel it bare against hers. I reached up and tugged my shirt over my head, dropped it to the floor with a soft thud, and ran my hands through her hair as she kissed my chest delicately.

"I love the way you smell," she whispered, her lips skating over my tattoo. "Is that weird to say?"

"No, it's a sign of compatibility. It's a primal instinct to be attracted to the smell of a potential mating partner. So in a way you just told me you want me to breed you."

Her eyes flared excitedly. "You don't even know the ideas you just put in my head."

She helped me out of my pants, and tugged down my boxers. I was already aroused; I had been since walking into her apartment with the understanding of the night ahead. I still made a point to give myself a few rousing jerks and get the blood flowing. Which came easily watching Natalia slip into her lingerie a few steps away.

"Are you sure about this?" Her attention flitted to the computer screen and back, landing on me with sobering, doe-like eyes. "One hundred percent?"

"I'm sure about you, Tal. I'm sure I want you. I'm sure I want all of this with you. I'm sure if you let me, I will make you the happiest woman in the world. I'm fucking sure, okay? I've never been this sure."

She kissed me with a force strong enough to knock me over, hopping up to wrap her legs around my waist. One small shift and I could slide home inside of her but instead I walked us to the desk and dipped down enough for her to hit play on the open window. Within seconds bubbles of viewers began popping up.

The live chat was filled with comments searching for us on the empty bed.

"Give me your consent," I said.

"You have it."

"Don't worry about me," I added quietly. "I'm exactly where I'm supposed to be right now."

Tally's mouth turned into a smile, a sparkle shone in her eyes, and she kissed me one more time before I took us both into the frame of the camera. Immediately the engagement from her audience doubled, small hearts dotting the page. The number of people in the server ticked upward steadily on a counter in the corner.

"Sorry I haven't been live in a while," Natalia spoke out loud to the viewers but never took her eyes off me. "It's because I've been enjoying this man so much, I couldn't go a night without him."

Comments started rolling in and I fixated on trying to read every single one of them. There was a feeling inside me that was new and uncharted. I wasn't sure how to respond to it, but my stomach rocked like a boat drifting out to sea until Tally tugged my chin toward her to bring me back.

"Don't read them, you'll get stuck there in your own head," she mumbled. "Focus on me, and follow my lead." She unfurled her legs and sat on the mattress, eye level with my hips, and glanced up at me for permission that I granted with a swift nod.

Then her mouth came down on me, swallowing me, and heat licked up my spine while my balls drew tight to my body. It was an instinct to thread my fingers through her hair, and just as naturally my touch wandered, down her neck to her chest, squeezing her perfect tits that I so desperately wanted to feel in my mouth. While she told me not to look, I was new and curious, and it was nearly impossible not to wonder what the people watching were saying on the other end of it.

This all relied upon me. Natalia already had a rabid audience, and my participation would either help or hurt her. I hoped for the sake of this relationship it was the former.

I turned her face toward the camera and we both watched my tip knock against the inside of her cheek while the viewer numbers rose, the comments hitting fast and frequently, positively enthralled with the addition of a live partner. My confidence spiked and I thrust to the back of her throat hard enough that a tear welled at the corner of her eye. My heart stopped.

"Christ," I bit out, swiping it away with my thumb.

Fuck. *Fuck.*

I was too rough, too fast. I let myself get carried away almost immediately when this was supposed to be about me easing into the act. I couldn't scold myself hard enough, and dropped my fingers out of her hair to caress her cheek, mouthing an apology. "I'm sorry."

What she did next was unexpected. Partly because I thought I blew it, and also because I was still learning things about Natalia every single time we were together. Learning her quirks and kinks and how she liked things, and apparently face fucking her hard enough to make her cry was a good thing because she pulled me down on the bed by my cock and cried out, "I want you inside me."

Every scratch of her fingers down my back was electricity, and each nip of her perfect little canines against my swollen lips had me fighting back as I took her under her knee, pushing her legs apart to fit, and finally drove myself deep inside of her. She gasped out in shock with wide eyes, but I didn't let her catch her breath. I broke into a rhythm of hard, plunging strokes, feeling it down every single inch of me while touching the most intimate parts of her. I had to close my eyes to focus on containing myself.

She kissed up my neck to my ear where her face was hidden from the camera. "Are you okay?"

"Just trying not to blow my load prematurely for hundreds of people to see, but you are so fucking hot I can't fight it."

"Let me get on top."

"That might be worse," I confessed quietly.

Tally nipped my ear and pushed out from underneath me, repositioning us so I was on the bed and she was straddling my hips. My cock was pulsing at the sheer loss of her tight heat around it, and the edging torture of being so close to finishing and having that ripped away was the most brutal pleasure I'd ever known.

The computer chimed in a steady succession and Tally's lips parted into a surprised, excited smile.

"What's happening?"

"People are joining. New subscribers. Dozens of them."

A weight in my chest alleviated at the sight of her pure joy. It wasn't just *her* doing this, it was *us*, together. People were here for Tally and me and the magic we were making as a team. She lost herself just enough, distracted by the screen, and I went for it. Needing her so badly, I slammed her down onto my cock without warning and we both cried out in ecstasy.

Her mouth dropped open and every sinful sound from her throat slipped right out and hit me somewhere deep and hungry. I palmed her tits and she bucked on top of me, riding me so fucking good my eyes rolled into the back of my skull and I saw nothing but black for a long, long moment.

Desperate to come, I sat up and wrapped my forearm around her waist, using the leverage of my other hand to bring her down onto me over and over again at my own pace. My muscles strained; her body heat against mine made the entire room collapse in on me in a fog and like she could feel me inside her swelling against her walls, she threw her head back.

"I'm going to come," she swooned. "Please, don't stop."

My lungs seized and she buried her face in my neck, slowing her hips to sit with me fully inside her as she made a noise so foreign that it shocked me. I'd had sex with Natalia and made her finish in several ways beyond it, but gone was that sweet, sexy moan of elation I was so fond of. Natalia faked an orgasm like she was expelling a demon. As soon as I realized it was her making good on our deal I hid a fit of laughter in a long kiss.

My erection slipped out of her and I rose to my feet, bringing Natalia to the end of the bed on her knees as I stroked myself. Her makeup was ruined, the blush on her cheeks was completely natural, and there was a twinkle of eager anticipation in her eyes gazing up at me. When she stuck her tongue out, waiting for it, it was over.

Ropes of semen splashed across her mouth and her cheeks, painting her hair. It dripped in beads down her chin and dotted her chest and mesmerized me. It was the most beautiful thing I'd ever seen. "Fuck, you look so goddamn pretty covered in my cum."

I couldn't tear my eyes away. She was the only thing in my entire orbit, the only thing that mattered. I forgot where we were, what we were meant to be doing, that there were potentially thousands of people watching this happen in real time, and I cupped her face in my hands and kissed the fucking hell out of her.

"Thanks, everyone," she said offhandedly. "See you soon. Hopefully Mat can join us again." She hopped from the bed and rushed to the computer, ending the stream, returning to me and running her hands down my arms and chest like she was looking for wounds. "How are you feeling? Are you okay?"

There was something frantic about it, like she was worried I was going to completely break down, but it was the exact opposite. I felt like I was on a high. I was still overtaken with adrenaline and all I wanted was to be there in that moment with her for as long as possible. A smile crested my lips as I tucked a sticky strand of hair behind her ear. "I'm perfect." I had never been more perfect.

With the stream closed, I steered her back to the bed and sat her right at the edge of it, dropping to my knees and hooking both of her thighs over my shoulders. "Need to take care of this pussy," I mumbled, flicking my tongue over her clit softly. Natalia's head fell backward as I slid a finger through her core, coating it with her own arousal before pushing it inside of her. The sweetest sound poured out of her parted lips. So sweet I added another finger and did it again, and again, until it was like a symphony I was orchestrating. I closed my mouth around her clit and circled that cluster of nerves until her elbows went weak, back bowed, and her cunt fluttered around me. "You did so good, sweetheart. Such a fucking good girl. Come for me, I know you want to."

I was insatiable, sucking and nibbling. Her thighs tightened around my head from the intensity and I wrenched them back open with my free hand.

"Matty, *God*, yes. I'm—" she tapered off as her orgasm rocked through her body and her pussy went from gripping to soft and pliant around my soaked fingers. Every muscle in her lower half constricted, there was a moment of dead silence, then a rush of shaking and writhing as she reached her peak and her moans filled the room.

Natalia collapsed backward, chest heaving and eyes closed, exhausted, satisfied, and absolutely glowing in the low light. I crawled up her body, peppering kisses all over her skin and stared at her until my own eyes threatened to close too. It could have been hours later when I lifted her into my arms and carried her across the hall into the small bathroom. The shower ran while I washed her face and body with a warm cloth, and then she let me bathe her slowly and thoroughly before she did the same to me.

Natalia made sure I was taken care of. She cared *for* me. The kind of care that you didn't extend to a friend. It was a care that challenged fondness, begging it to cross the threshold into something more permanent.

It was when the sheets were changed, and her room was put back in its usual chaotic order, and she was tucked into my side and fast asleep, that I realized something I'd been coming to terms with for weeks. I wasn't *fond* of Natalia Russo. There was another four-letter word for it. This woman wasn't passing through my life; she was there for good.

And I wasn't letting go no matter what.

chapter sixteen

Natalia

MY HEELS CLACKED up the marble steps of my parents' Palm Beach mansion as we arrived for my father's sixtieth birthday. Mateo trailed behind me looking clean and well put together, his parents ambling on his tail to keep up. At the helm of the double oak front doors, dwarfed by the sprawling white stucco home I grew up in, my father was waiting for us with a cardboard party hat on his head and half a rocks glass of amber liquid dancing in his hand.

The last time I saw my dad was before Christmas, when Mateo had secretly asked him for permission to marry me. Since then I'd received short updates on their holiday spent in South America and proof of life via social media activity. It's not like he and I had anything to talk about anyway, and any attempt would seem awkward or forced.

Our relationship was formal. I didn't find a common ground with my dad any time after puberty, and that was right about when he started spending more time at the hospital than he did at the house. Having four teenage daughters menstruating on matched cycles drove him into a fritz of overtime hours and drunk days off.

"Welcome to Villa Russo," he boasted, leaning down and kissing my cheek, then moving onto Mateo with a firm handshake that clapped and echoed off the atrium in the foyer behind him. A thousand teardrop crystals sparkled off a chandelier hanging from the ceiling.

"Happy birthday, Dad," I said. He seemed in a chipper mood, but it was only eight o'clock, and his breath was tainted with the sharp tang of bourbon already. I'd gotten used to that smell, but it still turned my stomach the same way getting sick off a liquor made you never want to drink it again.

Mateo cleared his throat and ushered his parents forward. "John, this is my mother and father, Anna and David."

"Pleasure is mine." My father grinned at the Durans as they gazed up at the house and took it in. It was the self-absorbed smile he wore whenever he got to show off his things.

"Beautiful home," David said, pressing on the crown molding around the door. "You buy this? Build it?"

Mateo laughed and nudged his father along. "Plenty of time for that later, Dad."

We shuffled down the long corridor hallway to the living room, passing arched doorways that broke off into the familiar nooks. A library, a formal dining room, a large sitting room with cushioned high back chairs in velvet pinks and greens. My mom had a gallery wall of expensive artwork that she switched out quarterly just for shits and giggles as a conversation piece for her haughty guests. The kicker about the sitting room was that no one ever sat in it; it was there to take up the wasted space in the mansion where my parents lived alone with their two dogs and a staff of housekeepers.

"There they are!" my mother crooned across the room, standing from the upholstered sofa in her floor-length blush dress, strappy heels peeking through the slit in the material as she clacked toward us. The cocktail attire for an intimate dinner in the dining room was a choice that I had no say in. Mom's bracelets jingled as she reached up to fix my hair, tucking the loosely curled strands behind my ears and pulling the rest over my shoulder the way she thought it looked best. I promptly flicked it back.

"Nice to see you again, Sistine," Anna said. "That color looks great on you."

"Doesn't it?" my mother volleyed back. "It's so nice to finally have everyone in the same room. It's like a test run before the wedding. But with better food." She laughed at her joke, I winced, the mumbled chuckles from the Durans spoke for themselves, and I looked around for a getaway car in the form of Mateo who was already engulfed in uncomfortable conversation with my father and backed into a corner of his own.

Mia peeked her head through the doorway that separated the dining room from the living room, *psst*ing at me like a cat and waving me in her direction. My mother had corralled the Durans into conversation and I tiptoed away, making it around the corner undetected only to come face-to-face with all three of my sisters in elegant cocktail dresses.

"God, what did I do now?"

"Dad is already toasted." Mia sipped her martini. "I just heard him telling Mateo about the psychology of grocery store layouts."

"Like he's ever been in a grocery store in his life," I snarked. "You'd think a man with a job reliant on sound-mindedness would be less of a blubbering idiot on his days off."

"Our jobs are stressful." Camilla fluffed my hair onto my shoulder just as Mom had and I again tossed it back. "Hospitals aren't for everyone."

"I'm just surprised he's already this far in the bag before dinner," Bella said. "This might be record time for John Russo bowing out of his own party."

"I give him until ten," I said, crossing my arms.

"I'll bet eleven." Bella shrugged.

Camilla inspected a piece of silverware on the table, shining it on the napkin. "Eleven thirty."

"C'mon guys, you know Dad." Mia laughed. "He'll have to

take a phone call at some point, and go puke in the bushes by the pool house before coming back for round two."

"We were all doomed from birth," I accepted out loud. "Please, if the three of you love me at all, keep him as far away from Mateo's parents as possible. I have three more months of convincing them I'm suitable for their son."

"Don't look now, but Dad is challenging Mr. Duran to a game of Operation," Bella said.

I spun, frantic, but she was only fibbing. My wide, distressed eyes narrowed into slits. "You're going to give me a heart attack."

"Good thing I'm a doctor," Cami added eagerly.

It was in my best interest to remove the threat at the source and put as much space between my parents and Mateo's as possible for the entire night. Letting them congregate in closed-off conversations was a bad idea. They might realize how starkly different our upbringings were and equate the delusory ivory tower for what I expected in our marriage. Anna already thought I was a step away from useless. Before I could let that happen I slipped back into the living room with Mateo and our parents.

The lull before dinner was the perfect time for a tour.

* * *

I STRATEGICALLY TOOK the long way through the expansive layout of the house. Even doing the rounds outside, through the garden and around the tennis court. I spent eighteen years of my life here, and yet it was like walking through a place you only see in dreams. Like you know it but you don't. The halls feel empty, the rooms cold. Even my childhood bedroom where I spent so much of my time hiding, locked away and keeping to myself, didn't feel like safety anymore. A cage with an open door. Sometime in the eight years since I moved out my parents had remodeled it. New off-white paint, neutral furniture, themeless space fillers for yet another guest bedroom. By the time we returned to eat dinner, my father had gone from a boisterous host to a second stage of drunk, sitting at the head of the table, stoically confrontational.

"Did you show them the wine cellar, Natalia?"

"Yep." I popped the 'p' and fluffed my cloth napkin onto my lap.

"There is a Bordeaux down there that costs more than your house," Dad said to me. "Are you two going to finally move out of there now? Find something a little more suitable to grow a family?"

"Something like this?" I circled my finger in the air, mocking the grand dining room and the hanging lights, the table so large you couldn't have a conversation with someone unless they were sitting on the same end as you.

"We have a great house." Mateo slid his hand down my thigh under the table, landing on my knee and squeezing. "It's only the two of us. We have a second bedroom and plenty of space to expand with an addition if we needed to."

A bright smile pulled Anna's cheeks taut. "I can't wait to be a grandmother."

My stomach tilted and an awkward laugh forced itself out of me. Children were always part of our plan, but having such an open discussion in front of my father about eventually being pregnant made me want to crawl out of my skin. Yes, obviously Mateo and I had sex. No, that wasn't a fact I wanted acknowledged at the dinner table.

Mom commented, "With you both in New York it'll be hard to be involved in a baby's life, won't it?"

"Well, let's not get ahead of ourselves," Mateo cut in. "We have a wedding to get through."

"Logistically speaking." Mom shrugged. "It's a conversation you have to have beforehand."

There was a hot bead of sweat accumulating at the nape of my neck and a quickly rising pulse banging like a gong in my ear. The chef my parents staffed regularly for special occasions swept into the room with hot platters of food and set them in the center of the table.

"We have talked about the distance," Anna mentioned. "David and I were thinking it might be worth it to look around for something a little more permanent."

Mateo's fork dropped out of his hand and clattered against his plate. "What do you mean?"

"Somewhere we wouldn't be in your hair," David added, stabbing a serving fork into the platter of filet mignon and dragging a juicy piece of it onto his dish.

"Like a timeshare?" I cleared my throat. "A vacation rental?"

"Buying is rough right now," Mia joined. "It's like a mad dash every single time a new home hits the market, especially in this area. You should hop on it as soon as possible if you're looking because the perfect place will be here today, gone tomorrow. I can get you in touch with someone if you need it."

"That's not necessary," Mateo said abruptly, turning everyone's head and squeezing my knee harder. Since the disaster at Sunday dinner last month I was quick to worry about him having another panic attack. His mother clearly had a way of bringing those suppressed, anxious emotions to the forefront and we were both blindsided at the moment. The Durans were enjoying their time in Florida, but now I had to worry that it was affecting Mateo considerably more than he let on. I threaded my fingers through his under the table and rubbed my thumb across the back of his hand in slow circles.

"That's very kind of you, Mia." Anna raised an eyebrow at her son across the table. "Between the four of you girls, if there's ever something your parents need, you have it covered."

Including me in that sentiment warmed my chest. You could easily argue a bank teller had significantly less pull than a pediatric oncologist, an attorney, and a realty mogul. Then again, my connections in the porn industry were worth even less for practicality's sake.

"We're very proud," my dad said. "One thing we always told

our girls was you've gotta be rich, or marry a man that gives you the world, so we're grateful to Mateo for making sleeping at night that much easier for Sistine and me."

"Lovely," I mumbled under my breath. Matty's warm hand caressed the back of my neck and his sympathetic eyes caught mine. I wasn't going to fight over something so trivial. I'd learned that biting my tongue was worth the mental sanity far more often than not. If I got out of this night with nothing but a few scratches that would be a battle won.

"You raised an incredible, indelible, hardworking, and compassionate woman. Traits she's honed artfully on her own, John," Mateo punctuated, and my first genuine smile of the night sprouted across my cheeks.

"That reminds me," Isabella said, dabbing at the corners of her mouth with her napkin. "Talia, did you look over that paperwork I gave you?"

Oh, *no*.

My little bit of joy snuffed out with one sentence. The room spun on an axis, like a Gravitron at a carnival with all the screaming and existential dread included. That legal binder was still shoved in the canvas bag I took for errands that day, and that bag was on the floor in the backseat of my car under the extra jacket I always brought but never needed and a garbage bag full of clothes I wanted to donate but never would.

"What paperwork?" Matty tilted his head and this time I avoided his eye contact.

"Nothing important." My nostrils flared and I lifted my knife slowly, drawing a 'cut it out' gesture at the hollow of my neck.

She ignored me. "The drafted prenup."

Fuck. Fuck in a million different languages. Fuck me with the largest alien dick imaginable.

The room stilled. I was too embarrassed to lift my head but I could feel the tension seeping off my future husband and his parents beside me. Mateo's hand dropped from my neck slowly and his body turned toward me in his chair. "This is the first I'm hearing about it."

"Christ, Natalia," Bella huffed. "I told you how important it was to get this sorted out so we could move onto the paperwork."

"Your sister is right," my mother said. "She took time from her busy work schedule to do something for you, and you're not taking it seriously."

"I never asked her to," I said, choking on the words as they fell weakly out of my mouth.

"I didn't know this is something you wanted." Mateo was still speaking directly to me, trying to draw my attention, but I was frozen in place. I couldn't look at him and bear seeing the hurt in his eyes that was evident in his voice.

"We never had a prenup when we were married," Anna chimed in. "It's considered a bit of bad luck where we're from."

"Where we're from, there's money and reputation involved, and I've seen things get really dirty when you don't take proper precautions," my father slung back. "It's not bad luck; it's common sense. Mateo might be smart to sign on the dotted line. He's got a business I'm sure he's keen on keeping if it ever comes down to it."

"It's nothing if not a safety net," Mom added.

"This is something I think we'll have to talk about privately," Mateo announced to the room. His plate of food was untouched and going cold, his knee bouncing underneath the table. I finally found the courage to look him in the eyes and they were frantic with the anxiety I was trying to keep tame. "Right, Natalia?"

"Well, it's no use now," David said. "Everyone has an opinion."

"I told you, I wasn't interested in the prenup," I said to Isabella, louder and more confidently.

"No, you said you would look it over."

"You were pressuring me. It was to get you off my back."

"Oh, Natalia, don't be a child," my mother scoffed. "Take some responsibility. You're twenty-six years old."

"It's very typical," my dad chided, amused in the most condescending, drunk, and arrogant way. "Not everything has to be a fight. You're getting married and you can't even make a responsible decision for yourself. Not even when it's given to you on a silver platter."

"There's no decision to be made if it's not a choice." I stood, my chair scraping hideously across the floor as I excused myself gracelessly from the table and headed directly to the exit with my gut churning.

There was a rustling behind me and Mateo's voice calling my name once before I turned the corner into the long corridor, made eye contact with the glass double doors at the end of it leading into the backyard, and took off running until I was bursting through and out onto the concrete pavers.

It was raining, soft warm rain that mixed with the humidity and fell like sweat as it came down on my head. My short sprint took more out of me than I expected and I keeled over to catch my breath. The longer I stood there, the more soaked my clothes became, until the material was stuck to me in every uncomfortable place. My feet throbbed inside my heels and I shucked them off and wiggled my toes on the wet ground.

There was so much noise going on inside my head, and though it wasn't reasonable the world might as well have been collapsing in on me. No matter what I did, it was wrong. Mateo's parents thought so, and mine only confirmed it. When I thought I was doing the right thing in keeping the proposed prenup from Mateo, it came back and bit me when I least expected it would. Every single turn I took, I hit a fucking wall, and the maze was only getting deeper and darker to navigate myself out of.

I was begging for the hits to stop coming and the chaos to quiet down.

A few feet away the pool was lit up and glistening aqua blue but the pitter-patter of rain made it nearly impossible to see the bottom clearly. I stepped forward, right to the edge. As a kid, it was so peaceful to submerge myself in the water and shut off the world around me. I wanted that right now, and so I did the only thing I could think of, and jumped in.

chapter seventeen

Mateo

I CALLED OUT HER NAME, but Tally was already through the tall open doors. Not stopping for anyone or anything. Not even me.

"Just let her go. She throws her fits and then she'll be over it in an hour like always." John resumed working on his plate, dusting off the mess he'd made in front of everyone. As if Tally was the issue here, and not our business being broadcast for the entire table to analyze.

Yes, I was extremely taken aback by the turn in conversation. There was never any mention of a prenup, and Natalia had a conversation with Bella that never made its way to me. I had questions, and I wanted to believe there were simple answers to them.

I tossed my napkin on the table and went after her. As I passed her father sitting unbothered at the head of his grand, lavish table—in front of his wife, and my parents—I took him by the collar of his rumpled dress shirt and pulled him close enough that I could smell the stale whiskey on the catch of his breath.

"Get your fucking hands off me," he barked.

"Make no mistake, John, she'll have my name soon. A name she's going to be damn proud to wear every single day of her life. So think about the kind of impression you want to leave behind on your daughter about how a man acts, and treats his wife and his family. The kind of father she wants for her own children." I paused. "One day there might be a baby that will never know a John Russo because I won't allow you to hurt them the way you've hurt her."

His eyes thinned and the cord of his throat struggled against my knuckles as I tightened my grip. I was playing it cool but my heart was working hard in my chest, adrenaline taking over for the anxiety I had been tamping down after my parents started talking about relocating.

A nerve had been struck, and the arrogance John usually carried with his daughters was undetectable now. I had scared him for the first time in his life. He glanced cautiously around the room and his jaw tightened. "You're out of line."

I let him go with a shove back into his seat. "There's no line I wouldn't cross for her."

John shook me off as I brushed past him and put his lips to his glass of liquor like it was a security blanket. Dinner might have been ruined—hell, it might be the last dinner I'd ever have in the Russo house—but it would be worth it. A thought crossed my mind, and I turned back around to the stunned silent room. "God help you if my wife is fucking crying."

Too determined to get to Natalia, all my emotional apprehension took a back seat. I had a one-track mind as I stormed out of the dining room and left everyone else to pick up the pieces. There was only one person I was worried about.

At the end of the wide hallway, one of the doors leading outside was swung open and I jogged toward it into the backyard. Wind whistled past my ears and raindrops spattered my face as I approached the dimly lit pool house and stood at the edge of the glowing water. My dress shirt clung to my biceps as rain ran down my neck and cooled against my back.

"Tally," I called out. "It's pouring." Her head peered out from beneath the water, dark hair floating behind her. I rubbed a hand down my face. "Get out of the pool."

She shook her head.

It was only about seventy degrees but the pool was heated. Steam lifted from the top of the water, making her look like a siren. She slipped back beneath the cloudy water and I lost her in the texture of the rain dotting it, nothing but a faint dark blob wading as she beat her arms to keep herself treading at the bottom.

I knew what she was doing, though. I'd been there before, wishing I could turn off the world around me, or at least turn the dial so that the volume wasn't so loud. It happened in our kitchen. Natalia and I felt in the same extreme ways. We were shit at controlling those emotions, but we had each other to lean on. That was why when she was losing her mind, I had to keep mine together.

We balanced. We were scales.

Which was also why I knew that there was only one way to get through to her, and that was meeting her halfway. Not waiting for her to eventually return from the place she'd gone, but helping her find the way back home.

"Damn it," I muttered to myself. I threw my phone on a patio chair, took a deep breath, then jumped into the water with her.

That startled her, because when I reached the bottom Natalia was already wide-eyed and waiting for me. It took nothing to gather her in my arms and kick off the hard stone floor, sending us both back to the surface.

"What are you doing?" she sputtered. I flipped my hair out of my eyes and dragged us to the ledge, underneath a circulating waterfall and a rock embankment built into the far side of the pool. We were shielded from the rain and hidden away. For once, all of John Russo's money was good for something.

Natalia's mascara was running beneath her eyes, but instead of red-rimmed they were soft and a bit dazed and she hugged her legs around my waist to stay upright. "My mother used to ask me all the time if my friends jumped off a bridge, would I jump off too?" I said. "I would tell her, 'No, Ma, I know what's good for me. I know right from wrong. I would never.'"

She smiled a sad, crooked little smile.

"I would jump off a bridge if you did, Tally."

"That doesn't make it the right thing to do."

"It doesn't matter." I squeezed her hips. The drenched material of her dress was glued to her body. "Even if it's wrong, I still want it. Because it's you."

Her jaw relaxed and her lips parted like she might fight that, too, and if she did I'd keep battling. I couldn't tell if there were tears in her eyes or if her lashes were wet from the pool. My hands slipped to her lower back and tugged her closer.

"There's something wrong with me," she choked out like it was stuck in her throat.

"No there's not, baby."

"I can't stand myself most of the time. I have all this hate inside me, Matty. All this rage. I'm so fucking angry and I don't know where to put that anger, because you are so perfect and when I met you I didn't have to be angry anymore. I got to be *light*. I didn't have to be on the defense all the damn time."

She exhausted those last few words as if she'd just run a marathon and they were too tiring to say.

"But that doesn't mean it's not still here, Matty. You don't find peace and automatically get rid of the anger. It needs somewhere to go and it just fucking waits until a night like tonight happens. I want to be so angry. I want to scream, but I can't so I end up *here*. In this pool, looking like a fucking maniac. Because that's what Natalia does," she said matter-of-factly. "Natalia makes everything about her. Natalia is a wreck. Natalia is lost. Natalia is lashing out again."

She tried to writhe away from me but I wouldn't allow it. I'd crawl inside her before letting her crawl out of her own skin. "Natalia is human," I said softly. "Natalia is thoughtful, and brilliant, and resilient, and fucking real. You are allowed to be angry. *I'm* fucking angry. You want to know why?"

She didn't look up. "Why?"

"Because it took me so long to get to you." I lifted her chin with my fingers. The rain around us had stopped, so I ushered our floating bodies from beneath the waterfall and back into a dark, cloudless night. It was quiet and warm and I hardly felt our clothes weighing us down. "I'm angry someone hurt you for so long and made you think that was okay. That it was love, and that's just how love works. That it hurts, and it's brutal." I shook my head. "It's not."

"I don't want to hate them." She sighed. "I don't. I'm just so resentful. Ashamed that this is what I have to offer you. Forever with in-laws that you can't stand, broken relationships, things I can't fix."

"They weren't part of the deal," I said lightly. "I was never worried about that. I don't care. My parents are no walk in the park either, Tal."

"That stupid fucking prenup." She tried to escape me again, but I held her steady in my arms. "I didn't ask Isabella to draw that up, I swear. She blindsided me that day we went for coffee, and I gave her some bullshit answer about looking it over but I ditched it as soon as I got home. I never planned on actually asking you to sign one of those."

Well, there it was. My tension around it eased. It was a misunderstanding that I was glad I hadn't let send me over the edge before I had the chance to hear it from Tally herself.

"I don't understand why you would keep it from me," I lamented anyway. "If it wasn't something you were worried about."

"I was embarrassed." She laughed at herself. "I am still embarrassed. Prenups are for couples who expect things to fail. My family values material things over their relationships. God forbid they lose their second house, but you can always find someone new to marry."

"We are not like them, Tal," I said sternly. "We got together and that was it. It was like the stars were aligning. We knew, from the very first date. And your family can't fathom that. They don't know what it feels like to be so sure."

Her eyes fluttered closed, wet lashes long against her cheeks. She looked absolutely endearing under the pale blue moonlight. "They're never going to. It's going to be a struggle for the rest of our lives. You're going to have to deal with them to be with me, and that scares me, Matty."

"I don't understand." My chest grew hollow, a large valley with wind whistling through it.

"We're strong right now, because whether we like to admit it or not, this is still new. We haven't been together long enough to test all these things. Now, we're starting to see how hard it can get and you're getting a taste of the bullshit I've dealt with my entire life. I'm scared that you're going to resent it eventually. And I can't help but wonder, am I worth all of this? Am I worthy of you? Am I capable of being the wife you deserve—"

"Stop." I was wearing a hole into the inside of my cheek. "Would I be treading water in dress attire in your parents' ridiculous pool right now if you weren't worth it?"

Her lips thinned.

"Your perception of worth is irrelevant," I said. "Do you want it? Want me?"

"Of course I do."

"Life is never going to be perfect. It's going to be really fucking hard. We're going to hit bumps. Our families are going to drive us to drink. I'm going to annoy the hell out of you one day, and then the next call your dad a sad son of a bitch and threaten to hurt him if he upsets you ever again."

Her eyes glistened. "You did that?"

"I would do anything for you," I said. "Including signing a prenup, if that's really what you wanted. Because if I'm ever stupid enough to make you want to divorce me, you can have everything I'm worth. All of it."

"I need an outlet." A lightness had returned to her and she curled into my chest, resting her head on my shoulder. "Some way to let this all out without screaming so loud I break glass."

"I am more than happy to take a rage riding from you, sweetheart."

Tally laughed, a little huff pushing from her nostrils. Anytime I amused her was like a pat on the back. "Tell me it won't always be this way," she sniffled, her warm breath skittering across the exposed skin on my neck.

"I swear it, Tally. Do you know what Duran means? It means endure. You were meant to have this name, because it's what you do. It's what we will always do, together."

Her upturned lips parted and her teeth scored my skin, then she turned in my arms and kissed me. A *thank you, I needed this* kiss. She seemed better, having worked through the moment, but there was something remaining. Something in her body language I couldn't pick apart.

"No more secrets, all right?" she proposed. "You're not going to get denied our marriage license because you married someone twelve years ago while you were drunk in the military and never filed a legal divorce, right?"

I jokingly pondered it and she elbowed me. "No, Tal."

"Good. I want us to be on the same page. Vegas is creeping up fast, and we don't need any more hiccups."

For a moment I thought about TechOps, and the work piling up while I put off hiring. How I was brushing off my mental lapses to avoid acknowledging a bigger problem. They weren't secrets, they were choices I had to make to keep the wheel turning smoothly. I was also convinced my parents had a significant effect on me, and the second they were back in New York, everything would return to normal. It was different. It was my mess. It didn't involve both of us.

"You're the boss," I settled on. "Now, can we get out of this pool before we both catch pneumonia?"

"That sounds like something your mom would say."

"How dare you." I pinched her ass as she swam to the steps but we both stopped short as Natalia's father stumbled out the back doors of the mansion and onto the patio. He trudged toward the side of the pool house, unbuttoning his dress shirt and mumbling something unintelligible and whiny as we watched on, completely undetected, intensely fascinated. He reached a thatch of neatly landscaped bushes, keeled over with his hands on his knees, and vomited into them.

Entirely unsurprised, Natalia clicked her tongue. "Damn it, Mia was spot on with that."

chapter eighteen

Mateo

PIKE

I didn't know you had a girlfriend Sam

WINK

I don't

ANGELO

Doesn't Natalia have like three sisters?

ECHO

That's what I said!

EASTER WAS TOMORROW, and for the first time in several weeks I was spending a Saturday morning at home instead of dedicating half of my day to the cyber security business. The second half of my Saturdays were blocked out for getting as much filming done with Tally as possible in what little time we had after Mom and Dad went to bed. Even then, what we could do was limited with the noise level, and the quality we were producing was nowhere near what Natalia was known for. The grit was gone, passion completely and utterly sucked out of the sequences. Apart from that, there was another problem: Recently, the *only* times we had sex were while on camera.

ME

Sister-in-laws are off-limits

ANGELO

You're a party pooper

My phone pinged with a picture of Tyler flipping off the camera and I snickered, kicking myself back further into the soft recliner. The house was quiet. Tally was out at the grocery store getting a few last-minute things for the holiday, and Dad had gone out to bingo with Gino Barry from next door. Mom had been milling around the kitchen cooking the last time I noticed her, but peering up from my seat I realized that was no longer the case.

A hot, unsettling wave licked up my spine and my hair stood on end at my neck. I turned my head over my shoulder.

"Jesus Christ," I gasped, my heart dropping into my stomach. My mother shot backward a step from creeping over me and I hid the screen of my phone against my chest. "What the hell are you doing?"

"Is that your brother?" she asked, flipping a dish towel over her shoulder nonchalantly. "I worry about him. He hasn't brought a woman home in years. Your father and I were starting to think maybe he swung the other way."

"How would you know that he hasn't had a woman over?"

"The basement ceiling is thin, honey."

I frowned. "Well, I wouldn't take anyone home with you two listening to my every move either."

Mom chuffed. "Like we didn't see the purple ding-a-ling you were shoving up your ass."

"Okay, all right, enough." The recliner slammed closed as I hopped up and paced away. "The point is that the man needs some privacy." I let myself out the sliding door into the backyard, more stressed than I needed to be, and dying for the day my parents packed up their shit and left my house and my wife and me to shove whatever the fuck we wanted up our asses in peace.

ME

Final count: Echo, no, Ang, no, Wink, yes

ANGELO

I want a code name

PIKE

You don't choose your call sign, your call sign chooses you

ECHO

In due time

ME

Everyone booked a flight for Vegas?

PIKE

Aye aye, Cap

ME

This fucking wedding shit is stressing me out

After the awkward dinner at Palm Beach for John's birthday, Tally's excitement for the wedding was noticeably withered. When Mom tried to talk to her about the details she was worn down by the responsibility of it. Her parents stole that girlish wonder away and replaced it with worry about every last choice that she made, and even my constant reassurance was barely scratching the surface. I didn't know how to fix it.

I ran a hand down my face, scratching at the shadow of a beard growing. Tally would want me to be clean-shaven for the big day, but I'd let it do its thing for over a week at that point because I hadn't had the time.

The yard looked like shit. Grass that was usually golfing green short was threatening to tickle my ankles, and there was a hive of shitty wasps making a home under the gutter pipe at the corner of the roof. I'd need to find time to do these things among everything else going on and the longer that mental list grew, the harder the knot in my stomach tightened. It was festering into dangerous outburst territory. Not a thing was in my control anymore.

My phone rang in my hand and Pike's name lit up the screen. I looked back at the sliding door and walked away from it, out into the yard and toward the tall wooden fence at the edge of the property. "What's up, brother?"

There was a beating of distant helicopter wings behind his voice, cueing me in that he was at work at the airbase in Colorado. He had a new job teaching military protocol to fresh pilots in training, something I was proud of him for pursuing despite the setbacks with TechOps I was facing on account of it.

After a crash that nearly ended his career and several lives, mine included, I wasn't sure he would ever have the confidence to fly again.

"What's stressing you out?" Pike asked.

"You got all day?"

He laughed that burly, infectious Frankie laugh I hadn't heard in so long. "Mom and Dad?"

"I'm losing my mind, Pike. I miss walking around the house with my dick out just because I could."

"I don't miss that."

"Things have gotten on top of me. I mean, work is hell, the days are long because I'm out late doing installs, and then I get home and have to do the other stuff with Tally with Mom and Pop down the hall. It's not looking good on the business end."

"The porn business?"

There was a splinter in the fence that I picked at. "Yeah. She was so caught up in every detail for the wedding and now it's like she's half with me and half somewhere else. Her family is fucking with her head. I almost had to fight her prick of a dad and I know that's weighing on her. We're just operating on different wavelengths right now."

"Well hey, you got help at TechOps, right? Training a new hire?"

I scratched at the back of my neck. "What if I told you I never hired anyone?"

His sigh crackled through the receiver. "Cap, what the fuck?"

"Listen, I know, all right? You gotta keep this to yourself. Tally thinks the hiring pool is dry, and I can't hit her with that mess right now, okay? When the wedding is over and all this shit dies down, I'll hire someone and figure it out. Right now, I'm too deep into the lie to claw my way out."

Pike was silent on the other end and I could almost see him with a judgmental hand on his hip. "I told you it was too much work for one person."

"It doesn't matter now. You know I can't trust people easily, especially not with things like my business. I wasn't ready to bring on a stranger."

"Are you going to tell her that you lied?"

"You're making it sound way worse than it actually is," I said. "You're supposed to be on my side."

"You're a dumbass," Pike replied bluntly.

"I know that." I rolled my shoulders and leaned into the fence, shredding the blades of grass at my feet with the toe of my shoe. My mind crept into the anxiety spells and how hard I'd been working to hide that from Tally as well. "Hey, can I ask you about something personal?"

"Shoot."

The right words were hard to find and I trampled over what I was trying to say before landing on it. "Do you..." Pause. "Are there times when..." Pause. I cleared my throat. "Have you ever thought that our time in the service might have fucked you up a little bit?"

"Cap, I had reconstructive back surgery after I crashed a helicopter."

I probably should have been more literal. "Not physically."

He quieted, shuffling farther away from the background noise. "You okay, Brother?"

"Yeah." *I don't know.* "No. But it's nothing crazy."

"Define not crazy," Pike said.

There was absolutely no reason for me to be embarrassed. Pike was my best friend. I knew what was happening to me was normal, but for some reason saying it out loud felt so vulnerable my heart was lurching against my ribs. "I've been having these episodes lately, where I kind of shut down. It happened in front of Tally and my parents. You know me, I'm always on. That never happens to me, and it certainly never happened in Delta. But a few times now, I get overwhelmed and the stress destabilizes me. I black out, and feel like I can't catch my breath. I don't know what to do, man. I'm always scared now waiting for it to happen again."

"Sounds like panic attacks," Pike said. "Have you talked to anyone about it? That might alleviate some of this. There's a lot of resources for veterans, Cap."

"You're probably right." I sighed. "I feel like I'm losing my grip on everything right now."

"You know O and I will do everything we can. You're balancing a lot, and you might think you've lost your touch, but you haven't. Your health is a priority."

Hearing that was simple, but effective. Now that I'd put it out there for Pike, there was no way I could deny or fall back on it, either. "I'll call the VA."

"Thank you for trusting me with that. I know the Swan boys would be right here with me saying the same thing. No shame in admitting you need some help. We lost too many already to pretend this shit doesn't exist for veterans."

"Thanks for having my back," I said. "I miss you around here."

"I don't miss those thin ass walls."

The corner of my mouth lifted and I pushed a sigh through my nostrils. "Yeah, well, not much to hear right now. Tal and I haven't had sex in weeks."

"Your job is having sex with her."

"That's not the same thing. That's not us. That's whatever character we're playing at the moment. I'm talking about her and me rolling around in the hay, having sex just to fuck. Not to film."

"That's not helping your stress levels."

"You fucking think?"

"We'll be in Vegas soon, Cap. You'll have a whole weekend to make up for lost time. It's gonna be fine. I'm here if you need me."

"I know the girls probably chat every day, but could you tell Ophelia that Tally's having a rough time? She won't say it for herself. Maybe she can talk some sense into her that I can't."

"Sure thing, man," Pike replied. "See you in Vegas in a couple weeks. Happy Easter."

"Happy Easter," I returned. "Later."

Before I went back inside I sat on my conversation with Pike. I wanted to be better, for myself and for Tally, and the only person who could help me...was me. That first step, as scary and uncertain as it felt, was necessary. I knew my harmless work secret had a time limit, and after that ran out, life would go back to normal. My house would feel like a home again, my fiancée would be my wife, and my life would be truly beginning. I was ready for that. More than ready for it. It was just a matter of getting there in one piece.

chapter nineteen

Natalia

I HAD ALWAYS BEEN a bed rotting queen. Mateo woke up before me every single day, Frankie even earlier than him when he still lived in the house. For the last few months I'd faked a morning routine several days out of the week to keep up my bank teller charade with the Durans, when all I wanted to do was stay in the comfort and warmth of my bed sheets until noon. But for the better part of this morning, my in-laws had been away on a boat tour with the neighbors and I was free.

Free to lie in bed and watch reality TV while shoving my face with food I definitely shouldn't be eating this close to my wedding. It also meant catching up on the film schedule. In the last month we'd lost over a thousand unique subscribers to the page. I was getting emails from clients requesting refunds on bookings we hadn't had a chance to get to yet, and DMs on our social media profiles asking if we'd broken up in response to Matty's scarce appearances.

It was hard not to feel resentment about how late he'd been working and how it was negatively affecting the cam business because I'd never had to share my time with him before. One simple hire could give me my partner back. According to Mateo it was much more complicated than that, but that didn't make the stress any easier.

Even sleeping didn't come easy. When I did, I'd only reach that first level of unconsciousness, where my brain wouldn't shut off completely and I would have dreams about falling off roller coasters or slipping through quicksand, or trying to punch a murderer in the face and my hand dissolving into Jell-O every time it made contact.

The longer I stayed in bed in the mornings, the longer I could avoid walking out into the living room and having a conversation with someone. It wasn't that I didn't want to bond with Mateo's parents anymore—they'd loosened up significantly since my father's catastrophic failure of a birthday party, probably taking pity on me—but my body didn't physically hold the energy for socialization.

The soles of my feet rubbed back and forth like a grasshopper over the soft cotton sheets in our king-size bed. I reached over blindly searching for Mateo's body, unsurprised to find him already gone. It was Thursday, the day before we left for Vegas and he was rushing to finish a last-minute installation. He promised that after this he was totally free from any work for our joint bach weekend. I was holding out hope that a long few days away from home was all we needed to rekindle the spark that had been missing between us emotionally and intimately.

Sun spilled in from a crack in the curtains and my phone started vibrating from somewhere underneath my heaps of pillows and blankets. I rooted around until I found it and squinted at the screen, seeing it lit up with the only person in the world I wanted to talk to at that moment.

"Phee!" I sat up, dazed and bedraggled. Ophelia's perfectly put-together face appeared in a video box on the screen. She was wearing a striped sweater and a lanyard around her neck, and a school smartboard was turned on behind her. She was likely in her classroom waiting for her students to arrive for the day.

"Good morning, sunshine." She cackled. "Sorry to wake you up at ten in the morning." Her skin was glowing, long brown hair swept up in a bun as her concerned blue gaze studied me.

"I need my beauty sleep."

She hummed. "Mateo might have mentioned something to Frankie about you living in a cave in your bedroom and making little voodoo dolls of your family members. So I figured a wellness check was due before tomorrow."

"Does my dad have salami-sized nipples yet?"

Ophelia swept a piece of dark hair out of her face and frowned sympathetically. "He might."

"Good," I huffed. "God, I can't believe I'm getting married in a month." There was no excitement at all in my voice. The process had completely drained me of it. At that point I didn't care about the details anymore, or the guests. I was counting down the days until it was over and my life could return to something resembling normalcy.

"Tell me what's going on," Ophelia said warmly.

I dropped back into the pillows and stared at the ceiling. "I think this is a bigger dick than I can suck."

"I think the saying is 'I bit off more than I could chew.'"

"Is it?"

"Yours works just fine."

"I'm trying to do it all," I said. "But I'm shit at balancing everything at once, between the wedding, Mateo's parents, mine, the cam business... Mateo is trying his hardest to be in two places at once, but it's not working anymore. It's almost like my thing isn't as important as his thing, as stupid as that sounds. I know he had TechOps before me and I had the cam page before him, but we're supposed to be partners in it."

"I know you might feel like you're losing control, but on the surface it doesn't look like that. You're so impressive, Nat. Mateo has a lot on his plate, too. You guys are just hitting traffic, but you'll still get there."

After the prenup debacle Bella hadn't pressed it again. Her dropping it was as close to an apology as I'd likely get. My sisters had been staying intentionally neutral on the entire thing, assumingly to not piss off our parents by choosing sides. "I know what my family thinks, but be honest with me, do you think Mateo and I are jumping into things? Are we doing this too fast?"

Phee shook her head. "When you know, you know."

"That's the thing. We *do* know. Before we decided to get married everything was perfect. Our life was so easy. There weren't families involved with all their opinions and planning. Inviting Anna and David to live here for six months was stupid, and Mateo warned me it was a bad idea for our relationship. I love the Durans, don't get me wrong, but..." I took a deep breath. "It's been a lot harder on both of us than I expected. Working with them in the house is impossible, and even when they do leave and I get some time to make content, Mateo isn't here."

"How's the camming otherwise?"

I rolled out of bed and padded over to the desktop, waking it up with a tap of the keys. "I'm a foley artist now. I've pretty much perfected silently filming sex. Do you know that I dubbed the sound of Mateo's hips slapping against my ass the other day? I added it after the fact with a raw piece of top round beef."

"Shut the fuck up." Ophelia clapped a hand over her mouth. "People buy that?"

I clicked a folder on the screen and pressed play, and the sharp slap of skin on skin filled the room.

"Wow, that is very natural, surprisingly. You're incredible at what you do, I give you that."

"I spanked the shit out of that thing."

Ophelia blew out a breath and pulled a block of sticky notes and a pen in front of her. "Let's focus on the now," she said. "What can I do to help you from Colorado? Want me to hand-write place cards? I'll do it. Call the florist? Finalize the setlist? Coordinate with the day-of planner? What do you need so that you and Mateo can go wild and get your work done without a piece of raw beef involved?"

I swallowed and dug my toes into the corner of the throw rug. "That's another thing. We haven't had sex."

Phee tapped the pen on her chin. "You mean *sex*?"

"I mean the difference between work and play." I sighed and covered my eyes, embarrassed. "I feel like a caged animal that hasn't been fed, Phee. I'm ovulating, which doesn't help. Because that man walks past me in a T-shirt with the sleeves a little too tight and his hair a little bit sweaty and my kitty is already purring."

"I know exactly what you mean."

"She's not purring, she's mewing."

"Growling."

"Ever since that dinner with my parents he's been gentle Mateo, sweet Mateo. Like he's trying not to set me off. But I want to be manhandled. Okay? I want to turn my dumb little brain off, and spread my legs, and have my hot fucking fiancé rag doll me around the bedroom like a plaything."

"I want that for you, too," Ophelia said. "Hell yeah."

"I don't want to hold onto the headboard, I want to be chained to it!" I cried.

She shrugged. "Some daddy issues are more extreme than others."

"I want to be spanked and choked within an inch of my life!"

Her eyes went wide, but supportive. "What kind of books have you been reading?"

My cheeks pinched with a smile and a tickled laugh burst out of me. "This is therapeutic. I can't wait to hug you tomorrow."

"Speaking of, you have a morning flight and I requested early check-in. A limo service is set to pick you up from the airport in Vegas. It's about a twenty-minute drive to the rental, and if everything is timed correctly, Frankie and I and the Swan boys will be there already. Your sisters fly in mid-afternoon, and I have dinner planned at six, followed by some light ice breaker games to get everyone a bit more acquainted, a poolside toast, and clay face masks before bed. Then a full schedule for Saturday."

"You and your lists." I chuckled. "I'm sure everything will go perfectly with you in charge, Phee. I wouldn't have it any other way."

"You still have to pack," she stressed, tapping around on the screen of her phone. "I'm sure the same can be said for Mateo. Go and take your time getting all your stuff together. I just texted you a checklist."

I scanned the perfectly curated and columned list of items of necessary items to be packed in my suitcase, along with suggested but not imperative belongings—everything from toiletries to electronics and unmentionables. "You know, I'm actually quite good at organization and task handling when it comes to my business."

"But when it comes to your personal life, you're a hot mess." She blew me a kiss. "I'm here to help you destress, remember? I don't want you to have to lift a manicured finger for the rest of the weekend unless it's to bring a margarita to your mouth."

I chewed on my bottom lip as it sprouted into a smile. "Fine." I gave in. The light at the end of the tunnel was dotting into view. Weight was not just lifted from my shoulders, it felt like years had been returned to my life. Vibrance dancing back into the dull, forgotten halls inside me. I was hopeful again, that every hiccup was part of the plan and the only one holding me back from enjoying the wedding was me.

"You know what else could really help you?"

"What?"

Ophelia leaned closer to the screen. "Maybe a little *you* time," she said quietly. "Without Mateo."

"Phee," I gasped. The last time I masturbated for the fun of it was so long ago I'd forgotten it. It was usually something I did after solo filming if I worked myself up enough and Matty wasn't home to finish me off.

"Play a little DJ on the downstairs turntables," she added.

I threw my hand over my eyes. "You're using my words against me."

"Take the edge off."

"Okay, I'm leaving this conversation."

"Like I don't know you've done worse in that bedroom!" she added in a hurry.

"Love you!" I doled back, ending the video chat with an amused shake of my head.

Packing was exceedingly more manageable and faster with Ophelia's list. I even gathered Mateo's things into his suitcase for him to look over when he got home from work. Maybe I was more like his mother than he thought I was. In a good way. In the nurturing, caretaking ways that weren't learned, but natural.

After scanning the bedroom a final time before zipping my suitcase, my gaze caught on the bedside drawer. The drawer I kept several of my and Matty's favorite toys and lubricants for easy access. The rest of our collection was carefully tucked out of sight in boxes, under the bed, in the closet. I ran my tongue along the backside of my teeth and tapped my fingers on my chin.

It'd been an embarrassingly long while since I had some provocative time to myself. There was nothing left to do before our flight tomorrow, and Mateo was still at work for God knew how long. With his track record lately it could be hours before he finished the installation. Taking a nice, long shower to relax wasn't the worst idea...

I'd already plucked my favorite thick pink toy out of the nightstand before I was done convincing myself.

The lock on the bathroom door clicked and steaming water spattered into the tub as I stripped in front of the mirror. For someone who spent a lot of time naked, I didn't spend much of it looking at myself. I ran my gentle fingers down my curves, over my breasts, drawing whispers of circles over my nipples. They puckered and darkened, and a lazy smile graced my mouth.

I kept going, sliding my fingers down to the apex of my thighs, dipping between them, tracing and circling until my breaths came faster. The toy was nothing fancy, a very standard dildo. Not like the rest of the things in our long-winded collection. There were no bells and whistles; it didn't even vibrate. But it was the pressure I needed. The familiarity, the size, the perfect escape.

All my muscles relaxed in my shoulders and down my back as I stepped into the balmy stream of water with it. Washing my hair, shaving and exfoliating with the promise of that penetrative orgasm to keep me on task. Then I started from the top again. I ran the toy over my lips, popping it into my mouth briefly, then slicked it over each of my nipples and down between my legs. A small tingle livened me as I slid the head over my clit. I widened my legs, propping my foot in the corner of the bathtub. The stream of water hit me perfectly, warm and forceful, and my head tilted back, a sigh leaving my mouth like a button popping off a pair of tight jeans.

My mind slipped to Mateo, his hands all over me, his cock teasing my core. That phenomenal thing he did with the curl of his tongue that somehow reached all the way inside of me when he went down on me. The skin on my shoulders bristled like static, the cool air kissing the parts of my body that the hot water couldn't reach as I slid the toy inside of me, meeting resistance before relaxing and welcoming it deep and full.

My eyes drooped closed and my chest hummed with satisfaction as I pulled it out and thrust it back all the way, twice, three times. A coil tightened in my lower belly and my knees weakened. The tiles on the wall were sweating as I reached out to steady myself, working the toy in short frantic motions to reach the peak building.

Concentrate. *Concentrate.*

My mind had snapped into nothing. I willed it back to muscles, and that V-cut of Mateo's tight waist, tangled hands in my hair, one around my neck. I held my breath.

That's it.

Veiny, sinewed forearms, peaks of pectoral muscle, a long canvas of a neck begging to be bit. Fingers unworking a belt buckle, that masculine way he pulled off his T-shirt over the back of his head. When that T-shirt made it all the way into the hamper and didn't die on the floor on its way.

Oh...oh god. My insides clenched around the toy.

The thought of him putting down a towel over the sink before he shaved and changing the roll of toilet paper instead of balancing a new one on top of the old had me groaning out loud. My chest heaved in short bursts and a wave of pleasure ignited at my core.

"Yes, more," I squeaked out.

More? I was on the precipice. I canted my hips to meet the shower stream and picked up the pace of my hand, drilling the toy inside of me harder.

What if he—my eyes rolled back at the glimmer of the thought—what if he listened to the videos on his phone at a lower volume?

"Fuck." My voice cracked. The fog in the bathroom made me feel like I was floating on a cloud, and my head was swimming in it. My pulse echoed inside my ears so loud I couldn't hear anything but the sound of my own breathing returning to a regular tempo. I couldn't hear the door to my bedroom opening, or the rummaging around. I couldn't hear the first knock on the locked bathroom door or the second. But that third sounded like a battering ram in an FBI raid at four in the morning.

I yelped, sliding the toy from inside me, shelving it on the hanging caddy with shaking hands. "In the shower!" I shouted. My heartbeat reached a higher metronome than it had at my near climax. "Mateo?"

"It's Anna," a soft voice answered. "We're back!"

"Can I...do you need something?" I panicked, squeezing my fists together.

"I'm going to run the laundry. Do you need anything cleaned before your trip tomorrow? I can grab some of this stuff off the floor."

Since my father's birthday Anna had been noticeably more present in helping around the house with small tasks like dishes and laundry—the things she was privately on my case about before then. Maybe she felt sorry for me in a way that only seeing my family dynamic would bring out, and normally I would be more perceptive to it, but I was currently teetering on the edge of an orgasm and chatting through the bathroom door.

"No, no, no. No worries." I opened my mouth to scream but nothing came out. "I'll grab it."

"You're sure? I can take it off your plate."

I couldn't think of anything worse than my mother-in-law washing my thongs, until I remembered just how R-rated the rest of our bedroom was if you went looking hard enough. Did I leave that bedside drawer open? The one with the cuffs, cock rings, nipple clamps, and bullet vibrator?

God forbid she swung the closet open and saw the hidden wall of sticky notes and the content calendar and started asking unanswerable questions. I whipped the shower curtain back in a rush, hopping soaking wet out of the tub and onto the bathmat, hardly drying myself before wrapping my naked body in a very short threadbare towel and opening the door.

"I'm positive." I laughed nervously. Anna was looking over Mateo's open suitcase skeptically. "He's all packed, did it myself."

"He never packs enough—"

"T-shirts, yeah. With Vegas weather in May, he's bound to sweat right through them."

"Exactly." She nodded. "Oh and also..."

"Advil, for inflammation. He tries to power through a hangover, but it's not the headaches that get him, it's the muscle pain."

Anna studied my face and a smile stretched across hers. "Right. Okie doke. If you need anything..."

"I know where to find you." I gave her an awkward thumbs-up and almost lost my towel.

She turned back the way she came, closing the door behind her, and I fell onto the bed with a deep, exhausted sigh. Not even the universe wanted me to get my rocks off.

Crisis averted though, I thought. For now.

chapter twenty

Natalia

IT WAS early afternoon and stifling hot when we arrived in Vegas. The wheels of our suitcases rumbled against the pavement in front of our two-level, white stone villa. It was absolutely gorgeous, fenced in by high walls, and bracketed by a deep back-yard where I could hear the pool water sloshing. We ambled up the pebbled driveway and let ourselves in the large wooden door leading to the side of the house. A massive in-ground pool lay in front of us alongside an outdoor bar dotted with stools, high-potted pampas grass plants decorating either end, and faux rocks that doubled as speakers stuffed into the backyard landscaping.

"Wow," I breathed out, looking around. I stretched my stiff legs from the flight and the ride from the airport, more than ready to get out of my frumpy airplane clothes and into a bathing suit. Mateo wrapped an arm around my waist and slipped his hand into the back pocket of my jean shorts, giving my butt a short squeeze. I was determined to enjoy myself this weekend, no matter what. Part of that determination included having my way with my soon-to-be husband. I was going to suck the stress out of him if that was what it took. It had been nearly five months since we made a promise to each other to prioritize our relationship as a caveat to all the ensuing chaos. Three rules: safe word, keeping the spark alive, and hiding our sex work. Somehow the spark was left behind and needed to be reignited.

"You're here!" The back door of the house opened and Ophelia popped her head outside with a giddy little laugh, and my heart instantly blossomed like a flower in spring. I dropped my bags where I stood and ran to hug her, hopping up and down like we were two lovers separated by war.

Mateo's burly laugh echoed behind us and he pulled Ophelia into a bear hug of his own when we parted. "This place is impressive, O. I don't know what I was expecting but it wasn't this."

"You only get married once." She beamed, tickled by the praise. "There's a hot tub around the side there, ping pong tables, an outdoor shower, and the mini fridge is completely stocked behind the bar."

"I'm in heaven," I said. "This is it, this is all I need for the rest of the weekend. I'm going to park my ass in that deck chair with a drink and wrinkle under the sun."

Matty cleared his throat. "Pike around here somewhere?"

"Frankie!" Phee shouted. "Where are you guys?"

There was a fit of laughter from above that we all turned our attention to seconds before a massive body leapt from the deck protruding off the second floor with a war cry. The tight, muscular figure curled together and cannon-balled into the crystal blue water in front of us, leaving no time to protect ourselves before the resounding splash drenched Mateo, Ophelia, and me all at once.

I stood there like a person a pigeon had just crapped on, too shocked to move and arms outstretched scarecrow style. My toes wiggled against my wet sandals as Tyler Swan in all his big-bodied glory surfaced and shook his buzzed blond head like a dog.

"Tyler!" Ophelia complained halfheartedly. He swam to the edge of the pool and hoisted himself out in his bright pink swim trunks, which were short enough to show off an upper thigh tattoo that twisted beneath the swimsuit and popped out again on his hip, then continued all the way up his ribcage and across his barreling chest.

"You motherfucker." Matty lunged, wrestling Tyler playfully into a headlock that softened into a brotherly embrace. "Missed you, you brute." The Swan boys had spent New Year's with us for a few days in Miami with Frankie and O, and though I'd only known them briefly, I considered them family the same way Mateo did. It was like we were all meant to be part of each other's lives in one way or another. It warmed my chest to see Mateo smile again— genuinely, excitedly smile, the same way I had when I saw Phee.

"Tally girl." Tyler opened his arms to me with a charmingly bright smile. "Get over here."

"You're soaked," I pointed out. Mischief splashed across his eyes and he laughed as he pulled me to his chest anyway.

"We told you not to get the girls wet." Another familiar voice rang from the deck above and Tyler's younger brother Sam came down the stairs alongside Frankie in their bathing suits.

"I can't help it," Tyler answered with a wink.

The Swan brothers couldn't have had more opposite demeanors, despite their physical similarities. Although Sam's body was more athletically built, lean and toned to Tyler's mass of crafted muscle, they had the same light, soft eyes and sharp jawlines. Personality wise, Tyler was the life of the party everywhere he went; he owned a bar in Salt Lake City and spent most, if not all, of his free time behind the bar there. He was larger than life, the center of attention, and a complete and total playboy. Sam on the other hand was quiet and observant, stoic, careful, and only comfortable in settings where he knew every detail and person. He preferred it that way. Slowed down. Their differences were their strengths in Delta according to Mateo because Sam was the silent sniper the boys referred to as Wink, and Tyler was a human battering ram—hence the nickname, Echo.

"Drinks for the guests of honor." Frankie reached the landing with a tray of plastic cups and handed Matty and me each a fruity cocktail with a paper umbrella.

Mateo squinted. "Is that a dick straw?"

"Yeah." Frankie smiled. "O thought of everything."

"Are there regular straws?" he asked.

"We thought you'd feel more at home with these ones."

"You were right," I said, sipping on mine. Rum and juice invaded my senses. "God, that's delicious."

"Made them myself," Tyler said, drinking through his little green plastic penis.

"This feels like an omen for how the weekend is going to go," Matty added, trying his.

Sam, Phee, and Frankie followed our lead and we all stood there in a circle with phallic straws in our mouths. When all the fondest memories of my life flashed before my eyes on my deathbed, this would be a highlight.

We filed through the French doors on the lower level of the house and Ophelia walked us through the layout of the expansive rental. Free floating pink and white balloons were dancing around the foyer, beach balls disguised as disco balls rolling over the floor. A metal spiral staircase took us up to the second floor, an open layout with a massive living area. There was a flat-screen television above a custom driftwood mantle; two deep-seated, L-shaped couches; and a bohemian-styled rug in various depleted shades of pink, orange, and blue. This floor was even more glamorously decorated—balloons scattered across the ceiling, more disco beach balls, pink flamingo-shaped neons, and casino dice. The Vegas disco theme was fun and well thought out, all the way from the tower of plastic champagne glasses centered on the kitchen island to the playing card napkins and Donna Summer playlist.

Frankie pulled a crown off the coffee table that said *Total Bach* in sparkling silver letters and placed it on my head.

"You should take up event planning, Pike." Mateo nudged his best man. "Who are you calling whipped now?"

Frankie stifled a grin. "So I blew up some balloons."

"He had some help," Sam said. "And about four pages of hand-drawn diagrams."

"Preparation avoids disaster," Ophelia justified. "My back-up plans have back-up plans."

"I, for one, am amazed at you both." I slung an arm around Frankie and Ophelia's shoulders and pecked their cheeks one after the other. "Show me more."

Ophelia swiped a clipboard off the counter and talked us through it as we walked out onto the expansive veranda Tyler had leapt off of into the pool. The deck was covered in a soft green turf and furnished with cushioned outdoor lounge chairs and bean bags, a dining table under the cover of a cantilever umbrella, and circular seating around a freestanding gas fire pit. You could see the entire backyard and poolside from up here and beyond, out into the pink and orange desert stretching toward the city.

"We're right on time," Ophelia said, checking something off her list. "Welcome party with drinks, house tour, and room assignments. The next two hours I blocked out for getting settled and comfortable, but then we dip straight into light refreshments and more alcoholic beverages when the rest of the crew gets in. Tonight is about friendship, but tomorrow is when shit gets real."

"You've really got this all mapped out?" Mateo raised an eyebrow.

"Tip of the iceberg," she assured him.

"When do the strippers get here?" Tyler plopped onto a lone bean bag and flattened it beneath his weight.

Phee perused her list, jabbing at it. "That's tomorrow."

Sam shook his head. "Don't get him all excited, O."

"Too late." Tyler shimmied into the bean bag and closed his eyes with a grin.

Frankie tugged Ophelia down onto his lap in a cushioned lounge chair and nuzzled his nose into her hair, whispering something that made a dark red shade sprout over her cheeks and a soft giggle catch between her lips. A longing twisted inside my chest. Jealousy. Jealousy for the first futile months of a relationship that felt so much like flying. The adrenaline rush, the need, that insatiable lusting. I *did* lust for Mateo. I never wanted anything more than him—in life, in bed, in my heart and soul. Our lust was quieter now, settled in. We weren't racing an invisible clock, weren't worried we would burn out. But I did *need* him, maybe more than ever. I missed him when we were standing in the same room. I was begging for him without knowing how to say it.

Mateo was watching me curiously when I looked toward him. Flames fanned my neck like I'd been caught with my thoughts in a bubble above my head. Maybe the lust wasn't gluttonous and greedy anymore, but his gaze still leveled me. It still warmed my core and felt like fingers ghosting down my spine. I swallowed nothing, the desert air dry and brittle in my mouth, my tongue like a cat's.

He looked so good across the deck in his soft white T-shirt, a tendril of his messy hair curling over his forehead, the tip of his tongue slipping between the seam of his lips, and I knew he was reading my mind.

"I'm going to go get our suitcases settled in the room." I cleared my throat. "See you guys soon." Sam and Tyler saluted me as I dipped quickly through the glass doors with Mateo's attention following me.

Our bedroom was the biggest in the house with a private bathroom and balcony, and large windows on three of the four walls on the west side of the house where the sun poured through at golden hour. There was a spread of gifts on the bed that included a bottle of champagne, a large sun hat that said *Bride*, sunglasses, sunscreens and skincare, organic dark chocolate, and a box of expensive cigars and mint gum beside it for Mateo. Then next to all that was a small folded towel that gave me pause as I picked it up and read *Cum Rag* embroidered in delicate script across the cloth. Beside it was a box of condoms, a bottle of personal lubricant, and a note that said, *Don't use it all in one place*, with a winking face. I tugged my bottom lip into my mouth.

There was no way I could admit to Mateo that I was having a crisis about our sex life. Our very versatile, not at all vanilla sex life. Not many couples spent their free time filming themselves having intercourse for money, and even complaining to him about our intimacy felt selfish when I already asked so much of him being involved in the cam business. To say we didn't have *enough* sex felt silly.

A few weeks in the grand scheme of the rest of our lives together was nothing. It didn't mean anything, like my insecurities were telling me it did. First I was worried all he saw me as was a warm body, and now I was worried he didn't even want that part of me. This blip didn't mean that my future husband was growing bored of me outside our scheduled sessions. It didn't mean he wasn't attracted to me unless I was pretending to be someone else. It didn't mean he enjoyed spending his free time alone rather than with me, or that my fear of him becoming complacent in our relationship and seeing me as a business partner rather than a life partner was coming to fruition.

It didn't.

That was not the reason he was staying later at work more often and telling me less about his days. He wouldn't *regret* getting involved with me after all this time; we were meant to be together.

I sat at the foot of the bed and chewed on the edge of my nails until the gel started to warp. God, I fucking hated my stupid brain sometimes. Most of the time. I was at war with my own train of thought. I was going to be the girl at the end of the altar asking my husband if he was positive when he said *I do*.

My head lifted at Mateo coming through the door. It clicked closed as he leaned back against it, and his eyebrow arched curiously. "What's going on in that pretty head of yours?"

"Could you hear me thinking?" I scoffed.

"I like to think I can." He was in front of me in three slow steps, sticking his hands into the pockets of his shorts. "You wear all your emotions like a badge."

"That's actually called resting bitch face."

"It's such a gorgeous face though."

My mouth slowly lifted into a smile.

"Really," Mateo continued, reaching out and running his thumb softly below my bottom lip. "We're in Las Vegas celebrating our wedding with our best friends. It's finally fucking happening. Some days this part, the *good* part, felt so goddamn far away, but you did it, Tally. I know it hasn't been easy, and I've been too caught up in work to give you the attention you deserve, but you still managed to do it all. I'm amazed by you."

My heart swelled, throat tightening as I turned to kiss the palm of his hand resting against my jaw and murmured, "Maybe you *can* hear my thoughts."

Mateo squatted down in front of me and put us at eye level. His thighs strained against the material of his shorts and momentarily, that was all I could focus on. "Is that why you're up here alone? Stressed out about every little detail? This is the one weekend you have to forget about all of those things, baby. It can wait. Enjoy this while we're in the moment. I want you to be here with me."

I pulled a deep breath in through my nose. "I wish we could get married right now. Forget all the fanfare and the flowers and guests. I want it to be simple, like this is. Just us. The closer we get to the wedding the more I'm questioning my motivations for everything. Don't get me wrong, it'll be beautiful, but it feels like it's not for *us* anymore."

"Are you regretting it?" Matty asked hoarsely, his face twisted in concern. He steadied himself with both hands on my knees, and skimmed his palms up my thighs and back down comfortingly. I was still on edge and that soft touch brought a wave of goose bumps to the surface of my skin.

"No, not at all," I rushed out. "Never. I'm admitting that I cared too much about sticking it to my family that I'm just as successful as my sisters by having a wedding that will impress them. The whole planning, the elaborate decor, the venue—it was all because my parents never thought I could do it without their help. But the only thing I care about anymore is that I'm getting married to you. The rest is this made-up thing I've been trying to convince myself I've wanted since I was a kid."

"Do you want to postpone it?" As much as that felt like what I was asking for, it wasn't what I wanted. The wedding had been months in the making, and there were too many factors involved to selfishly put it off for a theme change at the eleventh hour.

"I don't want to waste another day not being your wife, so absolutely not," I assured him. "It's all the little things adding up lately that have me thinking is all. There's a lot I've been wanting to talk to you about." His eyes flashed to mine as I put my hands over his and the air in the room thinned. I pulled them higher, meeting the bottom of my shorts, and Mateo's lips parted.

"All ears," he answered distractedly, playing with the loose frills of my jean shorts.

"Remember the ground rules we laid out, for having your parents stay?"

"Yes."

"We might be letting one of those things get away from us." I danced around it, feeling him out. The partial power trip of having him kneeling in front of me was giving me a boost of confidence. Mateo was so dominant intimately, I reveled in his softer, submissive sides when they peeked through. He turned it on and off so beautifully, like a switch.

His fingers slipped under the hem of the shorts on either side and squeezed my outer thighs. A sigh fell from my mouth in the quiet room and Matty's eyes glinted gold like sparks in a fire. "Say the word, Natalia."

The lube lying a foot away from us was so promising.

I thought too hard, for too long, and then there was a hand at my throat, tugging me forward until our noses connected and our unsteady breaths mingled. "I know you've been feeling this too, between us. I know what *want* looks like in your eyes. I could see it outside." His words skated across my lips and I pitched forward to claim him but he kept the distance like a cat-and-mouse game. A short whine erupted from me, pleasing Mateo into a grin.

"I want to get back to us again," I said vulnerably. My fingers skated into his long hair, pushing it off his forehead, behind his ears. His eyebrows threaded together like I'd pinched a nerve, then relaxed into understanding. We both underestimated how hard it would be to meld our separate lives into one. Our opposite upbringings, our distinctly different families. We were also naive to think we knew each other entirely without having stirred that pot. Love is never just about two people. It's about how two people take on the world together.

Mateo leaned forward and kissed me, blank slating all the thoughts I had racing through my head as my eyes fell closed, lashes fanning together. It deepened instantly as our lips made way for tongues to clash and a satisfied hum rumbled through Matty's chest and landed like a rock in the cavity of my stomach. This kiss was an 'I'm hungry for you' kiss, an 'if you don't stop me now, this is going to go all the way' kiss.

Half my shirt was over my head when the sudden slam of a car door in the driveway below our window followed by the incoherent rumble of yelling demanded our attention. I ignored it initially—my fiancé was kissing his way down my body and parts of me were completely checked out of reality. But another door slammed, and more disgruntled exclamations had Mateo perking his head up to listen.

"What is that?" I was flushed and breathy, and I ran my hand involuntarily through his locks like a tether to the moment, willing it to not get away from us again. But the chirping continued through the back gate of the house, getting louder and more animated and branching off into three very distinct voices that belonged to my sisters.

Causing a scene like clockwork.

I blew out a breath and ran my hands up and down my face with a groan. "Perfect timing as usual for us Russos."

"Ophelia can probably handle it," Mateo tried.

"I would never subject her to that." I slipped my tank back over my head and shimmied out from under Mateo's touch. He remained there on his knees with his forehead on the mattress, the blankets muffling his growl of frustration.

Jogging through the door and down the hallway, I met Ophelia out on the veranda where she was already trying to mediate my concerned and overwhelmed sisters. Camilla was wearing a sun hat the size of the deck umbrella and dragging a designer carry-on bag carelessly up the stone stairs.

"What's going on?" I asked.

"There's a *freak* that followed us here all the way from the airport," she spat. Mia and Isabella were making their way up the stairs close behind.

I looked down at an inexplicable number of suitcases abandoned poolside. "Followed you how?"

"He asked us at the taxi pickup if we wanted to carpool," Bella explained. "Yeah, no thanks. Women can't even walk outside alone without the threat of physical assault."

"I called him an ass-licking incel and then we jumped in the SUV and got the fuck out of there," Mia said. "But his car trailed us all the way here and parked outside. I think we need to call the cops."

"Who's calling the cops now?" Tyler and Sam stepped out onto the deck in tandem and the eyes on all three of my sisters doubled in size.

"Looks like the cops are already here," Bella lavished.

Tyler's eyes lit up and a smirk stretched across his handsome face. "You are going to get me in all types of trouble, aren't you?"

"Oh my god." I swallowed and put my body between them. "Where is this guy now? The boys will take care of it."

"Is your name Frankie, by chance?" Mia pointed at Sam.

"Have you forgotten that you just busted in here screaming about a potential stalker security risk?" I reminded her. "Focus, Mia."

Mateo and Frankie joined the group outside, glancing around

in confusion. My fiancé caught my gaze and lifted an eyebrow. "Everyone okay?" he asked.

"A car followed my sisters here from the airport. Can you four just go do a quick look around out front and see what's going on to ease everyone's mind?"

"Of course." Mateo nodded. He gestured his head toward the stairs and Frankie and the Swans followed the order like it was ingrained in them, filing one by one in a stealthy line toward the backyard fence. Us girls leaned over the veranda wall and watched from a safe distance.

"Should we keep score on the absolute fuck-assery that goes down this weekend?" I suggested. "Starting strong with this one. If someone's not in jail by Sunday it will be a miracle."

"No one is ending up in jail," Ophelia assured me. "This is a small hiccup. It will be sorted out in just a few minutes."

The wooden double doors on the gate squeaked open and the men below stopped, flattening themselves to the white stone walls of the house, disappearing from view.

"Oh my fucking god, he's coming inside," Camilla panicked.

My lungs jammed into my ribs, nervous energy buzzing. "It's okay, they're literally trained for this."

In a flash Sam reached out and pulled the gate completely open, shocking the person on the other side as Tyler in all his big boy glory dropped his shoulder and pummeled him into the ground. We heard the air leave the man's body in an *oof* as Mateo and Frankie crowded around the intruder who was splayed out like a pancake and groaning toward the sun.

"Oh fuck," Mateo cursed. "Shit."

"Babe, are you okay?" I yelled down.

"Yeah, are you okay?" Bella shouted all girlish and high-pitched. She nudged me with her elbow. "Ask Chris Hemsworth if he's okay."

"He does look like a Hemsworth," Mia agreed. "Good one."

Mateo helped Tyler to his feet before dusting the chest off the guy on the ground and offering him a hand to stand back up. I squinted, recognizing the stranger in his NY Yankees hat, a golden cross around his neck that matched the one Mateo always wore, and a beaten-up black suitcase still caught in the fence gate behind him.

"That's him." Camilla sighed in relief. "That's the guy."

"That's my fucking brother-in-law you absolute idiots." I ran down the steps directly to Angelo's side where he was still catching his breath from having the wind knocked out of him.

"So sorry, man." Tyler clapped him sympathetically on the back. "Our intel was wrong, it seems."

"Angelo, oh my god." Under his ball cap, Angelo's green eyes were pinched and he rubbed his right shoulder, rotating it. "Are you okay? Can I get you something? Ice? A beer? A restraining order against my sisters? I can't apologize enough."

"On it." Ophelia rushed to my side with a cold pack straight out of a medical kit and handed it to Angelo. "Is anything broken?"

"I mean, he's a big fucking guy, but I got some meat on my bones. I can take a hit," Angelo said lightheartedly. His disposition calmed my worry and he smiled at me, a bright boyish smile that wrinkled his nose. Then I was pulled cheek to hard chest and wrapped in a strong hug. "Hey, sis. Looking too good for my brother, I'll tell you that much."

"He's fine." Mateo punched out a laugh. "You'll be a cheeky fucking bastard on your deathbed, Ang."

My sisters ambled down the stairs with their heads dipped a bit lower than usual. "In our defense, we had no idea who you were," Camilla offered with an apologetic wince. "I'm Camilla, by the way."

"Bella," Isabella piped up, waving her fingers at him.

Mia cleared her throat. Her oversized designer sunglasses were covering half her face and she outstretched a hand to him. "Mia."

"Nice to meet you, Mia." Angelo reached out and took her palm in his. A grin sprouted on his lips. "I'm Ass-licking Incel."

chapter twenty-one

Mateo

IT WAS GOING ABOUT AS good as I'd expected it would. My brother was laid up on the couch beside me with an ice pack on the back of his head from his smack on the pavement. I wouldn't have wanted to be tackled by Echo if it won me a million dollars. There was a reason he was who he was to us in Delta.

An honest misunderstanding, though. Natalia's sisters were dramatic, but it wasn't entirely unlikely a schmuck would have seen a trio of women walk out of an airport with a train of designer bags and not identified them as an easy target.

We moved past it. The beer in my hand kept being replaced by another, the music was loud, and the mood lifted substantially. What I couldn't shake was the conversation that had been interrupted between Tally and me. Had I known she was so unhappy with the way the wedding planning was playing out, I would have done something sooner, stepped in somehow. It felt like yet another thing I was falling short at.

Ophelia bounced out of the kitchen with a tray of snack foods and dips, setting them on the large coffee table in front of everyone in the living room. "I was joking to Nat over Christmastime about throwing a joint bachelorette for her wedding one day, and now here we are."

"I remember you specifically saying how awkward it would be to do it alongside Frankie after you fucked him, though," Tally recalled.

"So awkward." Frankie swooped in holding a tray of champagne glasses and kissed Ophelia's cheek.

"Look at you now," I said, gesturing around the room at the decorations Frankie had helped set up for the weekend. "Martha fucking Stewart."

Ophelia put a hand on her hip. "He's a man of many, many talents, Mateo. You should know this."

Frankie plopped onto the couch beside me and whispered smugly, "And I know only one of us is getting laid right now."

"Cheap shot," I scoffed.

"Dish 'em and take 'em."

Tally sat on the large sofa, our wedding party between us, and my mind floated to what else had happened in the bedroom earlier. What *hadn't* happened at the height of it, the feeling of her thighs in my hands, the tiny shiver of her torso as I ran my lips down her neck. It was chewing at my nerves not to have her now, and I knew exactly how I wanted her. I had plans for us, and those big plans had me hiding a hard-on behind a throw pillow like a teenager.

I stared directly at her, through the murmurs of our friends and the room fell away like I was willing her bright brown eyes to catch mine. Her hair had grown so long it billowed like curtains over her shoulders and her soft tan legs folded under her body.

Look at me, Tal. Be vulnerable with me. Feed this possession.

Her throat bobbed, hand pausing with some sort of flattened pretzel halfway to her mouth as if she'd heard my plea, and through long eyelashes, her attention flitted across to me. The tension between us simmered like something lost begging to be found. *Need you*, I mouthed.

Natalia's skin turned a bright shade of pink and her teeth sunk into the plush pillow of her bottom lip. The visual went straight to my gut and I was halfway to taking her back upstairs with me to finish what we'd started when Ophelia addressed the room and Tally's gaze darted away.

"Let's go around the room and tell our favorite memory of the bride and groom," the maid-of-honor suggested.

"I've got something." Wink's blue eyes brightened, and he swung a tattooed arm across the back of the couch behind his older brother. "Oh Captain, my captain."

"Fucking spare me," I scoffed out with a laugh. The boys all replied in hoots, while Angelo looked on curiously and with reverence, like he couldn't wait to hear it. Unfortunately the call sign stemmed from something totally unheroic.

"I think it's time we disclosed how you got that nickname." Wink smiled brightly.

"It's because I'm always in charge," I explained.

"That's a lie," Tally said pointedly. "Don't get me started."

I stuck my tongue in my cheek. She was bold with an audience, but I loved that about her. "I'll deal with you later, princess."

"Sam, continue." Ophelia held out an invisible microphone for him.

"Captain Morgan," Wink elaborated. "Mateo loves boats, did you know that?"

"I like pirates." I looked down, into my lap at the beer I was holding. "Pirates are fucking cool, boats are their houses, and we spent a lot of time on the ocean in Delta."

"Cap got so tossed up on rum one night he thought he was a pirate, and we were stationed in a bay on our day off where there were plenty of boats. He carried his handle of Captain Morgan straight onto a charter and tried to take over the ship."

Echo snickered, reliving a night I couldn't even remember after the fact. All I knew was I woke up with the worst hangover of my life, stinking like salt water with my ID missing.

"He didn't take the boat, by the way. The poor guy on board barely spoke any English, and with a flick sent him over the bow. Luckily nothing too crazy. We pulled him out and shook him off. He did lose the handle though."

"Swimming with the fishes." I owned up to it, taking a long swig of my beer.

"I didn't know you wanted to be a pirate, babe," Natalia cooed. "I'm sure we could make that happen."

Frankie popped open the bottle of champagne and a stream of foam tilted from the lip and splashed the floor. "A toast to Captain Duran and his lovely first mate, Tally. May all your seas remain calm, all your ships sound, and all your rum barrel-aged."

"I'll drink to that." I smiled, watching my future wife raise her glass across the couch.

* * *

SAM LIT a fire in the standing pit on the deck after dinner. The girls were below in the pool, playing a game of tipsy chicken atop each other's shoulders. I was glad to see Tally seemingly back to normal with her sisters again. They always found a way to gravitate back into one another's good graces. I didn't hold the prenup against Bella, either. It was the way she was raised, and for all I knew her father put it in her head to begin with and she was simply following demands. At their core, her sisters were good girls. Definitely spoiled, but also insanely intelligent. It made me think Natalia might be able to tell them one day about what we did for a living and find support there.

I sat next to my brother on a bean bag and tousled his wavy brown hair. He batted my hand away, annoyed, and it sent me straight back to high school for a glimmer of a moment.

Angelo looked good—healthy, bright-eyed, strong. We were more similar now than ever before in our lives, and when I really looked at him I saw Dad, too. In the shallow smile lines around his eyes, the cleft on his chin. Aging was a mind fuck. Maybe I looked away for too long, but suddenly the image I had in my head of my parents, my brother, and even myself had softened and browned at the edges.

I put my feet up on the rail of the fire pit and felt the heat burning the soles of my shoes. "I've missed you, man. Catch me up on life in the Bronx. What's new?"

"Nothing at all." He blew out a breath and dug into his shorts pocket for a pack of cigarettes. "It's the same as the day you left. A few more gas stations. Settino retired so Mom had to find a new butcher. Pamela got married last fall, actually."

"Settino's daughter? That Pamela? The one with the toe thumbs?"

"That's the one," he said. "I was just as shocked as you."

"No shit." I chewed on my thumb. "What about you, though? How's it been with the house to yourself?"

Angelo sparked a lighter to life in front of his face. "Actually pretty lonely. I miss the constant yelling down the basement stairs to flip the laundry into the dryer. Don't get me started on the footsteps on the ceiling when I'm hungover at eight a.m."

I hummed out a laugh. "Now you understand. I don't get why you don't just move out, bro. Find a place. I know you have the money saved. It's a game changer."

"Soon, I won't have a choice," he said, reaching down to snuff out the ash from his cigarette on the stone floor. A habit he picked up working long construction hours with Dad. Our father had since quit smoking after his doctor scared him straight, but Angelo had yet to drop it.

"How's work been?" I asked.

"Slowing down," Angelo said. "Finally."

"Lucky you."

His eyebrows threaded together. "Owning a business is not all it's cracked up to be?"

"You should know. I've been spreading myself thin trying to stay upright since Pike left."

Angelo blew a plume of smoke toward the sky and turned in my direction. "Why are you doing it alone?"

"It's complicated." I bristled, glancing over the railing to the group of women by the pool none the wiser. Pop music bumped from the speaker and they were singing together. "I've been putting off hiring because I want it to be someone I know, and trust. Turns out my circle is a little too small for that, so it's been a long six months doing it all on my own."

"I'm glad I don't have to worry about fucking up anymore." Angelo sighed in relief. "Duran & Son couldn't keep up with the bigger companies anyway. Those contractors are owned by billionaires, and those billionaires own everything else in the city. We couldn't outbid them, so we got bought out every time. Dad made the right decision throwing in the towel."

My blinks slowed, and I sat up straighter. "What are you talking about?"

Angelo tilted his head at me, tossing his burning cigarette at his feet and crushing it with the toe of his shoe. "About the business closing, Matty. For the last six months I've been finishing up our open contracts and slowly letting the tradesmen go. What, did you think Dad just handed it to me after forty years? Yeah, right. You and he are the same in a lot of ways. He would have never retired if he wasn't forced to."

My brain was static. I scrubbed a palm back and forth across my chin trying to process the news. My parents had been feeding me a lie for months about enjoying their retirement and spending time with Natalia and me before our wedding, but didn't think once to include the fact that Duran & Son had gone under. Retirement denoted *choice*. According to Angelo my father's small, family-owned construction company couldn't stand up to the competition and that was somehow a big fucking secret.

It was understandable that Dad's pride had taken a hit and he didn't want to admit that the business was forced out of the market. They had to know that this would all come to light, most likely by their youngest, big-mouthed son.

"Nobody told me that." My jaw clenched. "Why?"

Angelo's brows furrowed in confusion. "I thought you already knew. Wasn't it obvious with them down there buying a house?"

All the air in my body stagnated. My gut pitched forward like it was trying to escape my body, and a cool rush fell down the back of my neck. I licked my lips and swallowed a knot in my throat. "Don't fuck with me right now, Angelo."

"I know better than that," he said. "They really didn't tell you?"

John's birthday. The briefest mention of finding a place in Florida over conversation at dinner. I gave it no merit, never even thought I'd need to, because a decision like that wouldn't be made in the dark. I realized that might have been the most fucked-up way for my parents to test the waters around the idea. My head began spinning on an axis.

"I've been lied to for months." I leaned forward to rest my elbows on my knees. I hung my head in my hands and tried to focus on the gray pavement and keep my breathing steady. The last thing I needed was to have an episode in Vegas in front of my entire wedding party. I couldn't. "Do you know how fucked up that is? Tally is going to feel used. Fuck, *I* feel used. What were we to them, a stepping stone?"

"The intentions were good, Matty, but the execution was shit. I don't know why they kept it from you. Mom has her own thoughts and plans, and Dad goes along with them. But they *did* go down to visit you. That was the reason for the trip."

"But it changed." I squeezed my eyes shut, tensed my fingers, and then my forearms and biceps, isolating the muscle groups like I'd read to do as an anxiety management technique. "There's really no excuse, Ang. It's typical Mom and Dad bullshit. I could have handled this in doses, I'm sure. Sorry that finding out our family business went under, and that our parents have been house hunting down the road in the same breath, is coming as a bit of a shock to the system."

He put his hands up. "I get it. I'm not condoning the lack of communication. I'm also fucking peeved that I became the unknowing messenger. That was probably their hope all along, to soften the blow."

"We both got played." My stress evened out and my attention

moved to Tally on the pool patio, wondering how I'd break this to her. That our lives would never truly go back to normal after the wedding if both my parents were going to be in Florida, having us accessible, meddling in private, isolated moments forever. I couldn't tell her here. Not in Vegas, not during our one fucking weekend that was supposed to be drama free and perfect and relaxed with our wedding party. It would change the entire mood, and there was nothing that could be done about it from Nevada anyway.

"Don't worry about it now," Angelo said, reading my mind. "I'll talk to them. I'm sure there's a perfectly good explanation for keeping you in the dark."

"Yeah, they knew I couldn't oppose it if it was already done."

The chair shifted like sand underneath me as I sat back and bit my tongue. This was just another thing I would have to deal with, another listed item on the docket. My life was becoming an endless to-do; when I checked something off, three more things materialized at the bottom. Our sticky note wall of clients, TechOp's installations, my parents, my anxiety attacks, my relationship with my future wife that needed tending to.

There were so many things that needed my attention, but only one that I could actually focus on while we were in Vegas, and it was long past due.

Natalia was sprawled out on a lounger, her crown high on top of her head, a plastic cup tilted to her lips against a small smile. She watched on as the boys jumped in the water and took a turn playing chicken. Ophelia was on Pike's shoulders wrestling with Sam mid-air while Sam was off-balance on his brother's, towering over her.

Tally's sisters bopped along in the small wake of the pool water, yelping and laughing. Everyone was perfectly distracted.

"Why don't you get down there and join the action?" I gestured with a nod toward the backyard. "Meet you there."

Angelo clapped his hand over my shoulder, shaking it empathetically, then slipped down the stairs to the poolside. I slid my phone out of the pocket of my shorts, keeping my eyes on Tally the entire time as I sent her a message.

ME

> Go upstairs to our bedroom, and be naked when I get there.

chapter twenty-two

Mateo

WE'D DONE this a thousand times before—more than that, by far. It was part of our life, a staple of it. Where there was a Natalia and me, sex followed. It had from the very first date.

This was different in all the ways I'd never expected it would be. It felt like a reckoning. Like coming home after a long time away, like I was returning us to a place we'd traversed so far from that we never thought we'd get back. In reality the past few weeks were nothing, and our life together would be long and full of hardships, but this was the first time we'd ever had to come back to each other. Fight for each other.

She was going to know exactly how much I missed the feeling of her underneath me, riding me, spread out, shivering, taking exactly what I gave to her. The thought of what lay beyond the bedroom door as I walked toward it was enough to have me half hard and full of adrenaline before I even turned the handle. But the image I was greeted with immediately pulled my cock to stand at full attention.

My heart thudded hard against my chest. "That is so fucking perfect, Angel."

Natalia sat on the bed, fully nude, knees parted just so to where the pink petaled center of her peeked out. I took a staggering breath and met her half-lidded, seductive eyes. She knew what she was doing to me, the same way I knew her. But this night was not going to be even. It was going to be fair. Fair to me was taking my place at the edge of the bed and wrenching her ankles apart so I could see what was mine.

She let go of a sigh, shocked and recentering as my hungry gaze devoured her, top to bottom. Her nipples hardened like I'd touched them, and the small bursts of air in in her chest jilted her abdomen. I could read her like a book. She was trying to stay aloof and that was *fucking* adorable. It only spurred me on more.

"Ran up here like a lovesick puppy when you got that text," I said. "Obedient little pup you are, Tal. You must really be wanting something."

"I know where I get my bones." She wrinkled her nose, and I swatted at the inside of her thigh, hard enough to make her jolt at the sting, but revel in the small promise of pain that it brought.

"I've been waiting to have you alone since this afternoon. I'm going to take advantage of this." I dragged her by the ankle to the edge of the bed. I was a step away from rocking myself into the cradle of her open legs. She was looking at the tent in my swim trunks as if she wanted exactly that. To feel the friction of my clothes and the ridge of my cock against her clit, to have something beyond the cool air in the bedroom. I pressed my hips forward.

"Fuck." Her head fell back, exposing her neck, and that long dark hair cascaded backwards and splayed out on the bed. "It's been too long, Matty."

"I know." I wandered a gentle hand up her body, fingertips scraping against her ribcage as she arched into it and ushered me to take a handful of her heavy breast. "I'm going to take care of that."

I thrust my hips forward again and took her nipple between my fingers at the same time, rolling the soft flesh, tugging it to the precipice of pain. Her limits waxed and waned. At the peak of her orgasm I could *hurt* her, and she'd beg me for it. I liked to work our way up to those moments as torturously slow as possible, because I got off on it, on my end. Edging myself on her pleasure, watching her come undone. The longer I could let myself go without being touched or being inside her, the harder I came, and it was never not worth that hard-earned euphoria.

Natalia started wiggling her hips toward my shorts, sliding herself over the bulge of my erection. I dropped forward and notched myself there so she could writhe and took the breast I wasn't already playing with into my mouth. Her legs latched around me and her ankles crossed at the small of my back, keeping me in place.

"So fucking desperate, baby. How does it feel to be so desperate?" I lifted my chin and found her gaze was focused on where our bodies connected, her eyebrows pinched together in frustrated concentration. I wanted to reach up with a thumb and iron out the wrinkle settling at the base of her nose, but instead, I pushed upward and surprised her with a hard kiss.

That kiss fell into another, and our lips parted on a dime, tongues tangling like they always did. Kissing Natalia was warm and familiar, but she could still take the air out of my lungs after all this time. We'd learned every single inch of each other's bodies, and our mouths were no exception. She pulled back and sank her teeth into my bottom lip, tugging on it, and my mind was made up about how the rest of this night was going to go. In this bedroom, locked away, compensating for the last few weeks of wasted time in only the ways that Natalia and I could. Because I'd never had a partner like her, I'd never been so comfortable with anyone this intimately before, and I'd never felt so confident to do what I was about to do with another soul besides Natalia Russo's.

"I have something for you," I murmured. "A surprise."

"Right now?" She ground her hips again and I hissed through my teeth. It was becoming harder to hold out. I wanted to feel her skin on mine in the worst way. I pinned her hip down with my palm so she couldn't continue to move against me and she whined insolently.

"Behave." I slapped her nipple, blowing on it afterward to relieve the burn. "There are rewards for girls like you," I said. "And there are punishments. It's entirely up to you which of those things you're interested in, Tally. Both suit me, because at the end of it I'm going to fill you with my cum so deep it gets you fucking pregnant." Her eyes rounded. They were the deepest, get-lost-inside brown eyes, and they turned even darker as she processed my promise.

Natalia's entire body dropped back against the bed, heaving, as I stood and crossed the floor to our discarded luggage. I pulled my T-shirt off over my head and tossed it, adjusting myself in my shorts to alleviate the ache as much as I could, but I knew it wouldn't go away until she *made it* go away.

"It's kind of funny," I started saying, "how forgetful you can be when you're in a rush. It's something we always stressed in Delta, tying up loose ends. Not leaving a trace or a trail back to you. It's a lot different when it's not life or death, of course. But some self-preservation is always a good idea. You don't want to get caught doing something you might have wanted to keep to yourself. You know what I'm saying?"

She had no fucking clue what I was going on about, which made it all the more exciting. I could see the confusion on her face clear as day. I grinned, pushing a breath of amusement through my nose, as I removed a travel bag from my suitcase and unzipped it.

"You forgot something, Tally." I turned back around, holding out the bright pink toy she'd left in our shower back home. The one I'd come nose to nose with beside the shampoo bottles after work the night before. Such a small mistake on her part that had been weighing on me for twenty-four hours while I waited patiently to get her exactly where she was right now.

Her expression reddened, sheer embarrassment blossoming in her cheeks and migrating down her chest.

"Were you fucking yourself in the shower, Tal?" I slithered toward her. "Did you put this in your pussy when you thought you were all alone at home?"

Her tongue darted out to wet her lips and I was back to standing between her parted legs, running the head of the toy from her thigh down to her knee. She tensed and I pushed back until she fell completely open.

"Answer me."

"Yes."

"What am I going to do with you?" I said softly. Natalia lifted her hips as I grazed the head of the dildo against her clit. We'd used toys in bed together before, so I wasn't startling her with anything she hadn't already handled. But there was a primitive difference between those times and now.

Her short gasp hung in the air as I slapped it against her wet flesh, rubbing the silicone against the lips of her pussy until it was glistening. I stopped when I was satisfied and ran the toy up her body, circling her nipples and dragging the head straight to the seam of her mouth. "Open," I told her. "I want you to taste how fucking desperate you are."

A pleased smile curled Tally's lips. She was loving every second of being told what to do and how to act. Submitting to me. This was our favorite game to play. She parted her lips and stuck her tongue out wide, batting long innocent eyelashes at me as she did. I let the toy slide over her tongue and disappear down the back of her throat, and she hummed around it, sucking slowly and letting go with a loud pop when she'd licked herself off it.

My pulse was alive and beating erratically, most noticeably in the erection I was fighting to ignore as it crested against the suppressive lining of my bathing suit. I wanted to fill her throat worse than anything. To feel her hot mouth around me, the sweep of her tongue massaging my shaft and balls. To take her by the hair and fuck her face until she was drooling.

"You wanted this, right?" I propositioned her. "You wanted to play, baby. So let's play."

I stepped backward, taking her by the hair at the nape of her neck and dragging her down to her knees on the floor. Rough and abrupt. Her spine straightened as she felt the drag of the toy again against her cheek before I pushed it back between her lips and started thrusting it.

God, I was going to fucking lose it. Precum was dripping inside my shorts. I was so uncomfortably hard it was masochistic to watch her brown doe eyes blow out and glaze with tears like the most grateful woman in the world to be used like this. I pulled it from her mouth, spit following, and she smiled her perfect, charming, elated smile, giving me the green light to push her even further.

Our bodies were so in sync that we worked in cues and beats, especially when it came to sex. I hardly needed to check in with her verbally. After over a year every single movement, whine, moan, tremble, and swivel of her hips was a language I was fluent in.

"I'm going to make sure every single one of these holes is filled properly," I said. "Would you like that, angel?"

Her eyes were level with the bulge of my cock. "Please."

I wrenched her forward and pressed her face to it. Her mouth parted, leaving sloppy kisses across the outline of my shaft. She hummed, and the vibration sent my neck rolling back and I stared at the ceiling, letting the feeling of her lips and her tongue crash and roll over me. "You own me, Tally," I found myself saying. "I worship you. I would spend my life on a leash for you, if that's what you wanted. And I know from that look in your eye, and that smile on your spit-stained lips, that you feel exactly the same way about me. I've known it for a long time. I know I can do whatever I want to you, and you'll let me. So prove to me, like the little cockhungry slut you are, just how badly you need your fiancé to fuck you."

"I need it—"

I pressed my finger to her lips. "*Show* me."

Natalia walked her long pink fingernails up both my thighs,

gaze never leaving mine as they hooked onto my waistband and tugged my shorts down to the floor. Before she could touch me I bent over, taking her pretty face in both my hands and crushing our lips together. Our tongues mingled briefly, before I pecked the tip of her nose and straightened back up. That kiss said all it needed to. That my deep respect for her would never waver despite how *disrespectfully* she was going to be ruined for the rest of the night.

Natalia lifted both her hands and wiggled her fingers. The shimmer of her rings glinted in the sunlight dripping over the horizon and casting the room in a deep orange glow. "Take these off for me."

I plucked two decorative gold rings off her pinky and middle finger on her right hand, tossing them aside, and then repeated the same thing on her left hand with a thick ring on her thumb and several stacked thin on her index finger. I paused at her engagement ring, rolling it between the tips of my fingers and watching it catch and blaze like fire in the sunlight, swathing the wall beside us in circles of color. I loved this ring. I agonized over it for weeks, unsure if she'd like it despite knowing there was something very similar hanging out on a Pinterest board she owned. I wanted the simple diamond to accentuate her own beauty, not demand attention. It was perfect for her and it made me proud every single day I got to see her wear it.

I left it on her finger, dropping her hand back down to her side. "As a reminder that I love you. Because I'm about to fuck you like I don't."

Her jaw fell open and I took that cue to drag her lips to the head of my cock and urge her mouth to widen. She swallowed the tip eagerly and a gruff, trapped noise broke through the cage of my chest. *Fuuuuck me.* I squeezed my eyes shut to recenter myself. I was going through something torturous from the outside looking in. Every ounce of pleasure in my body was in the twist of her hands as she brought them to the base and pumped me, her lips meeting the knuckle of her hand halfway, and then her throat chasing it back down.

"You are something else, Tal," I praised. "An absolute knockout on your knees. Keep sucking, princess. I know you've been thinking about this."

Her eyes flashed to me, and she grabbed me by the hips and unhinged her jaw, swallowing until her nose touched the patch of hair at my base. My dick twitched like it was on edge, and I was. I was so close to letting go.

"Stand up," I coaxed her, unwilling to let it get to that point. I wasn't coming anywhere but inside her, I would make damn well sure of that. She fell back onto the bed, crumpled white sheets billowing, the bright pink toy at her side and still that light of excitement glowing around her like a halo. The irony of that thought wasn't lost on me.

On the nightstand was the bottle of lube and our salaciously decorative hand towel. I brought them both back to Tally and my eyes hooded to find her fingers between her legs, circling her swollen clit gently.

"Look how excited you are for this. You can't even keep your hands off your pussy for a minute." I swatted her fingers away, replacing them with mine and a sweet, high-pitched moan squeaked out of her. "It feels much better when it's me though, doesn't it?"

"It feels much better when it's you inside me," she sighed petulantly. I was frustrating her with little whispers of a touch, brushing her clit and taking the sensation away. "Mateo, fuck me before a goddamn dust storm comes through this villa and cock-blocks us again."

I plunged a finger inside her and her spine bowed in answer. "Don't rush me, baby. I am going to take a long time with you because it's been a long time. I want to revisit some things." My finger pushed and pulled. I rubbed a small ridged part of her and she hissed, teeth clattering together. My thumb worked her clit in circles and in no time at all she was dripping to my knuckles, her pussy fluttering around my middle finger. So I added another.

"Please don't stop," she begged. "I'm going to—*fuck*." Her shoulders lifted off the bed and her stomach tensed. I continued fucking her with my fingers, recognizing the signs of her orgasm coming to a head. This was different, a build-up that came on like a freight train. She couldn't hold on to the climax in the same way. It shook through her hard, lifting her hips from the bed.

"Oh, do it for me," I begged her right back. My voice was hoarse with need, all of my focus on the rhythm of my fingers between her legs, not letting up at all. "Come on, Tally, do that thing you know I love."

Her lips parted, eyes rolling back, her entire lower half relaxing—and then I was covered in her. My hand and wrist, her legs, the bedsheet. She screamed out in ecstasy and thrashed as I thrust to the very last pulse, until her knees were buckling inward and she was clawing at my arm to stop, overcome by it.

"Fuck yes. Jesus Christ, Natalia, I'm gonna fucking ruin you like you just ruined these sheets." I didn't let her breathe. Possession took over and I palmed my cock, slid it through her pussy, and plunged myself inside of her to the brink. She was tight, and hot, unimaginably wet. The friction shot pleasure straight up my spine, goose bumps erupted down my body, and I was *home*. I was home inside of her. Reaching up I swept her sweat-slicked strands of hair off her forehead and kissed her as I rolled my hips over and over again. She tried to speak but I hushed the noise with my lips, swallowing whatever desperation was there. I was on another plane of existence, forgetting for a moment where I was, that I had a plan, that I couldn't fucking come yet, because I hadn't followed through on my promise.

I growled and straightened back up, gripping the base of my cock as I pulled out of her to the very tip, leaving it there to tease and poke at her entrance.

"What are you doing?" Natalia complained. Her long fingers

wrapped around me and guided me back inside her but I resisted. "Put it back," she demanded.

"Tell me about your shower." The top of the bottle of lube popped open with a flick of my thumb and I brought it between us. "I want to know everything. I want to know what had you so riled up that you needed to scratch that itch. So hot and bothered you couldn't wait for me to get home to take care of you."

The cold, viscous liquid dripped onto my shaft, and I pulled a breath through my teeth to adjust to the lube coating me. I let it drizzle across Natalia's core, rubbing it across her clit, and then watched it travel down to her tight ring of muscle.

Her breath quickened as I gathered more on my fingers and brought them to her unfilled hole, sliding one inside. I was aching to be buried in that snug part of her. It was far from the first time, but the sense of trust was always prevalent. We had to work our way up to this carefully.

"I was stressed," she said. Her voice wavered as I added another finger, pumping them slowly in and out. I picked her limp arm up off the bed, kissing the tips of her fingers, her palm, her wrist, and then down her forearm to lessen the pressure, to relax her.

"About what?"

She didn't answer me for several seconds, eyes squeezed closed, adjusting to the intrusion, ecstasy loosening her limbs with every in and out. She took a shaky breath. "Everything. The wedding, my parents, us. I thought it would—" A sharp breath whistled out of her. "I thought it would help me calm the fuck down if I just got off. It was innocent, I swear. I didn't even finish."

"Innocent?" I scoffed out a laugh. "Our interpretation of innocence is not the norm, Tal. Just because I've paddled your ass red, and tied you in knots for an audience, doesn't mean I'm not going to get jealous when you choose a plaything over me."

"It's not your enemy," she reminded me. Her fingertips skated to her nipples, pinching and tugging on them and I watched her pussy flutter in waiting, gripping at nothing as I worked her ass open inch by inch.

I poured more lube over us, drenching my cock in it, and then replaced my fingers with the tip, sheathing myself halfway inside of her ass in one push. I shocked us both, like ripping off a Band-Aid. Her legs trembled and I pressed them open wider, pinning her thighs to the bed. I could watch my dick splitting her in half every day for the rest of my life and never get bored of it. In fact, I intended to. Her body was mine. Her soul was mine.

"I thought your pussy was the tightest fucking hole on this planet, Tally. But fucking your ass is unreal." I thrust farther, letting her reactions to me set the pace, giving her my full length in slow, deliberate strokes. She was blissed out, a deep moan filling every silent second. The vein in her neck thrashed against skin as she tossed her head backwards. "That's it, love. Get lost."

I thought I couldn't handle having my cock in her mouth, but holding off on this woman now was an Olympic sport. My body was screaming to release. All this energy inside me had been pent up so long that when I let go, it was going to be uncontrollable.

Natalia's body started rocking against me on her own accord, her hips swiveling in small circles, inviting me in farther. I rubbed two fingers against her clit, working her in both places and sliding my touch down to her unused entrance, teasing them inside.

She thrashed, grabbing my hand and holding it there. "Please, Matty."

"Tell me with those perfect lips what you're asking for." I knew what she wanted, and I was going to give it to her, but I loved hearing her say it in my own torturously degrading way. "If you're going to be a slut, commit to it, Tal."

"I want both." She picked up the pink toy beside her and brought it to the apex of her thighs. I took it and slapped it eagerly against the hood of her clit. Jolts of pleasure racked her, and she rested a heel at the small of my back, bracing for the moment I penetrated her.

My hips bottomed out against her ass and I stopped, feeling

her whole body swell around me. Lust clouded my brain like a fog. "You want to be used, huh? One cock isn't enough for you?"

Natalia tugged her bottom lip between her teeth, shaking her head. She loved it when I spoke to her like this, but she still got shy regardless. I adored that willingness. I wanted her to have everything she desired in a partner out of me, and I cradled the trust she put in the palm of my hands to give her just that. Degradation wasn't for everyone, but she had her reasons, and I had my limits. We danced on the edge of that.

She sat up on her elbows and watched me slowly dip the first inch inside her. My own breath chased itself as I felt the intrusion through the thin layer of skin separating my cock from the toy. I puffed my cheeks, keeping my composure, and let her pussy swallow the dildo right down to the base where my knuckles met her flesh in a single stroke.

"Fuck me," I cursed, dropping my chin to my chest, overwhelmed by the act, the feeling, the rush, the fucking dynamic between us that widened my boundaries and rewarded every last one of my sick fantasies. Tally's fingers threaded through my sweat-damp hair, and my free hand tightened around her waist. The room was spinning; I didn't know up or down. I just knew my wrist was working the toy inside of her, and my hips were pounding into soft, buttery flesh.

"You fill me so good, baby," she mumbled. "I love feeling you everywhere."

"You say the prettiest things when you're being fucked like a whore." Her mouth fell into a soft *O* shape. "That's okay, honey. Because you're such a perfect one for me. Just like you should be."

Her body started to quiver and I knew the first waves of a building orgasm were barreling through her. She dug her sharp nails into my biceps, her sounds flowing more freely as I bared down, giving her everything I could in languid strokes and short snaps of my wrist. The mix of her arousal and the lube made everything so *wet*. It was hard to pace myself. I knew the second she started to come undone I was going to be right behind her.

The tightening in my groin grew more and more fierce every time I jerked my hips.

I wanted to punish her, bruise her, leave a mark for her to wear under her white dress while she ate breakfast with all of our best friends in the morning. I wanted her to still be sticky with my cum between her legs.

"You are fucking everything," I gritted out. "I want you to let go again when you come, Tally. I want to hear you scream my name, so everyone in this house can hear it, too." I guided her hand to the toy and let her take the reins. She did without skipping a beat, pleasuring herself to the same rhythm as my cock in her tight ass.

"Oh my *god*," she reeled. Another wave of trembling passed through her. Her legs stiffened, arms pulling taut, and before her neck could give out I grabbed her face with two hands and crashed my mouth over hers.

Tally wailed my name in drawn-out syllables, convulsing and squeezing me to a standstill with every one of her lower muscles. My hips had nowhere to go, my thrusts stuttered, and as soon as I felt her orgasm fully wash over, covering us both in a mess of pure ecstasy-driven arousal, my climax followed furiously.

I painted her insides, her ass as I pulled out, the pink lips of her pussy, the short hair between her thighs. I came so fucking hard that I saw white light flashing in my eyes and I forgot how to breathe until I was gasping for air and collapsed half on top of her.

What a phenomenal high to come down from.

We were both naked, flushed, and absolutely filthy but I laid my head across her stomach, pulling her thigh tight to cradle in one of my arms. I felt peace listening to her heartbeat settle behind her ribs, like ambient noise had finally leveled out our loud, overstimulated life.

This was a breakthrough for us, and I didn't want to let it get away again.

With gentle fingers I gathered what was dripping of me

between her legs, and like an afterthought pressed it inside of her. "Is it just me or was the other guy kind of quiet?"

Her sweet laugh lit up the room like birdsong, and it was better than music. To make my girl smile was one thing, but to make her laugh—it plucked at my heart in ways I never knew before I met her. It was my favorite sound, and like ocean waves, howling wolves, palm leaves in the breeze, and soft sighs in the late afternoon, it was the sound of us. If you put all of those things together, somewhere our story was written in the score.

chapter twenty-three

Natalia

I COULD EXPLAIN MYSELF.

There was probably a very specific, psychological reason behind why I enjoyed being degraded in bed. Maybe something about my childhood trauma, the chemicals in my brain, my self-esteem issues, or all those subliminal thoughts I had about myself and my career that floated about in my head, daily. I was sure that it was very closely related to my relationship with my father, and how I saw myself beside my sisters also contributing a small bit. But for me it really came down to one thing.

Safety.

Mateo was where I felt safe.

Calling a sex worker a whore in the name of sexual gratification was twisted in and of itself. If it were any other man, I would be running in the other direction. Actually, scratch that, I would be throwing a right hook and ball tapping the bastard at the same time.

But the difference was that I knew Mateo didn't mean those words. He was taking control of them, letting me be in charge of how those words affected me. When we're finished having sex, and the fog has cleared, it's just him and me and nothing but pure love. Those words mean nothing.

They do leave an ache though. As does being double penetrated and wrung out all night by a well-endowed man. I realized when the sun in Las Vegas brightened the bedroom to dusky purple the next morning that I could still feel the pressure of Matty between my legs. I'd slept like an absolute rock. His side of the bed was empty but there was a steaming cup of coffee on the bedside table, next to a glass of water, two Advils, and a mini Gatorade.

There was stirring on the floor below, pots and pans being clinked together in the kitchen, the muffled sound of conversation. A full, animated smile filled my face.

This was everything I ever wanted.

Engaged to the love of my life, fully satisfied sexually, the gorgeous Nevada desert landscape in front of me, all of my best friends to share this experience with waiting downstairs. It was going to be the best day of my life. I could feel it.

The shower was still wet when I ambled into it slowly. Mateo was a stealthy motherfucker when he wanted to be. I washed myself under the waterfall shower head, feeling every last place his hands had been on my body hours ago. The dull pain ignited my interest again, and I slid my fingers through my core with soap, hissing at the tiny sting and soreness where I'd been stretched open. I got dressed and twirled down the staircase to the second floor where everyone was bouncing around between the living room and the kitchen.

"Good morning, bride-to-be!" Ophelia beamed. "Breakfast is served, and you can thank Tyler Swan for these muffins. He was awake making them before I even got in here."

An impressed hum vibrated my chest as I circled the warm blueberry muffins and took a bite of one. "Wow, Tyler. I have to admit, I never would have pinned you for a baker."

You could maybe roll some dough out on his washboard abs that he never seemed to put away. Tyler and Sam both, perpetually shirtless, riddled with tattoos and endless charm. My sisters were the least bit coy about watching them from the couch across the room.

I took a muffin to the recliner out of earshot. "When was the last time you three got laid?"

Isabella turned to me wearing undereye patches with black coffee filling her mug. "We know when the last time you got laid was."

Heat crawled up my neck and I shot a look out to the veranda where Mateo was pacing on his cellphone. He turned and saw me, and a smile lit up his face.

"I have a very colorful sex life, thank you very much," Mia said. "I work with a lot of tradesmen as a realtor, and man are those blue-collared boys easier than opening a straw."

"Just put your tongues back in your mouths," I said. "I could hear you panting from the kitchen."

"Again, why are we not supposed to be flirting with the groomsmen? The *single* groomsmen?" Camilla elaborated. "They're flirting with us."

"No they're not." I rolled my eyes. "Mateo told them you guys were like sisters and sisters are off-limits."

"The forbidden fruit tastes the sweetest." Bella shrugged. "If you think walking around in shorts that short, hanging that low, baking us muffins, and doing it shirtless isn't flirting, I worry how you bagged a husband."

"Tyler made these muffins for me," I pouted.

Mateo finally filed in from the deck, shoving his cellphone into his pocket and walking over to the couch. "Morning." He leaned in to kiss me. "How are you feeling?"

"Good." I pulled my bottom lip between my teeth. "Little banged up, but I'll definitely manage."

A retching sound came from Bella and I swatted her arm.

Frankie and Phee joined us from the kitchen, followed by the Swans wiggling themselves onto the couch in the tight, open spaces. Angelo brought a plate full of food into the living room and bent over the coffee table, inhaling it like a garbage disposal.

"It's our only full day in Vegas, and we're going to need every minute of it." Phee hopped up from the couch and retrieved her clipboard. "Who's up to hike the Red Rocks early?" An awkward silence followed, and O pulled a pink disco ball pen out and scratched the top item off the page forcefully. "I guess we can go straight into the scavenger hunt."

The energy shifted and both Swan brothers sat up eagerly.

"We're listening," Sam spurred her on.

Frankie went to Ophelia's side with a stack of paper like a pop quiz was about to be handed out.

"We're going out to the Strip today, and while we're there I have these curated lists of scavenger hunt items to check off. It's supposed to be *fun*," she stressed. "But there are definitely stakes at play here."

Frankie passed each of us the list that was typed and printed on graphically designed, full color paper. There were cactuses and flamingo clip art, pink lettering, framed check boxes—the whole nine.

"You're fucking adorable, O." Tyler Swan grinned from his tight spot on the couch. He kicked his feet up onto the ottoman and got comfortable reading the items on the list.

"I know there's a few of these that some of us can't exactly partake in," she admitted. "But that just means the rest of your team will need to pick up the slack. Since it's even on both sides, that shouldn't be an issue."

"So it's bridesmaids versus groomsmen?" Camilla asked.

"Yes."

Mateo was already focused on his list when I started reading mine.

Photo with a street performer. Easy enough. There were hundreds of those walking up and down the Strip at any given moment of the day. *Blow Job shot.* I smirked and looked around at everyone else with their noses buried in their paper. *Switch clothes with a stranger.* Interesting, and not as simple as the first two. I was impressed with Ophelia's creativity. *Lap dance.* Mateo and Frankie wouldn't be caught dead. Similarly to the item *kiss someone you just met.*

There were several others. *Gather a crowd, sing karaoke, find an Elvis impersonator, find another guy with the groom's name, blow on dice at a gambling table,* and *get a DJ to play your song request* were just a few. I loved how much thought had been put into all of this. It was clearly planned for several weeks, months probably, knowing Ophelia. Mateo and I struck gold with our best friends, and it was the cherry on top when they also fell in love. It was honestly a matter of time before our roles were reversed.

There was a buzz of excitement around the room. "Some of these are..."

"Out of the question," Matty finished for me.

"Someone's gotta do it, so I'll take one for the team and get the lap dance, boys," Tyler said regretfully.

Sam shook his head. "These are pretty good, O. Sounds like a challenge, and I love those."

"What does the winner get?" Angelo asked.

"It's not what the winner gets, it's what punishment goes to the losing team," Frankie explained.

"Losers will have to choreograph a group dance to perform at the wedding reception," Phee announced.

"Oh fuck no, I do not dance," Mia spat.

"Then you better win," Angelo fired back.

Tyler stretched his arms across the back of the couch. "Ladies, I hate to break this to you, but there is absolutely no way in hell you can win this thing. Not even with tape over my mouth and my hands tied behind my back." Bella stood, taking her list with her. "You'd look even prettier like that, though."

"You two." Mateo gestured like he was spraying two feral cats with water. "Cut it out." His phone rang in his pocket and distracted him from the kittenish look my sister and his friend shared. I was too blasé to be irritated, and at the end of the day Tyler Swan was probably the best candidate for a one-night stand because the guy was a revolving door of women. *Godspeed, Bella.*

My fiancé put his palm over the receiver on his phone. "I have to take this quick."

"Is everyone good with this?" Frankie chimed in. "We can all go shower, get put together, and reconvene here in an hour."

Good? Yes. Scared? Definitely. Exhilarated? That was the closest word to what I felt. A bachelorette scavenger hunt in Las Vegas that would determine who had bragging rights for foreseeably the rest of our lives. I gave Frankie and Ophelia the thumbs-up.

"Perfect," Phee squealed. "Pink outfits today, girls. Minus you, Nat, white and glam. Do you need help?"

I laughed. "I can manage."

"Don't forget your sunscreen. Sunglasses, hair ties, lip balm, wallets. I'll have extra too."

"I could really use you on a day-to-day basis," Camilla said.

The room dispersed to get ready for the day, that little spark of competition like a shot of espresso in everyone's coffee cup. When I stood from the couch I noticed Angelo had started down the hallway toward where Mateo disappeared, and I craned my neck curiously as I watched him head up the stairs first.

chapter twenty-four

Mateo

"YES, I understand how dire this is, Stephen. But it's a Saturday, and I'm at my bachelor party in Las Vegas. This isn't exactly a remote job, especially if you're telling me the service is hacked." I pinched the bridge of my nose, inhaling an unsteady breath as I paced the bedroom in a circle. "Trust me, I would have a direct notification, and there are several firewalls in place to keep that type of thing from happening. Unless for some reason you have Edward Snowden on your case, I'm fairly confident what you're experiencing isn't a breach of security. Have you checked with your service provider? Outages happen this time of year, especially in a storm."

The crackling voice of the elderly man who owned a family-run hardware store in Coconut Creek berated me on the other line. He was one of my newer clients, and so far had me doing pro bono computer tech work for him despite that not being the job I was hired for. Guy was a Korean War veteran, though, and you could call me a sucker but I couldn't tell him no—no matter *how* ridiculous the request got. My email was set to be out of office for the weekend but it hadn't kept him from dialing my personal cell-phone number for office-related issues.

He likely didn't even check his email, and the address he'd given me was for the sake of completing my onboarding.

"No, no, no, I can't help you with a wireless outage. I know we were due for a tropical storm, that could be it."

A beat passed.

"Well if it's raining cats and dogs like you say, there ought to be a whole block of internet out. Trust me, Stephen, you are not being hacked. Your security is perfectly fine. No one is gathering your personal information to sell to the government."

There was a knock on the bedroom door and I dropped the phone to my chest, covering the receiver. "Yeah?" I called out.

"It's me." Angelo pushed inside the room.

I lifted a finger toward him and put the cell back to my ear. "Okay, yes. Yes, definitely check in with the ladies at the coffee shop next door, or use the landline and call the cable company. I'll be back Monday if this is still giving you a problem. Great, perfect, I will tell my fiancée you said so. Okay, Stephen, right, thanks, bye. Oh, don't you worry about that, thank you, I'll behave...bye now."

I tossed my phone onto the bed and squeezed my eyes shut until I saw shapes.

"Work?" Angelo walked over to the large window and leaned against the sill.

"I can't catch a break." I sighed.

My brother crossed his arms and twisted his lips. "You know, I was thinking... Maybe I could be the one to help you out."

"How so?"

"You haven't hired anyone because you want a guy you know and trust, you said it yourself. Frankie was that partner for you, and now you don't have him, but I'm willing to give it a go if you're looking to fill that spot. I'll put in the work. Dad had enough faith in me to let me tie off loose ends for D&S and I understand this is something just as important."

My eyebrows threaded together and I turned toward him fully. "How the hell are you going to work for me if you live in New York?" I'd shocked myself by not completely shutting the offer down as soon as it left his mouth. I was desperate, or hopeful, something in between.

"That's the thing." Ang opened his hands and started waving them around in the way I often did when I talked, the way our mother and father did, the only way we knew how to properly articulate ourselves. "You're down south, Ma and Pop are going to be there now, and Duran & Son is caput. I know I can find another trade skill or carpentry job to do in the Bronx, but I miss the family."

My hard stare softened.

"If you're all in Florida, maybe I might do well with a change myself. I'm not going to fucking move in with you or anything crazy," he stressed. "But I'm pretty quick to learn new things, and I want to be helpful. We could make Mom and Dad proud seeing both their sons finally working on something together like they always wanted."

I opened my mouth to protest, closed it, opened it again, and my thoughts of how terrible that idea was languished on my tongue. "It's something to think about," I said. "I'm not even supposed to be having this conversation right now. I'm supposed to be downstairs enjoying a fucking party, getting ready to go do ridiculous things in Las Vegas for the next twenty-four hours, and having sex with my fiancée without our mother down the fucking hallway for the first time in five months."

"I can tell how badly this is stressing you out," Angelo said. "And I thought taking the burden of hiring someone off your shoulders might loosen you up a bit. You can't do it all on your own." He shrugged. "Well, you can, but look where that's gotten you. Taking work calls in the middle of your bachelor party."

"I'll deal with it," I shot back. "After this weekend we can revisit you coming to work for me and this whole thing about Mom and Dad buying a house in Florida. Now's not the time."

The bedroom door that was left cracked open creaked on the hinges and Natalia slid out from the shadow behind it. My blood froze, and my heart leapt into my throat.

"Your parents bought a house?"

"Tal." I stepped toward her. "I was going to explain everything to you when it was a better time."

Her jaw tensed and relaxed and she looked back and forth between Angelo and me. "You were never trying to hire anyone, were you?"

"Of course I was." I rubbed the back of my neck. Thinking on my toes was once my strongest suit. Now I was tripping over all the excuses and lies piling up in my head trying to make two things meet in the middle and soften the blow. It was past the point of that. I couldn't do it anymore. "I mean, I wanted to. There were a lot more semantics involved, and it wasn't the right time."

"You had *months*," she emphasized. "You watched me struggle without a partner at home, left me out to dry, fending for myself thinking *I* was the one being selfish for wishing you would come home for dinner when you had so much on your plate at work. You were staying away on purpose. To punish me for inviting your parents to stay, or something."

My entire body recoiled. That had never crossed my mind, nor did I think Natalia would ever come to such a ridiculous conclusion. I had actively tried to keep my parents on a leash around her. "Do you really think I would do that?"

Tally's face paled and her lips parted in small surprise. She dragged a thin breath through her teeth. "I don't understand why you would lie about it, Mateo. I thought we talked about this. I thought we agreed that the *secrets* were over, the *lies* were over. Or was that just referring to me? I can't hold onto things in our relationship, but you can?"

"No," I said. "It's not the same thing. This...this is not...this is *work*. Okay? It had nothing to do with you; it had no bearing on anything. You were keeping a fucking prenup from me, Tally. That is between us, very much so between us. You can't possibly compare the two."

"Does your parents moving into our backyard have no

bearing on our relationship?" she spat back. "Because you had plenty of chances between rounds fucking me last night to tell me that, and you didn't. So I'm going to assume it was another thing I didn't need to know, according to you."

"I'm gonna..." Angelo gestured to the doorway and slipped quietly from the room, shooting me a sorry empathetic expression on his way out.

"That's not fair," I scoffed, leaning my hip against the wooden dresser. "Everything I do has a purpose, Natalia. All the decisions I make, the things I keep to myself, it's for a reason. You didn't need to know about my parents yet, because I was trying to save the weekend from crashing and burning. But I should have fucking known it would anyway."

"You don't get to decide what I need to know, Matty. And lying about actively interviewing is a pretty big fucking deal, regardless of if it affects me or not. And it did, by the way. It affected everything. You've been missing from our life, stressed, working late, abandoning me with your parents..." She squeezed her little fists together and closed her eyes. "I know it was my idea to have them stay, but we agreed to take it on *together*. We made a fucking promise. We made a lot of promises that *I* am the only one honoring."

I bit my cheek so hard I tasted iron. We were both angry, and hurt, twisted too tightly to communicate, and I was a stubborn yank who wanted her to trust me, blindly, because I loved her and I would never hurt her purposely and I couldn't see why she wasn't understanding that. My chest was so tight it felt like I was choking on air, clawing my way to a surface that was farther and farther away with each reach. I had to clench my palms to keep my fingers from shaking.

"Why did you lie?" she asked. "What is the purpose you're so adamant about?"

"To protect you," I said sternly.

"Protect me from what, Mateo?"

"Me! To protect you from me. From all this shit going on in

my head I didn't want you worrying about. You have enough going on." I sighed out a long breath and several shorter, more stilted ones followed. I swallowed a wave of nausea and focused on a crack in the wooden floorboards trying to ground myself.

"I *want* to worry about you," Tally stressed. She was too far away and my hands ached to grab her and pull her to me, shake her into seeing where I was coming from. "I *want* to get through things with you. I *want* you to look to me for fucking support." Her voice caught and my eyes darted from the floor to her face.

"I do." I took an urgent step forward and she took one back that stopped me in my tracks.

"We're supposed to be partners, Mateo. Partners in this, in life. Figuring it out together. We are getting *married* in less than a month, and you're still worried I might not be able to handle parts of you. When I said yes, it wasn't to a ring, it was to you. Everything that comes with you. Everything you haven't dealt with yet. I didn't realize there were caveats and exceptions."

"Don't do that," I said. "Don't back away. Don't *try* to hurt me when the pain you're feeling was unintentional."

"It was mediated!" she snarled. "You knew I would react this way eventually, and you were putting it off. You were trying to save your precious bachelor party from Natalia getting angry and losing her shit again."

"I found out about my parents yesterday," I reasoned. "If I knew trying to save this weekend from turning to shit would make me the bad guy I wouldn't have done it. I would have told you everything instead of letting you enjoy Vegas with your sisters and your girlfriend."

Natalia put both hands on her hips and threw her head back, staring at the ceiling. "You know what, you're right. I am going to enjoy my weekend in Vegas. I'm not going to let this get to me, because I deserve it. I'm going to win a fucking scavenger hunt, too."

She stormed past me toward the bathroom like a gust of wind, setting me off balance. Before I could argue with her the door slid closed and the lock latched.

I knew I fucked up. When Natalia was in her moods she was deep in them. We butted heads over ridiculous things like laundry and watching a show while the other was at work, but this was more real than that. We didn't *fight* like this. We'd never had grounds to more than disagree with each other; it was one of the reasons we were so compatible.

Maybe this was inevitable, like she'd said. I still wasn't convinced that my intentions were *all* misguided. She was making me second-guess everything I'd done in the last six months while trying to save us from this exact thing happening. I'd sabotaged myself worrying about everyone else.

Approaching the bathroom door gently, I rapped my knuckles against it. "Tal, I'm sorry."

There was silence, and I held my breath hoping she might come meet me on the other side. Leaning in, I pressed my ear to the wood. She was thinking about it. I knew she was. We were stronger than this.

A moment later the hair dryer thrummed to life and snapped my hopefulness in half. It was a tight fist squeezing around my lungs.

If she needed the space I would give it to her. Unhappily, but understandably. This wouldn't last forever, but we would. I held onto that as I left her to get ready for the day, and slipped back downstairs alone.

chapter twenty-five

Mateo

"THE GIRLS LEFT HALF AN HOUR AGO."

Sam held his phone out, staring at the screen while my groomsmen and I waited at the edge of the villa driveway for our ride to pick us up. Try as I might to shake off the blow of the morning and pretend like everything was fine, the gallery of sorry looks when I came moping down the stairs said all they needed to.

"They're determined." Echo cracked his knuckles and did some calisthenic stretches on the scorching blacktop like we were running a marathon. The desert road was broad and pale, dust picking up with every shuffle of a step. "It's cute they needed that little head start. I wonder which thing on the list they're after first."

I checked my own phone with a sigh: nothing from Natalia. I'd watched her from the window in her white mini dress and sparkly ankle boots and nearly choked on my saliva. It was so perfectly her, flirty and tiny, feathers on the short skirt that showed off her toned tan legs. The other four followed into a Suburban wearing different shades of pink, and the saving grace was that they'd be easy to pick out in a crowd looking like a pack of flamingos.

Pike came to stand beside me, slapping a silver flask against my chest. "Drink."

My attention sliced toward him out of the corner of my eye and I took a generous swig without argument.

"It will blow over," he assured me. "You have to man up and take your licks. Won't be the last time."

Wink shoved his phone into the back pocket of his tan slacks. "What happened, anyway? Everyone seemed great this morning, then Tally came downstairs like a tornado and I'd hate to be the man that got in the way of that storm. What did you do?"

"You wouldn't survive it," I grumbled. "She overheard a conversation I wasn't ready to have with her yet."

"I was trying to help." Angelo shifted on his feet, fragments of pebbles and sand crunching beneath the rubber soles of his shoes. "For what it's worth, we didn't know she was being a little eavesdropper."

"It's her party, she's allowed wherever she wants to be." Angelo avoided my eyes, adjusting the collar of his shirt and plucking a string of lint off his chest. "Now I'm in hot water, and I'm not going to be able to think about anything but my impending groveling on the one day I didn't think I would need to. Leaving the families in Florida for the weekend was supposed to leave the drama behind too, but look at that, it just follows me around."

Wink shook my shoulder and wrapped an arm around me. I shrugged him off lazily. "You are strung tighter than a wire spool, man. Think about it this way. You and Tally are getting married, right? That's happening. You're deeply fucking in love with each other, and a little misunderstanding isn't going to throw that away. You both need to let off steam and find your way back. Let's do it the way we know best, which is getting drunk and scavenging. Friendly competition. I don't know about you guys, but this is my bread and butter."

"Hell yeah." Echo nodded. In the distance tires popped over gravel and an SUV started down the long flat road toward us like a mirage, heat bouncing off the hood in waves.

I wasn't operating in the present. All I could think about was hours from now talking to Natalia again, the days from now when we got home to confront my family, a month from now at our wedding, every year of the rest of my life and every moment that could be stressful: having kids, anniversaries, gatherings, vacations. My anxiety controlled me. I didn't want it to control this day, either.

The boys stared at me apprehensively and I threw everything to the wayside and stole the flask of rum back from Pike, taking another long drag of the sweet liquor as the taste burned down my throat.

"Boy howdy." Echo laughed. "The captain has boarded."

Pike waved at the approaching car as it pulled up to the curb. "Come on, Cap. We're going on a treasure hunt."

* * *

WE LET out on a busy sidewalk and were immediately lost in a crowd of early afternoon partygoers and performing buskers. The wind whistling through the tall alleys between hotels and restaurants was a reprieve from the heat, but despite it, my neck was clammy with sweat as I put a palm to it and turned in circles, orienting myself with the street signs and landmarks.

I found myself looking for Tally, too. Just a glimpse of her in the crowd somewhere, standing beside the spouting marble fountain, ducking into a hotel lobby, her feathery dress and sweet laugh mixing in with honking car horns and the distant bass of a drum thumping. I'd recognize that sound anywhere.

There was no Natalia, but there was a very intoxicated mime tripping over himself attempting to stand inside a glass box.

"First stop is drinks," Frankie suggested. "It'll make embarrassing ourselves more appetizing and hopefully unmemorable."

"All right, liquid courage," Sam said. "I've benefited from it a time or two."

Tyler scoffed, licking his lips. "We don't need any help. The drinks are purely ambiance. Some of this shit on the list is a regular fucking day for me."

"God, I pray one day you find a woman who puts you on your ass and turns you into something redeemable, Ech," I said.

He stretched, jutting his arms out and flexing them with a brutish grin. "Never going to happen."

My eyes rolled as I pulled the scavenger hunt list out of my pocket. "You guys go, I'm gonna try to map this out. It'll give me something to do to keep my mind off the other shit. Bring me something back though." I waved a finger between my groomsmen.

"I'll keep you company," Angelo said.

The last place I should have been was standing alone with my brother. I might think too hard about all the grief he'd caused me with my Natalia, and wring his neck in broad daylight. Despite it, I nodded and gestured to Pike, Wink, and Echo to take off so we didn't lose any more time.

My Delta buddies turned and started in the opposite direction, bumping shoulders as they disappeared into a sprout of people. I watched them for a few seconds too long, partially entranced by the bright lights and flaring neon signs, squinting to adjust to the hue of pink and orange reflecting from the massive hotel windows onto the street and realizing when I started smiling like a little kid that I was already nursing a buzz.

"I never said I was sorry." Angelo saddled up beside me. "I promise I'm going to do everything I can to win this little hunt for us. Your wife can't be mad at you and do a choreographed dance for you at the same time. It's scientific."

"If there's one thing you need to know about your sister-in-law, it's that if she wants to do something she will."

"Let's see the list." He plucked it from my hand and studied it with the same demeanor as our father reading the *Times* on Sunday mornings. Vague confusion, a pinch of concern. "Natalia will get over this, I know it. She'll realize you have her best interests at heart, the same way I did."

"Same way you did?"

"I was pissed at you too when you joined the Army and left me with Mom and Dad and a family business neither you or I wanted." He chuckled. "Maybe I didn't act like it a lot back then, but you were the only person I ever cared about not disappointing."

I cut him a glare. "You used to steal my ID to buy cigarettes at the bodega."

"You used to flush them down the toilet so that Mom and Dad didn't find out."

"Because you're an idiot and I wasn't about to be an accomplice."

I thought about being eighteen again, right before I left for boot camp, still sharing a bedroom with Angelo who would reluctantly, but always, get up and make his bed after I did. The same kid who would leave his beard trimmings in our sink but never leave the house without a clean shave like mine, and hop in the passenger seat of my beat-up Pontiac and put his feet up on the dash but never try to change the music I liked to play on the radio.

"Every stupid thing I did was to try to get your attention. If you didn't throw the cigarettes out, it meant you didn't care. Even if you chewed me out for it, it was better than you not giving a fuck about what I was doing."

"You've been getting yourself in trouble long after I joined." I looked over his shoulder at the scavenger list but I wasn't reading anything. "When I wasn't there to pay attention."

"Yeah, and then I realized that no one else did. I was pissed at you for leaving me because you were doing the one thing that I couldn't follow. I had two more years of high school, and by then I was...bitter." The word came out like it was stuck between his teeth. "When I could have enlisted, I didn't because Dad would have killed me, Mom would have guilt tripped me, and I was checked out, involved with the wrong people. You know the story. The easiest thing I could have done was stay in the basement with my guaranteed union job and hand-me-down business, because at least that made me feel important."

I pulled in a deep breath and lifted my chin toward the sky, watching the spattering of long, thin clouds draped over Sin City amble slowly in a direction I couldn't place. When considering how leaving for the military affected my brother, I had lapsed—significantly. He was too young and proud to be this honest with me way back then, and I was too clouded by the need to get the fuck out of New York to care about anyone but myself. I'd kept that same energy until this past year. I realized that leaving and putting a barrier between my new life and my old one was selfish. It was childish, it was running away from the problem. Which I was still guilty of because I'd been doing it for the last six months with Natalia by purposely keeping her naive to the real, penetrating mental health issues I was ignoring.

Figuring this all out while drunk wasn't ideal. I needed to tell *her* this, but she was so pissed off at me she was probably somewhere across town getting a lap dance by a Chippendale and checking boxes off. Enjoying herself, like she said she would.

"You know, I was jealous of you, in a lot of ways," I confessed.

Angelo's cheeks dimpled. "Me?"

"Yeah, because in Mom and Dad's eyes you couldn't do anything wrong. You got the youngest child treatment, squeaking by in life. No rent payment, no strenuous responsibility, a regular eight to four—"

"I'd like to see you haul sheetrock without breaking a sweat."

I punched out a laugh. "I wanted to be home so many times when I was deployed. Literally yearned for it. My bedroom, the sounds of the city past the window, the homemade meals. I'd hear all this shit about you getting involved with the wrong people, getting in trouble, and it looked like you were just throwing the privilege away, and it fucking aggravated me. I wanted to have my cake and eat it too, and I'm sorry."

That was something I'd never said out loud. I pretended I was aloof so I didn't have to come to terms with being homesick, with being envious of my brother for having it easier than I did, even though I made the decision to join the Army all on my own because I'd already convinced myself I hated home. Anything else was unacceptable, a weakness. Now that I'd admitted it, my chest opened like adding a link to a chain, loosening the gate it was keeping closed.

"Now this shit is happening with Tally for the same reasons, because I wanted to impress everyone with how perfectly I held it all together. I didn't take any accountability and now I've ruined the entire trip and she wants to kill me."

"You are the man, Matty boy. The fucking man. Don't think for a second you're not." My brother gave my shoulder a squeeze, and his light eyes softened contemplatively. "She's in love with you, she's perfect for you, and she's going to come around when you get your big Italian head out of your ass. You just have to give her space for like..." He checked his watch. "More than two hours. This is some Romeo and Juliet shit."

Giving her space made my hands itch. Distance from this woman was like being weaned off an addiction. I couldn't go two whole *minutes* without thinking about her, and it had nothing to do with her being angry at me. That's just where my brain traveled, to Tally. What she was doing, thinking, wearing, saying. To marry a woman I was this mind-numbingly obsessed with was the real privilege.

The night before in the bedroom replayed like a highlight reel in my head, and it would until the day I fucking died. But it felt wrong to fantasize about it on a city sidewalk knowing she was so pissed off at me. Like I didn't even deserve to think about her naked. I needed to punish myself. Go to mind jail.

"Okay, the list, the fucking list." I tapped on the paper and squeezed my eyes hard enough for a manual factory reset, sending a burst of color into my vision.

"Right, right. Back to that." Angelo tutted, scanning the columns as two women in barely-there clothing sauntered by wearing large, extravagant wings and rhinestone heels. Their faces were painted and jewelry ran up their arms and around their necks. My brother's face lit up and he shoved the list into his pants pocket. "Here we go, we can check this one off right now. Photo with a street performer." Angelo waved them over. "Would you ladies take a photo with my brother? He's getting married."

"No, come on, not me." I backed away, but the two women surrounded me in a fit of giggles and posed.

Angelo pulled his phone out. "It's all in good fun."

My glare intensified as a foreign hand landed at the small of my back. "You get in here instead."

"Too late, say cheese."

His camera shuttered with a flash. I didn't smile. I didn't fucking move a muscle. My hands remained at my sides like a little kid whose father took him to Hooters on his bi-weekly custody visit.

Angelo leaned in awkwardly and cleared his throat. "You got a couple bucks on you?"

"Are you serious?" I deadpanned.

"I mean, you gotta tip the ladies. Look at this." He fluffed a pink feather on one of the performers and jingled a hanging bead with his fingers. "Extravagant. Gotta be hell to dry clean."

"After all that mushy, pour-my-heart-out shit and you're still a goddamn pain in my ass, Ang." Tugging my wallet from my pocket, I handed the girls a few bills and they skipped past my groomsmen who were heading back toward us juggling several tall drinks. Echo broke his neck to take them in from every angle.

Pike handed me a cocktail so strong it hit the back of my throat and burned like battery acid all the way to the empty pit of my stomach. "You guys good? Everybody sorted? Let's get this party started."

"One down," Angelo announced. He rooted around in his pockets, looking for something, then came out with a tiny nub of a carpenter's pencil, crossing our item off. "Street performer."

"What's the game plan?" Wink was casing the streets with both brows furrowed, a habit he would probably never shake.

Not that we ever let our guards down, but when he was around it was easier to. Sam had a distinct way of keeping us all at ease. He didn't miss anything weird, out of place, unidentifiable. Perks of being a special operative sniper.

Pike swiped across a map screen on his phone, clicking on a dropped pin I realized was Ophelia's location. I rubbed my bottom lip between my fingers, the necessity of knowing making my pulse thrum eagerly in my neck. "Where are they?"

"I feel like watching their every move on a map is cheating," Echo pointed out.

"Like they're not doing it, too." Pike edged Tyler away with an elbow, shielding his screen. "Just keeping an eye on them in case."

"Let's ask ChatGPT," Angelo suggested as the swooping sound of a text being sent came from his phone.

"Now *that* is cheating," Tyler doubled down, pointing an accusing finger at my brother. "And insulting. We don't need a fucking robot telling us how to win a hunt. We *are* fucking hunters."

"Calm down, John Rambo. You can eat a cheeseburger without shooting the cow yourself. It's not telling us how to win, it's guiding us in the right direction."

"O purposely made the list AI proof. These aren't tourist tasks," Pike said. "Let's start at a casino."

"Is that where the girls are?" I asked.

"Cheating," Tyler added once more.

A text pinged in my pocket, then Pike, Echo, and Wink's phones simultaneously. I all but wretched my cell out of my pants. We all stared down at the message sent from Angelo to a group of the entire wedding party and a chill brushed across the back of my neck. "Angelo, what the fuck did you do?" My eyes snapped in his direction.

There on the screen was the photo of me between the two scantily clad street performers and the message, *On to the next one,* right underneath.

"What?" My brother looked around confused. "What's wrong?"

"'On to the next one'?" Pike pinched the bridge of his nose. "She's going to fucking peel the skin off his sack, man. You don't know Tally."

"On to the next one, like, the next item on the list," Angelo explained, a sliver of panic making his voice tremble. "How are we supposed to win if we don't send our proof?"

I paced the dirty concrete sidewalk, feeling my blood pressure rise. The fear of death was somehow easier, and more peaceful, than the fear of my fiancée and what she could unleash if she ever saw the need. I was afraid of her in the healthiest of ways. The way a man *should* fear his woman. "I have to kill you," I decided, taking a lunging step toward my brother.

"Woah, WOAH. Wait!" He threw his hands up, defending himself from mine finding their way around his thick neck. Sam put himself between us, and Pike pulled me back.

"It's the only way. She'll see it as a necessary sacrifice and forgive me," I reasoned. I broke free of Frankie and grabbed ahold of my brother's earlobe like we were children, yanking him harshly once before Echo stepped in and stiff-armed us both in opposite directions. "I'll make it quick and painless."

"This isn't doing us any good," Pike said. "Take a breath. We'll fix this. We'll find them."

A sharp cramping feeling hit my gut. I swallowed the panic in slow gulps, recentering by reading the names of the businesses on the buildings around us, counting the tips of my fingers tapping against one another. I'd gone from one less than ideal situation to an even more intensely rupturing one. The post had moved, but the goal remained the same: win back my wife.

chapter twenty-six

Natalia

IT TOOK everything in me not to fling my phone into oncoming traffic on the busy central highway through Vegas. My expression was unbothered, save for the slight twitch of an eyeball that I was sure none of my bridesmaids had caught. If they had, they were doing an admirable job pretending they hadn't.

Maybe it was unfair of me to expect Mateo to come begging on his knees for forgiveness after I'd given the explicit impression that was the last thing I wanted. It was me who ignored his apology. Me who left the villa without him, me who ignored him gawking out the window. I put that metaphorical space between us because I would always stand my ground.

But receiving a photo of my future husband sandwiched between two beautiful, chest-blessed women was fanning a tiny flame into something much hotter and more dangerous to put out.

"Are you sure you don't want that prenup?" Bella snorted. "I still have the draft."

"It's fine." I tucked my phone back into my bag with an annoyed sigh. "We just have to beat them at their own game. If Mateo wants to be petty, well, he knows who he's dealing with."

Ophelia squeezed my hand. "For what it's worth, it was Angelo who sent the text. Could all be a huge misunderstanding."

"I can't wait to give that mafioso weasel a piece of my mind," Mia said. She paced the crosswalk where we stood and slammed her fist against the signal button. "They're baiting us. Men are all the same, and unless you go down to the dirty, dingy ball sweat crawl space that is their level, they'll never get the hint."

"We'll find you some strippers, Talia," Camilla said. "It's only fair."

I scoffed. "Mateo would lose his mind."

"Exactly." Mia flailed her hands. "No one said we were playing a nice game. This is war, as far as I can tell. They took the first shot, and now we have to send one right back over. The first shirtless guy we see, it's on."

"There's a difference between vengeance and desperation," I countered.

Bella rolled her eyes. "Russo women are never desperate. We're *calculated*."

"Let's stick to the list," Phee suggested. The crosswalk signal beeped and we shuffled across the long two-lane highway, heels clacking against the pavement and sequined skirts glinting in the bright sunlight. "There's a pool party, and a DJ. We can strike a few of these off in no time and have them scrambling."

My bag started to buzz and I flung my dark hair over my shoulder, pulling my phone out. "It's Mateo," I said, skidding to a stop to search the crowds around us. Of course he wanted to reach out now, and similarly, every instinct in my body was telling me to pick up the phone, regardless of how much I wanted to throttle him. His name and a photo of us from Christmas day was staring back at me as I let it ring. "Should I answer?"

"No!" Mia lurched for the phone but I tugged it away.

"Don't give him the satisfaction," Camilla advised. "You're not at his beck and call."

I tugged my bottom lip between my teeth. "What if it's an emergency?"

"Oh, it's an emergency all right." Mia scoffed out a laugh.

"He's urgently trying to fix his screw-up. He can suffer until you're ready for him to crawl back."

"If it were an emergency Frankie would have called. He's under strict orders," Ophelia said. "I hate to say it, I'm with your sisters on this one."

There was an internal fight thrashing around in my head. I wanted to talk to him, and I *also* wanted to scream at him because I knew he would just listen and let me. I wanted to hear his voice, while *also* violently shaking him. I was a median on a busy high-way, two concurrent flowing forces beckoning me in either direction. I was so good at icing out everyone in my life, except for Mateo. He softened me to butter. He owned me. He was the only person I cared about caring about me, even after I put up a convincing-as-hell front this morning.

My phone skipped to voicemail and seconds later lit up again with another call from Mateo. I twisted my lips.

"Let me talk to him." Mia reached for my phone again and I let her take it. She folded an arm across her chest and stuck the receiver to her ear with an agitated sigh. "Yes, Mateo?"

I scooted closer but the only sound I could hear was a muffled voice full of panic. "Put it on speaker."

Mia pushed a waiting finger toward me, rolling her eyes at the voice on the other line.

"What is he saying?" Bella pressed.

My sister mockingly made a chatting hand movement, bringing a reluctant giggle to the tip of my tongue. "She doesn't want to talk to you," she said. "She's busy, with these guys who said they're in the Navy or something. Oh yeah, big sailor boys. They said they'd show us the best spot for a lap dance."

"Mia." I choked out a laugh, reaching for the cell, but she twirled in a circle away from me.

"Oh, that's going to chap some asses." Phee's eyes widened. "We've got minutes before the SWAT team arrives."

"'On to the next one'? Ariana Grande would be rolling in her tanning bed," Mia continued. "Hope you don't get a rash from those cheap-ass Temu rhinestone bras those girls were wearing, and tell your brother I can smell his bodega cologne all the way from the MGM Grand."

"Jesus, Mia," Cami snorted. "Tell him how you really feel."

"I mean, the audacity," Mia added. "You must be fucking high—oh, you're drunk? You know what, that's so rich, trying to find a cop-out. You're not getting off that easy."

"He said he's drunk?" I bit my tongue.

Mia clipped the phone between her shoulder and her ear and put two hands out, forming air quotes. "*Allegedly.*"

I was exasperated, and Mateo was clearly having his fun. It was my turn to throw that type of caution to the wind. God, I'd never been so frustrated with him before, and it hurt me more than I realized it could. *He* hurt me more than I realized he could, and I was unable to process it while trotting around Las Vegas on a bachelorette trip. All I knew was I wanted to make him feel the way I felt.

I grabbed Ophelia's hand and tugged her toward the sparkling facade of billboards on crystalline hotel blocks and the sign for a beach club calling out to me like a sermon. "You can hang up, Mia. We've got a game to win."

"Hope you guys got your fun little giggles in, because this is war now, *brother-in-law*. If you think you five play dirty, there's nothing quite like a woman scorned with a tag team of vengeful Russos...and Ophelia."

"Thanks." Phee shot her a pair of finger guns for support.

"You won't even know what hit you until you're two-stepping across the dance floor in Key West. Ciao."

I snatched my phone, Mateo's desperate voice called out my name in a last-ditch effort to sway me, and I ended the call before the little voice in my head convinced me to answer him back.

chapter twenty-seven

Mateo

WE WALKED twenty blocks with blind hope that the girls were a handful in the thousands of people swarming the pools and dance floor at a massive exorbitant beach club. Sand vibrated beneath our feet and anxiety beat like a low drum in my chest trying to wrangle the level of overstimulation. I tamped it down forcefully to keep my head on straight as it swiveled searching for my fiancée in the sea of inebriated ravers.

Pike threw his arm around my shoulder and tugged me into him. "They're here somewhere."

The only lead I had was the little bit of information my sister-in-law decided to give me in that god-awful, albeit warranted, phone call. Which brought us to the biggest, loudest, crowd control fiasco of my wildest nightmare. A *Where's Waldo?* would be easier than this.

"Mia mentioned the MGM Grand," I said. "They have to be. Let's just scope it out and move on. We might need to divide and conquer, though. Frankie, we'll take Angelo out toward the DJ. Wink, Echo, you two float around the pools and the bar."

"Roger." Tyler tugged his T-shirt over his head and tucked it into the waistband of his pants, letting it hang. It came as no surprise to anyone that it took Tyler less than five minutes to start stripping off his clothes. You couldn't teach an old dog new tricks. Especially not one at a busy dog park.

"They're out for blood with this scavenger list, so keep that in mind and don't be like my fucking brother." I glared at Angelo. "I swear to God if someone takes another photo of me with a woman even standing in the background you're going to find me floating face down in the fountain at Caesars Palace."

"Didn't she say they were with a bunch of Marines?" Sam asked. "I think you have bigger problems, Cap."

The thought of Natalia surrounded by a group of ogling men sent fire through my veins. I didn't mind the attention she got when it came to the work we did on camera. It wasn't the fucking same. She was safe with me, behind a screen, in our own home with a set of rules and boundaries, a pre-existing understanding of what's going on, and a partner who respected her more than anything in this world. I was well aware of how stunning my fiancée was and that given the option, she could have any goddamn man on the planet. Not for a second was I okay with being more than an arm's length away from her in a barrage of fuckboy bachelors trying to get laid in Las Vegas.

"Navy." I pushed the word through gritted teeth.

"At least it's not Marines," Angelo offered with a faint shrug. "Could have been Marines."

"I'm calling their bluff on that one. O knows better." Frankie shielded his eyes with his hand and lifted onto the balls of his feet to look over the crowd. My best friend had his heart broken once upon a time, but Ophelia had picked up all those little shards and hot glue gunned them back together in a way that changed him permanently. "Check your phones," he said. "Half an hour."

The Swans broke away, their tall, broad bodies still inches above the people around them after getting swallowed into the shuffle toward the pools. They were easy to pick out, yet effortlessly blended into whatever background they needed to when necessary, and I had trust in them the same way I trusted Pike. Plus, if anyone were to take this scavenger hunt to heart, it would be Sam and Tyler. My conscience breathed out a sigh of meta-phoric relief knowing the two most shameless competitors were on my team.

The venue split itself down the middle, and my brother and Frankie led the way through a plume of fog into the pit of people in front of the DJ. I stopped attempting to speak to them beyond hand gestures and facial expressions as a mind-numbing bass gonged in my ears. Through what game of charades we were play-ing, I understood we were circling the dance floor, making our way to the other edge and avoiding the shower of champagne from the bottle service models standing over the crowd at the edge of the stage. By the time we got there I'd had two drinks inadver-tently spilled on me, a high heel speared through the top of my foot, a puff of vape smoke that smelled like cotton candy hotdog burps blown in my face, and the will to live drained like a toddler with a Shirley Temple from my veins. No Natalia to be found.

That wave of anxiety was growing again. The loud music and tight spaces filled me with an untamable dread I could only breathe through until we arrived at the end of our search, still coming up empty.

"Fuck this!" I yelled out. Frankie followed me through the maze of bodies like an anchor until we hit a paved edge leading into a row of cabanas and ridiculous ride-on animals. I tugged in a jagged breath of air only the slightest bit less polluted, and Pike pointed ahead to a dark head of hair wearing a sparkly crown with a veil attached.

My ears popped from the pressure change. "It's not her."

"You can't even see her," Angelo said. "How do you know it's not her?"

"I just fucking do. That's not what the crown of her head looks like. Her hair was curly when she left the house, and that girl is too tall to be Tally. Keep moving. I'll know my wife when I see her."

"It's another bride." Pike shrugged, pointing at the list. "We have to find another bride."

I stuck my tongue in my cheek and put both hands on my hips. "Fine." I let up, reluctantly. The eagerness to win the game was still there despite the hiccups. "Quickly."

We shouldered through to the circle of women, and somehow unsurprisingly, the first voice and face I landed on wasn't a stranger at all. It was Mia. Standing there in her sequined mini skirt and familiar indignant scowl that should have been a warning in and of itself, but instead perked me right up.

Natalia was close.

The noise around me dissipated and I beelined toward my future sister-in-law who had already caught the attention of the other bride in that feminine, girl power way Natalia described a drunken bathroom stall visit was like for women. All giggles and handholding, complimenting each other like they'd known one another their entire lives. "Where is she?" I demanded.

Mia popped a hip out and stuck her hand to it as she slowly turned toward me. "Look who decided to finally show up."

"Well you didn't make it very easy, now did you?"

"You were busy." She squinted. "Now if you'll excuse me, I was taking a photo with this gorgeous, gorgeous girl and winning a scavenger hunt." She turned back to the brunette in her veil and lifted her phone to take a selfie. A moment later my phone buzzed in my pocket. Said photo, sent to the godforsaken group chat Angelo had started. Mia gave me a deprecating pat on the shoulder. "Maybe she doesn't want to be found, Mateo."

"Maybe not, but she'll have to send me away herself if that's the case. Quit making this harder for me to fix, Mia." I felt my brother and Pike at my back and strangely enough Mia's scowl deepened and her glare turned dark looking over my shoulder.

"Don't kill the messenger," Angelo chided.

"You greasy little meatball—" She pointed a sharp finger and I caught it right at my ear. You couldn't have pinned two more fiery, cocksure people against each other if you tried. Mia was a brat and Angelo was a dick. If taking on Tally didn't put me in an early grave, mediating these two would. They started fighting like siblings the second they got the chance, which should have been endearing, but this was a different kind of loathing I wasn't touching with a ten-foot pole.

"Little?" Angelo scoffed, taunting her. "Ain't nothing little here, sweetheart."

Mia stuck her pinky in the air toward him, and Pike and I turned our laughs in the opposite direction.

"Mia, please," Frankie cut in. "Point us in the right direction. We promise to be on our best behavior." He jutted his bottom lip out, and I recalled how charming and freshly kicked puppy my best friend could become if he really wanted to. It was a secret weapon.

She regaled him, crossing her arms and looking around. I followed her line of sight as though it would lead me right to Natalia but the crowd behind us was boundless and ever-changing. I could hardly see three heads away. "Tell you what," she said, tapping her lips with her finger and then gesturing toward the row of rideable animals only someone who lost a bet or was stupid drunk would be caught dead on. "If Mr. Gabagool can stay on that mechanical bull over there longer than me, I'll walk you right to her."

Alas.

I stuck my tongue in my cheek.

"Who's Mr. Gabagool?" Angelo asked.

"It's you," I said.

"Me?"

Mia cackled. "You."

Angelo scrubbed a hand down his short beard. "You know, that's kind of racist."

She was extremely proud of herself. There was no lack of venomous wit when it came to the Russo girls, I'd learned first-hand. Probably something to do with their upbringing; comedy came as a natural salve to the slow burn of childhood trauma.

Angelo pushed past me, knocking my shoulder and squaring right up to Mia and I could have sworn I saw a smile twitch at the corner of her lips. I braced for some sort of impact, because it felt inevitable, but my brother just tilted his head down toward her short frame and said, "You're on, little nightmare."

* * *

"THIS IS GOING TO BE BAD." I chewed the corner of my thumb as Mia stomped up to the mechanical bull attendant with the confidence of a sorority girl walking into a bar without a wallet.

"Entertaining," Pike supplied instead. "How's the anxiety?"

"Lethal." I was being honest. If anything else in my life went wrong I'd likely collapse under the unbearable weight of it all. "I don't know where my normal thoughts end and my obsessive, intrusive ones begin. Because not everything can be the end of the world, right? I am acutely aware of how much I stress myself out, in comparison to how much stress these things actually put on me, but I've yet to find that happy medium."

"Self-aware king."

I raised an eyebrow. "What the fuck did you just say?"

Pike's little smile flatlined and he cleared his throat. "It's nothing, just a dumb inside joke I have with O."

"Is this what Colorado is doing to you?" I shook my head. "What happened to the stoic, killer instinct, badass Delta fighter pilot I used to get in firefights with in the desert?"

Out of the corner of my eye I saw him shrug nonchalantly.

"You became a self-aware king?" I tossed back. "Man, what are these women doing to us?"

"Yours convinced you to fuck her in cosplay on camera."

We continued watching Mia chat the ear off the attendant. Angelo was a few feet behind, waiting his turn with a rapt determination—and a flare of annoyance. Finally, she kicked her heels to the side and looked like she might mount the thing, but at the last second realized how impossible it would be in a mini skirt without putting on a whole different kind of show.

She said a few indecipherable words, pointed to her ass, to the bull, back at the man—who looked just as happy to field her antics—and what I thought was an easy win for me and a step closer to getting back to Tally was stalled when the guy shimmied his own blocky beige cargo shorts off his hips and handed them to her.

"What's going on over here?" Bella and Camilla appeared with drinks in each hand. They noticed Mia at the receiving end of our attention, right as she pulled a complete stranger's clothes up and under her skirt, then unzipped it and stepped out, handing it to the attendant standing there in his underwear.

"Where's your sister?" I parried.

"Wouldn't you like to know," Bella quipped. Her short hair was in two tiny buns on the top of her head that I stifled the urge to tug on like a doorknob if someone didn't tell me where the fuck my fiancée was.

Mia hopped atop the bull in her new outfit and threw a mocking wink down at Angelo as the machine started to sway, bucking her slowly. I wasn't a betting man, but I'd say my luck dried up the same time Mia went from two hands on the saddle to one in the air like a cowgirl.

"She's done that one before." Bella whistled proudly. "That's my twin!"

Having never wished ill on a woman in my entire life, it was amazing how eagerly and unapologetically I wanted my future sister-in-law to get violently tossed like a rag doll off a mechanical bull. The longer she stayed put, the slimmer Angelo's chances of winning their little wager. Even Camilla, who was the most uptight of them all, was beaming proudly at her younger sibling as she got thrown side to side in concerning jerky movements.

She was more impressed with Mia dry humping the leather saddle than she was with Natalia's engagement. That said all it needed to about how far out of a hole I'd need to crawl to get my sister-in-laws to help me with Tally. I stole a drink out of Bella's hand and swallowed the throat-numbing liquid, immediately regretting it. "What the fuck is that?"

"Vodka water," Camilla said. "Gets you drunk, keeps you hydrated, and saves all the calories."

"Sometimes I wonder how you four ended up the way you did, and then I'm reminded you were hardwired to hate yourselves to the point of mixing hard liquor with water to appease your parents. Put some fucking cranberry juice in that cup and live a little bit, doc. It'll save you and Mia the UTI she's probably gonna have from grinding all over that dude's sweaty dick shorts."

Camilla frowned. "God, say what you really feel."

"You don't want me to."

Mia survived another ten seconds, which felt like ten minutes, before losing her grip and slipping gracefully off onto the foam pads below her. She skipped toward Angelo, dusting her hands off arrogantly, knowing her time would be hard to beat. Interestingly enough, my brother leaned down to her ear to say something that caught *her* off guard instead. Mia froze, eyes narrowing as he stepped around her with a grin on his face.

"Sweaty dick shorts or not, she knows what she's doing." Bella smiled. "Switch clothes with a stranger, check. Looks like you boys have some catching up to do."

The list felt like a rock in my pocket. I pulled it out, looking for an easy win while Ang climbed the bull in the distance. Mia returned to us like the female lead singer of a ska band in her mismatched outfit and wind-tousled hair, heels dangling from her hand.

"That is the most unironic walk of shame I've ever seen," Pike said. "Bravo."

"It's called taking one for the team." She looked back toward Angelo, crossing her arms over her chest. His clock had just started and the bull was already jolting him back and forth aggressively.

My phone rang in my pocket and tore my attention away.

Before I could get a word out Wink was already speaking. "We got eyes on Tally."

"Where?" My eyes darted toward Pike's and he nodded, understanding we were about to be on the move.

"Poolside bar with O. We'll step in, but you're gonna want to get over here, brother."

Fuck.

That meant one thing, and I wasn't in the headspace to deal with it sanely. In fact, I was in possibly the worst headspace I'd ever been when it came to Natalia, and I wasn't about to fend off drunken, handsy men around my woman calmly or collectively like I might in any other circumstance. I could handle the attention she got because it fed my ego to know other men wanted what I had and could *never* have themselves. But this time I was a little bit too over the edge. Too desperate.

Hurrying in the direction of the pools, Pike followed on my heels.

"Where are you going?" Bella yelled. "You're just going to leave your brother?!"

He would understand. Taking one for the team and all. We moved without turning back, without an answer, and the huge crowd swallowed us once more as I braved the living obstacle that was pushing back through to the other side.

chapter twenty-eight

Natalia

THE COVERED tiki bar was packed solid. Half of it dipped into the pool where there was a swim-up ledge with stools floating in the water and cocktail waitresses standing in the wake serving drinks. I squeezed my way through on landside to the sticky wooden bar top, wedging my elbows in and waving my hand at the woman behind it with a bottle of tequila flipped over, draining through a metal topper into a plastic cup. She twirled another bottle, bumping hips with a coworker as they both danced around each other making cocktails.

"Be right with ya." Her blonde bubble-braided pigtails slapped her shoulders, and the button on her jeans shorts was undone, showing off a peek of a bright blue bathing suit. She passed by, reaching for a bottle of orange juice out of a mini fridge and then backpedaled to a sliding cooler where she grabbed three glass bottles and wedged them between the webs of her fingers. Then she was gone again, to the far end of the long table top.

"Excuse me!" Phee uselessly called after her. A hundred grabby hands were waving at the bartender for attention, and ours were getting lost in the mix.

"What's a girl gotta do to get a drink around here?" I huffed. "If I'm sober I'll lose all the go-fuck-yourself confidence I've built up this morning, and we can't have that."

"Your go-fuck-yourself confidence outscales mine at its base, so I wouldn't worry too much about that."

"I don't think I've ever been this mad at him."

Ophelia's lips thinned. "Does this have to do with some X-rated stuff you don't want to talk about, because I totally get that and I'm not pressuring you at all, but it might feel good to let it out and get another perspective. I'll listen like a therapist, not a friend who's seen you doing the splits in reverse cowgirl."

My lips curved at the corners. "Have you been watching our streams?"

"I subscribed to support you, but curiosity got the best of me." Phee hid her face while mine lit up in a bright cackle. "I swear it was just one time. You told me about the steak slapping and I needed to see it for myself."

"That's true love. That's soulmate level shit, Phee. I can't believe I ever thought you might see me differently for my career choices." I threw my arm over her shoulder and she laughed alongside me. "How did it look, though?"

"Literally stunning. The lighting, the athleticism—you're unmatched."

"Mateo and I have something special," I sighed. "And it's not *all* about that. Our fight. We're just on completely different pages. He lied to me about how much work he's been doing at TechOps since Frankie left, and his parents bought a house in Florida without telling anyone, apparently, and he didn't think I'd be able to handle it. I know he's struggling, but he won't let me in."

Mateo's anxiety attack was at the tip of my tongue. I stopped myself before I went too far. It was his story to tell, and though I could use a person to confide in, the only one I would be helping was myself. I wouldn't break that trust no matter how hard it was to watch him take it on alone.

"You'll come out stronger together on the other end of this, Nat. I know you will, because Mateo is fucking obsessed with you. What you need to do at this moment is get a drink, remember you are that man's everything, and then beat him in a scavenger hunt so he has to perform an interpretive dance to prove his undying love for you in front of his entire family. We're already two steps ahead."

"You're right." A jolt of positivity needled up my spine, straightening my shoulders. This was still my bachelorette party; it was what we made of it. I adjusted my veiled crown purposefully and caught myself looking around at everyone perched on the edge of the circular bar, hoping my eyes might meet soft, familiar hazel ones.

"Of course I am." Ophelia's arm flew out, waving toward the bartender again.

"It's hard to get their attention." A man beside me brushed his arm against mine and I peeled it back, staring up at him. It might have been an accident, but the crooked smile said differently. One of his bottom teeth was jagged, there was a gap between the two middle, and he was wearing a bowling shirt with the name *Lance* sewn into the breast pocket. The hair at the top of his head was visibly thinning through a combover. "Let me buy that drink for you. Wedding gift."

I turned away, looking for the bartender. "No, thanks."

"Come on, what are you, here for a bachelorette party? Where's the rest of you?"

"In a much luckier position, I'm sure," Ophelia edged back.

I leaned away but the crowd was so thick it was difficult to fully move. "Uninterested."

"Don't be like that." He chuckled. "Isn't it the last night out or something? Final fling. What happens in Vegas stays in Vegas. It's just a drink."

"I said no." I turned back toward him with heat in my eyes. I'd gotten exceptionally good at telling men to fuck off online, but it was always nerve-wracking in person. You never knew how they would react. My guard was constantly up, unless I was with Mateo. "What is with you putrid predatory losers and the lack of comprehension? *No* is a full sentence, now find a hole in the desert and fall into it before someone does it for you and makes it look like an accident."

The guy looked me up and down with amusement, a snarl poking out between his chapped lips and I crossed my arms over my chest as a shield. Something caught his dark gaze behind me then, in his periphery, and his face paled. Brows arching, he stumbled back and bumped into the person behind him, sending their cup and a splash of red liquid onto the sand, and then he was quickly shoved sideways and out of the immediate area by a new throng of people competing for a sliver of pine at the bar top.

"Yeah, that's what I thought!" I boasted, giving Phee an impressed nudge. As I was patting myself on the back, two large bodies saddled up beside us, unbothered and slurping noisily from a straw. I didn't even need to look to realize it was in fact *not* me, but Sam and Tyler, who had scared the creep into a speechless, fumbling mess. The two stones of ex-military concrete known as the Swan brothers stood behind me and Ophelia like a blockade.

The bartender materialized out of thin air, glancing at the boys with a smirk. "Can I get you guys something?"

"We'll do two Blow Job shots," Sam said. "You ladies need a refreshment?"

"Please, vodka sodas," Phee ordered. "Doubles."

I blanched at Sam. "You're not serious."

"Thank God we were here." He clicked his tongue.

"I had that handled."

"I'm sure of it." He smiled in that sideways, charming way I'd only ever found harmless coming from Sam Swan. I could see how it might not be so harmless to any other woman in the world. "You're lucky it was us and not the other two."

He was probably right. The most intense I'd ever seen Mateo was when he stood up for me, and he very well might have taken Camilla's Chippendales comment to heart despite how ridiculous it was. Our emotions were heightened. Petty is as petty does.

"Does he even care?"

Tyler scoffed mirthfully. "You women are so smart, yet so unbelievably self-deprecating."

The bubble-braided bartender returned with our drinks and two frothy shots and placed them eagerly in front of the Swans.

"You're actually out of your mind," I said through a reluctant grin. "Can we get this on camera, actually? I'm saving it to warn the poor women you marry of the eye-shielding embarrassment they're getting themselves into."

"Put on the flash. We're in it to win it, baby." Tyler muscled to the table. It seemed like everyone around us dispersed to make room for the two of them to have their space. "Check it off the list, too."

They weren't kidding. I watched with a mix of pride and mild humiliation as my future husband's groomsmen, special forces veterans, and two of the most masculine men I'd ever met stood at the edge of the bar on either side of me, put their hands behind their backs, and deep-throated a whip-cream-covered shot glass without a shred of hesitation. A giggle bubbled from my throat as they lifted the glasses off the table with their mouths and threw their heads backwards, shooting the creamy liquor without spilling a drop.

My eyes pinched closed and a smile spread across my face. The whole thing plucked at something hopeful inside my chest, regardless of how it put our team at a disadvantage in the scavenger hunt. I didn't grow up with brothers, but I figured this was what it must have felt like. The ridiculous antics, the air of protectiveness, coming to my emotional rescue when they know I needed a pick-me-up.

Tyler licked his sticky fingers clean and ran his forearm across his mouth.

"Showboater," I said, elbowing him.

He shot me a wink.

I turned my back to the bar and looked out into the crowds of people around the pool. A significant area beneath a platform at the edge had been cleared to make room for something. People floated around in bright-colored tubes and flamingo-shaped floats. Like a magnetic pull, my eyes wandered to the opening in the dance floor as it split, and Mateo and Frankie poured out of the dense crowd. A pang hit my chest, like a single piece of thread being tugged, a sewing needle through my heart pointing toward his with the remaining stitch.

His wide hazel eyes found me in an instant. There was something hurt, but hopeful, in them, just the same as mine, and a flush of panic subsided to calm when he realized it was the four of us standing there.

"Did you tell them we were here?" I gestured toward Frankie and Matty.

"Of course." Tyler checked himself out in the sunglasses sitting on top of Ophelia's head. "Stop running away, girls. We'll always find you. Whether you want to be found or not."

The commotion at the pool reignited and Sam watched with rapt attention as a tall man in flagrant chrome sunglasses and layers of beaded necklaces hopped onto the small wooden stage with a microphone. The man waved his hands and the poolgoers cheered expectantly. "Who here's got the best belly flop in Las Vegas?"

"Oh, Jesus," I snorted. "Who in their right minds would ever voluntarily do that to themselves? In front of thousands of people, no less. We should get out of here before this gets too crazy. Looks like the entire place is about to be standing around this pool any second."

Sam glanced past me at his brother, then back to the pool. My face dropped. Not Sam. He was reverent, and quiet, an *observer*, perfectly melting into the background. The liquor shot was likely going to his head because a wicked grin stretched across his face and he pushed off the bar and started for the pool.

"He's joking, Tyler. Tell me he's joking." I took one worried step toward Sam and then looked back at his beaming brother. "What is *with* you two and public humiliation? This has to be some sort of kink."

"Wink never jokes about winning." Tyler whistled at him. "Hey, shirt! Pockets!"

Sam stalled briefly to peel off his shirt and strip down to his black boxer briefs, showing off trim muscle that accentuated a body full of traditional American tattoos. I caught his clothes clumsily as he tossed them back to us, and then he continued toward the water.

chapter twenty-nine

Mateo

A KNOT in my chest unfurled knowing Tally was within reach, in my sight, and there was no prowling creep in the vicinity—despite the way Wink made it feel like I would have to emerge from the crowd throwing fists.

Sam headed down toward the belly flop competition at the pool, taking his clothes off on the way. From early on in our military career it became obvious he had a motive for everything, so questioning that confidence was something I never stopped to do anymore. I did, however, tilt my head like an older brother watching his sibling make a mistake he would have to learn from.

The good news was it didn't look like Tally wanted to kill me anymore. Not as much as she did stomping away from me this morning, anyway. I wasn't stupid enough to think that meant anything close to a reconciliation. Natalia, like any other woman, had a very specific and intricate code pattern, and if you didn't hit every button precisely it was back to square one.

We both said things we probably regretted, and we'd both have to figure that out like adults do. We fought, we fucked up, we needed a little bit of time to let rash emotions form careful solutions, and the silver lining was that we had all the time in the world. I would approach this with a heed of optimism.

Pike started for the bar and I threw out my forearm to hold him back.

"Wait," I said. "Ask her if she'll come talk to me. I don't want to come off like I'm backing her into a corner she can't escape."

Pike's dark eyebrow arched. "You're overthinking this, like you always do."

"I'd rather be an overthinker than an underthinker and embarrass myself."

"This is so high school." Frankie heaved a sigh and scratched the hair at the back of his neck, walking away reluctantly.

A platform hung above the pool water where Wink waited in line with a handful of other men, looking entirely out of place among the rounder bellies. He stretched his arms above his head, then did some standing twists and a few high knees to limber himself. Natalia's sisters finally caught up, cutting through the crowd beside me with no lack of colorful complaints following.

I hushed them, pointing down at Sam.

"What is he doing?" Camilla asked. "Do you think he knows how many grown adults are peeing in that water?"

A grimace stretched across my face and I shook it away. "He's gathering a crowd, ladies. Looks like you're falling behind again."

We watched Sam step up to the edge of the stage to a chorus of cheering and whistling. It was unclear if this was a competition of who had the best flop or who could stay in the contest the longest, but I was putting my money on my sniper either way.

Frankie trudged back across the sand toward me with O and Tyler and I held my breath waiting for Tally to come, too.

"He's the most competitive person I know," Echo boasted. "And he also hates to dance, so he's taking this thing personally."

"There's an art to belly flops." Bella tilted her head. "You can do it without any pain if you land the right way."

"And you know this from experience?" I lifted a brow.

"Research."

Pike handed me a drink and a bar napkin with a scribble of pen on it. I squinted at it. "Tally wanted me to give you this."

She stared at me across the way as I unfolded it, and as easy as it was to read her mind when I was inside her, this was more of a reach. Judging by her choice to keep our distance, I might have been better off answering my own question.

Beckoned by a man? I'm not a dog.

Shit.

My lips twitched and I stuck my tongue in my cheek. The attitude on that woman would never cease to entertain me, if not turn me on. It was like a secret weapon she'd honed. She knew it all too well by the self-assured look on her face when I dared to find her gaze again.

Not my best move, in retrospect.

The rowdy host by the pool introduced Sam and the crowd went wild for him as he readied, spreading his massive wingspan. The muscles on his sides rippled and the sun beamed down on his handsome face. We all held our collective breaths as he jumped, flattened in the air, and fell into the water with a *clap*.

The mob recited a collective *oof*, Tyler and Pike cheered, and Sam swam to the surface, pumping his fist triumphantly as the crowd erupted in applause. More and more people poured over, filling out the space around the pool until it was just as thick with partygoers as the dance floor.

I rapped on Pike's chest with the back of my hand. "Go back over there and tell her I said, 'You've worn a collar for me a few times.'"

"Yeah right, man," Pike scoffed, pushing me away. "I like my balls where they are."

"I see where your loyalty lies."

"I'm not getting in the middle of this love note erotica game. I do not consent."

A disgruntled noise rumbled out of me. Sometimes you had to do things yourself if you wanted them done with any dignity. I set out for the bar just as Angelo found us, and before I had time to apologize for leaving him behind he brushed past me and toward an uncharacteristically quiet Mia. He pushed her forgotten sequined skirt into the center of her chest wordlessly and expectantly, and her eyes widened in shock. The next thing I knew she was tearing the garment out of his fist and stomping away to go put it back on.

I'd never seen two complete strangers take such a firm dislike to one another, but I couldn't worry about them now. Instead of going directly to Tally I found an open space farther down the bar and asked the bartender for a pen, pulling a cocktail napkin off the edge of a caddy.

> You have every right to be upset about Angelo's text.

"Could you send this napkin and a cosmo with a splash of orange juice down to that woman in the white dress, please?"

The bartender looked me over. "Okay, but you do realize she's getting married, right?"

I fought back a smile. We were strangers here. I'd worshipped every inch of that woman's body with my tongue, brought her to the edge of ecstasy, held her trembling body while she cried in pleasure, washed my cum from between her thighs under the rain of our shower, in *our* home—but right now, she could be anybody. I could make her mine again for the first time.

"Yes, I realize," I told the bartender. "Don't let your fiancé keep you from meeting your husband, am I right?"

"I'm just here for the tips." She sauntered away to do my bidding. I glanced out of the corner of my eye, elbows stuck in something unsavory on the wood of the bar top, as she placed a martini glass in front of Tally and handed her the note.

I enjoyed this little cat-and-mouse game. Normally, Natalia would too. I lived to please her. She lived to give me a headache and a complex and remind me that a love like ours wasn't easy, it was formed like a diamond under pressure. We were just in the middle of one of those duress timelines.

"Congratulations." The bartender returned several minutes later, dropping a gin and tonic in front of me with another napkin. "She answered your pigeon post. Her soon-to-be husband is a lucky guy."

"You have no idea."

> Is that all I have the right to be angry about? A cosmo isnt an apology, by the way. Any man at this bar is up to that task.

Crumpling the napkin in my fist, I flicked it toward the wet mats. Tally was hiding a smirk under her hand when I looked toward her again, that shiny rock I put on her finger glistening in the fiery sunlight. I picked up the drink she sent over for me and lifted it toward her. She did the same with hers, and we both took a long, hostile sip of liquor together.

Touché.

Cheers to her undying spirit, her incredible grudge-holding stamina, her smarts, her wit, her pure vitriolic refusal to come out on the bottom of an argument even if it meant spending the entire day in Vegas trading snide commentary and heated glares.

At the pool Wink leapt from the platform again, higher and larger than the first, thwacking against the blue-green water to another chorus of *humphs* and *oofs*. When he broke the surface with a smile, waving his arms up and down, motioning for the crowd to get louder and louder for him, they answered in waves. The music was an unbelievable beat of bass and techno spurring even the least likely Pike to sway from one foot to the other with an arm wrapped around Ophelia. I pulled out another cocktail napkin.

There's not another man on this planet that could handle you, and we both know that.

P.S. The bartender thinks you're throwing your marriage away for me so we might as well give her a show.

The woman in question reluctantly swiped the message out of my hand with a roll of her eyes on her next sashay by me, dropping it in front of Tally at the other end with a pointed glare down at her engagement ring. I couldn't help the chuckle that rumbled out of my chest.

Tally scribbled something out on a new napkin, and I analyzed the twitch of her lip and the involuntary way her tongue poked out at the corner of her mouth. This was more painless than facing my hot-headed fiancée head-on after the morning. I might be dumb but I wasn't stupid. She folded the napkin while the bartender waited in front of her and sealed it with a big, dramatic lipstick kiss. My grin was as wide as the state of Nevada.

When the bartender returned she pushed the napkin back to me with one slow finger, leaning over the bar with it. "It's so much easier to go sit next to her."

"Debatable." I opened the note quickly and she tugged the napkin holder out of my reach.

The only show you're going to be putting on is a dance number in Key West. I'm feeling extremely motivated to prove just how hard I am to handle at the moment.

I turned toward Tally instead of wasting the time writing it down, and I could tell she was just as surprised as the people between us at the bar as I shouted over them, "So you still plan to marry me then?"

Her dark eyes flared golden for a short second. All that mischievous playfulness I knew so well showing up like a break in the clouds. I let her sit with it.

Wink stepped up to the platform a third time. It was down to him and one other very large, red-bellied man. His opponent lifted a beer to his mouth, chugging it in three repulsive gulps, and crushed the plastic cup against his bald head.

Our wedding party chanted for Sam, and the cheer picked up steam until more than half of the onlookers were hooting his name in unison like a battle cry. Wink beat on his chest, unscathed apart from a tinge of rosy skin on his stomach. He took a deep breath, centering on the platform, then bent his knees and leapt, getting enough air to tuck into a full front flip, level completely horizontal, and land belly down in the pool like he'd been practicing for the moment his entire life. The crowd went wild, splashing and screaming; the chants of Sam's name got so loud they drowned out the electronic music beating through the speakers.

Natalia stood, heading back down the sand toward our friends but she stopped briefly beside me, not letting herself look up, though every fiber of my being begged her to. "Marrying you was never the question," she said. Her soft perfume floated over me with the breeze she left in her wake and I watched her every stride as she walked away.

chapter thirty

Natalia

MATEO COULD CHARM the pants off a department store mannequin, but for all intents and purposes, today I was a Victorian era lady-in-waiting. He would have to get through layers of me. Corset, chemise, bodice, those really long fucking underwear made of wool that were virtually impenetrable.

We left the pool party, mid-afternoon siphoning into a cooler early evening, and our party of five dipped into a dazzling casino with the boys hot on our heels. I didn't mind that they were keeping us in sight; it was easier to manage the scavenger items, and it upped the pressure to perform. The Swan boys had proven they were willing to do just about anything to win.

"Let's play to our strengths," Phee suggested. "Gambling tables, men, *drunk* men, money, pretty girls in dresses—" she rambled off. "One of you Russos is our only chance at checking dice blowing off the list."

There was no shortage of card games on the vast carpeted floor. The stench of cigarettes and citrus was overwhelming as little billows of smoke lifted out of ashtrays beside the sedentary customers at the poker tables. The last I'd seen Mateo, he had disappeared between a row of slot machines the size of SUVs with his brother and the time was as good as any to try to get ahead.

Camilla straightened her pink dress at the seam and tightened the halter, lifting her boobs just so. I was so used to seeing her in more conservative, pediatric unit hospital garb, it was almost alien watching her let her too stiff slicked-back ponytail down for the night. Having fun was something I didn't know she was even capable of. For my entire life she was all business. The perfectionist eldest daughter. A lot of the time it felt like the world wasn't serious enough for her, but she might not have had the chance to experience it any other way.

"Dad taught me how to play craps when I was a kid," Cami said. A game was ongoing nearby. A small crowd had gathered to watch a pair of dice being tossed into a deep-set green felt table.

"Did he really?" I asked.

"I think it was his very misguided way of finding a common interest with me. Or one of those rare times he actually had to parent and didn't know what to do without a nanny or Mom around."

Bella laughed sardonically. "Sounds about right. Gambling 101 with John Russo. I'm convinced Mia and I were only born to entertain you like a pair of Baby Alive dolls."

"And Natalia was their last attempt at a boy," Mia added.

"Explains the resentment," I mumbled. "At least you got a cool party trick out of the deal, Cami."

She jokingly bowed to us. "I'll go do my civic slutty scavenger hunt duty. Looks like this guy could use some luck anyway."

"We'll be here cheering you on," Phee spurred her. "I believe in you!"

Camilla walked purposefully over to the game table, lingering on the outskirts with one of her French-tipped fingernails to her lips as though she was in deep, thoughtful contemplation. The man waiting drearily for his next turn couldn't keep his eyes off her. Sneaky, diabolical, doe-eyed Camilla. The easiest way to hook a man was by making him think he could teach you something.

Sure enough, the idealistic betting man in his oversized suit jacket and salt-and-pepper hair crooked a finger at Camilla and called her over to his side. She started asking questions, pointing at the lines and the curves on the table, basically shimmying herself right into the man's side pocket, and excitement surged in unfamiliar ways inside my chest. Yes, because I realized she was a shoe-in for the ticket item, but also because I might have had something in common with my older sister. She turned on the charming confidence in ways I recognized in myself, like I did on camera. It was all for show. A hidden talent, a secret superpower.

On his next toss, Camilla shuffled to the edge of the board, gesturing at the two red dice in the man's hands. She leaned in, breezing her luck and charm all over them and my mouth parted in a cheek-splitting grin.

Hook, line, and sinker.

"Did you get that on camera?" I tapped on Ophelia's shoulder. She was holding her phone horizontally, zoomed in and recording the entire thing, then zipped it away into the group chat before the roll had even settled on the table. Cami and the mystery gambler exchanged a very awkward double high-five as it was clear he expected more, and Mia took it upon herself to step in and save our oldest sister from her suitor.

Camilla ambled back to the group and without even thinking about it, I threw my arms around her neck for a hug. I couldn't see Camilla's face, but judging by Bella's pinched eyebrows and clamped teeth, she was just as confused and uncomfortable as we were.

We did not hug.

Unofficially. Our family was not doting, or tender. It was just how we were raised. Thinking about it, I hadn't seen anyone in my family show affection in a physical way. It was like getting my fingers caught on a piece of tape and flicking my wrist until it flung off.

Shockingly, Cami slowly but surely returned the embrace, tightening her forearms at the center of my back.

"I got that on camera, too," Phee announced just as the flash shuttered. Cami and I parted, brushing each other off like a film of dust. "Oh my god, girls, is it hug time?" Ophelia pressed forward with open arms and my sisters curled in on themselves. "I knew I could successfully orchestrate team bonding."

"You are exactly like that little Troll doll," Mia said. "The pink one that sings and makes scrapbooks and drives everyone crazy."

"Poppy," Ophelia said proudly. "My students love that movie, so even if you mean it differently I'm taking it as a glowing compliment."

"As you should," I assured her. "Any type of acknowledgment from Mia is a compliment, because she will simply pretend you don't exist if she doesn't like you."

A deep laugh rumbled behind me. It was familiar and conceited and could only belong to Tyler Swan, who had snuck up on us holding a soft pretzel. The remaining men were close behind. I ripped off a sliver of the salty bread and shoved it in my mouth.

"So she likes us," Tyler repeated. Mia huffed and tried to take a piece of the pretzel but Tyler pulled it close to his chest. "This cost fifteen dollars, and legend says if I don't eat it I'll turn into a big green monster in purple shorts."

"Took a snack break?" I asked. Mateo's eyes were on me, and my throat dried. *Don't look at him, Tally. He's trying to intimidate you. Be stronger than that.*

I looked at him.

Unsurprisingly, his hazel eyes were as handsome and soft as ever, and my stomach fluttered in betrayal.

"We figured we would let you girls catch up," Frankie said. "Make this at least a little bit interesting."

"Not so cocky, Maverick." Ophelia threw a warning at her boyfriend. Frankie's eyes narrowed toward her, but he held his tongue.

"Well, there's no more pools to jump into, unfortunately for you one-trick ponies," Bella quipped. "Was it worth the day-long swamp ass?" She gestured to Sam's shorts.

"You think I didn't ditch the wet briefs?" Sam said. "Anyway, people piss in their chairs so they don't lose their turn at the slot machines here. I'm the least of their worries."

Angelo's nose scrunched. "Is that what I smell?"

"That smell is fear." Tyler sniffed in our direction, and I pushed him away by his big barrel chest. "These girls reek."

Ophelia nudged me with her phone, showing an address for a karaoke bar only a few blocks away. My eyes flared, but I quickly schooled my expression and cleared my throat, giving her a subtle nod of approval. The cocky groomsmen entourage was like sharks in the water; we couldn't let them follow us.

"I have to use the restroom," I said.

I tugged on Phee's hand. The longer we stood there the harder it would be to outrun them, and the one leg up we had was that sneaky women's telepathy keeping us all on the same page. We started walking. Naturally, my sisters caught on and followed.

Mateo's head tilted, zeroing in on me, and I avoided him in the most obviously up-to-something way. He could always tell when I was lying; it was a real pain in the ass when it came to any kind of surprise for him. I could feel the heat of his pressing attention trying to pin me across the casino floor.

We pressed forward to the first public bathroom in sight, leaving the men precariously aloof. In a perfect world they'd get bored and wander off, or leave to try and figure out another way around the scavenger hunt, but in reality we had about four minutes to get our shit together and find a way to the karaoke bar without sounding the alarms.

"What's really going on?" Bella turned against the marble vanity and plucked a round mint from a bowl.

Women filed around us out of the bathroom stalls, checking their makeup in large round mirrors, shoes pattering on the tiled floors. The sound of the hand dryer was loud to hide our voices beneath thundering gusts that seemingly never stopped.

"We need to get to this karaoke bar." My sisters leaned in as Ophelia showed them the map on her phone. "It's four blocks away, but the guys are watching our every move. I don't know if we should just make a run for it or call a car and try to disappear into traffic and hope they don't catch on."

"The second we leave this place they're going to know something's up," Mia said. "Half of the fun for them is chasing us down. It's like a whole different kind of hunt."

"Four blocks are nothing. We'd spend more time in an Uber trying to get there than it would take to walk," Camilla reasoned. "I say we just go."

She was probably right, and I was probably overthinking it. But this had become so much more than a game of bragging rights. "What if they're right outside?"

"Then we run," Bella said.

Ophelia fixed the creasing sparkly eyeshadow on my lid with the pad of her pinky finger as if she was donning war paint. "While we're here though, does anyone actually have to pee?"

"No, Mom," Mia said mockingly. Rather than annoyed, though, it was charmed, appreciative. My two deeply separate lives crashing together in a gooey, warm way. Like melting s'mores. Maybe it was just the drinks, the circumstance, or my own wishful thinking, but I had stars in my eyes hoping there was a future of harmonious friendship between my best friend and my sisters, and whatever this was, it was a start.

"We're going to beeline straight out of this bathroom to the far doors at the front of the casino, then hang a left," Ophelia instructed. "Don't hit pause. Don't get distracted. Stay together."

I shouldered the heavy black bathroom door open and led the group, keeping my head down. One foot in front of the other, my eyes remained on the patterned carpet until we were halfway there and onto sparkly tile. I felt my sisters at my back, Ophelia to my right with her arm linked through mine. We all had the same idea, shrinking into ourselves, as if the parade of hot pink and sparkles wasn't a full giveaway. I chanced a look up at the revolving glass doors as we inched closer and the pink skies outside looked like a fresh, well-earned freedom. In four strides we were there, in another few we were galloping through the vacuum of partitions, and when my short boots finally hit that pavement outside I let go of a breath that had been holed up in my chest for what felt like an hour.

Night was creeping up on Vegas quickly. All the lights were that much brighter, the streets busier. There was a pulse picking up in the city and my own heart was an echo of it. Adrenaline skipped through me in anticipation for the shoe to drop, for the plan to be wasted, but when we all finally stopped to look around, the coast was clear. There was an audible sigh of relief.

"Holy fuck, why am I so nervous?" I laughed. "We did it."

"Keep going." Phee ushered me forward. My sisters kept up the pace until we got to the edge of the block and pounded the button on a long, busy crosswalk. Once we made it to the other side, finding us would be like finding a needle in a haystack.

The streetlight changed from green to yellow, and I was rocking on the balls of my feet as it hit red and the cars rolled into complete stops. The crosswalk signal gave us the go-ahead, and I don't know why—maybe that invisible string tugging me in his direction—but I turned back to the casino just as Mateo burst through the doors and outside.

He saw me, and a muscle in his jaw ticked. And then a wide, bright smile split his face.

One word left my lips. "Run!"

chapter thirty-one

Mateo

SHE WAS REALLY RUNNING.

All five of them in their hot pink skirts and thin heels, squealing with laughter and dodging people on the busy sidewalks through Vegas as if outrunning us was even an option. Had we not looked away for two minutes to watch Echo pull a slot handle on a Monte Carlo machine, they wouldn't have even made it out of the bathroom. But this was fun now. I had a rush of adrenaline after seeing that shock in Natalia's eyes and I had every intention to use it.

Their head start across the highway dwindled quickly. Our legs were just longer, steps brisker. Tally kept checking over her shoulder, maybe hoping she didn't see me when she looked back, and the last thing I needed was for her to catch a crack in the sidewalk and go ass over tits. God I fucking loved her, but graceful and agile my fiancée was not. Wherever they were headed, we were headed, and for all we knew that could very well be a gay bar or a male strip club, or something equally impossible to talk ourselves out of. I hadn't asked, but I was pretty sure there was a cap on how far *taking one for the team* would go if it came down to it.

Plus, I wouldn't put it past those women to set us up. They were educated, and diabolical, and a little bit drunk, which was a frightening combination.

Suddenly I was slowing my strides and rethinking the eagerness in which I was leading myself and four grown men into uncharted territory. Ahead of us the Strip was thick with restaurants and stores, neon spectacle signs extended from the buildings. I was anticipating their next move, but at the same time I couldn't give a damn where we were headed as long as it was in line behind *her*. My brain had two tracks. One was always Natalia. The other one was often, also, Natalia. But the deeper, more regulated, day-to-day things played out there as well. She was like a film filter over everything.

Another two blocks on the right, a door swung open and a few people filed out with cigarettes hanging from their mouths as a cacophony of shrill singing and a Joan Jett instrumental thumped loudly through the brief opening. Before it shut again Tally squeezed herself through the door and disappeared with her pack of flamingos close behind.

A fucking karaoke bar. I swiped a hand down my face. "Who here can sing?"

None of my groomsmen volunteered but Pike threw an arm around my shoulder with a shit-eating grin on his face. "There's really nothing you wouldn't do for this girl."

He was right about that. Despite the dread, there was no keeping us from stomping right into the dimly lit karaoke bar. It was long and thin, like it was built between two already standing buildings and the owners threw a roof over the alleyway and called it a day. At one end there was a stage and tall bar tables scattered in front of it. A projector was casting moving lyrics against the wall and the DJ stood behind his booth with a queue of eager amateur singers waiting to give a request.

Bella was in that line.

The other four had found a table nearby and were already pointing at items on the menu. My brother, Pike, and I made ourselves at home in the empty spaces beside the girls, wiggling in like unwanted pests. I set my elbows on the table and my arm pressed flush to Natalia's, but she didn't move away like I expected her to. Her posture straightened, her bicep went stiff, and then she relaxed, ignoring me and the small connection there altogether.

I wasn't going to get my hopes up over an arm touch like I was in fucking middle school. But we were headed in the right direction. We'd gone from taking separate cars into the city to sharing a sticky bar table with minimal castrating side-eye. Progress.

"That whole sneaking away thing was very cute." I plucked a menu out of Mia's hand across from me and dodged her long fingers attempting to snatch it back. I'd spent thirty-five years without sisters, and now I had three of them, so I considered my instigating as making up for lost time.

"Try a low crawl in the future," Frankie suggested, tugging Ophelia into his side and wrapping her in a playful headlock. Her brown hair fell in her face. "You have these massive heads. They're impossible to miss."

"You're one to talk," O shot back at him, giggling.

"*Tally* is impossible to miss," I said. That inside thought cartwheeled off my tongue before I could catch it. The table stilled, but Tal and I were the object of everyone's attention. Feeling bold, I grazed the side of her pinky finger with mine and tacked on, "Always has been."

For a second I thought I had her. That she might give in and turn around and we could figure it out somewhere quieter and more private while the metronome of shitty off-key karaoke ticked in the background. But the moment was gone as quickly as it presented itself. Sam and Tyler were suddenly there, hollering at each other and backing us all away from the small table top to slosh down ten plastic cups of pale yellow beer they'd somehow managed to carry with only two sets of hands.

"I don't understand what the big fucking secret is," Echo pecked at his brother.

"It's none of your business who I take on dates." Wink

shrugged. He reached over and plucked the menu out of my hand and studied it too closely to be reading anything at all.

"Sam has a girlfriend?" Tally wiggled her eyebrows.

"Sam doesn't have a girlfriend," Sam replied.

"Sam has a date to your wedding that he's keeping under wraps like she's a celebrity or something," Echo snorted, then pointed a long finger at his brother with wide eyes. "Oh shit, have I fucked her before? Is that it? There's no hard feelings here. Wouldn't be the first time a girl got the Swan brother special."

"Watch your mouth." Wink's head shook.

"Is that on there, somewhere?" Mia pointed at the wobbly laminated menu in Sam's hand. "I didn't see that one."

"Shameless," Angelo mumbled.

"I'm just saying, you're bringing a new girl into a pretty chaotic situation. I hope she's up to the task." Echo put his palms out as if surrendering. "First date at a wedding that you're in across the country with all of your best friends is pretty fucking bold."

A comeback was at the tip of Sam's tongue but he tapped it back down and put his beer to his lips.

Wink had girlfriends in the service but nothing that lasted more than a few months. Amy, Megan, Stephanie, Eloise—a revolving door of the same story. The lifestyle in Delta was intimidating to most women. We were gone for half a year at a time, in dangerous conditions, with hardly any communication, and for the vast majority of that experience we didn't yearn for anything more than a warm body to pass the lulls. Even outside the Army, acclimating back to civilian life and finding a partner who understood that most of the scars were internal was tough. Pike and I had been extraordinarily lucky in that.

"If she's meant to be, she'll fit right in, Sam," Tally said.

"Agreed," I added warmly. "We'll be on our best behavior."

"Don't feed the boy lies," Echo insisted. "Just like today is a circus, that day will be a more expensive one."

"I wouldn't call today a *circus*," I argued passively. We may have been drunkenly gallivanting around Las Vegas playing an immature game and ignoring the astronomical elephant in the room that was me and Natalia—but that was neither here nor there.

"A circus is a show," Mia pointed out with a proud tilt of her lips. Bella had made her way to the front of the line of singers and was flipping through the catalog of song choices. "This is a game, and you are losing."

"You wish." I took a beer from the center of the table and tossed it back, the entire goddamn thing in four sloppy, dribbling gulps, and wiped the damp foam from across my mouth with my sleeve. This was the worst idea I'd ever had, but I was quickly running out of them. I left the table and skipped into the line beside Bella as if I'd always been there with no shortage of impatient, frustrated side-eyes aimed at me.

"Hey, sis." I threw an arm over her shoulder.

Isabella's brows knitted together, and her short hair tickled the back of my hand. "What the hell do you think you're doing?"

"Karaoke, of course." I pointed to the list of songs, choosing one that was suitable for a duet on a whim. I gave the DJ a charismatic nod and dragged Bella up the small set of stairs and onto the stage before she could put up too much of a fight. With the spotlights shining it was almost impossible to see the audience not directly in front of us, but I shielded my eyes and found the table of my fiancée and friends watching raptly.

"You can't just hijack my spot," Bella spat.

"Just did. You can either sing with me or forfeit."

"Do you even know this song?"

There were two microphones beside each other on a stool and I handed her one. "Do I need to know the words if I can just read them off the wall?"

A piano ballad started and the crowd hushed. My nerves were doing somersaults over one another but there was no time to fully panic as the lyrics began moving across the screen. I could do this; I was a natural in front of a live audience. A live audience had seen my balls, for fuck's sake. Singing a P!nk song was the least vulnerable thing I'd done for the entertainment of someone else.

Bella was unimpressed. She crossed her arms, turning awkwardly away from me as she softly sang the opening line—which was a clear and mortifying confession of love.

Oh, hell...

A hot, uncomfortable burn, like a slap in the back of the neck, hit me as the words continued. It was too late to stop it from happening. I put a substantial distance between us, thinking that might dissuade anyone from getting the wrong idea, but Bella was a phenomenal fucking singer and people were taking notice. She hit the first chorus of the song and turned toward me with wide, and understandably angry, eyes.

"Don't look at me," I mouthed.

Her forehead creased down the middle and she threw a hand out to the side as if to say, *Where the fuck am I supposed to look*, and I realized much like Natalia, the other Russo women had their own unique, cutting language that required nothing but violent intent and the fear of God to communicate.

This had to be rewarding for Tally. It was like thinking all the presents were opened on Christmas morning and then finding one hiding at the back of the tree. My total humiliation was a fun little quirk of the scavenger hunt. Or karma's fucked-up, sister-wives way of getting even.

The second verse started, and as soon as it was my turn to sing Bella dropped her mic to her side to scold me. "You fucking idiot," she seethed. "'Bohemian Rhapsody' was right there!"

I waved her off, staring intently at the lyrics as each word was highlighted, crawling inside my own skin with every shaky syllable I managed to sing. I'd heard "Just Give Me a Reason" a million times on the radio when it was popular but never actually acknowledged what it was about. Standing up here was the worst time to figure it out, as I was seemingly engaging in an intense lovers' quarrel with my fucking sister-in-law.

"I'm going to kill you," Bella seethed through the world's

fakest smile. "I'm going to find a way to sue you for this. Emotional damages, something."

I stuffed a hand in her face, meaning to muzzle her as my notes carried on, but the little fucking animal bit the palm of my hand. I ripped it away and the last line of my verse dropped off a cliff.

"Ou-CH." I shook out my hand. "Do I need a fucking tetanus shot now?"

We were seconds away from throwing elbows at one another when the chorus lifted once more and we both harmonized through our disdain like a musical theater number.

"She's my sister," I said into the microphone, pointing toward Bella. To which a couple "eughs" and "what the fucks" returned from the darkened room of people.

"Please stop," Bella sang.

One day, we would laugh about this. Maybe not one day *soon*, but someday, when we were old and sentimental and youth was lost, there would be a story about Las Vegas and a karaoke love song. Maybe by then Bella would even like me, and I'd have paid off that lawsuit she promised to throw my way.

Through the haze of lights I could barely make out Natalia's silhouette at the back of the room but my chest felt lighter knowing she was there. My finger snapped in the direction of our table, to Tally, hopefully. With a metaphorical beer blanket draped snugly over my shoulders, I dialed it up to ten and sang my goddamn heart out. At the very least, I'd make her laugh at how ridiculous it was. On the other hand, it might be enough to win her over. If I was willing to make a fool of myself in a shitty karaoke bar there was no saying how far that desperation could extend.

All I knew was that I wanted the song to be over so that I could return to our group with what little dignity I had left and a point for the boys to fall back on. Bella was singing me in circles, but there was no rule saying I had to be good at the task to mark it off the list.

As the final keys played, my future sister-in-law abandoned her mic on the stage and bounded away from me with her hand covering her face. The audience's reaction was lukewarm, but our friends and family lit up the room with an embarrassingly long standing ovation to really hammer in the most awkward four minutes of my life.

If I was lucky the floor would open and swallow me. But I was the opposite, and when I traipsed back over to the table, not only had I completely embarrassed myself in the name of love, but that love of mine was nowhere to be found.

Mia hung over Ophelia's shoulder, looking down at a piece of paper keeping track of the score. "We're tied," Ophelia announced.

Mia tossed a hand on her hip. "That's bullshit. Mateo stole that right out from under us. We were here first, so we should get the point."

"That's not how a scavenger hunt works," Angelo pushed back. "It's how many, not how quickly. Everything on the list is fair game."

"I'm sorry, what exactly have you contributed to your team?"

A low whistle rang out and Camilla high-fived her sister. Angelo scrubbed an impatient hand through his short beard and Mia squared up to him with a self-righteous tilt of her head. So far, this weekend had been the catalyst to every problem. No one seemed nearly as concerned with Natalia's whereabouts as I was; my palms were clamming waiting for her to reappear. I tried to voice that concern—the words were on the tip of my tongue— but instead I was silenced by the sight of my brother wrapping a hand in the hair at the nape of Mia's neck, and tugging her mouth onto his.

The kiss dragged on for a questionable second before Mia ripped herself away, and if that hadn't already left us speechless, the slap of her palm connecting with Angelo's cheek did the job just fine.

"Oh fuck, you deserved that," I said.

"One hundred percent," Pike agreed.

Sam shook his head. "Am I missing something?"

"My contribution." Angelo was grinning, even though his cheek was pink with the imprint of a thin set of fingers. There, at the bottom of the list, was the line *kiss someone you just met.* He stole Ophelia's sparkly pen right out of her grip to write his initials next to it.

"He did not," Bella scoffed.

Mia pressed her plump lips together and folded her arms over her chest. She wouldn't make eye contact with anything but the ceiling, and the only thing more concerning than a vindictive Mia was a silent one.

"Does that...count?" Tyler mumbled.

Angelo shrugged, tossing the pen on the table nonchalantly. He'd successfully thrown a live grenade into our already uncultivated bridal party and then turned toward the bar. "Anyone need another drink?" No one replied. "Suit yourselves."

My brother left the table, and Mia spun in the opposite direction, stomping toward the bathrooms with her sisters hot on her heels.

Reality folded in on itself, and I blinked. "Where's Tally?"

"I'm not exactly sure," Ophelia said, but I knew her better than that. At least enough to say she'd never blindly allow her best friend to take off in Vegas alone without some kind of plan. Tal was having a field day making me chase her.

"Try again," I offered kindly, while my hand tightened on the wooden backrest of her chair. "Come on, let me go get my wife, O."

Her lips twisted, fighting to hold something back. She breathed deeply in through her nose and let it go as a sigh. "All she said was that she was going to find Elvis, and she needed to do it alone."

Elvis. So this was a scavenger thing. She was trying to get ahead again.

Wracking my brain for somewhere I might find an impersonator, I came up short, and desperation struck. Pulling my phone out of my pocket, I Googled it. My pulse picked up, thudding in my neck, because there were several results, but one very specific one nearby that stood out against the rest.

I knew exactly where she was headed.

It was where we'd been heading this entire time.

chapter thirty-two

Natalia

I STARED upwards at the buzzing white sign and yellow bulb lights. Elvis was there dancing with a red acoustic guitar across his waist and smiling down at me like he knew a secret.

There was a gold awning at the front of the building, white steel fence posts with hearts embellished on the spokes, and an old pink Cadillac parked in a twenty-four-hour wedding drive-thru bay.

The irony of this being the sole place within walking distance to find an Elvis impersonator was not lost on me. It was some kind of divine intervention, forcing me to face the music—no pun intended. There were obviously more romantic places to get married, but after planning a wedding and nearly losing myself in the process, I understood exactly why this kind of place existed. Those people were geniuses. They knew what they wanted, and they went and got it.

Safe to say, letting anyone interfere in our wedding was the biggest mistake Mateo and I had ever made. It complicated every-thing, it made us question each other, and it clouded our choices, bringing us to this.

Mateo had made it clear that he was ready to put the hard work into whatever the hell *this* was to fix it. I wanted to let him, and a little part of me knew that when I walked out of the bar alone it would only be a matter of time before my fiancé showed up to reel me back to him.

The chapel doors swung open and I peeked inside, hoping to catch a glimpse of what was happening beyond the gold ruching and red roses. There was the slightest breeze that made the hair on my arms stand on end and I rubbed the chill away as a couple walked across the green carpet with their wedding license. He was wearing a white dress shirt two sizes too large and a bow tie that barely clipped together at his neck, and he swept his blonde bride in her red tube dress and feather boa into his arms, kissing her so hard her lipstick painted his mustache when they finally pulled away.

That spontaneity and lust was electric. It was how it felt to be in love with Mateo. Simple, yet unconventional. We weren't ever going to fit in a box, but we'd spent the last five months trying to force it, and hurting ourselves in the process. I'd known that, but it hit me all at once, watching longingly as the newlywed strangers walked down the sidewalk into their new lives, together. And I realized I was *jealous*.

"Tal."

The voice spun me around. Mateo was there, standing alone with his hands in his pockets. Wind had mussed his hair the way the beach back home always did, and that paired with those despairing, soft brown eyes took the air out of my chest. My heart hammered against my ribs; blood rushed to the tips of my ears.

He stepped right into my space and blocked everything else out around us. The bright lights in the chapel sign formed a yellow aura around his head.

"I figured you'd find me." It came out no higher than a whisper. My gaze landed on his throat and I studied the familiar beauty marks that peppered him all the way up to his jaw.

"There's nowhere you could go that I wouldn't." Mateo took a hand out of his pocket and timidly reached for mine. I let him. His thumb grazed over the diamond ring on my finger, sliding the band back and forth. "I'm never leaving you alone, baby. No matter how mad you are, no matter how distant we might find ourselves, no matter how impossible it might feel to patch all the holes. I'm going to do it, Natalia. I'm going to show up."

My lip quivered traitorously. A burn threatened at the back of my eyes, and Mateo's grip on my hand tightened as he tugged me forward and my ear connected with the soft linen over his chest. For a man so deliberate in his words, Mateo's heart was racing.

"That ring on your finger means something. I am *yours*. Not the other way around. Like you so earnestly reminded me at the beach club, there's a man with a drink and a man with a ring waiting for you everywhere you go, but you wear *mine*."

"I was being a teensy bit bratty when I said that." I pinched my thumb and pointer finger together.

"We'll deal with that later," he promised, wrapping both arms around my shoulders and crushing me against his body. His scent draped over me and set my soul on fire, and my eyes closed as I got lost in the protection of it. "I don't want to be at odds with you anymore. And I don't think you want to be with me," he guessed correctly. "But if you still do, then fight with me, Tally. Yell at me. Get it all out. Tell me I'm a piece of shit who doesn't deserve you, call me a misguided momma's boy, remind me how badly I almost fucked this up, make me beg. Just don't be done with me. Okay? Because I won't survive that."

"I'd never call you a misguided momma's boy," I said, hiding my smirk. "But I'm glad you're self-reflecting."

He jostled me. "Punk."

"I wanted to blame you for everything this morning, because I'm so used to having to defend myself to other people, and justify my anger, but that's not fair to you. I should have been paying more attention, reading the signs, realizing you were struggling. I don't know how I became a person you couldn't talk to when you needed to, and whatever I did to make you think you had to keep things from me, I—" My voice trembled. "I'm sorry, Matty."

He tried to brush it off, shaking his head. His thick fingers threaded through my hair, scratching gently against my scalp.

"Let me say I'm sorry to you, please." I stepped back so I could pour all my grief directly into his hard gaze and make him hear me. "You don't always need to take things on the chin, you know. You're *human*. It's not your job to solve other people's worries and problems, because you're not a brick wall, Mateo. You're allowed to say you've had enough and not feel smaller for it. *No one* would ever think you're smaller for it."

"I would, though," he mumbled. "That's the problem. This has nothing to do with you and everything to do with me, Tally, I promise you. I can't be...less than I was."

"In Delta?"

Matty glanced away from me. "I'm the fixer. People looked to me for that. I had the answers, I made the right choices, every single time. If I can't figure something out now, then what am I, really? I'm a shell, a fraud. I had that panic attack in front of my parents and ever since then I've been pretending that the anxiety isn't controlling me, and hiding it from you, hoping it would just go away."

"You don't live in fight or flight mode anymore." I slid my hand through the coarse hair on the side of his head and pulled him back to me. His cheek felt heavy in my palm. "This isn't war. You're allowed to make a mistake and fail. You're allowed to ask for help."

Mateo took a deep breath. His hand latched onto my hip and his thumb drew circles, likely to anchor himself while he spoke. "This whole thing with TechOps and putting off a hire—it's because I can't trust anybody but my boys, my *team*. They were the only people I had for so long, Tal. It's a different type of loyalty, and I don't expect you to understand it. I realize how insane it is to not be able to hire a person more than qualified for the job, but the security company is *mine*, like the cam business is yours. I didn't realize how much stake I put into that until Pike left. Then my parents showed up, and the wedding planning became exhausting, and the sex work suffered, and our relationship grew strained. By the time I realized I couldn't do it alone like

I thought I could, it was too late. The lie was dug too deep, and I couldn't take it back." His eyes were glossy and wet. "I didn't want you to look at me like I wasn't the same man you fell in love with anymore."

My chest caved in on itself. It hurt to swallow. God, I hated myself for not giving him a chance to talk to me this morning. I hated myself for assuming everyone in my life was going to hurt me, that it was inevitable, that Mateo was even capable of doing something like that. I hated my parents, briefly, before I reeled it back, but most of all, I hated that there weren't enough words to articulate how wrong he was about the limitations of my love.

"Mateo, when I look at you, I see everything I've ever wanted." His tears were a dagger in my chest, and one fell quickly before he rubbed it away. "I mean it when I say I wasn't fully *me* until I found you. I was waiting for the blank to be filled in for my entire life, and you showed up and wrote your name in it. There isn't a version of you that I would feel any different about. I want to know everything. I want to be let in. Please don't hide from me again."

"I swear," he whispered. "It's the way I feel about you that takes my fucking *sense* away." His breath played across my lips with each word, his thumbs resting in the hollows beneath my rib cage. "It scares me more than anything ever has, because it makes me weak and stupid, Natalia. I would do anything to have you. I'd walk into a firefight unarmed if you were standing on the other side. I need you. From the moment I saw you I've needed you."

"You're not the only one who's made a bad choice in the last few months," I reminded him. "I pretend I'm not desperate for my family's approval, but this entire wedding has become about me proving a point. I don't know why I care so much."

Somewhere deep down, I knew it was hoping that one day I could have a relationship where my family would support me regardless of how niche and uncomfortable it might be. If I could be both the successful, put-together daughter and also the private seductress, the first one may cancel out the other.

Not so much my parents, for obvious reasons. Really, I longed for that connection with my sisters.

"I'll never forgive your father for what he did to this pretty little mind." Mateo tapped my temple. "We got so caught up trying to placate our parents and play nice as if this isn't the most important day of *our* lives. No one else matters, and losing each other in the madness was the one thing we said we wouldn't do. If you want something different, Tally, we can do that. We can figure this out."

"The venue is paid for." I smiled meekly. "The catering is booked, and people have bought flights and suits and blocked out rooms in the resort. It's happening, Matty. It will still be perfect, I'm not worried about that. I'll love it because it's the day I get to marry you. I know I can be a little crazy but I'm not cancel-a-wedding crazy."

He leaned in and planted a kiss on my forehead. "But you'll always remember it as the day you settled for because you didn't get what you really wanted."

When the smoke cleared, and the ice sculpture melted, we would be back to our regular, reclusive lives like the last six months never even happened. It was a blip in the tapestry. The only thing that would always remain the same was us, and holding onto that would get me through Key West in June.

"All I want is me and you like it's always been. Like it will always be," I said.

Mateo scooped up my hands and brought them to the center of his chest. His eyes were dark and dilated. He swallowed hard, and his cheeks dimpled as a thought crossed his mind. "Then marry me. Right now."

"What?" My short laugh was entirely full of disbelief.

"Marry me," he said again, a full smile curving across his handsome face. "I don't need any of that other shit—the flowers, the seagulls, the fucking DJ. I don't need my parents or the boys or some random officiant with a little binder full of poems he reads to every single couple that comes through. I need you, though, and what's more me and you than saying fuck everything else?"

Mateo turned us toward the little white chapel and all its dazzling lights that sparkled against the setting purple skies in Las Vegas. Everything else in my mind went blank. My heart pounded like a drum. My stomach flipped. I couldn't place what was happening inside of me. Anxiety, excitement, rebellion. It was like running and being chased but wanting to be caught for the thrill of it.

My mind was quickly made up. "What will we tell everyone?"

"Nothing." His teeth caught his bottom lip. "Who needs to know?"

My mouth opened but nothing came out. We could have everything. A secret, intimate, spontaneous nuptial, *and* also the wedding everyone was expecting, but on *our* terms. Already married, and simply there for the party. There was nothing else I wanted in the world more.

"Okay." I nodded, my voice breathy and rattled. I threaded my fingers through his, squeezing tightly. "Let's do it."

Mateo picked me up bridal style, the feathers of my dress ruffling beneath his large, warm hands as they settled on my back and thighs. I crossed my heels at the ankles and threw my head back, laughing. When I came up for air Mateo stole it from me again, kissing me hard, opening his mouth over mine as our tongues swept against one another and my arms latched around his neck.

"Are we doing drive-thru or counter service?" he asked. "We don't have a car, but I'd let you ride me through it."

My eyes rolled playfully. "I came here for Elvis, didn't I?"

"Then Elvis you shall get."

Mateo walked us across the threshold of the building, and surrounded by pink stained glass and red rose petals in an empty room, I became Natalia Duran.

chapter thirty-three

Mateo

MY WIFE TUCKED herself into my side—*my fucking wife*—as I pushed a strand of her dark hair behind her ear and pulled her warm, smooth thighs against mine in the backseat of the SUV.

"Say it again, Tally." I kissed her neck gruffly, begging to hear the words tumble from her lips. There was only so much I could do without getting banned from rideshare services indefinitely, and the drive to the nightclub our friends had migrated to was in stop-and-go traffic.

Her skin pebbled beneath my mouth. "I'm your wife."

The blunt tips of my fingers curled around the inside of her thigh, and she squeaked out a noise that had my eyes cutting to the driver's in the rearview mirror. He quickly bowed his head. I wanted her to keep saying it, engrain it in my ears, speak it into permanent existence because I still felt like I was dreaming, floating on a cloud.

"Do you think he wants a show?" I asked softly, deliberately brushing my lips along her earlobe. Her head fell back on my shoulder. "Because you're driving me crazy."

She clamped her hand over mine as it inched toward the hem of her dress, but not before I felt the heat underneath, and my fingers twitched. "You can wait."

"I can't." I turned her face to me and captured her lips with mine as my slacks tightened at the zipper. Of course we *couldn't*. That didn't keep me from pushing it, swelling her lips with my teeth, drawing a pretty little mark to the surface of her skin where it would be hidden by her hair. "I want to fuck my wife."

She ran her fingers up my shaft and I sucked in a breath. "Behave, husband. The night is still young."

That was the problem. We had to show face for the rest of the night, because the scavenger hunt wasn't won, and there were people waiting patiently for us to find our way back to them. But I didn't give a single fuck about any of that at the moment. I wanted to call it quits and drag Natalia back to the villa with her hair wrapped around my fist. On the other hand, it was our only day in Vegas, and Ophelia and Pike had put in a lot to plan this. We owed them our participation.

"I know Phee is practically a minute away from sending a search party," Tally said. "I promise it will be worth the wait. Let's not blow our load too early."

"When I do I'm filling your mouth." I grabbed her chin and jammed my thumb in between her lips, feeling her silky tongue lap at the pad of it. She bit my finger and I wrenched it away, wincing.

"They're going to have questions," she said. "We weren't even speaking to one another an hour ago. Clearly something happened."

"What they're going to assume is that we solved our issues one way or the other—emphasis on the *other*—and now we can all enjoy ourselves drama free." A tiny problem I'd forgotten about reared back to memory, and my face pinched together.

"What is it?" she asked.

My touch danced along her kneecap, and a spot she'd missed shaving prickled my skin. "My brother might have kissed your sister."

Natalia's face warped the same way as mine had. Her manicured eyebrows shot to her forehead. "Which—"

"Mia."

"On purpose?"

"Out of desperation." I tilted my head. "For the scavenger hunt."

"Oh, fucking hell."

"She may have slapped the shit out of him."

She was less surprised by this. "And then what?"

"I don't know." My shoulders lifted and fell. "I left to find you before the fallout."

"You didn't stay to get the tea? You didn't want to know what was going to happen? Did she seem vengeful, or just perplexed? I mean, the slap was purely consequential, you don't just kiss people. The two of them have been going at it for two days, though. This is bad."

"Bad as in, he kissed her, and she slapped him."

"Bad as in, if he's not in the hospital by the time we get back, there are more evil spirits at play."

"You're perplexing *me*, Tal. It's not our problem. Angelo has a habit of getting himself in trouble and this is no different. But this is to say I'm sure our showing back up hand in hand won't be the most talked about thing in the room."

She relaxed. The lights and billboards filled the leather interior with a rainbow of colors, and Tally leaned over me to gaze out the window at the advertisements and neon. For the first time in months my body turned like an ignition key and idled. Hummed. I wanted to bottle this moment and keep it on a shelf like rare whiskey. I wanted to age with it, revisit it, show it off, take tiny, secret sips. My wife in my arms in the backseat like this. All the noise was outside and we were watching it pass by, unscathed, like a bubble.

"I'm so happy right now," she said. "I can't explain it."

I pressed a kiss to her hairline. "I was just thinking the same thing."

Natalia's eyes sparkled with the bright reflection out the window as she looked up. She pointed toward the sky but I was completely caught up in the button curve of her nose and the natural pout of her lips. Lost somewhere admiring how fucking beautiful she was and how badly I wanted our future children to look just like their mom.

"Look, Matty."

I reluctantly followed her voice.

Full moon.

Of course.

Everything in my life was a circle, folding back in on itself at all the right times. Following me from one substantial event to the next like a time marker. Reminding me to slow down, perhaps. Urging me to feel everything as deeply as I did because it didn't make me weak, it made me real.

I held her tighter. "Do you remember when I told you that story about being a kid and howling at the moon because I could pretend I was a wolf, and it just made sense? There was something so childlike and innocent about giving in to an impulse like that, and no one ever questioned it either?"

"That was our first date. You should have known back then I wasn't going anywhere because instead of sending you home, I dragged you up the stairs to my apartment."

"Well what I didn't tell you was that, when I was deployed, I would do it too. I would be scared and alone on a post for the night, wondering if it was going to be the last full moon I ever saw because there was no saying what the next twelve hours would bring, let alone another month. And I'd howl to remind myself that that little kid still lived in my chest, his soul was in there, he was going to be fine, and he was going to make it back home."

Natalia scratched her fingers softly through the hair at the nape of my neck.

"But the real reason I went to hell and made it home was because you were waiting for me here. Like fate. Then I told you that story that night and you turned around and howled at the moon with me and goddammit, Tal, something dormant in my body woke up for the first time. It all connected."

"You're the first person who ever stopped and made me look," she murmured. "I needed you just as much."

Our car cruised through lighter traffic and Natalia unfurled herself from my lap, waving toward the driver. "Excuse me," her sweet voice called out as she knocked on the sunroof. "Can you open this?"

The large window retracted and I grabbed Natalia at the knees as she stood, poking her head and shoulders through the vast opening. "Baby, what are you doing?" I couldn't help the smile that split my mouth in half as she looked back down at me through the feathers on her dress, completely taken with herself.

"Come on, Mateo, be my big bad wolf."

"Will I even fit?" I laughed and stood. Our bodies pressed flush against one another, which did nothing to tamper that earlier incessant lust as she inadvertently straddled my thigh. I hoisted her higher and held her hips against the edge of the open roof.

There was a mumble of protest from inside the car but it got drowned out by my wife filling her lungs with air and bellowing toward the bright yellow Vegas moon like the tiny she-wolf she was. My chest hurt with happiness. Everything in my body hurt, like my emotions were trying to burst through my skin and getting stuck. I could combust with it. "Fuck, I love you."

"I love you, too," she said softly.

I followed her lead and let the sound rumble to life deep in my chest before howling toward the sky. We took turns letting it out, all the way to our destination.

* * *

WE FOUND our wedding party in the dark nightclub and Pike sighed out in relief as if the last two hours of his life had aged him twenty years. "All good, I assume?" he asked.

"All is great, brother." I smiled so hard I felt my dimple deepen in my cheek. So much for playing it cool. I would keep our little wedding chapel secret for as long as I needed to, but fuck if it wasn't going to be hard not to tell my best friend. I wanted to shout it. My lips thinned awkwardly and Pike tilted his head. "We worked it out."

"She chewed your ass out, didn't she?" He glanced down at a mirthful Natalia. She was loving every second of that assumption, because Pike was used to watching her give me hell. He'd been on the other side of the wall to it for over a year.

"She laid it on really good," I fibbed. "We had a lot on our minds."

"Where'd you two run off to?" Echo shouted over the music, then reached down attempting to ball tap me but was thwarted by my hand. "Got anything left in there, Cap?"

Ophelia swatted his arm. "Leave them alone, Tyler. They love each other again."

"I could go all night, pretty boy," I said. "You could learn a thing or two."

Natalia squeezed my fingers and blinked her long eyelashes at me and I leaned down to ravage her with a kiss that quickly put everyone in the wedding party on the same page. Back to our game and our night, at a club somehow louder and more packed than the previous two. Vegas was becoming one blur of lights and thudding bass with our scavenger list items stuck like pins through a map.

Angelo's eyes were hidden in a plastic cup full of beer and I crooked a finger toward him. He silently, reluctantly, stepped up to the plate. There was a nervous glint in his eyes, but there was nothing left to say. He knew exactly why I was summoning him. The same way we knew as kids that our father was going to discipline us for stealing gum from the corner store, or riding our bikes down the train tracks. We answered the call, and suffered the consequences. I sighed, because it hurt me as much as it hurt him, and then I gave him one good slap on the side of the head.

His lips thinned and he rolled his neck on his shoulders. "I deserved that."

"Mia is a hard fucking limit."

"I'm not interested," Ang replied, so quickly it gave me pause. "I just don't feel like doing a jig at your wedding. You should be a little more appreciative."

"We'll see when we win." There wasn't much left on the list to make a fool of ourselves with, thankfully. A few less daring objectives, and one more salacious one. It wasn't like we had to do everything there; we just had to do *one* more thing than the girls, and I'd lost count of them anyway.

We found a large round booth to sit at and ordered another round of drinks. Every one of us had crossed the threshold from sober to sentimental, entering that weird fuzzy limbo where the trips to the bathroom were like getting off a carnival ride and finding your feet again. My heart was fueled, my chest was warm, I sipped my gin, and across from me my bubbly wife got lost in a martini glass and teased her tongue over her lips to lick off the excess.

Dammit if I didn't think about licking it off myself.

Natalia's heel inched out and grazed my shin below the table. When the toe of her shoe crept up to my knee, I snatched her ankle, drawing patterns in the bone with the pad of my thumb. I couldn't touch her like I wanted to, which was becoming a problem for my body. My manhood was rebelling against my wish to remain cool and collected and instead was playing the pop-a-boner-in-public game. I needed something to alleviate it. A brisk walk, a cold shower, ice down the back of my shirt, anything. I dropped Tally's ankle and stood.

"Does anyone need anything?"

Everyone at the table declined and I sped off before anyone decided to join me. A small alcove beside the bar was empty, and I stood in it with my hands behind my head and my eyes closed, picturing mangled, boot-bound athlete's foot and the unattended barracks bathrooms at Fort Liberty.

Yep, that'd do it.

For the time being, at least. Until I caught another glimpse of Tally and my cock decided it wanted to be a real boy again.

I pulled out my scavenger list as a distraction. *Get the DJ to play your song request.*

That was easy enough, right? What kind of DJ didn't take requests? The stage he was on was the most challenging part. It was higher than the dance floor, made to look like a bird cage or maybe a jail cell, with a tiny ladder in the back and an opening through the bars to come and go. There was hardly enough standing room for one guy and all his equipment, and I wasn't entirely confident in the stability of the thing after watching him jump to the beat of a bass drop and rock the floor like a boat.

My first try was shouting through cupped hands toward the guy with no luck. I wasn't going to throw a drink, but I wasn't seeing too much of an option outside of climbing the ladder myself. That would likely get me ripped down by a meathead bouncer and thrown out of the club entirely. I opted to back up enough into the crowd to wave my arms like I was directing airline traffic. After a solid two minutes of lifting eagerly onto the balls of my feet and doing my sedentary jumping jacks, I caught his attention. He lifted one of his headphones off his buzzed head and beckoned me up toward him.

The second I reached the top of the DJ platform, I could feel a thousand eyes on me from below. I easily picked my bridal party out in the crowd, watching me skeptically. Natalia had a worried, confused dimple between her brows.

"You okay, man?" the DJ asked. Below the booth was loud, but inside it was deafening. My brain recalibrated taking in all the switches and knobs, the buttons glowing green and red. I clocked an open laptop at the center of the setup and squinted at a Spotify playlist actively running. This dude wasn't even fucking mixing at all.

The platform we were on started to sway and I cut to it. "I have a request."

"Nah, man, I don't do that. I have a pretty strict setlist. You don't want to mess with the flow, you know? Can lose the whole crowd that way."

My attention darted to the laptop again, and he took one step in front of it, blocking it from view.

"I won't tell anyone your secret if you play one song for me—for my wife," I added, knowing if anything he'd care more about her. His blue eyes sliced toward the buttons and he pushed one back and forth as if he were actually doing anything. "We just got married. Think of it as a first dance song. The crowd will love it." I was a few inches taller and about fifty pounds heavier than him, and I used that size and practiced intimidation to make it seem like there was no ultimatum. "Please," I tacked on.

He scratched the back of his head and stuck his tongue into his gums. Another beat picked up, skipping over itself, and the music man twirled his fingers around a turntable and threw his fist out in the air. Tapping a button, an airhorn screeched, followed by a blast of smoke on the busy dance floor. This was the equivalent of an adult sensory table.

"What song," he shouted. There was no question, just reluctant acceptance.

"Good man." I clapped his chest.

My song request was personal, somewhat of an inside joke but more an anecdote of Natalia and me. And despite thinking it might *ruin the flow*, or whatever unremarkable words he used about the stolen setlist, it slipped into the tracks like it always belonged. It met the alluring vibe of the club right in the middle between sensual and euphoric. I waited for the first few bars of the song to play before slipping back down the ladder and into the crowd toward my wedding party, feeling extremely pleased with myself and awaiting the reaction of my bride.

chapter thirty-four

Natalia

Mateo had not only snuck himself into the high tower of the DJ booth to request a song and cross another item off the scavenger list, he'd picked one that I used frequently in our live cam sessions, almost so often that the response was Pavlovian as soon as the deep bass ruptured the room. My body replied in a stomach flipping, nipple perking, cunt fluttering way. It was like he'd done it on purpose. Which, clearly, he had, based on the surly way he rejoined our crew, watching me arrogantly, like he could see right through my skin to the blood in my veins rushing around trying to find a place to settle with nowhere to go but down.

My ache to get him alone was just as needling, but I was more demure about it. I could keep a poker face in a crowded room. Mateo on the other hand was unapologetically horny, but our group was too tipsy and blithe at that point to realize there was something else going on between my husband and me.

My husband.

My cheeks actually hurt from smiling.

Mateo sat across from me, a smirk on his lips. "I picked your favorite song."

The chorus bellowed and I could picture the way I usually moved my body along with it, rolling my hips like a wave, running my hands through my hair, arching my back. It became obvious Matty was imagining the same choreography we'd practiced before, except he'd seen it half naked and on his back.

An idea poked at me. Not poked, it stabbed me urgently. If Angelo could kiss my sister for a point on the boards, I sure as hell could give my husband a lap dance to accomplish the same. I tapped Phee eagerly, grasping for her scavenger list and the little pen she slid into the spandex shorts under her dress. She didn't even blink an eye. The queen of fashionable and functional struck again. I circled the lap dance item and slid out of the booth beside her. My hot thighs peeled off the leather in the least sexy way possible, and I let out a shaky breath.

Find yourself, Natasha.

This might have been the most mortifyingly embarrassing thing I ever did. Not because I couldn't pull it off—that was easy —but because for the rest of my life I'd need to make peace with dry humping Mateo in front of his brother, his best friends, and my sisters. It was best that I just rip the bandage off and treat it like any other day at work. I was used to doing this completely naked with a hard dick between my thighs for paying subscribers, for fuck's sake.

Matty was gawking at me, taking his time tracing my body up and down with heat simmering in his stare and a wrinkle between his big russet eyes as I stood in front of him. I kicked his thighs apart with the toe of my heel and stepped between his legs, draping my wrists over his shoulders and clasping my hands together behind his neck. I tugged the long tendrils of hair at his nape, forcing him to look up.

God, I'd seen that expression a million times. The far-gone glazed eyes, his defined brow bone flattening, jaw flexing. I felt so powerful. Mateo's hands slid up the back of my thighs, warm and calloused. My heart thumped, and the nerves between my thighs begged for some attention.

"You're going to be a bad girl in front of all these people, Tal?" he whispered. The song continued and I closed my eyes, using the familiar feeling of Mateo's body to put myself right back in our studio at home. I climbed over his lap, rolling my hips sensually, eliciting a tortured sound from the depths of his throat. Matty's chest rose and fell faster against mine.

My dress climbed up my thighs, and Mateo's hands splayed over the bottom of my ass, keeping my modesty hidden as much as physically possible, and that little quirk of possession pinched me somewhere deep and lust-filled.

I swirled my hips again, catching against the seam of his pants just enough to make my eyes roll back. Fucking dammit, I knew this would rile him up, but I sincerely underestimated the way my professionalism would go flying out the door once I felt even a tidbit of an erection. My shoulders dipped backwards, and I held on around his neck for dear life as I let my long hair and head roll, pushing my tits forward and dragging Matty's face down into my cleavage.

There was a chorus of good-natured giggles from our booth, and a clear-as-day "You go, girl!" from Tyler Swan. I couldn't look behind me for fear of losing all my newfound vodka-aided conviction. Mateo pulled me closer to him, leaving a trail of kisses from my chest to my neck, until his mouth was hot against my ear. "I'm going to fuck you so hard," he whispered. "So deep, Tally. You're going to feel me on your body for days if you keep this up."

My clit thrummed. There was a distinct clench and release going on internally that made it clear if I didn't have this man inside me soon my petulant little Kegel workout was going to be for nothing.

I pushed him back onto the booth, leaving my hand against his chest like I was warding off a predator. At that point, I was. Another hot sentence out of his mouth and I wouldn't care who was watching anymore. Mateo's gaze was burning, so serious and savage I couldn't bring myself to match it. Mateo lifted his hips ever so slightly and I choked on a groan. He was reading me like a motherfucking book. Reading me to filth. He reached between us and adjusted himself, brushing his knuckles so fucking close to the apex of my core it was like someone blowing out birthday candles. Except the candle was my fucking clit and the breath was too weak to blow out the flame.

The song started the bridge and I unwound my legs from him, turning and placing my back to his chest and my palms on his outstretched thighs, rolling my ass over his lap. That earned me another animalistic grunt from the depths of his stomach.

I made the mistake of looking up and immediately regretted it when I found our entire wedding party watching intently. Not just them—we'd earned the attention of quite a few people in the club who might have thought we were part of the club's entertainment. All but Frankie, who had clearly learned his lesson from Christmastime and was hiding his eyes behind his hand and staring at the table. My sisters were somewhere between pride for how seriously I was taking this scavenger hunt item, and the sheer inability to look away. I knew I had that effect on people, based on hundreds of thousands of dollars of experience.

"We're going," I heard uttered gruffly. Mateo's hands slipped around my body, one pinning my waist down so I couldn't move it anymore, the other over my thigh like a seatbelt. His fingers drummed on the inside of my leg impatiently.

"Going?" I squeaked. "Where?"

"Oh, baby girl." He said it so sarcastically, condescendingly. "How does it usually end when you put on this little show?"

With my feet tickling my ears? A stack of pillows under my hips? My head hanging off the edge of the bed and my mouth wide open? We were at a borderline rave where none of those choices seemed like an option, but I wasn't underestimating Mateo's creativity. Not with his possessive hands on my body and that determined dark stare—the one that only came out for a very specific reason and didn't go away unless that reason was satiated.

He wouldn't, I dared to think. It would be so goddamn obvious why we were leaving and what we were about to do.

The music mixed into a different song and Mateo's grip tightened just before he hefted us both off the leather booth, keeping me pressed to his body, no doubt hiding the boner I could still feel pegging me in the back. I was deranged enough to smile about it even though he could swipe a finger between my legs and put me on blast just as easily.

"I don't know whether I should clap or not." Tyler held his two palms about a foot apart from each other. "It was almost like you've rehearsed that before." I sent a silent *thank you* into the universe for giving Mateo friends who were outwardly unabashed because it made the pregnant awkwardness of the lap dance coming to an end *that much* more bearable.

That was short-lived, of course, as my darling husband pushed me forward by the small of my back, steering me like a grocery cart with a wonky wheel *away* from everyone. Ophelia was amused; my sisters were baffled; Angelo avoided eye contact like an animatronic with a loose screw, unsure of which direction to turn or what to do with his hands; and Sam was buried in his drink, unfazed.

We were one hell of a dysfunctional group.

"We're going to sort something out," Mateo announced. My cheeks flushed, and my lower half buzzed in anticipation as I tripped over myself adjusting to the quickness in which he turned us toward the dark hallway leading straight to the bathrooms.

Two steps later, we were screeched to a halt by a strange man and a deep voice that chilled me straight to my bones.

"I thought I recognized you two."

chapter thirty-five

Natalia

MY HEAD WHIPPED to the side and I was blindsided by a man my father's age. Dark hair, the hint of a beard circling his thin mouth and sharp chin. Light eyes that literally cut the air from my lungs in half when I glared into them, because I didn't know that face, but he very clearly knew mine. The recognition made my stomach turn over as I realized he knew us for all the wrong reasons.

No, not here. Not *now*.

I'd never had to face a subscriber in the wild. We'd been lucky despite the online popularity to remain under the radar. This was a thousand times worse considering it was happening in front of my sisters, our friends—people who were none the wiser.

My heart thudded so violently my ribs felt like they might crack. One of our streaming rules was to keep personal lives *personal*. The only information we asked for was valid identification, and a lot of the time the men I did requests for were trying to keep themselves incognito too. They had wives, and kids, and very important high-paying, travel-dense jobs that made splurging for my service possible, but a dirty little secret. The less I knew the better.

I'd gone rigid, and Mateo noticed. His shoulders widened,

and he stepped in front of me, putting a very large, intimidating body between the man and me. "Do we know this guy?"

"No," I lied. Maybe that would be enough to get him to walk away. Make him think he'd mistaken us for someone else, or realize this wasn't the time or the place and he was stepping over a boundary I'd never had to verbally place before.

Don't be fucking stupid, I thought to myself. *Walk away with a shred of stolen dignity, dude.* My breathing stuttered as our wedding party became more aware of Mateo's protective body language and the uncomfortable conversation.

"Mat and Nat, right? Sorry if you're trying to keep it lowkey, I watch your stream every week," he retorted with a disturbing amount of charisma. His unsettling stare raked down my body slowly as if he was reminiscing on the skin beneath my clothes and I felt so exposed knowing this man had that intimate knowledge of me. Like I was nothing but a toy. "The little lap dance is what gave it away. I *knew* I'd seen that somewhere before. But I had to get a closer look. Natasha and Matthew in the flesh. Had I known you were doing live shows I'd have brought some singles."

"Forget you saw us," I said through gritted teeth.

He recoiled, a flash of confusion spreading across his face. The man had clearly had a few drinks and was looking for more from the both of us, like we were purely entertainment and expected to behave like we did online.

"Everything okay?" Sam came to our aid, flanked by the rest of our group who I wanted to stay far, far away.

Mateo's attention flitted to mine and I tugged on his hand, trying to walk away, but the man stepped in front of us again, reaching out to grab me by the arm. His eyebrows pinched together to form a deep wrinkle and he frowned. "Can I at least get a picture? My buddies aren't going to fucking believe this."

"Get your fucking hands off her," Mateo spat, tearing the guy's fingers from my bicep and shoving them toward the floor. "She said no. It will be a mistake to make her say it again."

The older man ignored him, growing more annoyed and

vindictive as a result. "Are you serious, man? I pay good money to watch your girlfriend take your fucking loads and you can't take a simple photo with me? I should have cancelled my sub when your content went to shit these last couple months."

Mateo stepped forward and dug a finger into his chest, pushing him. "You better back the fuck up. I swear to God, I have no problem sending you out of here on a cold stretcher."

He threw his hands up, a vile smirk playing on his lips. "I thought you weren't a jealous guy, considering."

"What's this guy's issue?" Bella asked beside me. I had no explanation, a dumbfounded look on my face, my mouth gaping open and shut like a fish out of water searching for air. The entire situation was out of my control.

"I'm pretty sure she made it clear you weren't welcome breathing her fucking air. Things change." Mateo pushed him back once more, harder. Before the man even had the chance to steady himself again Frankie and the Swans were at Mateo's sides, putting a wall of unmoving bodies in between us.

"Uh…" I shrugged, panicking. Maybe the absence of the screen was making him bold. I no longer had that safety net. I couldn't close the server, couldn't end the stream. "He's confused. I have no idea who he is."

"You're really going to pretend I don't know you?" The man scoffed out a laugh, and Mateo stepped forward again aggressively. This guy was inebriated; he *had* to be to see five fully grown, large men circling him and still choose his next words. "What's wrong, Natasha? You're too good for me with your clothes on? Or do your friends not know you get naked online for money?" He spat that out and it landed like a bomb. My ears started ringing; the ground shook. I waited for a sinkhole to appear in the floor, but it was just my legs wobbling defiantly.

Mia's confused glare cut to mine. "What the hell is he talking about?"

"You're way out of fucking line." Frankie's harsh voice rang out, surprising me. He didn't have to step in, but one thing about

Frankie Casado was his loyalty to Mateo, and that extended to me. We were *all* family. I had no doubt the Swans were on the same page. Still, the swell of unease inside me could combust my entire chest.

"Come on, Nat." Ophelia laced her fingers with mine and tried to usher me away as if the damage hadn't already been done. "He's crazy. We don't need to entertain that. I'm sure the guys will figure it out."

"Natalia." Camilla's voice was stern. She crossed her arms over her chest, brows furrowing. She looked so much like our mother it made the room spin. It was like I was back in school again, standing in the shadow of my bedroom while my parents scolded me from the door, my sisters peeking out from behind my dad's long legs and sneering at me. "Is that true? Are you..." She looked like she might vomit out the words. "*Selling* yourself?"

Her bite of disgust scorched me to the bone. More so than the fact that she seemed to be believing every word out of this random stranger's mouth. She didn't even think to question him; she'd made up her mind almost instantly. It was more heinous for someone to be a sex worker than to be harassed for it.

"It's more complicated than that," I rushed out.

"How could it be?" Bella countered. "Do you even know how crushed our parents will be when they find this out, Talia? They're going to lose it."

"That's extreme," Ophelia cut in. "She's a grown woman."

My body was vibrating. "It's none of their business."

"But what if they do?" Mia added. "Wouldn't you rather it come from you and not one of the doctors Dad works with telling him they've jerked it to his daughter doing porn?"

I swallowed hard. "God, Mia."

"So you're not denying it?" Camilla asked again.

I bit my tongue so hard I tasted blood, but couldn't bring myself to fully walk away as the stranger continued throwing insults. "Really great business model the two of you have. Matthew, right?" he taunted a seething, silent Mateo, and I caught the Swans shooting each other an addled look. "You loan her out to other men to use and manipulate, lead us on to think we mean something, but pocket our money and discard us like trash once you've gotten what you wanted. I think there's a word for men like that."

"Don't you fucking dare," Mateo warned, his fists balled up at his sides.

My sisters had gone still. Stone cold, deadpan. I could pinpoint the exact moment I knew they were never going to accept me. All that work we'd done, the change I'd felt within myself and them, the closeness I swore I'd never feel that had come so fucking close to reality, disintegrated between the spaces of my fingers like fine sand. I wasn't just shocked anymore, I was fucking angry. Humiliated. Tears burned in the corners of my eyes, and it made me want to disappear, because I couldn't stop them from welling there no matter how hard I tried.

"You're nothing but her pimp," the man barked. "And she's worth a hell of a lot less in person."

My face fell, Mateo lunged forward, and every single one of us moved like pieces on a chessboard crashing to the floor. Tyler hooked Mateo around the chest with his forearm, keeping him from making a mistake that would land him in jail, and Frankie and Sam closed in aggressively. But it was Angelo, who before that moment hadn't said much, that took one determined step forward and uttered, "Nobody disrespects my sister like that."

Then cocked his arm back, and punched him square in the jaw.

chapter thirty-six

Mateo

IT WAS four in the morning when Angelo finally stumbled out of the Las Vegas police department where they had booked him. His hair was a mop of tangles, the buttons of his wrinkled shirt undone to the center of his chest, golden Catholic cross hanging down. He rolled his neck, yawning, rubbed the sleep from his eyes, and got one good look at me.

"You look like shit, brother."

It was telling that he was the one dragged out of a nightclub by security, thrown against a wall by Metropolitan police, and arrested for assault, yet I was the one with the haggard where-withal of a man who got mugged and kidnapped at gunpoint. It also could have been that Tally and I had spent six hours on a bench outside waiting for the bail money I put up to clear and Angelo to be let loose.

She sprang up and threw her arms over his shoulders, rocking him back and forth. "Fuck, I'm so sorry, Ang. What were you thinking?!"

"Guy had it coming." He hugged her back with one arm. The other held a plastic baggie filled with his belongings. The knuckles of his right hand were still inflamed.

"You didn't have to do that," I said. "I would have taken care of it."

"And ended up in the slammer at your bachelor party? No way. Besides, your record is clean, and mine is like a McDonald's bathroom. What's one more splash of piss on the seat?"

I shook my head, giving away a grin for the first time in hours. "Thank you, I guess."

"Where is everyone?"

"Sleeping, probably," Tally said. "They went back home. Everyone's flights are at different times today. After what happened tonight I'm pretty sure the entire mood was killed and the weekend was ruined, so I don't exactly blame them."

I'd spent every second since we got to the station thinking about how I would approach this conversation with Angelo. It was awkward as hell for Natalia, and the words that guy used to describe her made me sick every time I replayed them in my head. The scumbag would be fine; he was assessed by EMS outside the club, blubbering like he hadn't been asking for someone to clean his clock, and from what I could tell a little cosmetic dentistry would do the trick. It wasn't like he couldn't afford it. I was more disappointed that *I* hadn't been the one to do the damage. It was probably a good thing, because once I started I would have done a hell of a lot more harm than that. Angelo saved my ass by stepping in.

My brother looked up to me, though. Not that what Tal and I did for work was anything to look down on, but it was taboo, and he was allowed to be hesitant about it. Pike had decided what I did in my free time with my girlfriend was none of his business, and we were better for it. I just hoped that Ang would react the same. As we'd figured out, Natalia's sisters were much less inclined.

"This is a bit awkward." I cleared my throat, scrubbing my hand over the dusting of hair on my chin.

Angelo looked from Tally to me, sliding his hands into the front pockets of his jeans. "Look, I don't need to know anything. If that's your gig, that's your gig. But I do dabble in the fine arts, so we're going to have a problem if I accidentally scroll past a

Reddit post of my brother's dick and balls while I'm trying to relax. *Capisce?*"

"Jesus Christ." I pinched the bridge of my nose.

Tally's hand flung to her mouth to conceal a laugh. Her chilled pink cheeks blossomed into a darker shade. "Got it."

"You don't have to worry about me flapping my gums to Mom and Pop, either," Angelo said pointedly. He reached into his plastic baggie and pulled out a crushed box of Marlboro, putting a cigarette between his teeth. "Nobody needs to know my brother splashes his little soppressata all over the internet. They'd tell the priest, and you know Father Aldo loves his church group gossip. What happens in the confessional most definitely does not stay in the confessional. I'm a son of a bitch, not the devil."

"Nothing little about my soppressata," I argued.

Natalia looked about ready to cry again and Angelo pulled her back in for another hug that made my chest tight. "You're gonna be fine, sis. It's all gonna be fine."

I took a deep, grateful breath. I spent half my adult life ignoring my kid brother, while the other half I thought he was a directionless punk. He deserved more than that; they both did. I was as guilty as Natalia's older siblings, but I wouldn't make the same mistakes. My feet scuffed the pavement and I circled my arms around them both, dropping my forehead to my brother's. Natalia's frizzy hair tickled the underside of my jaw.

"Can we go home now?" Angelo said, the unlit cigarette muffling his lips. "I gotta take a fucking shit so badly it's about to sprout legs and walk out of my ass."

Natalia wiggled herself free of our embrace. "On that note…"

* * *

THE HOUSE WAS quiet when we got back. We crawled into bed and managed less than three hours of sleep, though I'm sure Natalia was wide awake for all of it, before the first snick of a door closing on the floors below us rang out. The footsteps that followed were trailed by a rolling suitcase and then another. Tally had been listening, too. She unfurled from my arms and hopped off the bed in a panic, throwing a sweatshirt over her tank top and rushing out the bedroom door.

The early sun rippled through our curtains and slanted orange squares of light across the white duvet. I tossed it off my legs, pulled on my sweatpants, and followed her. Tally's family needed to know that she and I were united in this, and if there was anything they wanted to say to her, they'd have to say it to me, too. We were adults. We did an adult job, and we'd continue doing it as long as Natalia wanted to. No one would make her feel like that wasn't an option.

Her sisters were dressed for the airport, bags in a pile at the door. They had the earliest flight but part of me wondered if they would have slipped out without a goodbye if Tally hadn't come down to meet them first.

"I know this is a shock," Natalia said. Her fingers dawdled on the kitchen countertop. "It's not new, and it would have never come out if this hadn't happened. All I'm asking is for a little bit of understanding. Let me explain it, and I promise you'll see it differently."

Camilla let out a deep sigh. She looked tired, but still over-dressed in a long sweater dress, heeled boots, an expensive designer watch, and her hair slicked back into a bun. "How? At the end of the day, you're doing *one* thing, no matter how sophisticated you make it. You have to see that."

"Did you need money or something?" Bella questioned. "If you needed money, Talia, all you had to do was ask us, or ask Dad. We would have helped you."

"I didn't need the money," Tally shot back. "Even if I did, I'd never ask Dad. Because then I have their favor hanging over my head. I can't owe them anything, don't you understand? If I took money from our parents it would mean they have control over me. They'd use it to guilt me, and make me feel ungrateful and unappreciative. They're fucking narcissists, and you three know that. You're not immune either. You've just learned to take their abuse, but I wanted out."

Mia crossed her arms, shoving her tongue into her cheek.

"But, *sex*?" Camilla remarked, calling me out across the room. "Aren't you a business owner? Aren't you afraid of the repercussions? Someone could plaster you all over the local pages. You have neighbors and family who didn't sign up for this. Did you not think about those things?"

"Sure we did." I joined them under the dim kitchen lights, beside my wife, laying a soft hand at the small of her back. "We're careful, we don't use our real names, and there's nothing tracing back to our home or personal lives. We vet every individual client. There's clear and concise rules, contracts, and consent. It's a business, and Natalia is remarkable at what she does. Would you have had any idea at all, if that hadn't happened?"

Camilla's mouth twisted. Her shoulders rose and fell but there was no argument. Apart from this hiccup, our career had never posed an issue in our personal lives. And let's face it, a man being publicly splashed for doing porn meant nothing. I would still be a business owner, I would still carry clients, and hell, I might even gain a few. The double standard was insane.

"I've been doing this for years," Tally confessed. "Despite the stigma surrounding it, I feel more respected and admired than in any other job I've ever had. Sex *sells*, and you're naive to think it doesn't. I'm taken care of with or without a man in my life, and isn't that the whole point? Isn't that what the three of you strived for and accomplished all on your own, just like me? I've been taking hits from our entire family since I graduated college because you all assumed I wouldn't figure it out on my own, and that I started dating Mateo and got engaged because I'm desperate for a man to keep me afloat. I *let* you think that, because my pride is less important than keeping the peace. Let's not disrupt it any further."

A car horn honked outside. Isabella flicked her wrist out, checking the time on her smartwatch. "We don't know what to think," she said. "All I know is that we need time, Talia. It's a lot at once, and I don't think you can blame us for needing to process it. You're asking us to keep a huge secret here, too, you know."

"But you'd do that for your sister, right?" I looked at each of them. It wasn't a threat, it was an expectation. A loaded question. "You'd do that for someone you love."

There was a flash of guilt in all of their eyes. That, or they'd really had a number done on them by male authority—their father, presumably—because the smallest bit of contention out of me rattled something loose. "I want to make something clear, too," I said. "I have never given this woman an order or made her do anything she didn't want to do. She has control over me in every aspect of our work life. I support her with my entire chest."

A corner of Natalia's lip twitched upward at me and she turned to her sisters again. "I understand if you need time. That's perfectly fine. Just...don't do anything that might—"

"Ruin the family?" Camilla tossed out.

"That would be far from what ruined it," I shot back. "There's already plenty to blame."

Mia picked at her cuticles with her head down, her lack of an unsolicited opinion entirely out of character. There was no way she had nothing to say, and yet it was like her lips were sewn together. The hangover couldn't have been that bad. Even my headache was mild and I'd outdrank every woman standing in this room.

The car honked again and we all looked to the door.

"Let's revisit this when we're all home," Bella suggested. "Clear our heads." She threw a carry-on over her shoulder and gripped the handle of her suitcase so hard her knuckles lightened a shade.

"I think that's best," Camilla agreed. She followed her younger sister toward the door, pulling her own suitcase.

Mia was the last one to grab her bag and she stalled with her foot keeping the door open in the threshold. "I have to show some properties this afternoon," she said. "Buyers are really persistent."

"Okay." Tally tilted her head. "Yeah. Good luck."

"But I'll see you soon."

My eyes twitched. She was hesitating, stuck on what to say. Then it occurred to me Mia might have wanted Natalia to know she was leaving for a work commitment, not a personal reason. She was cracking a window, casting a line, leaving the dialogue open. Tally took a few steps to meet her.

"If someone's going to bring Mom and Dad into this, can you at least convince Cami and Bella to let it be me?" she asked. "I swear I will, but they should hear it from me first."

Mia nodded. "I think they'll agree with you on that." Bella called out to Mia from the driveway, and she rolled her eyes. "I have to go. Tell everyone I said bye."

"Safe flight," I said.

Mia pulled the door closed behind her, and Tally stayed in the thin window watching the SUV pull away on the dusty desert road.

chapter thirty-seven

Natalia

I WAS SPIRALING.

Partly because I couldn't bring Ophelia home with me, as I watched her from the brown leather armchair across the bedroom while she packed away my entire suitcase. She folded my silk pajama pants into a neat square and tucked them in the main pocket, then moved onto the matching button-up shirt. I swung my legs over an arm of the lounger, resting my neck on the opposite one, and stared at the ceiling. "I wish I was an only child."

Phee snorted. "Then you'd only have one bridesmaid. You don't have any other friends."

"First of all, *ouch*. Secondly, I don't even know if I have more than one right now. The jury is still out. My sisters haven't landed in Florida yet where they can choose to ruin my life or never speak to me again. Maybe they'll do both," I sang. "Maybe I'm free!"

"You're not a whale being let loose into the ocean." A zipper opened, followed by rustling. "Clean or dirty?"

I dropped my head to the side to see Phee holding out a plum purple thong. "Clean."

She rolled it into a more compact size and packed it away, next to a small family's worth of unworn socks, four bathing suits, and three different bras for our whopping two-night stay.

"Seriously, what do I do? I need one of those *Men in Black* mind eraser flashbulbs," I joked. "I can't believe I actually thought they might be cool with the sex work thing. I'd imagined Bella might be a little more open-minded, being a lawyer and all, but she was all moral compass this and that, like she doesn't represent sleazeballs in the courtroom weekly."

"I'm a little surprised by it all, too," she murmured. "But hey, at least you're not a flop. If they found out you were a cam girl and you only had like two subscribers it would be way harder to plead your case. Thousands of people want to see your bits."

"I'm no cheap whore," I croaked. "Say my dad does find out, shuns me from the family and removes me from the will, what would really change in my life anyway? I'm already one foot out the door. It might even be a breath of relief for them to be able to say I went off the rails instead of being forced to face that they're just shitty parents. I can hear it now. *'We tried our best with that one, but we don't know what went wrong!'*"

"They'd probably tell people it was a cry for help." She laughed. "That you were in a dark place and the only way out was through copious amounts of twerking on your boyfriend."

"The only way out was through the field of bubblegum butt plugs."

"You just had to follow the yellow dick road."

I cackled but it tapered into a little growl of frustration. "Is this my villain origin story?"

Ophelia abandoned the bedside and crossed the room to the closet, swinging it open to look inside and finding it empty. "You are surprisingly high-spirited through all of this, so I don't think so?"

"I'm not high-spirited, I'm processing trauma through humor like a normal person."

"I think a normal person would be panicking. You seem like you're in the stage of acceptance, maybe. Or you're a possible masochist. Are you turned on right now?"

Frankie swept into the room, knocking his knuckles gently on the door. "Am I interrupting something?"

"I was just about to fuck your girlfriend," I said without sparing him a glance.

"Nothing says foreplay like folding laundry."

"We were just chatting about the odds that Nat will be exiled from the Russo family if her sisters force her to come clean about...you know." Ophelia gestured vaguely.

Frankie's lip curled. The hat he always wore was resting loosely on his hair, a single brown curl falling down the center of his forehead. "They can't exile you if you exile yourself first."

If only it were that easy. Part of the reason I could even make light of the situation was because Mateo and I were already secretly married. Half the pressure of having the wedding was gone. If the entire thing blew up in my face I could at least rest assured knowing we were no less legally bound.

Ophelia disappeared into the ensuite bathroom with an empty toiletry bag, flipping on the light with a gasp. I'd forgotten to put away the pink sex toy after that first night, and honestly, I didn't think I'd have to explain myself now. "Why is this thing suction cupped to the mirror?"

"It's air-drying," I called out. "Avoiding shrinkage."

"You can pack it yourself," she shouted back. "I love you, but not that much."

"That's fair."

"Gross." Frankie knocked my legs off the arm of the chair so he could sit.

"How is it that everyone in this house is perfectly fine with the sex thing except for my sisters?"

"Are we talking about that?" The Swans appeared at the open bedroom door, entering the same way Frankie had. Tyler hopped onto the bed, spreading his long limbs across the comforter, and Sam leaned against the dresser with his hands in his pockets.

"No," Frankie answered Tyler.

"Because I have some questions," Tyler continued, ignoring him. "Starting with, how much money are we talking? Because I definitely have a sex tape or two somewhere on the internet."

My eyes creased and my lips turned upward. "You'd make out handsomely, pretty boy."

Sam drummed his fingers against the wood grain on the dresser. "I never would have guessed, for what it's worth. And I'm pretty spot-on at figuring things out."

"He really is." Phee shoved my shoes into a separate bag at the top of my suitcase that I never knew was designated for shoes. Apparently luggage was not as self-explanatory as it made itself out to be. That, or I was best friends with Marie Kondo.

"You never would have guessed, or you never wanted to know?" I asked rhetorically.

"Are there any solo vids of Cap?" Tyler tucked his hands behind his head on the pillow and crossed his legs at the ankle.

Frankie shuddered. "Why the fuck would you want that?"

"Oh come on, you're not curious?"

"Curious enough to watch my best friend wank his dick on camera? Nah, I'm good."

Tyler scoffed out a refute. "Well it's not like we can watch the ones with Tally in them. I'm just supporting the biz."

God bless him, the big himbo whore. It didn't make me want to crawl into my asshole any less, but at least I knew the respect was there and that's honestly all I could have asked for.

"I didn't know we were all hanging out in here." It was Angelo's turn to show up outside the bedroom, sticking his head in timidly. He shimmied inside and found a spot against the windowsill. The room was collapsing in on itself, but I welcomed it. It felt so much less lonely and gave me some hope that I still had family, even if family came in a different packaging. These men didn't need to be here, keeping me company, making jokes, lifting my spirits. Yet they were.

"Is that what you're wearing to the airport?" Ophelia pointed at my sweatpants, tank top, the threadbare zip-up sweatshirt I had hanging off my shoulder, and my hard-soled moccasin slippers. Effectively: my pajamas. And yes, I would most certainly be wearing them because if I had to slip my shoes off in a TSA line, I'd do so without causing a scene.

"Yes, Mom," I replied.

Phee took to zipping my suitcase closed, struggling with the final edge of it and then hopping up on the bed to sit on top of the hard pink shell while she wrestled the zipper completely closed. Tyler looked bemused and impressed.

"So, how does it work? You just...you flip on the ring light and fuck?" Sam piped up.

"Sometimes." I couldn't believe I was having this conversation. I'd given Mateo a lap dance in front of everyone in this room less than twelve hours ago, so talking about the details of running a sex cam business was tame in retrospect. There was no visual to go along with the explanation this time at least. "I guarantee you that whatever you're imagining is exactly what it is."

"You don't want to know what I'm imagining," Angelo said. "I can get really weird."

"I'll fill in the blanks for you so that we never have to talk about it again." Frankie pinched his nose and took a dramatic centering breath. I could tell that with even over a decade in special operations, Matty and I had still given him a pinnacle moment of trauma, and I'd wear that like a prideful badge of honor. "The only reason I know about this little side gig, and you guys don't, is because I walked in on Cap dressed as Santa Claus porking Mrs. Claus under my own goddamn roof. That shit you don't forget."

"It was our highest-paying video of the year, for what it's worth," I added. "Even better than the leprechaun."

"What's the romantic counterpart of a leprechaun?" Phee mused. The boys thought hard, their eyes creasing inquisitively. Frankie's frown deepened and his head shook back and forth like someone trying to erase a picture off an Etch A Sketch.

"You'll never know." I grinned big.

"I need to know," Angelo complained. He scrubbed a hand down his face as if the riddle would haunt him. "Female leprechauns don't exist. So if you're not doing your research, there's bigger problems at stake here."

"Didn't Mateo tell you? That job he's hiring you for is actually *director* of video content."

"I'm taking my name out of the hat."

"Where the hell is everybody?" a voice called from the hallway a second before my husband lumbered into the room, stopping short and looking around at all of our friends gathered in several places. His thick eyebrows drew together and steam wafted from the mug of coffee in his hand. I gestured lazily when he found me in the chair. "Is this an intervention?" Mateo asked.

"We didn't want it to come to this, but you forced us." Sam dropped his head and put his hands on his hips. The room fell silent, confused. He was a man of very few undeserved words, and the tone was a touch too serious. "We're worried about you. Doing porn with a cock that small has to be some level of self-harm. Are you okay, Cap? We can get you the help you need."

We exploded in laughter. A warmth rushed through me, like medicine aiding an aching, cold heart. It would be okay, all of it. The secret being let out, my family, our wedding, the future of this, no matter what it looked like. Because I had them.

Maybe it didn't always feel like it, but I deserved this happiness. Not for small glints of time like drops of rain in a pool, all the time. I deserved to swim in it.

"Maybe I was supposed to have brothers," I muttered. The swell of attention was back on me, and Frankie placed a hand on my knee and shook it. Beneath the lip of his faded ball cap there was that beholden kind of love brightening his dark eyes, and a small smile tugged at his full lips.

"You do have brothers," he said.

I put my hand over his gratefully, fighting a whole shelf of emotions from being knocked down and trying my hardest not to cry, because when that started it wouldn't stop. But then I favored a glance at a reassuring Angelo, and an agreeable Sam, and landed on an already teary-eyed Tyler and the dam burst open.

"Look what you did, Pike." Tyler sniffled. "You made her cry."

"Oh, Jesus Christ, Ech. Get it together," Mateo said, crossing the room to lean down and kiss me on the top of the head. I swiped my tears away with the sleeve of my sweatshirt. When we finally got home I'd need a full detox and an uninterrupted forty-eight hours in my bed. Vegas was going to be a dark strike on our vacation destination list for the foreseeable future.

At that point I was practically aching for South Floridian humidity and the familiar coastal palm trees. My coffeemaker, my car, to get back to work and throw myself into it. I could tell I wasn't the only one chomping at the bit to be home. It might not be any better than here *emotionally*; we had to have hard conversations with both his parents, and mine, and though I'd never be ready for that the same way you'd never be ready for death, I was less afraid.

Angelo pushed off the windowsill and to the door of the ensuite bathroom. "You guys got any tissues in here?" He closed the door behind him, right before flicking on the light. I looked at Ophelia, but she was already staring wide-eyed at me with a wicked glimmer.

"One...two..." I counted on my fingers.

A deep shriek rang out, followed by a tormented, equally as boisterous "*What the fuck!*" Ophelia buried her face in the crook of her elbow. Mateo hid his own in his hands.

"Well don't scream at it," I shouted back. "It's not going to jump off the mirror and fuck you."

chapter thirty-eight

Mateo

PART of me wished that if I ignored the problem long enough it would just go away. If I ignored my parents in my home, hanging their towels on the clothesline that was definitely not there before I left for Vegas, it would just go away. If I ignored the freezer full of frozen loaves of bread, or the mini goat milk soaps on the sink in the hallway bathroom, or the new doormat with the tropical flowers on it that I had to step over with my suitcase when we returned, it would all disappear.

Poof. Gone. A figment of my nightmarish imagination.

I managed it for a week, because I couldn't muster up the energy to have the conversation that needed to be had as soon as we got home from Nevada. I had to recover, return to some sense of normalcy at work, which was kicking my ass, and evaluate the situation. To be honest I was waiting for one of my parents to tell me about their newfound homeownership first. But after seven days of radio silence, I realized it wasn't going to happen, and the longer I walked around pretending I didn't know the for-sale sign on the house in the development one road over had come off the lawn, the more resentful I became.

Angelo was back in New York tying up loose ends with Duran & Son and every time the phone rang with him on the other line, I felt like there was some big secret I was purposely not being let in on. He'd told me everything, and I was being updated daily on the changes happening in the Bronx, but my parents didn't know that. So they were purposely keeping me in the dark.

Well, fuck you, Mom and Dad. I had a flashlight.

There were chicken cutlets sizzling on the stove top and a pot of sauce simmering with a delicious mix of garlic and tomato that made every porous surface in the house take on the smell of three-in-the-afternoon Sunday dinner. Dad was in the living room watching the Yankee game on the recliner, and Natalia was curled into the corner of the couch with her phone in her hand.

I hadn't rehearsed exactly what I would say to my parents about what Angelo had told me. Them buying a house in Florida was a bigger decision than simply moving. I didn't need to do much with the physical aspect of it, sure, but the implication was that I'd be going from seeing my parents in short visits and controlled bursts of time, to them having uninhibited access to me. If the last five months were any indication, I craved my personal space and Natalia and I needed it to function properly. It was about more than privacy. It was about sanity. If it was going to happen, which seemed inevitable given the facts, I had to grow a pair and put my foot down firmly.

Mom came out of the kitchen, wiping her hands off on a small towel and tucking it into the string of her apron. Her short curly hair was frizzy from standing over the frying pan.

"I bet Angelo can't wait to get you back home cooking for him again." I cleared my dry throat. "Few more weeks."

They didn't even look up. My mother hummed, and Dad sighed in frustration as a player struck out swinging. Tally glanced up from her phone and gave me a pressing flare of her eyes to try again.

"He was saying that work has really slowed down," I continued, finding a spot on the couch. I put my elbows on my knees and weaved my fingers together. "Not much going on contractually."

That earned a sideways glance from my dad. He shifted in the chair, and a spring somewhere beneath it panged. "It's the slow season."

"Really?" I volleyed. "June? I remember this being the time of the year it usually picked up for you. Good weather and all."

The next batter on the screen swung and popped a long fly ball into center field. Dad smacked his palm on his thigh, ignoring me.

"Did you notice there was a house for sale on Leatherby?" Tally tucked her feet under her thighs, sitting up straighter. My parents finally turned their heads at the mention. "Pretty sure someone bought it already."

"Yeah," I rushed out. "It's hard to find a good price like that around here. Total seller's market." Mom inched into the room behind my father and kneaded her thumbs into his shoulders. "It got me thinking, actually."

"Thinking about what?" Mom asked.

I shrugged, absolutely spitballing. "Thinking about selling our house."

"What?" Dad let go of his white-knuckled grip on the remote. "Why would you do something like that?"

The chord was struck. I would needle this confession out of them with the help of my wife if it killed me. "Move back to New York," I lied. "Be closer to family, better schools, more help if there's grandkids."

My mother drew in a gasping, stuttering breath as though she'd been stabbed. Her fingers dug into my dad's shoulders, scoring his polo with her nails. The mere mention of a baby spun this woman's world on an axis. It was a low blow.

"What's wrong?" I asked. "I thought you'd be excited. We could all be back together again, a big happy family. Of course, I'd never do something like close the business I built from the ground up and sell my house to move into your neighborhood without running it by you guys first. That would be crazy."

Dad craned his head to look up at Mom. Guilt splashed across her face in pink splotches. And not because she was overheating from the oven. "Mateo..." Dad lifted a hand, offering an explanation.

"I definitely wouldn't pretend to be in town to visit my dear, loving parents for six months because I missed them, and wanted to spend time with them before a very important event in their lives, while I was actually scoping the realty landscape and going to open houses in secret," I said as dryly and sarcastically as humanly possible.

Mom tutted, her hands going to her hips. "We were going to tell you, but after the wedding. We didn't want to make it all about us. I don't think that's a crime." At least they weren't trying to deny it anymore. That made things a hell of a lot easier. I could stop speaking in metaphors, and I'd definitely garnered all of their attention because my father actually clicked *off* the baseball game, which I hadn't ever seen happen—unless the Yankees were getting their asses kicked and he couldn't bear witness to it anymore.

"You didn't think that I might have an opinion?" I pinched my shoulders to my ears. "New York has been your home for your entire lives, and don't try to tell me you've grown bored of it, or you wanted to retire somewhere warm. Even if you decided you love it here after the last six months, that wasn't the reason you came. Angelo told me everything."

"Angelo doesn't know what he's talking about. We did come here for you two," Dad said, gesturing toward Tally and me.

"Then why lie?" I leaned my hands on the back of the couch. "You didn't retire from Duran & Son and pass the torch to Ang. You closed up shop because you couldn't keep up. There's nothing wrong with that, Dad. You've done hard, solid work for decades. I don't know why you couldn't be honest about it with me. With us."

My father's face warped, and Mom's lips thinned.

"Business dried up and you were planning on moving here to be close to us, and you knew how I might feel about it, so you didn't tell me. I've been living my own life, and now I'm going to be married and starting a family and you didn't want me to have a choice."

"Why wouldn't you want to be close to us, too?" Mom asked. "Especially now. We want to be in your life for big moments. To help Natalia when she needs it. To be the kind of grandparents that see the kids more than once a year."

"But this is more than that. This is manipulation. And guilt. I love you both," I pressed. "I want you in my life."

"We both do," Tally added. She reached up and laced her fingers through mine at the top of the couch.

"But I'm not a teenager. I'm not the eighteen-year-old that left for the Army. Hell, I'm not even the same man I was a year ago. You can't make decisions for me and expect me to fall in line. You can't expect no pushback, no dialogue, no boundaries. We should have had a conversation about this. I shouldn't be hearing it from my brother like an afterthought at my bachelor party. What you've done is wrong on so many levels, and it's going to take time to gain that trust back. I know it's happening, and that's something I'll come to terms with, but I couldn't let this go without telling you both how I really feel about it."

This was the first time in my life I'd had a conversation with my parents that felt like I was the lecturer. My voice was rising and falling, that anxiety knocking on the inside of my chest. I was fighting hard against the principles with which I was brought up to make it clear that things were going to change. They needed to, not just for my sake but for Tally's. I was protecting what was mine.

The air was explosive. Thick and tense. My father's throat bobbed but he wasn't the argumentative type; he let my mom do the talking and sat back stoically, processing. She was the matri- arch, the one pulling the strings knowing anything she decided would be supported. That's how it always was, and that's how it'd likely be with Natalia and me. It was about trust.

"I'm sorry our timing wasn't the best," Mom said softly. Surprising me. Tally's fingers tightened around mine. "You're right, we should have discussed it. Maybe in the back of our minds we assumed that it was something everyone would benefit from, and being your mother, making decisions for the entire family has been more than half of my life."

"You did your job," I assured her. "You did it well. There's no need to grip so tightly. I might need a kick in the ass sometimes, but I found the right woman to do it. Trust me, there isn't a damn thing I can get away with. You don't have to worry about that."

Natalia laughed quietly, and her lips grazed my knuckles with a kiss.

"We made the wrong decision by hiding the house from you both," my father added. "I think we were so excited about the possibility of being around more that we only saw it from our perspective, which is having our son back."

A knot formed in my throat. "I'll take blame for not coming home as often as I should have. I forced you to hold on as tightly as possible to the way I used to be. Your kid and your responsibility. It might take time, but you don't have to carve out a space in my life, because you're already there. I regret making you feel like you had to. We could have avoided all of this."

"I think this goes without saying," Natalia added, "that you raised the best man in the world. He's caring, and soulful, selfless, open-minded and hearted. He makes everyone around him better. He would never turn his back on your family, *our* family. I promise to take care of him forever."

My fingers slipped into Tally's hair, then ran down her neck and back up, and she leaned into the touch. "I think it's great that you bought the house. Really." I was as sincere as I could be. This wasn't a *bad* thing, it was an adjustment. We'd been warming up to it since January. "As long as you call before you stop over," I rushed out. "No more surprise visits."

"We learned our lesson," Dad said jokingly. "No more surprises."

"You can enjoy the fruits of your labor, finally. If Angelo accepts the job I offer him, he might find his way down here, too,"

I said. My parents perked up, exchanging a shocked but elated glance with one another.

"You offered him a job?" Dad sat up. "Doing what? He doesn't know anything about cybersecurity."

"I can teach him," I said. "If he's willing to put in the work and get serious about a career with me. He's still young, smart, and I'm not worried at all about his reliability." Not after lying in a holding cell all night so I didn't have to, but we'd keep that to ourselves.

My mother left my father's side and waddled to me, wrapping her short arms around my waist and shaking me back and forth. "That made me the happiest mother on the planet just now."

"The Barrys next door are going to be so thrilled," Tally chirped. Then she and my mother shot off talking about the neighborhood, interior design and garden landscaping, my mom's brand-new dream kitchen, and throwing a housewarming party once we got back from our honeymoon. My dad reclined in the chair once more, shooting me a wink and turning the game back on.

Grade school joy sparked in my chest where a weight had been lifted.

chapter thirty-nine

Natalia

MATEO and I both agreed to take a short hiatus after the wedding to enjoy married life, go to a beach that wasn't Pompano, and focus on each other fully. Which meant three weeks of long nights, content filming, and finishing the projects we were contractually obligated to.

During the day when his parents were home, Anna and I had coffee together. I showed her how to use Pinterest for all of her decorating ideas, and built her a wall of boards for things like recipes and holidays. She broke out the ironing board that was collecting dust in the hallway closet to teach me a skill I'd never bothered to learn. When I was younger the dry cleaner took care of it, and when I was in my early twenties, I wore wrinkled clothes or threw rumpled outfits in the dryer for an extra cycle hoping that would magically fix them. One day, I showed her how to use the streaming remote, because she'd only ever had cable, and Spotify so the radio wasn't her sole option. She came home from the store with a floral spiral notebook the next afternoon and sat at the counter writing all the meals Mateo grew up eating in perfect cursive with ingredients and measurements and left it next to the stove for me.

Most of the time, though, Anna and David were busy like

Mateo and I were. After the wedding they still had to go back to New York and sell their house and pack it, which would take a few months. Angelo would be there to make the transition as smooth as possible, but things were moving at a pace that both scared and thrilled me. When they were out of the house I worked in the privacy of a quiet bedroom.

Our inbox was flooded with requests after Vegas. I'd never gone more than twelve hours without checking the messages or updating myself on subscribers, so being gone for two days set us back. I was writing skeleton scripts all day, testing lighting, choosing costumes, doing my solo client requests in between, and faking so many unearned orgasms I was lightheaded. My clit was chafed from the vigor of my wand vibrator.

Immersing myself into my work was the only thing that kept my mind off everything else. But it had to have been a good thing that a week had gone by without a phone call from my parents, right? Every time the screen lit up I had a small panic attack, my lungs seizing and my muscles stiffening. There was no way that level of anxiety was good for my body, being in full fight or flight mode constantly. Part of me wished that if they were going to out me, they would just fucking do it already instead of pawing me around like a toy. But this was probably part of the satisfaction, having something to hold over my head until they felt like kicking me in the cunt.

Slipping into one of Mateo's long, soft robes I crossed my legs and sat in the computer chair to edit the week's worth of scripted content we'd filmed. I got to have fun with the pre-filmed scenes during the mixing and polishing process. I always liked the look of the videos more with cuts in time, specific framing, and at least two angles. I could tell a story artistically, make it more eye-catching, the sounds more pleasing, the payoff even grander at the end. When I analyzed the viewership and interaction data, I knew exactly what videos did the best, and could replicate our best performances visually and physically.

For example, our most popular video included zip ties; a sloppy, spit-string face fuck; my tits; and an impressively long cum shot. I was more than happy to find a plethora of ways to reinvent the wheel there if it meant keeping our viewership as happy as they were when that one hit the internet.

I knew I'd never get my sisters to *applaud* my work. The same way I'd never want to see one of them having sex, though I'd absolutely walked in on Camilla with a hand beneath her sheets when she was in high school. I was too young then, but I shuddered at the thought now. It did give me hope, though, that my oldest sister wasn't as frigid and uptight as I'd thought. She did indeed have a pulse, and sometimes it even thrummed between her legs.

But would curiosity get the best of me if I'd found out one of them had a popular porn business? Would I need to entertain that little piece of my mind wondering what the hell it looked like?

A twinge of discomfort built in my gut, spreading like static on a limb after lying on it for too long. That tingling, gnawing sensation found its way into my ribs, and then my throat, and before long I was scrolling through our recent subscribers, searching for an email I recognized. I found nothing, but they also would have never been stupid enough to subscribe to our page with their real names. If they could even find it.

Their only lead was Matthew and Natasha, and one thing Mateo had done when we first started filming content together was bury the chances of anyone stumbling upon us in a preliminary Google search by manipulating the SEO.

That didn't sway me from falling down a search bar rabbit hole.

We were lost somewhere in the deep web all thanks to Mateo. The only results I garnered were other couples with similar names, several hyperlinks to that one unethical competitor site, and a barrage of cooking blogs claiming to have the "Easiest, Best-Tasting Italian Meatballs."

Cracking my knuckles I pushed away from the desk on squeaky chair wheels and dropped onto the bed on my stomach, scooping up my cellphone from the fluffy sheets. My finger hovered over the group chat with my bridesmaids, but after everything that went down I didn't know how to casually converse with all of them as if the entire wedding party hadn't self-imploded.

Ophelia's text chain was pinned at the top of my messages and I clicked into it.

ME

Do you think my sisters are snooping on my page?

PHEE

What makes you say that?

ME

Because it's the perfect ammo to humiliate me

PHEE

Is it more humiliating to be the one getting dicked down by your man, or to be the one watching your sister get dicked down by your brother-in-law?

ME

It depends

PHEE

??

ME

Maybe they're watching the one where we're dressed as Bo Peep and Woody from Toy Story

PHEE

The kid's movie?

ME

Bo Peep and Woody are ADULTS

PHEE

There has to be some kind of copyright law against that

ME

Then the people at Pixar would have to explain how they found it in the first place

PHEE

Talk about covering all your bases

We *had* covered all our bases. I had absolutely nothing to worry about, and yet I couldn't shake that feeling that somehow Bella was using her lawyer connections to find and compile a damning testimony against me and my nether regions. If not to bring it in a binder of hot-off-the-press computer paper to our parents, then to present it back to me as a form of reverse revenge porn self-reflection.

Ophelia texted me again.

O

You should just ask them

ME

I haven't even talked to them in over a week

O

Maybe they're waiting for you?

The last thing Mia said to me was that she'd try to talk Bella and Cami into letting me do my own dirty work. They could have agreed and were waiting for me to hold up my end of the bargain. If that was the case I still had some time left to convince them *not* to ruin our family, because if they thought I'd be outing myself to anyone before our wedding reception was over, they'd be sorely mistaken. That way I could fuck off forever and never have to show my face to anyone in the Russo lineage ever again.

It'd be for the best.

It would also haunt me until the wedding if I didn't find out what was going on with the three of them and where we really stood in all this. They were still my bridesmaids; no one had rescinded their invitation. We were possibly the most dysfunctional bridal party in America, but at least there was no groom-cheats-on-bride-day-of-wedding drama like in the movies.

Mia was the most receptive, if you could call it that. I singled her out and decided to skip over waiting for a text back and hit the call button in her contact. It rang enough times for me to question whether or not she would pick up, but on the fifth ring she did.

"Hello." Her voice was low, but soft. A jingle in the background sounded like her car keys rattling around on her finger.

"Hey," I said, letting out a deep breath. "I don't want this to be weird."

She punched out a laugh. "That's a good way to not make it weird."

"I don't want you to get penalized for finagling with the enemy. But if I have to be in the dark about what's going on for another hour I might scratch myself out of my skin."

Her heels clicked against the pavement. It was the middle of the afternoon so she was probably coming or going from a property showing. "Have I become the more approachable older sister? I made a wrong turn somewhere."

"*Approachable* isn't the word I'm thinking of, but empathetic, possibly?" I squeaked. "The only one who might pick up the phone, at least."

"I was worried about you," Mia said. I was taken aback by it, and before I could catch up she filled the open space. "What's the verdict on that guy Angelo punched? Is he pressing charges?"

"No, thankfully. I think he sobered up and nearly shit himself when he realized there were four more men waiting for their turn. Angelo got a ticket for disorderly conduct, but that's far from the first time for him."

Mia was quiet on the other line for a moment, a short hum sifting through the receiver. "So that guy harassing you was... what? A...fan?"

"A subscriber. *Former* subscriber."

"I'd say."

"That's never happened to me before, just so you know," I rushed out. "I've never met a person from my online life in my real one, and neither had Mateo. It was all such a freak coincidence. I'm sorry again that you were there for that."

"Doesn't it scare you?" she asked quietly. It was the furthest thing from accusatory—more profoundly concerned, and whimsically curious. "That these men are complete strangers but they think they own you? The parasocial aspect of it has to fuck with you."

I sat up straighter on the bed, crossing my legs into a pretzel. I pulled my phone away from my ear to check that it was in fact Mia I was on the phone with before placing it back. This was not the way I thought this conversation would go. It wasn't even the way I was *hoping* it would, but I was more than happy to continue because in a screwed-up way I liked that she cared. That she even wanted to be on the phone with me to begin with.

"It used to," I told her. "When I started, I was doing it alone and had no idea how easy it was to be taken advantage of, even behind a screen. Once I realized how liberating the power was, that I was the one in control of everything and I could be any person that I wanted to be, it wasn't scary anymore. I'm not in any danger, if that's what you're asking."

"I'm just still trying to wrap my head around it," Mia said. "You're my baby fucking sister. In my head you're still playing dress up in Mom's formal gowns and cutting your hair with the kitchen scissors."

"That's the problem," I sighed. "I'm twenty-six years old. I'm not trying to say that means you should have known I was a cam girl, and I'm not even saying you should accept it. What I'm saying is, if I'm doing adult things, as an adult, I should at least get a proper hearing before being voted out."

"You really shocked us," she said.

"I know. I totally get that, and it's been a week of well-deserved silent treatment. Now I'm in wedding panic mode, and spiraling, so I guess what I'm asking is, is there a world where we pretend nothing ever happened and everyone is none the wiser?"

She made a small, exasperated noise. The chirp of her keys unlocked her car and the heavy door whooshed open and thudded closed before the radio blared to life. Mia quickly dialed the volume down as the engine in her BMW thrummed to life.

"You know I can't speak for Cami and Mia. I also can't say that this isn't questionable at best from my point of view. I mean, are you dead set on making America's Horniest Home Videos for the rest of your life?"

A laugh escaped me. "Who knows?"

Not even I did. Tomorrow I might wake up and decide that I never wanted to make any new content ever again. That creative bug inside me could die, Mateo could change his mind about it, I could put my energy into working behind a camera instead of in front of it. Life could become busy in other ways.

"All I'm really asking for is solidarity," I said. "Does that work?"

"If that's what you need," Mia said. "Don't mention it,

because this is as much for me as it is for you. God knows I don't ever want to be on the receiving end of John Russo's wrath. I'm stockpiling karma points."

My lungs lightened. There was a breath caught in my throat that I pushed out heartily. I hadn't won anything, but it felt like I should be crossing a finish line, or at the very least finishing a very tumultuous leg of a race.

"I'll win them over." Though it was an inside thought, I spoke it out loud.

"Is that why you called? To figure out how deep of a hole you had to crawl out of?"

"Because my wedding is in three weeks, and I needed to know if I had to hire stand-in bridesmaids off Craigslist."

"Your saving grace is that this wedding is a reflection of the entire Russo family. If we don't look like one cohesive unit, it tarnishes Dad's image, heaven forbid." I could hear her eyes rolling. "He's been way more self-aware lately, so don't hold out for a drunken rehearsal dinner speech."

"What's the point of the dinner then?"

"Spending a thousand more dollars as quickly as humanly possible."

"Oh, I did have one more question." I pinned the phone between my shoulder and my ear and played nervously with my cuticles. "You didn't try to look me up online, did you?" A beat passed, and my fingers stilled, eyes widening. Her non-answer was all the answer I needed. "Mia!"

"How are you going to drop on us that you're some high-profile sex worker with people recognizing you out in Las Vegas nightclubs and not expect a little research to be done?"

She had a point, but it didn't make it any less difficult to swallow. My tongue felt like a paperweight in my mouth. "And?"

"And we didn't find anything, so you can unclutch your pearls."

Relief rushed out in a sigh. The very first thing I was doing when Mateo got home was kissing his perfect cybergenius mouth.

"More reason to leave Mom and Dad out of this. They would literally never know."

"Yeah, yeah." Mia's voice bottomed out. "I have to go. I'm meeting a seller to take photos for a listing. My advice is to give the other two time. Bella is a snob, but she's not without compassion. Camilla needs to get laid. Don't go on Craigslist."

"I won't," I replied with a little too much hopeful glee. Very kid in a candy shop with an empty plastic baggie and a dream. The line dropped and my phone plopped onto the comforter, me going right down with it and burying my face in a pillow to let out a dramatic muffled scream.

chapter forty

Mateo

I BACKED into an open space at the back of the car lot and threw my truck into park. My hand lingered on the key fob like I might make the decision to rev it up again and peel out of the local VA hospital. Natalia squeaked against the seat, her thighs tacky on the hot leather as she twisted in my direction with a proud, empowering look on her sweet face. That face could make a man do anything. Like buck up and walk into an appointment with a government-mandated therapist for the first time.

Veterans Affairs medical services ranged from therapy and mental health services to general practitioners, preventative measures, illness, injuries, dentists, you name it. I had never used any of my benefits out of pure laziness. Really, if I was ever sick it was easier to be seen in an urgent care than jump through the hoops of making appointments for the same result. I was like any other adult turned off by the idea of making phone calls and filling out paperwork unless it was damn near detrimental.

But when I made the choice to finally talk to someone about what I'd been going through, finding someone qualified, who knew the minds of men and women who had been deployed, felt like the smartest, most natural thing to do.

"Are you nervous?"

"I guess you could say that." Ahead of us the gray double doors of the brick building opened and closed. Another guy around my age walked out into the stifling June sunlight in an olive drab T-shirt, squinting and sticking his hands in his shorts pockets.

"Don't be," Tally said. Her soft, tiny hand reached over to rest comfortingly on my knee. I hadn't realized it was bouncing until it stopped. "Just be yourself. They're professionals. Remember that nothing you say is wrong, because it's not a test to pass or anything like that. You're going to do great."

The corner of my lip twitched upward. "I don't know what I'm supposed to talk about. I don't want to waste this guy's time, either. What if this is all just normal everyday struggles and I've chalked it up into something it's not?"

"Just because your trauma isn't the same size as somebody else's doesn't mean it deserves any less attention," she said. "Some people need an unbiased sounding board, and if that's all this is for you, then that's fine, too. There's no mandatory life-altering prerequisite to therapy."

The stigma around it was what had deterred me for so long. I thought I didn't have enough of a reason to seek out professional help when there were real veterans struggling, real statistics showing how hard the acclimation from military back to civilian life really was. In my mind, if I wasn't in danger of becoming one of the twenty-two a day, I was wasting time and resources. But what I never thought about was how there was a time each of those vets was in the same boat as me, embarrassed to ask for help, unwilling to self-reflect, hoping that they might be able to figure it out on their own.

My commitment to showing up today was a step in the right direction. Maybe the beginning of something completely unexpected if it went well enough. The difference in my life from just six months ago was stark, and glazed with potential to be a point that I looked back on years from now as the beginning of every-thing. The turning page from part one to part two. The day we got engaged, the world shifted on an axis, and like dominos, the rest fell loudly and chaotically into place.

For the most part.

I put my hand over Tally's and squeezed it gently. "I won't talk about our thing," I told her. "If you don't want me to."

"I want you to talk about whatever you need to. It's a big part of your life, and if it unlocks some kind of doorway to understanding more about yourself then I would never tell you not to. This is strictly about you, Mateo. Be as selfish as possible. It's all confidential."

She was so adorably supportive, and I hated myself for ever thinking this would be a burden for her to manage. Lifting Tally's fingers to my lips, I kissed each knuckle, then flipped her hand and pressed my lips to each of her fingertips and her palm. She slid her open hand against my stubble, resting it on my jaw and running her thumb across my cheek.

"Selfish, got it."

* * *

DR. HENRY BRINCKLER replied to every answered question with another question. It felt very much like an adult conversation with an inquisitive toddler. The kind that had you questioning the validity of your information after the sixth consecutive, "Why?"

My expectation was to be picked apart and scrutinized, but it was more like getting stripped down to the core aspects of myself. How old I was, what I did, where I was deployed, my family dynamics, why I decided to show up at therapy for the first time and then why I thought this was the right time to take that step.

Doctor Brinckler, Brinck, as he told me to call him, sat across from me in a matching dark green velvet chair with a round coffee table between us. There was a psychology textbook and a geode in the center of it that I couldn't stop staring at, and I caught myself sliding my palm up and down the arm of the chair several times while I was answering his open-ended question.

Doc had a pad and pen resting on his crossed knee, but didn't use it, like it was more decorative than functional, and I found that I was waiting the entire time to say something interesting enough for him to record. Until it was all that I could think about, and I was irritating myself with how much I wanted to feel like a real, damaged case and not just another veteran coming into the office with the same story he'd heard a thousand times before, and the same advice to be given.

I told him about Angelo, and that spiraled into the misplaced resentment I once felt for my brother, and how we didn't see one another for years, then the wedding planning, the best man debacle, and Vegas a couple weekends ago when he stood up for my wife and got himself thrown in jail overnight to defend her honor.

My tangent lasted fifteen minutes before I ran out of material and even then Henry stared into my soul with a contentment that was more blasé than impressed and more curious than interpretive.

"You don't want to write any of that down?" I gestured to the pen and paper.

His head tilted. "Do you want me to?"

Lodging my tongue in my cheek I hid my chagrin. My arms crossed over my chest. "I thought that's what we were doing."

Doc's bright blue eyes narrowed and his jaw twitched so quickly into a smirk I almost missed it. Then he picked the pad up for the first time and scribbled something short and direct onto it. Which was just about the worst thing in the world that he could have done. Now instead of worrying over why he wasn't writing anything at all, I was twice as worried over the few words in black ink that somehow defined everything about me.

"What was that?"

"Very important notes."

I let my head fall back on the soft edge of the chair and started counting the points on the popcorn ceiling. Maybe therapy wasn't for me. Or maybe I'd watched too much television that portrayed going to a psychologist as some mind-altering, eye-opening experience where the doctor said one slightly poetic, riddle-esque thing and the plot came crashing down around them. Everything all of a sudden making sense. Like Fleabag.

I did not want to fuck a priest, so my problems might be unsolvable.

"Do you think you seek validation from the people in your life as a grading system for your worth?"

Oh, fuck. I stood corrected.

I readjusted in the chair. "I think I feel valuable to my friends and family when I'm providing for them."

"Do you need to provide something to feel valuable?"

"Isn't that how it works?"

"Should you not be enough on your own without a form of currency attached to it?"

"Are you going to answer everything I say with another question?"

He scratched another word onto the lined pad and my skin started to itch. Not because of the writing anymore, I was more worried over the thought of attaching all my value to acts of service. It brought me back to Delta, being the point man for my unit, because being the go-to in a high-stress environment like that *did* make me feel like I was providing something invaluable to the men I served with. Being the leader, the captain, was the most important and worthy I'd ever felt. When I came home the rush of that depleted. I wasn't a soldier anymore, not in the way that I was used to. The full heart, body on the line, dying for my country soldier. I was a civilian, and there weren't many things I could do in life that felt as *important* as that. The high was what I'd been trying to recreate. To fill my cup with, and I was struggling hard with the reality that I might never do something that would make me feel quite as indispensable again.

It was why I was afraid of letting down my family, why I couldn't say no to anything. I wanted to be all the things I could possibly be at once. The best son, the one who didn't complain, the one who was available, the one who had space in his house for extended stays, and a beautiful wife, and possibly grandchildren. It was why it was so fucking impossible for me to give up control at work and hire someone to help me with TechOps after Pike left. My clients expected a certain level of quality from me and I couldn't chance letting a new face, or a new hire, half-ass it. I felt valuable for offering Pike that job, and I'd feel valuable again when I hired Angelo.

Then there was Tally. I never thought about why I was so accepting of the sex work, so eager to join in on it, so open to it. I always chalked it up to...being there for Tally. I wanted whatever she wanted, and would do anything for her, so being part of her life in that way was never something I hyperanalyzed. But maybe the reason I agreed to join her on camera was because it would make me more *valuable* to her. Until two minutes ago I also never viewed myself as a good to be exchanged, either. I wasn't fully convinced I did, but I was more inclined to pay attention to the way I interacted with the people in my life on account of it. Did I think that she might find me expendable if I never started sex working with her? Was that the driving force in becoming an online pair? That if I didn't do it, she might find someone else who would? All the memories of our first conversation surrounding it came rushing back.

No.

That wasn't it.

I loved working with her. It was as much of a joy for me to make her films as it was for her to do the directing and choreography. We were well oiled, no pun intended, and we cared deeply about one another. I had all the free will in the world with Tally, and if I truly wanted to stop working on camera tomorrow, she would never ask me again, no questions.

But I didn't want that. I was certain I didn't.

"The military has been half of my life," I said. "It was the only thing that mattered, until it didn't. That change was like jumping off a cliff and hoping I missed the rocks at the bottom and landed on something soft or wet." I found a piece of bark on the tree outside the window to stare at. "Maybe you're onto something, Doc. I could be trying to recreate a familiar feeling, but if I'm being honest I was the kind of kid growing up that was more worried about pleasing my parents than anything else. I joined the Army and that was the worst thing I could have done, because it was the first time I'd chosen a thing my parents didn't completely approve of. They made that very clear. Then I got discharged and instead of going back to New York I moved to Florida to avoid them for even longer."

"Because you thought if you avoided them you couldn't be responsible for disappointing them? Or the burden of value would become too heavy?"

Something about that hit a nerve, but felt correct. True.

"Maybe," I agreed with a low murmur. "There's a lot of stress that comes from it, that provokes other kinds of panic. I shut down when I don't feel—"

"Worthy?"

I swallowed, tugging the collar of my shirt away from my hot skin. Doctor Brinckler wrote one more thing down on his notepad and uncrossed his legs, placing it on the table between us. He rolled his sleeve up and looked at his watch.

"That's about all the time we have today," he said. "It goes quick, doesn't it?"

"Time flies when you're trauma dumping," I jeered.

Henry stood and his crow's feet deepened with his smirk as he headed toward the door, swinging it open and stepping a foot outside. His voice carried and I could hear him telling his receptionist he was taking an hour for lunch.

He was out of sight, and I couldn't help myself as I passed the notepad on my way to the door, needing to know what he wrote down. After all, he'd left it in plain sight on the table. I glanced at the paper, turning it toward me to read what was important enough to write down. As soon as I did a humored scoff gusted out of me. The top of the page said *Grocery List* and below it he had listed bread, milk, and condoms.

My tongue clicked against my teeth, and I reached down, tearing the yellow page from the legal pad and shoving it into my pocket. I half expected him to be standing in the doorway as a witness to the little joke, but he never came back.

Before I left the office I made another appointment.

chapter forty-one

Natalia

THE LAST TWO weeks before the wedding flew by. I picked up my gown and the rings, confirmed all the final touches and head counts with the venue and my vendors, did a trial run on hair and makeup with my stylist, and put together the gifts for our wedding party—given I still had a wedding party.

We were driving to Key West in three days, and I hadn't had a full conversation yet with Isabella and Camilla. One group text, verifying that everyone had their dresses, was the most I'd received. I couldn't care less if they showed up in their birthday suits, as long as they showed up. They'd had more than enough time to figure out how they felt about me and my little secret. It was either going to work out, or it wasn't. I had become resigned to the latter.

I left the house to go shopping at the grocery store, attempting to try out a recipe Mateo's mom had written down for me. It turned out cooking food instead of ordering it *was* in fact more financially responsible and nutritious, although I hated to admit it. Somewhere, a food delivery service was going bankrupt in my absence. I wasn't gone long but when I pulled in the driveway, an extra car was there parked on the road beside the mailbox. Bella was sitting on the small concrete step on the front stoop.

My heart skipped over itself seeing her there. Pattering hard and then falling into the pit of my stomach just as quickly. My mind went to disaster immediately. My sister was no coward, so she'd likely come to tell me that my time was up and either I came clean to our parents or she would. Bella pushed her cat eye sunglasses into her short bob of hair as I approached carrying two arms full of heavy paper bags. I stopped at the edge of the stone walkway with a raised brow.

"Are you going to invite me in?" She stood and brushed her hands off on her sleek blue suit pants. Her matching blazer was perfectly fitted on top of a white silk tie neck blouse. "I've been out here for like twenty minutes."

"Depends." I brushed past her to the storm door, wedging it open with my hip and wrestling my keys out of my pocket. "Are you a two-thousand-year-old vampire?"

The lock clicked and I pushed inside the house into the open foyer, dropping the bags onto the small entryway table along with my keys. Bella was on my heels, not taking no for an answer. I hadn't spoken to her in three weeks yet here she was, unannounced, at my and Mateo's home for an unknown reason. One I was too afraid to ask about.

Her attention darted around, from the open concept kitchen and living room to the sliding glass doors leading into the backyard. The house was empty, but she was clearly looking for another person to pop out from behind a wall. When she realized we were alone her shoulders dropped from her ears and the rest of her body unspooled itself from the invisible tight wire tugging at it.

"Not what you expected?" I asked.

"Not what I thought a sex dungeon would look like," she pondered. Her long, sharp fingernails swiped down the counter of the kitchen contemplatively and snatched a lone apple from the ceramic bowl at the center of it.

I choked out a laugh. "Sorry to disappoint you. I'll make sure the bull whips and bondage chains are hanging from the fucking mantle next time you drop in for a visit. Is this like...CPS for sex workers? You're filling out a case report on how unfit I am to exist in society?"

"Delightful as ever, Talia," she shot back playfully, sinking her sharp white canines into the flesh of the apple and sending a spritz of juice to the floor.

I busied myself unpacking the grocery bags, taking the meat to the fridge and restocking an empty drawer with produce. "Sorry if I'm a little confused, I guess. The last time we talked you were walking out of a villa in Vegas basically promising to ruin my life unless I ruined it for myself first."

"I was making suggestions based on my assessment of your situation." She shrugged. "If I'm remembering correctly my reaction was tame compared to Camilla."

"Tame?" I stood from being hunched over in the refrigerator. "You basically insinuated I was so poor I needed to sell myself for money."

"You're telling me you do it for the creative freedom?"

"Yes!" I flailed.

Bella sank into a barstool at the kitchen counter with her apple, eyes softening to a doughy light brown. She sighed and pinched the bridge of her nose, and in all my life I'd never seen Isabella struggle to find the right words for what she wanted to say. I'd at least never seen her care enough to use the right words with *me*. It was so easy for us to fall back into the childish back-and-forth and put off adult conversations, because it was too real, and too uncomfortable, and none of us were raised with that lovey-dovey, sibling gene that some families seemed to have. Serious discussions made my tongue prickle like an allergic reaction.

"Look, if you came here to pick my brain about what I do based on a handful of misogynistic stereotypes I'd rather refer you to a friend. I'm sure they could answer all of your questions without confirmation bias."

"Do you have a lawyer?" Bella asked.

"What?" A spark of shock zipped up my spine, straightening my posture.

"I think it's smart to have a lawyer on retainer for your line of work. Especially if there's contracts involved, the verbiage needs to be airtight so that you can protect yourself. So that if something like what happened in Vegas with that creepy fucker happens again, you have every one of your t's crossed."

A baffled noise ripped out of me. It tapered into a confused hum and I steadied myself on the countertop. I'd gone into the conversation with my walls built all the way to my ears, expecting the worst, and hoping to be let down easy, that my body was still in fight mode. Bella had gone from telling me three weeks ago that she needed time to think about how my porn career would affect us, to now offering a legal liaison to lock the shit up like the family jewels. "Did I miss something?"

"I came off cold in Vegas, I know that. But it was because I didn't know what to do with the information, and I needed to process it on my own, like I said I would. I'm pretty good at playing the pros and cons game, and even if the thought of it dries up my pussy with a burning hot coal, you're not doing anything morally inept by fucking your fiancé on camera."

I leaned back against the fridge with my arms over my chest. "It just feels too easy," I admitted. "This all solving itself."

"Is it really that hard to believe grown adults can find mature solutions to their problems? I'm thirty, Natalia. I'm a fucking attorney. This doesn't have to be hard. Let yourself have something for once."

"Mia didn't have anything to do with it?"

"She was a little gnat in my ear, and Camilla's. She said you were going to come clean all on your own." A disbelieving jeer fell from her lips. "Why?"

I threw my hands up. "I thought it was my only option."

"You're not the only one who steers clear of our father. You just do it in the most dramatic ways. Trust me, I'd rather contract pink eye from a fucking hotel pillow than drum up a conversation with John Russo about porn."

A grimace curled my lips and I started pinching the skin beneath my elbow. Bella scrunched her nose. "What are you doing, freak?"

"Making sure I didn't fall asleep in the middle of the day on the couch again and I'm not being visited by a sleep paralysis demon."

"The lawyer," she reminded me with a roll of her eyes.

"Oh, right. No," I said. "I don't have one, officially. I mean, Mateo has a lawyer for TechOps, so I figured if we ever needed one he's there."

"No, no, no," she rescinded, standing from the stool and turning in circles in the kitchen with her apple core pinched between her fingers. I pointed to the cabinet beneath the sink where our garbage can lived and she tugged it open. "That's not good enough. I don't want to know what you're doing and I'm not asking for a spot on the quality assurance committee, but let me at least sleep soundly at night knowing my legal responsibility to you is fulfilled."

"You want to work for me?" I smirked. My hands slid from my chest to my hips. "Is this you making up for the prenup?"

"That prenup would have been a mess considering all your extracurriculars." Bella leaned against the edge of the counter. "Is that a yes? Are we in business?"

There wasn't a reason I could think of to turn her down. Isabella was family, and proved her loyalty by showing up at our house to talk everything out. I was still adjusting to the change in the tide, and Camilla was still up in the air, but I didn't want to push Bella away and risk losing my sisters all over again. She knew things about the industry I never would. She was smart, cunning, fierce, witty, and she took her job very seriously. It was the one thing that Bella prided herself on the most in life. To extend that to me and Mateo was incredibly generous, and something I would be stupid to refuse, especially after the incident in Vegas.

"We're in business." A pleased grin brightened my sister's face as I extended a hand. Then I drew it back, spat into my palm, and presented it to her again.

Her smile flatlined as she looked down at my wet skin. "You're pretty good at that, huh?"

My eyes widened expectantly, and I jutted my hand out farther. A giggle was at the tip of my tongue as she slowly brought her palm to her mouth and spat onto it. I couldn't help myself as I mused, "Must run in the family."

We shook two damp hands together, and Bella immediately took off to the sink to scrub her skin clean as the front door knob wiggled and Mateo came barreling through it. "Hey, baby, you know whose car is parked outside?" He rounded the short wall and found me and Isabella standing in the kitchen and his steps slowed, eyes slicing from hers to mine inquisitively. "Hey, Bells."

She dried her hands on a dish towel and swiped her purse off the counter. "I was on my way out. Talia, keep your phone on. I'll be sending contract drafts your way and will need some preliminary information from the both of you. And listen, this is a referred case, so let's keep it between us." Bella brushed by Mateo and patted him on the shoulder, his confusion getting more apparent the deeper the crease between his brows became. "See you in Key West this weekend, *bro*."

Laughter shook my shoulders as she disappeared into the foyer and the door closed behind her with a whoosh. Mateo doubled back, his jaw cracked open, mulling it over. "I'm guessing whatever the hell that was went well?"

I shrugged, but my lips tugged upward. "I guess it did." I couldn't pinpoint my emotion exactly, but Mateo didn't need me to. He opened his arms and let me melt into the firm cavern of his chest, resting his chin at the crown of my head. My cheeks started to ache with a smile.

chapter forty-two

Mateo

PALM TREES SWAYED at the entrance of the pristine Key West oceanside resort, and salty air caressed us the second we stepped out of the car and a valet unloaded our bags under the stone porte cochère. Inside the lobby, the white marble was so shiny I could see my reflection in the floor, and massive gold-framed mirrors decorated the walls from ceiling to crown molding. It was bright and Grecian, and a hotel concierge was waiting for us with a bottle of prosecco before showing us to our bridal suite. What more could you ask for?

Most of my family was flying in from New York in batches, some trickling in throughout the morning, and I was mentally preparing myself to be reacquainted with people I hadn't seen or heard from in several years. I had to remind myself that it was my wedding, and I needed to take time to enjoy it without the pressure of entertaining my guests, at least not the *entire* time. I didn't want to be the married couple who spent their reception hopping from table to table making small talk while everyone else got drunk and had fun, and I would absolutely make sure that wasn't Natalia. She did all the work, and she deserved to enjoy it.

In the first few hours at the hotel Natalia met Uncle Tony, Uncle Enzo, and Uncle Sal and his son Sal, who I hadn't realized just graduated from high school. The last time I saw him he had been walking around the backyard in a pull-up diaper full of shit. My mom and dad were having lunch at one of the cabana restaurants with my nonna Maria, my mother's sister Victoria, and her new husband. They had their moment fawning over Tally, and how she was "even more stunning than the photos online" because all they'd ever seen of her was a passing reposted picture from my mother.

After that it was my cousins and their spouses. Most of the people I was introducing to Tally were also introducing me to their own partners; I'd been gone so long I never even met them myself. Angelo showed up at the hotel just in time to be a backboard for those conversations so I didn't feel entirely out of my element.

When he walked in I almost didn't recognize him. He'd cut his hair from the scraggly, curled mop of brown to a short taper, and his beard was as trim and neat as I'd ever seen it. The pressure of all the family photos must have gotten to him—that, or the promise of a resort full of women in bathing suits for a whole weekend. Either way it was good to see my brother growing into himself, filling out. Giving a shit, to put it bluntly. My parents reacted to seeing him for the first time in months like he was their long-lost son returning home from war. That irony wasn't lost on me.

Our rehearsal dinner was at seven o'clock, and by four o'clock my other groomsmen had arrived. We met them out by the oblong pool as the sun started dipping lower on the horizon. A new, foreign addition to the crew caught my attention immediately, sitting beside Wink. He stood and she followed suit, wringing her hands together at her waist like she didn't know what to do with them.

"Holy fucking shit, he really did bring a date," I said, tugging Sam into a rough hug. "I'm shocked."

She was a pretty blonde. Her hair fell just past her shoulders in waves, freckles speckled her cheeks beneath light green eyes, and I almost missed the cochlear implant hiding behind her ear. They complimented one another, but their body language was too stiff to be comfortable. It was how I imagined two people on their first date would act. Too unsure to touch, too new to play. Or maybe I was reading it wrong and Wink was as gentlemanly outside of the bedroom as I imagined he was in it. A true good boy.

Natalia hugged her right away. "Hi, I'm Natalia. So nice to meet you."

"Hailey," she replied warmly. "Thanks for having me. This place is incredible. Congratulations, by the way."

"He's been hiding you from us," I said. "Where did you guys meet?" Sam's tongue perused his bottom lip and he looked to her like he didn't actually know the answer. My eyebrow raised. "Trick question?"

"He doesn't want to tell you that Hailey's his boss." Echo spread out in a lounge chair, tucking his hands behind his head. "You might accuse him of sleeping his way to the top."

"War Paws is a nonprofit," Wink cut in.

"What, does that mean you only do it doggy style so it doesn't count?"

Hailey snorted, and Sam's jaw twitched as he glared down at his brother. The animosity was palpable between them, but Hailey's ability to laugh at Tyler at her own expense meant she was going to fit in just fine with the rest of us. You had to have thick skin and roll with the punches. That was why Ophelia was such a perfect fit for Pike, and Tally and I would last a lifetime.

"Just because all the women you have sex with want to do it face down doesn't mean the same is true for your brother," Pike added. "Sam is a hell of a lot prettier than you, blockhead."

"Younger brothers usually are," Angelo tossed into the mix.

"Younger brothers get the shorter sticks." Echo laughed. "I mean the short *end* of the stick."

I shot a finger gun at him in solidarity.

"You boys are going to scare her right back to Utah." Ophelia shook her head. "Ignore our vulgar counterparts. I promise they're not always this misbehaved."

"Yes we are" rang out in a chorus of deep voices.

"I'm used to it. My two older brothers are Marines, and my dad was too. Trust me, there's nothing you can say that would make me blink an eye."

Echo opened his mouth, lifting his finger.

"That doesn't mean try it," Tally rushed out frantically, and Tyler deflated into the cushioned chair with a mischievous smirk.

Ophelia took a seat on Frankie's thigh. Her arm draped over his shoulder, and his fingers got lost right under the seam of her flowy sundress. "Can you believe it's finally here? You're getting married tomorrow!" she sang giddily.

"It's surreal." Natalia squeezed my hip. I dragged her in front of me and hugged her tight around the waist, planting a kiss to the side of her head and her body decompressed against mine.

"Hey, who ended up winning that scavenger hunt, anyway?" Angelo asked.

"I think the game ended when you got arrested," Pike noted.

My brother shrugged. "Wouldn't be the first party I've ruined."

Ophelia sank her teeth into her lip. "It was tied before that. But I never got an answer about the Elvis impersonator. Did you end up finding him, Nat?"

Natalia stiffened. The tiebreaker was our trip to the Little White Wedding Chapel, and technically it was a draw, because we'd both found our sweaty, bloated, wig-wearing King of Rock 'n' Roll at the end of the makeshift altar, together. That was our big secret in a world of little secrets between us. The cam work used to be the most important one, but with that cat abruptly out of the bag, this was what he had left that was ours.

Tally was the mastermind, though. She went to the chapel, and I followed because I always would, because I needed to have her back no matter how much groveling it took. It ended up being the most chaotic, spontaneous, memorable, purely magical moment of my life. My greatest victory.

I heaved a deep sigh and cleared my throat. Later, I'd make her promise to take this to the grave for my own well-being when it came to my groomsmen. They'd never forgive me for what I was about to do to them.

"Tally found him fair and square," I announced. "I was too late."

Natalia twisted in my arms, big brown eyes staring glossily up at me. Her perfect lips parted and I sank mine down on top of them to hush whatever protest I knew she was seconds away from hollering.

She would let me have this whether she wanted to or not. It sat right in my soul.

If the worst thing I ever had to do to keep my bride happy was dance like an idiot in front of her, I was luckier than most. I already did that any chance I got. Down the line there would be more weddings, more parties, and a whole hell of a lot more shenanigans where this group was involved, I was absolutely sure of it. Even now, the night was still promisingly young.

"So the girls won." Ophelia clapped her hands together. She bounced one too many times on Pike's lap in excitement that he had to reel her back in. "You guys have a dance to rehearse!"

"I want a recount," Echo complained. "Are you telling me I did that Blow Job shot for nothing?"

"For the memories," Tally replied. "Don't act like you didn't enjoy every second of it."

I blew a raspberry through my lips. "I can't believe I missed that."

Wink hunched over on his chair with his elbows on his knees and his hands over his eyes, swearing under his breath. Hailey rubbed the space between his shoulder blades in a way that was less consoling and more encouraging, a sparkle in her emerald eyes.

"I think going to jail should count for two," Angelo mumbled, crashing down into a lounge chair. He peeled a cigarette out of his pocket. "Just saying."

Natalia's tiny hands fisted my shirt, and she leaned in close to my ear. "You didn't need to do that."

"I know." I brushed my mouth against her temple. "I love you."

"Does love make you crazy?"

"*You* make me crazy." I ran my thumb down the curve of her nose, dragged it over her lips as they curled into a smile that showed off her straight white teeth. "The love was just an added perk, but man am I fucking glad you decided yours was for me."

Loving her made everything easy. Even the hard stuff. Even the things that would break most other people and brittle their relationships. Because at the end of the hard thing there was an even bigger, brighter thing waiting for us.

chapter forty-three

Natalia

CAMILLA WAS like the final boss in a violent video game.

I'd actually all but forgotten about seeing my parents for the first time since the disaster that was Dad's birthday dinner. Instead, all of my anxiety was tangled in a heaping, agita-inducing ball of nerves about soothing the hemorrhaging relationship with my oldest sister. If I could get through to her, then it would all be worth it. My expectations were as low as physically possible, so low I wouldn't blink an eye if she walked in the room wearing off-white. At least then we could talk it out.

The restaurant hosting our rehearsal dinner was Tuscan inspired. The walls were vaulted and behind the bar counter, wine bottles lined wooden shelves backlit with yellow ambient light. Vines twisted around the room's columns and through rustic trusses as a pianist tucked into the corner played melodic classical music. I was winning all the brownie points with the Durans for this one, and caught my reflection in a pane of glass between the bar and the private event space to give myself a pat on the back.

One long dinner table took up the length of the room with place settings and placards on each plate. I'd opted to hire the venue's event coordinator to make sure everything went according to plan, and she'd gone ahead and separated each side of our family into their own respective end of the table so there were no awkward musical chairs as our bridal party arrived.

My sisters were already there, floating around the hors d'oeuvres waiting for us. The bubbly prosecco I'd drank in the hotel room to calm my nerves settled like a sunburn in my chest. I squeezed Matty's knuckles so tight he hissed. "Fuck, sorry."

"You good?"

I swallowed the lump in my throat. "Great."

Mateo tugged my chin toward him, the touch of his fingers lingering there as he swept a long strand of my hair behind my ear. "Do you need me?"

"Go buy me some time with the rest of the guests. My mother and father should be here any minute, unless they double-booked this weekend somehow." My head twisted toward the doors, looking for them.

Mateo swatted my ass, sending me in the direction of my sisters. "Even I don't think they'd stoop that low."

I feared we might not have reached the pinnacle of lows my parents would find in our lifetime. I was, however, ready to tackle anything with my husband by my side without the loneliness that was conquering it myself as a young adult.

My sisters were crowded together and made room for me to step into their small circle in the corner of the room inconspicuously. They were all in different floor-length floral cocktail dresses that matched the vibes of Key West in June perfectly. Cami wouldn't look me in the eyes, and I plucked a stuffed croquette off a small crystal plate in Mia's hand and shoved it into my mouth to prolong the silence further.

"Thanks for coming," I managed around a mouthful of soft-shell crab. It was hotter than I anticipated and I crouched over, *ha-ha-ha*ing the burning appetizer. Mia shoved her plate under my chin and I let it drop unattractively from between my teeth.

"Careful, that's hot," Bella joked.

"No one saw it," Mia assured me.

I wiped the scorch off my lips and blew out a breath. Camilla looked at me then. Her soft brown eyes were just like mine, but more tired from long days working in the hospital. She was the most structured woman I'd ever known, even as a kid. Keeping codified planners, picking outfits days in advance, turning homework in early, managing being a multi-sport varsity athlete. She was a lot like Ophelia. A true planner and doer. The weight of the world was on her shoulders as the first daughter of John and Sistine Russo, and my guess was her spite for me at the moment had a lot to do with that.

"We should talk," I said to her, leaving the floor open. I'd understand if she didn't have much to say to me, but I'd rather clear the air than wait until after the reception, or worse, never broach the subject again. Camilla's plum lips thinned but she nodded agreeably.

Mia and Bella peeled away from us on cue, leaving the spit-up croquette plate on the edge of the table to be swept away by the waiter. God, this was uncomfortable. It was like playing a game with a black bear, staying as still as possible hoping it might see you as a friend and not a foe. I thanked my wilderness exploration elective in college for that.

Camilla was not a black bear, though. She was in her own bracket of the food chain.

"First off, thank you," I started, treading on the side of caution. "For not making a rash decision for the entire family and giving me some time to reflect on how hard this has probably been on all of you, too. I've been keeping that in mind, how I'd feel about it if the roles were reversed, and to be honest I can't give you a straight answer. I'd like to think I would be free of judgment, supportive, proud, and maybe curious. But the truth is I'll never be able to put myself in your shoes because we live entirely different lives. Sometimes I think about you, and what you do and have accomplished, and I can't even believe we share DNA."

She twisted her rings around on her fingers, a pop of color splashing across her cheeks in the low light. "Did you know that Dad hasn't had a drink since his birthday dinner? Completely cold turkey. Not even a glass of wine on Sunday afternoon with Mom. It's like a switch flipped or something."

A chill brushed over me. In twenty-six years my dad hadn't gone more than two days without a beer in his hand or a shot of Baileys in his coffee. She was lying, or mistaken. She had to be.

As if she could sense my disbelief, she continued.

"Yeah, whatever Mateo said to him changed something. He's a different person. I noticed it right away because he lost some weight, and he was in a better mood on his days off. When we were both in the hospital at the same time, he'd come find me for lunch or just to say hi, which was absolutely foreign." She scoffed out an annoyed noise and stretched a long finger toward me. "But then I realized it was you."

"It was more likely waking up in a pricker bush by the pool covered in his own vomit that drove him over the edge."

"Nope." Camilla shook her head. "It was your fiancé. It was the threat of losing you to a bigger, better man. And that really shouldn't have, but it pissed me off," she admitted gruffly. As if it made her angry with herself. Her attention flitted around the room briefly and then refocused. "I've been begging him to care that much about me for my entire life. I did everything he and Mom ever wanted: the grades, the extracurriculars, Ivy League, medical school, residency, fucking unintentional celibacy because no one in their right mind would want to be with a woman who works as much as I do. But none of that was important enough to get sober. Not my graduation, or white coat ceremony, or my honorarium. You'd think a man who spent half his time under a surgical lamp would be more proud."

"He is." I lurched for her hand, entangling it with mine. "I agree he has a funny way of showing it, but I know you're his golden girl, Cami. You're perfect, and you do it all on your own, which is why he doesn't have to worry about you. I lived for your approval as a kid. I still do," I pressed. "I'm standing here seeking it right now, because I didn't look up to Dad growing up, I looked up to you."

"And here I am, jealous of you," Camilla said. My head tilted, mind spinning to process that. "You have everything I've ever wanted."

I reeled back, almost speechless at the thought of Camilla envying anything about me. But based on the soft sincerity in her eyes, she was being completely honest. This was the most vulnerable she'd ever been.

"I'm kind of at a loss for words," I murmured.

"I thought I was getting over it. Well, *coming to terms* with it over the last few months. When everything came out in Vegas, it put me right back in that headspace again. I was so spiteful, and judgmental, more angry than I knew what to do with because you are...doing what you do, and you still get to have the life of your dreams. You don't have to worry about Mom and Dad, you're engaged, you have a home and a business and a best friend who clearly already knew your secret and celebrated it. Don't get me wrong, I love my job and I wouldn't change anything, but goddammit, there are no rewards for being the patron saint of Russo."

"It's not fair, you're right," I rushed out. "I get it, Cam, I really fucking do."

"Then I realized it's not Dad, and it's not you, it's not the twins, and it's not even Mom." She sniffled, dabbing her finger softly at her lower lash line. "It's me regretting something I never had. I might have never even wanted it, but I didn't get to make that choice. It wasn't right to leave you in the dark for the last few weeks, and I'm sorry."

I understood everything. Camilla was the first born, the eldest daughter, the role model. She was right, she didn't have a choice because she was born into the position. By the time my parents had me six years later, it was like all that expectation had been divvied out already. The pressure she had on her trickled down onto Mia and Isabella, but merely sprinkled onto me. I took it for granted, and for the same reasons I resented Camilla for being the most important person in my parents' lives, she envied me and my freedom.

My teeth sank into my bottom lip. A fresh wave of emotion blurred my vision and before I second-guessed it I was wrapping my arms around Camilla's thin frame and resting my chin on her shoulder. She met me in the middle, letting go of a deep, stuttering breath. "We're more alike than you think," I said.

Her hand rubbed a soothing circle between my shoulder blades. "I know. We're two sides of the same coin. I would probably never take my clothes off for thousands of people, but I share a similar passion for other things."

A curt laugh darted out of me. "I'm not asking you to be a fan, by the way. I know it's a lot to accept, and I can't even really ask you to keep it to yourself. I just don't want to lose you over it."

Camilla stepped back. She fixed the strap on my dress that had slipped down my shoulder and ran a finger sharply across my winged eyeliner to keep it intact. "You know that thing Mateo said in Vegas, how we'd keep a secret for our sister because we love her? Well I do love you, Talia. Even if I won't be asking you how work has been on the holidays."

"I can live with that." I beamed. My throat was dry, and my mouth still felt weird around the words, but I made it a point to say, "I love you, too."

Camilla's lips twisted, eyes glossing over again, but she cleared her throat and looked away, finding our parents walking into the room to wave at. "We're good, sis. Go have fun and enjoy your party."

Mateo had already started a conversation with my parents across the dining room by the welcome sign, and Camilla wasn't kidding, color had returned to my father's entire body. Gaunt eyes plump and alert, structure had returned to the bones in his face that were so often swollen. He was sharper, yet somehow softer at the same time. Warmness in a usually cold gaze, awareness that made it seem like he was finally looking at me and not straight through me.

"Dad," I greeted him and leaned in for a side kiss. "You look great."

"I was just thinking the same thing," Mateo added.

"Thank you." He stuck his hands in his chino pockets, staring at the ground. "Quit the booze. I've never felt better."

Mateo's eyes flared toward me, as shocked as anyone. "That's huge," he said. "That's great, John. I'm stoked to hear that."

"Being at a wedding isn't easy for sobriety," my mom chided, tugging me into her for a long hug before putting me at arm's length and giving me a once-over. "Love the dress, honey."

"Not easy, but we'll make sure you have whatever you need," I promised. I wanted to see this through for my father. He deserved that support. This wouldn't only be valuable to him, it would change the entire dynamic of our family. It would be like starting fresh, new. For the first time in my life my relationships with my siblings and parents had a chance to really matter. New beginnings. Opportunities. Things to look forward to. Hope was blossoming inside my chest like flowers sprouting in the spring. Everything changing from grayscale to technicolor. I was Dorothy landing in Oz.

The same way my mother looked at Mateo the first time she met him, with a curious awe and hand-over-heart admiration, was how she reacted to the Swans when they introduced themselves. I had to give it to those two, they were absolutely astounding on paper. Respectful, charming, well-adjusted, and the perfect amount of mischievous to keep Sistine laughing like a schoolgirl with a crush. Even Dad was impressed. Frankie stuck with Mateo while Ophelia and I traversed arm in arm, and I let her chew my ear off about details and timing, the hairdresser, the makeup artist, every last minute of the next day until I reminded her I had a day-of planner and she was off the metaphorical clock.

My sisters floated around the room making their own introductions, and my worry washed away like the ocean tide I could hear through the windows of the restaurant. I should have kept in mind that Italians would migrate to other Italians, the one common denominator enough to unite whole cities of people. It always turned out that through a friend of a friend, or a cousin in college, a business partner, a second marriage, we were all three degrees separated.

By the time dinner was served, the placeholders were gone, and the table was a glorious mess of intermingled family and friends all in the same room to celebrate the same thing. I didn't expect the night to be so emotional. After so many years building a wall to protect myself from being let down over and over again, fearing that I'd never have the connection to my family that I craved, that closeness and camaraderie, the tears I'd shed for all the wrong reasons were making these tears I shed for the right ones fall in spades.

Everyone toasted Mateo and me, and even in my white dress, with my husband's gentle fingers drawing hearts into my skin, surrounded by the people who meant the most to us in the world, I was overwhelmed with the feeling that the best days of my life were still yet to come.

chapter forty-four

Mateo

THE CHOREOGRAPHED dance was going to go as badly as you could imagine. After the rehearsal dinner I took my reluctant, mildly drunk groomsmen across the resort to an empty conference room to put something together. Echo was as uncoordinated as he was wide; grace eluded him entirely. Although Pike was a fighter pilot, he apparently couldn't distinguish his right from his left, and Angelo's go-to move was something he learned watching *Jersey Shore* as a teenager. Staying on beat, even putting one foot in front of another in a sequence, was as difficult to solve as a Rubix's Cube. Wink was the only one of them worth his weight, unsurprisingly. Sam Swan was a jack of all trades.

Ophelia hadn't given us any rules to abide by, and after an hour sweating and frustratedly trying to come up with something original to perform with no luck, I decided to pull up an old classic on YouTube to mimic instead. One we'd all seen a dozen times. Then it started to click. For two more hours the five of us watched the *White Chicks* dance battle scene on repeat until we nailed it, flips and all. If that didn't get the people going and satisfy the girls, nothing would.

It was after midnight when we were finally satisfied and exhausted. Echo went to grab a nightcap at the bar, which was code for finding someone to warm his bed for the night, and Pike and Wink left to rack out with their women. I, on the other hand, was stuck trailing my brother back to his hotel room for a sleepover while my wife spent the night alone in that big, beautiful, king-size bridal suite.

Fuck the wedding traditions.

I'd said it before and I'd say it again, there was nothing conventional about Natalia and me. Weddings were evolving. Couples didn't even wait for the bride to walk down the aisle anymore; they were doing *first looks*, and I only knew this because the option was sprung on me and I stared at Tally like she'd grown two heads while she was forced to explain it.

Angelo's room was on the same wing of the resort as mine and Tally's, directly below it and facing the oceanside to catch the morning sunrise over the Atlantic. Meaning I'd have to stare at the ceiling all night wishing I could ram a hole in the drywall and crawl through the floor to her. We were rattling on about our hockey team's recent playoff run when Ang shouldered us inside the doorway and flipped on the recess lighting. My shoes came to a squeaking halt on the wood floors.

"What the fuck is that?" My already low expectations plummeted further as I gaped at the bed against the wall. The *one* bed, against the wall. This could not be fucking happening to me. My hands found my hips. I spun around, searching for a cot or a pull-out couch, but the only other things in the room were a cuck chair and a coffee table.

"We're cuddling, brother." Angelo leapt onto the bed, ruffling the white comforter. "Isn't this everything you ever dreamed of the night before your wedding?"

My finger wagged back and forth at him. "Don't mock me right now."

"Are we going ass to tip or ass to ass?" He tapped his finger on his chin, a smirk showing off all his teeth. "Tip to tip?"

"Flat on your back, and if you so much as scratch the underside of your balls I swear to God I'll maim them."

Two grown men in a queen-size bed was too close for

comfort, and I'd spent weeks in a six-by-six tent in the jungle with Pike, unshowered. The difference was I didn't have a choice with one of them.

"I don't like this any more than you do." He hopped off the bed with his hands up. "You're making it really hard for me to get laid. I could be prowling at the bar like Tyler but instead I have to tuck my big brother in and read him a bedtime story. I didn't even get a choice. You were put in my room *without* my knowledge."

"Ang, if it were you and Echo sitting at a bar, what chance do you really think you'd have of getting the girl?"

Angelo scratched the back of his head, clearly unused to the shorter curls. "Some girls prefer a man with a little more pasta on his bones than meat. I'm warmer in the winter."

"You keep believing that." I smiled.

He snatched a toiletry bag off the top of his open suitcase on the floor and trudged into the bathroom, jarring it closed.

Not an hour later, Angelo was snoring beside me. I was under the covers with my fists pinning the sheets to my sides like I was a cadaver on a gurney, trying not to make any sudden movements and catch a hairy limb that didn't belong to me. Even if my body was tired enough to sleep after a long day, my mind was still racing, and the ticking of Angelo's watch on the dresser was keeping me just unsettled enough that my only option was staring at the wall.

This was complete and utter torture.

I snagged my phone off the nightstand next to me and opened our text thread.

ME

You up?

The three little dots on my screen showed up a few seconds later.

TALLY

Damn, I haven't gotten a 2 a.m. text like this since college, and on the eve of my wedding no less

ME

Send pics

TALLY

Once a fuckboy always a fuckboy

ME

A domesticated fuckboy. I used to be for the streets

TALLY

You are pretty well house trained

I smiled at the screen.

ME

I can't sleep without you

TALLY

Me either, I don't like rolling over and not feeling you

ME

I'm going to instinctually try to cop a feel and end up with a hand full of beanbags

I swore I heard her laughter spill out from the floor above. That or I was consciously trying to materialize her next to me.

ME

Go out on the balcony

Throwing the covers off my body without so much as a stir from Angelo, I draped myself in his hotel robe and slipped quietly out onto the stone deck and into the warm, salty air. It was so tranquil the only sound was the wind blowing through the palm trees, shaking their leaves, and the ocean crashing onto the shallow sand. I walked over to the edge and put my elbows on the railing, taking it all in. The whole resort sprawled out in front of me in a U-shape, pool deck, cabanas, and lounges where we'd sat earlier with our friends down below. The lights inside the restaurant on the ground floor opposite me were dim. A trail of wooden fence posts marked a path to the beach access and disappeared behind a dune, poking back out at the open wedding ceremony space where Tally and I would be standing tomorrow.

The sliding glass door a floor above me opened and shut. I could sense the hesitation in Tally's steps as she trekked onto the balcony. "Mateo?"

"Down here," I called out.

"Have you been underneath me this whole time?"

"God, I fucking wish."

I glanced up and saw her fingers curled over the banister, but the architecture of the patios was designed to give every guest ample privacy and the rest of her was obstructed by the angle. "Don't worry, we can't see each other. I know it's technically our wedding day."

"I always said tomorrow doesn't start until you go to sleep."

"Did you work everything out with Bridesmaidzilla? I mean Camilla?"

"Thankfully. Did you dance your little heart out?"

"Wouldn't you like to know?"

"It's keeping me awake."

I smirked, running my fingers over my dry knuckles and the calluses on my palms. "I've had a lot of time to think while I was staring at the ceiling and I'm wondering how we're doing the kiss."

"Is that why you called me out here?" A sweet laugh trickled out of her. "We can't exactly practice."

"Are we keeping it PG for the parents? Throwing a little tongue action in there? Should I dip you? We only have one chance for the cameras. We can't fuck it up."

"I don't know." She giggled again, soft and dreamy. I could tell how tired she was by how loosely her words flowed, the muddled sound of her voice. "We should do whatever feels natural. Not stick to any scripts. Let's just be us. We're generally very good in front of a camera lens."

"Can't argue with that, Ms. Duran."

"I can't believe it's our wedding day," she marveled. "Or that we're all still in one piece. It's crazy how much planning goes into a day of your life, and then it's there and gone in a blink. Even crazier, after all this, I don't care if every single thing goes wrong tomorrow. I already have what I always wanted."

My chest warmed and swelled. I was desperate to reach out and touch her, bring her into my body, smell the fruity shampoo she used on her hair. Tangle my fingers in it.

"You put together an unbelievable wedding, Tal. We're going to enjoy every minute of it, and the guests are going to be talking about it for the rest of the century. But getting married to you in that little chapel, just the two of us in a moment as raw as that, was exactly how it was meant to play out. I have no regrets."

"Not even tipping Elvis a thousand dollars?"

I tilted my head. That momentary lapse of judgment had been stuffed into the back of my mind like a discarded tissue. He had caught me in the most vulnerable and ecstatic hour of my life, and naturally I wanted to spread the love. Schmear it, generously. "I regretted that a little bit when I found out how much Angelo's bail was."

"You can't put a price on love." I could hear the shrug in her voice.

A cooler breeze whipped over me and I stuck my hands into the pockets of the robe. We were silent for several seconds, watching the foam caps roll onto the beach and sweep back into the dark ocean without knowing where the water stopped and the night sky began.

I had a feeling we were both stalling going back inside. Falling asleep would be hopeless for me even when I did, so standing on the balcony with Tally until the sunrise was all right with me. It wasn't fair to her though. She needed to rest before the morning because as long as today was, tomorrow would be twice that.

"I don't like this rule," I said. "We break all the rest of them, anyway."

"It's more of a superstition," she sighed.

I looked up again and her hands were still hanging over the railing. "What are we stitious about?"

She rushed out a laugh. "They used to think if a bride saw her groom before their wedding, it would give her more time to run away."

"That's not a superstition, that's called forcing pre-pubescent girls to marry grown, gout-stricken men who didn't shower."

"Well, when you put it like that."

"I think that I'm the logic to your limerick, and that's why we work so well together."

"I didn't realize I was married to a poet," Natalia mused.

"I can be whatever you want me to be, baby. A pillow, a blanket, a sock that gets lost under the covers at the foot of your bed, you name it."

I pictured her shy, dimpled smile in the darkness even though I couldn't see it. She probably had her bottom lip wedged between her teeth, wanting to give in, but fighting that last bit of resolve I was plucking at like a guitar string. An ultimatum, perhaps.

"You should sleep, angel," I murmured. "We'll both be so busy in the morning it will fly right by. Then I'll see you at the altar."

"You're right." She sounded disappointed, and the corner of my mouth tugged upward impishly.

My voice dropped lower, and I added, "But maybe before you slip under the covers, you tiptoe over to the door and leave it unlocked."

Tally's breath hitched. That I did hear loud and clear. Silence followed, like she was gathering too many thoughts together to articulate only one. I peeked up again and her arms were pulling away from the railing, footsteps retreating toward the door. "Good night," she called out.

"Good night," I answered. I waited until I heard her close the slider before darting back into Angelo's hotel room. He was turned over on his stomach and snoring into the mattress, oblivious. He didn't hear me tug my slacks back on without bothering to hinge the belt buckle, or hastily throw my dress shirt over my shoulders, leaving the buttons all undone.

I snuck out ready to be disappointed, and if that was the case I'd be okay with it because Natalia was getting what she wanted. You miss one hundred percent of the shots you don't take, as they say. This was no different than every other part of our relationship. The chase, the give-and-take, the teasing. It was almost always worth it to test each other's boundaries.

Nearly two in the morning, the hotel hallways were just as quiet as outside. I bypassed the elevators and pushed open the stairwell, taking the steps two at a time to the next floor to avoid waiting a second longer than I had to.

I rounded the tight corner, nearly losing my footing on the carpet, and skidded to a stop, panting with my hands on my knees in front of the bridal suite. The swing lock was wedged in the doorframe, and I threw up a victorious fist as I walked right in.

chapter forty-five

Natalia

"HAPPY WEDDING DAY!"

My eyes flung open in a panic and met Mateo's already blown wide and frantically looking back at me under the sheets. That was all the warning we received before the white duvet was violently ripped off the bed, exposing us in all our pre-marital, naked glory.

I yelped, tugging the top sheet over my chest and Matty wretched the fluffy pillow out from behind his head with a brutish howl, using it to cover himself as he scampered up toward the headboard.

Our screaming cued screaming from my sisters, who stood at the foot of the bed with horror-stricken expressions. They put their hands up like they were bracing for a car crash, which would have been a hell of a lot better than this.

"Oh my god," Phee cried out. "I didn't know!"

"How did you even get in here?!" Mateo cried back.

"Nat gave me the extra key!"

I winced, having forgotten that little fact. Though I'd not expected to be ambushed first thing in the morning by my bridesmaids. In their defense, it would have been really delightful in a different circumstance. The only thing that would have made it worse was if my mother was here.

"What is with all the damn hollering in here?" A feminine voice crested the doorway.

Fuck me.

"Shit, shit, shit." Mateo grabbed a second pillow and pressed it over his nipples as my mom pushed between my sisters.

"Oh, for heaven's sake, Natalia Emile," she guffawed and smacked a manicured hand over her eyes. "It's your wedding day, not your birthday. Don't you know this is bad luck?"

"I was just leaving!" Mateo slid off the bed with the pillows still snug to his nether regions, sidestepping around the group of women to keep his backside out of sight. His clothes were scattered across the floor, but Bella gave him no time to gather them as she pushed him toward the door the same way you shoo seagulls away from food on the beach. "Wait, wait, wait!" he protested. "I'm naked!"

Anna Duran appeared in the doorway with a bottle of champagne in one hand, ready to join the pre-wedding festivities, and bumped right into Matty. Her light eyes widened and took him in from messy bedhead to his socks. "Get!"

"Mom—"

"Mateo David Duran, you are not supposed to be here!" She shoved her son out into the hallway without a second thought but before the door could fully slam closed in his face he stopped it with his palm.

"Please just give me my clothes," he begged.

Camilla swiped a pair of pants off the floor and threw them into the hall, nailing him in the gut. Mia followed with his wrinkled shirt crumpled in a ball and smacked him right in the face.

"Okay, I guess I'll—" His sentence was cut off by the door flinging shut.

My teeth clamped together. I'd never been caught under my parents' roof sneaking around with boys as a hormonal teenager, but somehow Mateo and I were making it a habit in adulthood. A very bad, unbreakable habit that was somehow more mortifying every time. The room turned their attention back to me.

In my signature fashion of making light out of the awkward, traumatic moments in my life, and because I would probably never learn, I clicked my tongue against my teeth. "Mimosas, anyone?"

* * *

THE DAY-OF COORDINATOR showed up an hour later, toting our professional photographers and videographer along into the bridal suite to bounce around filming the morning. Room service delivered a cart of catered breakfast, and soon after that the hairstylist and makeup artists set up and got working on my bridesmaids. We danced around the room in our matching silk robes to a mix of my favorite house music, and all the pressure of getting married and putting on a wedding that would exceed expectations melted away.

I wanted it to be memorable, of course, but like I'd said to Mateo out on the balcony, there was nothing that could happen today that would sully what we had. This wedding reception was just a cherry on top. A big-ass fucking party to celebrate the union that already existed in secret between us. It made me love it even more. Our two lives diverging into one in the most perfect, story-book way.

Ophelia hung my gown beside the bridesmaid dresses on a tall rack, and it all became so real. They looked effortless and elegant together. The black flowy floor-length dresses my sisters and Phee chose for themselves brought out all the details in the simple embellishments of mine. My bridal gift to the girls was matching white pearl earrings and a bracelet that went perfectly with the rare blue ones my sisters gifted me to wear. Ophelia texted Frankie to come grab the matching cufflinks Mateo had chosen for his groomsmen for the ceremony, and I realized I wasn't even worried if they wore them or not.

Eloping was the shit.

Morning turned a corner into the afternoon, and the girls

were dolled up, hair curled, slipping into their dresses while I got my makeup done with curlers in my hair. My mother looked stunning as usual in a pretty coral dress that accentuated her tan skin, and she hovered around me as the makeup artist tapped eyeshadow onto my eyelids.

"Is that too dark?" she asked.

I looked in the mirror at the light brown blend of color at the outer corner of my eyes. "I like it," I said. "Trust the process."

"You want to look natural," she added. "Glowy and bright. Less is more. You're so beautiful, you should be highlighting your natural features."

My tongue drew circles into my cheek to keep from chewing it off. "Thanks, Mom," I bit out. "Don't worry, it will be exactly how I want it." The makeup artist nodded her to death until she took a step back to watch from the comfort of the cushy ottoman a few feet away.

Anna came out of the bathroom and surprised us all with a long sage green off-the-shoulder gown that hugged her body and ruched in all the right places. I steepled my fingers in front of my mouth, squealing. With everyone's encouragement, she did a few spins, showing off the completed look proudly. She didn't wear makeup at home, and seeing her eyes glaze over as she took in her reflection in the mirror pulled at all my heartstrings. It had probably been years since she had a reason to dress up, and this was way different than any other event. It was her son's wedding. She deserved to feel beautiful.

Knuckles rapped against the door and Frankie ducked inside, looking devilishly handsome in his suit and tie. I knew he cleaned up nicely, but Ophelia lit up like fireworks on the Fourth taking in his long, combed-back hair without the usual hat on his head and a pair of superbly tailored pants.

I blew out a low whistle. "Francesco, you look like a million bucks."

"Very nice," Camilla added to a chorus of hummed agreement and impressed nods.

A blush crept from the collar of his shirt up his neck and pinkened his cheeks. He dropped his head bashfully, studying his shoes, and for a second I forgot why he was standing in the threshold of the suite altogether until Ophelia pranced over to him with the cufflinks.

"Oh, right." Frankie cleared his throat, gazing down at her and getting lost all over again. He lifted Phee's chin and pressed a soft kiss to her mouth. The room shrank around them in their private, intimate moment.

"Young love," I teased. They had the same type of special that Matty and I did. The worlds had aligned when we all ended up in Coconut Creek together at the same time. It was fate. Fate was the culprit of everything.

"What have you guys been doing all morning?" Mia asked.

He listed it all on his fingers. "We went out for breakfast, hung by the pool, played a little bocce ball. Sam went for a run, and Angelo was still asleep the last time I checked."

"The ceremony is in two hours," Anna stressed.

"I'll make sure he's there, Momma D." Frankie reached into his pocket and took a white envelope out of it, waving it in my direction. "For you. From the mister."

The pulse in my neck thrummed and warmth crept across my cheeks. I shot my arm out and made grabby hands until he brought it over to me. It was a small white card, printed with two delicate gold rings on the outside, and when I opened it, I recognized Mateo's handwriting.

"We'll finish this after." The makeup artist stepped away with a warm smile.

I swallowed a hard lump forming rapidly in my throat. I didn't want to cry this early, but I was an emotional woman with easily provoked tear glands. Plus, ugly crying in front of a room full of people was as embarrassing as it was unattractive, and the videographer was laser-focused on me. Steadying myself with a deep breath, I silently read the letter.

Natalia,

My world will forever be split into two parts; there was before you, and now there's after. I know even in the next life I'll crawl to wherever your flowers are planted to water them. I'll end up on your doorstep somehow ringing the bell. We'll be two butterflies circling one another in a field, or two worms digging side by side in the dirt. If you're a falling leaf I'll be the wind that carries you, and if you're a passing face on a train I'll recognize you. My soul is yours to consume, my body yours to own, and my heart beats only because you bring it to life. You are as much a part of me as the blood in my veins. Mine to cherish, to hold, to possess, to love. From now until the ends of the earth, Tally. I promise to be your warmth in the cold, your torch through dark tunnels, the man who follows you into the water when you want to jump or wades at the edge waiting for you when you want to swim. The wolf beside you howling at the moon.

For pleasure or worse.

I love you, Natalia Duran.

How's that for poetry?

P.S. Don't cry, you know there's only one way I like to ruin your makeup.

Big fat teardrops were cascading down my face before I even got to the final line, falling and ricocheting onto the card. I read it again, and then again after that, each time thinking I might keep my composure and fooling myself. When I finally got it together I folded the message back up, slipping it somewhere safe, for me and only me.

The makeup artist told me that crying as much as I did gave my skin a dewy glow that couldn't have been recreated by her products. So in the end, it worked out better than planned. In fact, I was inspired to cry as much as possible for the remainder of the day if it meant my natural blush could have its moment in the sun.

I sat back while the hairstylist took over, removing all the tight curlers from my long dark locks. It was no shock how hot it was in June, even being on the coastline, and the temperature for the evening wasn't dropping below eighty degrees. I wanted my hair off my shoulders and back, to not have to worry about the wind whipping through the beach and sending it in a hundred different tangled directions during the ceremony, to be able to dance like no one was watching at the reception, and for my dress to be the center of attention—all while maintaining a flawlessly messy updo.

This displeased my mother greatly.

"Curls," she protested, fluffing the back of my head. "You have such luxurious hair, Talia. It's so much more feminine to leave it long."

"I think it'll be just as good pinned back," I rebuked.

She frowned at me in the mirror. "What do you girls think?"

Mom opened the floor to my sisters and the only thing she received was uncomfortable humming. That was a complete one-eighty from my god-awful dress fitting so many months ago. No one was outright taking her side, and that was equivalent to catching a stray bullet for Mom. Her ego was immediately struck. She wasn't used to that.

"Camilla?" she pressed.

My sister popped a grape into her mouth and shrugged. "I think a low bun is trendy."

"Big curls are timeless," Mom fought back. "Your face looks rounder when your hair is pulled back. Length elongates the jaw." She turned to the poor hairstylist retreating away farther and farther by the second. "Tell her."

A tiny scoff shot out of my throat. "It's my day, shouldn't I get to choose how I look?"

"Yes," Phee cut in. "Totally agree."

Mia and Bella nodded. There was a blood vessel twitching in the side of my mom's neck, threatening to burst.

"I don't want you to regret it when you're looking at photos from today wishing you would have listened to your mother. No one else is going to tell you what you need to hear."

My jaw clenched, and I didn't even try to hide the roll of my eyes. "You're impossible sometimes."

"It's my job to be."

I heaved out a sigh. "I'm having it done how I want it."

Mom didn't get it, and never would unless someone spoon-fed it to her on a gold platter. There was no getting through to a person so deeply invested in their own self-importance. Sistine Russo had great moments in motherhood overshadowed by the simple unwillingness to take a step back from underneath the shining disco ball at the center of the room. Sometimes I wished I'd known my mom before she had kids. I wondered if she was always this way, or if it was a cry for help. A vie for attention she'd been fighting for since having four daughters.

She crossed her arms petulantly. "You have long, beautiful hair that you're going to hide away, Natalia. You might as well just cut it all off."

I mimicked her posture and pushed out of the chair.

What a fine fucking idea.

There was no time to dissect how crazy it was, how my first instinct when overwhelmed was to do something manic like jump in a pool with all my clothes on, and this was fitting in the same unhinged category. I'd already decided that it didn't matter if everything went wrong today, anyway. I was embracing that. Maybe a gesture like this was what it would take to finally, *finally* break through to my mother.

Without putting any more thought into it I grabbed the pair of styling scissors tucked into the bag beside me in my dominant hand and twisted my hair into a ponytail with my other.

"Oh my fucking god, Talia, what are you doing?" Mia stood like she was going to stop me, but it was too late. I chopped away at the hanging hair and felt it skim my shins and fall at my feet.

When I snipped through the last piece the room fell utterly silent.

"I guess there's only one option now," I quipped, shaking my hair out like a dog.

Camilla popped another grape into her mouth. "This wedding needs its own reality TV show."

The video crew and the beauty team were trying to become one with the walls and I couldn't blame them. I would end up in a trending Instagram reel as the bride who lost her shit and gave herself a jagged bob an hour before her wedding. Mom still hadn't recovered her jaw from where it had fallen to the center of her chest. I delicately put my hands on her shoulders, staring into her warm brown eyes and seeing myself in the reflection. It might have been a bit dramatic, but I succeeded in my intention.

"I love you," I started. "But I'm not *you*. I've been trying to tell you this my whole life. I want to make you proud, Mom. But I want you to look at me and be proud of what you see because I'm *not* a mirror image. Because I became something different, all on my own, and I didn't need a handout or a connection to the Russo name. Because I found happiness in my own imperfect ways. I don't want you to loosen the leash, I want you to let go of it."

She inhaled a short breath, swallowing it down, and her fingers crept up my shoulders and tugged lightly at the freshly cut ends of my hair.

"We can fix it," I told her, then turned toward the hairdresser. "We can fix it, right?" She gave me a weak thumbs-up.

"It's very French," Ophelia noted.

I sucked in a hissing breath. "Yikes."

"I am very proud of you," Mom said then. "I'm only ever trying to do my best and help you succeed. Sometimes that's the only way I know how to be close to you, but it falls short."

"I read something once that said, "Be kind to your mother because they're also living life for the first time." I should remember that. There's time for everything. Change, growth," I added with a grin, motioning to my head. "You did your job with me, and I think I turned out pretty okay—for the most part. Maybe the spontaneity could use a little reevaluation."

"Everywhere it counts." She patted the underside of her eyes dry with the pad of her finger and squeezed my shoulder.

There was more to talk about, a whole world of unpacking under the surface. I had a feeling my mom knew it'd only been scratched as well. As long as she was willing, I was hopeful. Even if the change didn't happen overnight. At least for the time being I'd unlocked a door that we could step inside.

"I hate to rush anyone," Phee cut in, fidgeting with her hands, "but we are seriously running low on time to get Nat ready and do photos before the ceremony."

"Oh, fuck." I checked the time on my phone. "Quick, bring it in, group hug." My sisters flitted a short distance across the room and wrapped their arms around us. Ophelia squeezed in, and Anna gussied up to her side. "You guys, too." I motioned for the photographer, the hairstylist, the makeup artist, and the coordinator. We were all huddled together like a team.

I had no idea how I was going to explain my impulsive new haircut to Mateo, who had seen me five hours before with a mane down my lower back. But I sure knew how to keep it interesting, and walking down the aisle to him was going to be interesting to say the least.

chapter forty-six

Mateo

THERE WERE three instances in my entire life that I felt complete and utter calm. When I was seven, my father carrying me half asleep from the car and tucking me into the warmth of my bed after a whole day at Coney Island. Again in Delta, the day our helicopter went down in South America with Pike in the pilot seat, because in those final moments with my brothers around me I had accepted death.

Then this moment.

Waiting for my bride to walk down the aisle to me.

The ceremony was everything Tally had planned. Cozy yet sophisticated, elegant and effortless. The ocean was the most jaw-droppingly beautiful backdrop to the altar, and a string quartet plucked away at their instruments while everyone was buzzing in anticipation in their seats.

Pike was beside me, Angelo rocking back and forth on the balls of his feet to his right, then Wink in his perfectly tailored suit and Echo adjusting the sleeves of his jacket because there wasn't one big enough to fit all of him just right.

"What time is it?" I murmured.

Pike flicked his wrist out to look at his watch. "Almost four."

Any minute now.

Frankie motioned me toward him to straighten my tie and

tuck my folded pocket square into the breast of my suit jacket. "So this is it, huh? You're leaving me for real. Name off the deed, mail forwarded, separate taxes next year."

A chuckle rolled out of me. "You're one to talk."

"How did this even happen?" he lamented with wide eyes and a grin. "One day it was just you and me watching *Trailer Park Boys* reruns on the living room couch, and now we've got these women spooling us around their fingers." Pike pointed to the string quartet. "Did you ever think you'd have a cellist at your wedding?"

I smirked, looking down at the remnants of a seashell cracking under the pressure of my shoe. "I'm about as fancy as a two-dollar slice and soda deal from the corner pizzeria."

"But you're a damn good time like one, too."

When Pike left for Colorado with Ophelia my brain always assumed he would be back, because we were side by side for fifteen years and it was something like losing a limb. Sometimes I walked into the kitchen and expected him to be there eating a bowl of cereal, or looked out the window and imagined he'd be mowing the lawn. I missed him being there all the time, but we were both exactly where life needed us. Going in different directions was the end of an era and the start of a new one.

"Are you going to cry?" he asked.

"Are you going to throw sand in my eyes?"

"O told me if you weren't crying on your own when you see Tally I have to."

I leaned away from him. "I believe that."

"Listen, if you cry it's going to rub off on me and I'm going to start crying. It's like when you see someone yawn and then you can't help but yawn, too."

"I think the more crying men around Tally, the better. She feeds off male fragility like a demon."

Pike chuckled. "Did I ever tell you that the two of you were made for each other?"

"You didn't have to." I gave him the most ear-splitting grin.

The string section splintered abruptly in the middle of a Taylor Swift cover and recouped to play the recognizable sound of "My Girl" by The Temptations. All the murmuring from the people in front of me hushed to a stop and heads turned toward the top of the aisle. My spine straightened. I sucked in a deep breath and held it in my chest until the sound of my heart was thumping in my ears.

I wasn't nervous, but there was something twisted about this level of anticipation that made my stomach feel like static.

My mom was the first person to come ambling around the corner of the trees, and I thought I had it together—I really fucking did— but that pure, proud look on her face was all it took to crack me. Goddammit, I thought I could at least hold out for Tal, but seeing Mom in that dress that was her favorite color of green, sparkling in the sun with a smile that made her eyes disappear, brought it all on like a wave. I'd never seen her in anything like it. I hadn't even seen her wear more than a dab of lipstick all my life. I peeked over at Ang and his eyes had glossed over as well, no doubt thinking the same string of things.

Sistine came next, glowing, warm, and tropical as she found a seat opposite my mom. Camilla walked slowly behind her in a black dress, then Bella ten steps later. The rhythm of my heartbeat was erratic by the time Mia took her turn smiling down the aisle, and Ophelia was just as emotional as I was with rosy cheeks and quivering lips the second she saw me standing at the end of the long path.

O blew Pike a whisper of a kiss and lined herself up on the other side of the officiant with a giant bouquet of white flowers resting between her hands. It was like the changing of the guards. There was some silent understanding between Ophelia and me that I'd given my best friend away to her last Christmas, and she was here returning the favor with Natalia now.

"I'll take good care of her, O," I murmured. That was a given, but I wanted to say it out loud. She sucked in a little breath and her eyes watered some more.

"Showtime, Cap." Pike nudged me as the guests began to stand and turn toward the open space where Tally floated into view between the palm trees.

Nothing could have properly prepared me for the moment I saw her in that white dress. She was so devastatingly beautiful that it almost brought me directly to my knees. I scrubbed my hand over my mouth and down my face, but it was fucking useless to hide my jaw falling open and the way I was damn near debilitated by her. She was my total undoing.

I blinked my eyes clear and I realized that she didn't only look beautiful, she looked different. Her hair was chopped to her neck in soft waves that sent my eyebrows skyrocketing and my pulse racing. It was bouncy and sharp, sexy and playful. I didn't even have time to question it, I was too busy shifting my attention from her head to her toes, taking it all in. I could spend all night admiring the details in her dress, and I would do that. I would trace every last bead with my fingertips, every single score of lace after that. There wasn't a world where I'd let this woman in this dress go unmemorized.

Her father was at her side, offering his elbow to hold, guiding her closer and closer to me. Tally was a diamond in lace; the curves of her body were a Renaissance painting, and I was a beggar just trying to exist beside her, still not entirely sure how I ended up the man privileged enough to be her husband.

Fire caught in my heart and burned up my throat, stinging my eyes until they were blurry with tears. I had to wipe them away as fast as they were falling just to make sure I didn't miss a second of her walking toward me.

While my eyes were transfixed on Natalia, the rest of the people were turned back around and trained on me. I could hear the sniffling under the melodic string music and say confidently that there wasn't a dry eye in the entire house. Not my mom, or Sistine, or the bridesmaids. Not the audience of distant cousins and hopeless romantic aunts, or Natalia's old bank coworkers, or the two women behind cameras making sure they got every single angle of the whole thing.

Pike's hand came down on my shoulders, consoling me with a tight-gripped shake and when I looked back, all four of the most masculine, hard-souled men I'd ever known were in total fucking shambles behind me.

That picture painted a thousand words.

But Tally, God, it was no wonder we were all in tears. The way she looked was religious. Churches would erect in her image; people would pray for a woman like her. She was my angel. I held my breath until she was standing directly in front of me and then forgot how to breathe entirely when she gave her father a curt kiss on the cheek and took her place beside me right where she belonged.

One tear swelled at the corner of her eye and rolled down her cheek. I flexed my hands and fought every urge to swipe it away.

"You're going to ruin your makeup," she whispered.

My breath rushed out of me in a laugh and all the blood in my body that had stilled in those hypnotic few minutes began pumping again. For her. Always for her.

"You are so gorgeous," I murmured back, reaching gently to tug the short strands of her freshly cut hair. I loved it. "Fun morning?"

"I'll explain later," she promised.

"You know how much I love our pillow talk."

The officiant cleared his throat between us and opened a thin binder of ceremony scripts and a blush crept up Tally's chest like she'd forgotten we weren't the only two people there. Because it felt like we were. It always did. Even in front of a thousand sets of eyes, it was only ever us.

"Are you ready to get married?" he asked. I wanted to laugh. So ready we'd already committed to it. So ready we were two tea kettles on the verge of boiling over trying to keep our arduous secret to ourselves.

I shot her a secret wink. "What do you say, Tal?"

"Let's do this thing." She nodded back.

Then I married my best friend for the second time, and when it was time to kiss her I held her face and swept her off her feet because it was the most natural thing in the world to have her cradled in my arms, crushed against my lips. And if I ever had the chance I would do it again.

And again, and again, and again.

chapter forty-seven

Natalia

NOT TO TOOT my own horn or anything, but my wedding was the best damn wedding I'd ever been to, and it wasn't even close. While I might have planned it with the sophisticated tastes of the richest Russos in mind, there were enough personal touches that the black-tie dress code still felt cozy and casual.

There were long elegant dining tables and string lights that swept above our heads from tree to tree. A dance floor was laid for an all-night party and cocktail hour was currently buzzing, which I was sorely sad to have missed the majority of while our bridal party took photos out on the beach. There was delicious expensive champagne in a seemingly endless supply. Every time I finished a flute there was another to replace it, and the music had even the oldest Durans spinning in circles between meal courses.

My heart had never been more full.

This was that feeling I'd been trying to convince myself that I deserved. As if speaking it into the universe made it real, I manifested this moment, this life, this love after such a long time standing in the dark. Once I started believing I could have it, something miraculous took over. I was closer to my sisters than ever, my relationship with my mother was mending, my father was sober, my friends were happy and healthy, and Mateo and I were husband and wife.

My world was healing itself, patching up the holes, rubbing dirt in the scratches, sewing thread through things that had torn and needed attention. I was coming out on the other side of these six months a fuller person than I was before it.

Natalia Duran.

Fuck, I loved saying that. It made my entire body giddy like it was hopped up on Pop Rocks. It just felt *right*.

The best part of the wedding though, by far, was watching my gorgeous husband float around the reception in that perfectly tailored suit that made my limbs feel weaker by the minute. He was so confident and charismatic, the perfect host, the most adoring partner, and I should have been focusing on other things, like chatting with guests or dancing with my bridesmaids, but all I could think about was the way his dress shirt hugged his chest and how I was going to run my tongue down every inch of skin behind those buttons later.

It was only a matter of time before Mateo caught me staring at him from the other end of the table, and his face lit up, a playful, wicked grin tantalizing me. He put his hand on the shoulder of the older woman he was talking to and she squeezed his arm back gratefully before he turned, in my direction.

"See something you like, Mrs. Duran?" Matty slid into the seat beside me at the head of the long table. There was a centerpiece in front of us that said Mr. and Mrs. and our chairs were draped in floral and gossamer ribbon. He laid his arm over the back of mine and rubbed soft circles over my skin until I erupted in goose bumps.

"How much longer until the consummation?"

His eyebrow lifted at the same time the corner of his lip did. "Good to know I'm not the only one who's been thinking about how quickly I can get that dress off you."

Heat and anticipation stirred in my lower half. I tugged his wrist toward me and made a show of staring at the watch he was wearing. I'd gifted it to him for his birthday last August and he almost never took it off, but it wasn't ticking at all. "Hey, I think your watch is broken."

Mateo was unsurprised. He glanced down at it and back up at me, shaking his head with a boyish grin and warm eyes. "It's not broken," he said. "I did that."

"Did what?"

"I stopped it from moving the second you said 'I do.' I wanted to immortalize it."

The shock of that curled around my lungs and impacted a place deep in my chest. I was speechless trying to process something so sentimental and romantic, and that he even thought to do it at all. He was still wearing it regardless of how useless it had become when he could have easily left it at home for another functional watch.

"In Vegas?" Emotion scratched up my throat.

"I'm surprised it took you this long to notice."

"I've been a little busy," I croaked. "I don't even know what to say."

There were no words proper enough. When I thought I'd reached the epitome of my husband, and there were no other things he could do to make me love him more, or respect him deeper as a person and a partner, he went and proved me wrong over and over again. There was no end in sight. Happy little surprises followed him in every direction we weaved.

This, though. *This* was something out of a movie.

Mateo laced our fingers on the table and leaned into me. Our noses brushed and our foreheads tilted together, boxing us out from the reception into our own little world briefly. "That's the thing, Tal. I'm never looking for anything in return. You love me loudly enough without words. Let me love you quietly too."

"I love you every way humanly possible."

He kissed me tenderly, feverishly, with a sweeping tongue and a moan on the cusp of his lips that only my ears could hear. It was over too soon, and when we sat back he felt miles away when all I wanted was to melt into him again.

Metal tinged against a glass softly and stole our attention, and we tracked it to Frankie in the center of the dance floor with a microphone in his hand.

"A little birdie told me I had to say something tonight as the best man."

Mateo sat up straighter, tugging the leg of my chair closer to him until I was basically sitting in his lap. Our other bridesmaids and groomsmen came shuffling back to the table to sit beside us, and the guests quieted for Frankie to continue.

"I'm generally a man of few words, and I don't do well with lots of eyes on me like this, but if there's anyone in the world I'd suck it up for, it's you, Cap."

Matty smiled wide enough to show off a dimple.

"For those of you that don't know, my name is Frankie, and up until January, Mateo and I lived together for almost fifteen years in and out of the military. So it's actually a miracle that it's not the two of us up there making out at the end of the dinner table."

Laughter erupted around us, and Frankie's shoulders dropped away from his ears. "Some people thought we were swinging the other way for a bit, so I'm glad Mateo decided to propose and finally clear the air about that. I was running out of ways to defend the length of his shorts to the neighbors next door."

"Nothing wrong with showing a little thigh!" Matty called out.

"Either way, to keep this short and sweet, because there's dancing to be done, and drinks to be had, and an ice sculpture by the oyster bar melting at a rate absolutely everyone in here saw coming—" He sobered, taking a deep breath, and then began again. "I'm so glad you found your person, Cap. There is no one more deserving of happiness in the world. You care so hard and so much for the people around you, and it's beautiful to see Natalia be that counterpart for you, and make you a better man, give you hell, and provide you new purpose all at the same time. And I knew it was you, Tally," he addressed me and my heart lagged a beat. "The day Cap saw you in the bank was the first real day of his life, and he never looked away again. If you're lucky, you guys will live a thousand lives together. I'm just honored to be here, a part of this one, having seen the two of you grow together from the beginning. I want to be there for every milestone, because you both mean the world to me. I'm going to say it was fate all along, because your happiness gave me mine." Frankie's soft smile and deep gaze swept to Ophelia. "I guess giving my best friend away isn't so bad if I'm giving him away to you, Natalia."

My nose stung all the way up to my eyes and I placed my hand over my heart, so grateful that we had such amazing people surrounding us. That peace of mind was worth more than Frankie knew. He picked a flute of champagne off the table and raised it, and Mateo's fingers tightened around mine.

"To the Durans!" he cheered, and a chorus of applause and clinking glasses followed.

Ophelia's chair scraped lightly against the wood floor as she pushed away from the table beside me with a folded piece of paper in her hand. "Who let him go first?" she grumbled. "I've been working on this for three months and he just winged that off the top of his head with nothing but a Red Bull and vodka."

"You'll do great!" I slapped her perky little ass on her way to the center of the floor where she stole the mic from her boyfriend. He looked both enamored and terrified of her all at once, and it was the most satisfying enigma to watch. She was the world's most conscientious woman and fell in love with the man who flew by the seat of his pants; they would balance each other out until the end of time.

"I'll rough him up for you, O," Tyler shouted, tugging Frankie down next to him and putting him in a headlock that split a grin across her face. What was it about weddings that made everyone sentimental? It wasn't like the boys weren't rowdy together in their own ways—we'd seen enough of that to outlast ten weddings—but there was a sense of something deeper between everyone.

Family.

Well, maybe not everyone. Definitely not Mia and Angelo, who hadn't so much as snarled at one another over their steaks the entire day. It was honestly for the best.

Ophelia tapped on the top of the microphone. "*Hellooo*," she sang into it, adding a curtsy that put a winsome smile on my face. Her long light brown hair curled over her shoulders and the pearls around her neck were the perfect timeless edition to her strapless black dress. "I'm Ophelia, the other best friend. We decided to do this funny little thing where we dated another pair of best friends, and now here we are in Key West making speeches."

A mumble of laughter washed over the tables. She looked down at her paper briefly and then folded it back up in her palm. "I was going to read this long-winded thing I wrote, and tell you all about how Natalia was in college and the way we became friends, and our embarrassing corkboard in our dorm room with pinned photos of Chris Evans on it. Which is equally as embarrassing when you think about the fact that Mateo was probably somewhere in a desert trying not to step on an IED at the same time."

"Are you calling my husband old?" I poked at her.

"I'm calling this all miraculous." She gestured around. "That we've all made it here to this exact moment, a series of perfectly timed events and circumstances that truly makes love feel exactly like magic. What happened for the two of you can only be described as that. I always thought Natalia would end up with someone who was the male version of me, to be quite honest." Another humored murmur sifted across the floor. "Someone who would make sure she doesn't sleep in too late, tell her she can't live off of iced coffee and the passing carb, and remind her that an inappropriate joke has a time and place, and one of those places is not while getting a bikini wax. But it turns out I was so wrong.

"What she needed was the person who was going to slow down life to be with her, not try to get her up to speed. The guy who would sleep in beside her until eleven, order that late-night takeout with no remorse, and be the Bob to her Lucille, even if it means traumatizing an unassuming esthetician. And Mateo is that man.

"You are absolutely perfect for each other. There are some things in life that find you when you expect them the least and need them the most, and sometimes you don't know what you need until it's standing right in front of you, and I think both of you ended up in the right place at the right time. I know every single person at that table agrees with me." She pointed to our wedding party, and everyone reacted with a smirk while biting their tongues.

"Before I screw this up, let's toast to you both." Glasses lifted into the sky. "For a love that lasts forever, and a party that lasts all night."

A *whoop* shot out of the crowd. It was Tyler; it was always Tyler. He was like a human ball of serotonin, but he worked the room as effortlessly as Ophelia nailed that off-the-cuff speech. Tyler stood like he was about to take his turn with the microphone but Sam grabbed him by the elbow and yanked him back down into his chair.

"I love you so fucking much." I leaned into a hug from Phee, squeezing her so tightly she couldn't breathe. "Both of you." I reached for Frankie next. "Seriously, this wedding wouldn't have been half as special without the two of you long-distance directing the entire thing and showing up every single time we needed you. We promise to repay the favor." My eyebrows wiggled at Frankie and I swore there was a faint blush and a hidden smile in return.

"If it weren't for everything I tried to plan going wrong, I don't think anything would have gone this right," she mentioned humorously. "It's been perfect, and you should reap the benefits of a well-earned reception by getting so drunk you pass out on the beach later. I'll be right there with you."

"Can I bring my husband?" I joked. Mateo's hand slid from my hip to my ass and gave it a small squeeze. I still hadn't stopped wondering what he'd look like naked with nothing but his wedding ring on his finger, so the gesture stirred something awake inside my lower belly again.

Shoving him into a cabana closet for a blow job was not entirely off the table.

Phee twisted her lips. "I guess he's invited."

"Then I'll be there with a bottle of rum and my pirate boy."

* * *

WE DANCED FOR HOURS, laughing, drinking, and fumbling over one another in the bathroom as my sisters and Phee tag-teamed unbuttoning my dress in the stall so I didn't pee myself—on more than occasion. The music was so electric that it thudded through our bones and roused our tipsy, satisfied friends and family to their feet. Even my parents, who I was pretty sure hadn't shared a dance since their own wedding, ventured out onto the floor to sway in each other's arms when it was time for Mateo and me to have our first dance. Tyler took my sisters with him on a conga line into the thrum of cousins and coworkers, and even my father-in-law came out with his shirt unbuttoned down his gray-haired chest to twirl Anna in circles under the twinkling lights.

I tossed my bouquet into a very energetic swarm of women, and like the fate she spoke about in her maid-of-honor speech, Ophelia caught it. She stuck her hand out and closed her eyes and the bramble of flowers landed perfectly in her open palm. So when Mateo sat me down in front of the entire squealing reception of people to slide his deft hands up the inside of my dress and work my white lace garter belt down to my ankle in the most lethally antagonizing way possible, he didn't even bother flinging it. He walked it right over to Frankie to fulfill the tradition.

"I think now is the perfect time to have the boys pay up for losing the scavenger hunt." Mia saddled up beside me with a sinful grin. Her body was glistening with a sheen of sweat from the dance floor, and her hair was clipped on top of her head, keeping her shoulders cool.

I'd completely lost track of time. It'd been at least an hour since I'd slow danced with Dad, and more than that since I had a conversation with Mateo. I searched the outside venue for our bridal party, counting them off on my fingers like sheep. Bella and Cami were sharing a conversation with our aunt Loren, Ophelia was with my mom, Mateo was already in a little huddle with his brother and Tyler and Frankie near the bar, and Sam was nowhere to be found—though he was presumably with his date, Hailey, who was also missing when I glanced around for her, which could only mean one of two things.

They both excused themselves to the bathroom separately, or they excused themselves to the bathroom together, and there was only one way to find out.

I borrowed the microphone from the DJ and he cut the sound that was playing with the scratch of a record. "I'm requesting a much-anticipated group dance from the grooms-men," I called out. Mateo and the other three at the bar deflated on a whim, like pulling a pin out of a balloon. "You didn't think we'd forget about the bet, did you?"

Mateo did the same cursory glance I did a minute ago, scanning the entire reception space looking for Sam. His results were the same as mine. "We can't do it without Wink." He shrugged, delighted by that change in fortune. "Sorry, baby."

"Sam Swan, you are being summoned!" I announced through the speakers. "You can shove your tongue back down her throat later!"

There was a yelp by the oyster bar, and then a commotion of dishes and silverware that whipped me and everyone else around toward the noise, seconds before the unthinkable happened and the massive flamingo-shaped ice sculpture crashed legs over feathers onto the floor. Shards of ice ricocheted as far as the toe of my heels.

"Well, throwing a temper tantrum about it seems a little dramatic," Tyler commented.

Hailey was standing there in her long red dress, reaching her arms out toward the mess, eyes wide and mouth agape. She looked a second away from breaking down in tears from embarrassment while the venue staff rushed around her with a broom to sweep it off the platform and into the sand. "I am so, *so* sorry," she managed to squeak out. Sam stood behind her, fingers laced together at the back of his head. His pale cheeks were dusted pink, and his neck corded on a long swallow.

The sculpture falling left me momentarily speechless, but then the shock turned into pure, unbridled amusement and a cackle bubbled from my throat, cutting into the awkward, pregnant silence. As soon as I started laughing, everyone else did, too, as if they were granted permission. Hailey's body relaxed slightly, though she was still clearly mortified by what had happened, and I couldn't blame her for that. I would have felt the same way in her shoes. Getting caught doing *whatever* I was doing with my date, and then taking out an expensive, frankly obnoxious wedding decoration, was going to go on her list of most embarrassing moments, if not shoot straight to the top.

I, on the other hand, couldn't have cared less about the damn thing. Three months ago, this would have sent me into a spiral. But letting go of the expectation around the wedding had made even a pretty massive flub the least of my worries.

"Hey, at least it wasn't the cake," I said to her, throwing a shrug and a warm, understanding smile. "We were just going to send Pinky off to sea later anyway. This was so much more Shakespearean. I personally live for theatrics."

"I swear I'll pay for that," she promised. Her fists were balled together, and she was looking at Sam with such hopelessly apologetic blue eyes it made me want to drag her behind the ice sculpture and kiss her, too.

"I'll take care of it, Tally. It was my fault." Sam took the blame.

I'd never seen him so frazzled in his life, and not by the unfortunate accident—by the woman in front of him. I could nearly see his pulse beating out of the vein in his neck. He reached out to put a hand on the small of her back, but decided differently, and my brows pinched together. I'd make my own assumptions and leave the rest alone; these things always had a funny way of working themselves out.

"I'm collecting payment right now, Casanova." I beckoned him over and Mateo and the rest of the groomsmen made their way to the wide-open dance floor, ravenous for the opportunity to give him hell. Frankie and Tyler took turns shouldering Sam until he was so beet red and blushing that I was worried for his health. Eventually they split into two halves facing one another, Mateo on one side with Sam and Frankie, Tyler and Angelo on the other.

"Don't say I never did anything for you," Mateo tossed my way with a sweet smirk. Little did he know that taking the loss for the Elvis impersonator had earned my selfless husband a free pass to anything he wanted for life. Which was just as thrilling for me when I thought about it, because that man lived to please.

I joined my sisters and Phee back at the table to watch the reward of our hard-won scavenger hunt with a front-row seat. The music sparked to life, playing the first few jazzy notes of a classic Beyoncé song.

"Don't blink, ladies," I said.

My chest swelled with nervous, excited anxiety, the overwhelming kind that felt like adrenaline but wasn't quite. Cellphones around the room were lifted and recording, and our photographer was zeroing in on the dance floor.

Someone, somewhere, was fighting with their significant other to hold open a door for them. Mine was dance battling against his military buddies like the Wayans brothers in wigs in front of two hundred people to see me crack a smile.

And they *really* fucking did that.

Or something vaguely reminiscent of that. They might not have synchronized at any given point during the entire thing, and

I was pretty sure the threads holding Tyler Swan's pants together split while he was trying to do a flip that would feel like a train hit him in the morning, but the comedic timing was worth every muscle ache and back spasm. Sam committing to breakdancing after a few too many liquor drinks and a filet mignon dinner was really the cherry on top, proving all the expected effort was there.

It would have been tragic if we'd lost the bet, based solely on the fact that there was nothing we could recreate that would top watching my brother-in-law erotically slap his own ass in front of his grandmother.

We were on our feet applauding them, making it metaphorically rain, and when the music hit its final beat Mateo looked right at me with my favorite smile, a crinkle of happiness creasing his eyes, and blew me a kiss.

It felt like a lie now every single time I said it, but I had never loved him more than I did in that moment.

* * *

MATEO LED me to a small round table at the far edge of the reception space where our wedding cake was on display. Just beyond it, the floor let off into the sand and a small private beach. Waves broke gently onto the shore, illuminated by the string lights hanging off the trees. You could see every star in the sky, each blinking light of a passing plane, the full, spectacular moon. All the noise around us dulled.

"Was it everything you ever wanted?" he asked.

What a loaded question. This day? Our week? The last six months? Or maybe the past year and a half of my life that was like something out of a storybook? Not the Disney kind, the kind you had to ask the bookstore clerk about without looking them in the eyes. Still storybook, technically.

With any of those, though, my real answer would be, no, it wasn't. It was nothing like what I wanted when I was sixteen, or eighteen. Definitely not at twenty-two, or even at twenty-five.

Because I hadn't known what I wanted until it happened exactly the way it did. I hadn't known I wanted *hard* love. The kind you worked at and fought for. The kind that made you question why you ever settled for anything less than it before, and made sure you never settled for it again. We were two completely flawed people, and that hadn't magically ended when we met. We just learned how to love each other through those things. Not in lieu of them.

Everything I'd ever wanted was standing in front of me.

"It was more than that," I told him. "Even after the hair, and the sculpture, because it wouldn't have been *us* if everything went right. Too boring."

"Entirely." Matty picked the long knife up off the table and the soft white linen napkin it was wrapped in. Two little people embraced on the top of the two-tiered, marbled buttercream cake.

It was bittersweet, watching it all come to an end after the roller coaster ride to get here. One day went by in the snap of a finger after what felt like years of work, and tomorrow we'd go back home and continue life as just the two of us. The quiet solitude was already creeping in like the Sunday scaries. As ready as I was to resume our life and be able to enjoy one another fully, I could feel myself already mourning this unique time in our lives that we'd never experience again. As if it was a time capsule we'd been filling and now it was time to bury it.

I was somehow nostalgic for the present.

That would change. I knew the feeling would wash away, because our future was already building its blocks in front of us. Anna and David would be living down the road, and all the wheels were in motion for Angelo to join us when the time was right. There was a brightness ahead making up for lost time with my family, and turning the house Mateo and I lived in into our home. We had clients to make magic for, ideas to see through, dreams to bring to life.

The possibilities were an endless, invigorating blank slate, and I couldn't wait to get started.

"We did it," I said. "Butt naked and screaming, but we did it."

"Don't get me hard while I'm cutting the cake, Tal. Everybody's looking at us."

My mouth twisted into a grin, and I put my hand over Mateo's on the knife as he guided it to the cake and made the first cut while our closest friends and family gathered watching. He swiped a dollop of icing onto his finger and held it out in front of my lips for a taste.

"Didn't you just say not to get you hard?" I murmured. He plopped the buttercream onto the tip of my nose with a deep chuckle and dark eyes challenging me, and his perfect teeth split into a full, breathtaking smile. The sweet smell of sugar wafted through over me. "You don't know what you started."

I swept some more icing off the top of the cake and dabbed it onto Matty's nose, smearing it down and across his cheek. He gasped, breathy and amused, and tried to wipe it off but got even more of it on the sleeves of his dress shirt instead. "Oh, come here, baby. Give me a kiss."

Mateo caught me by the wrist when I turned to dodge him and planted his lips smack onto mine, rubbing his nose and his cheek across my face in a messy waterfall of kisses. I reached out blindly and took a handful of the cake and smashed it into his hair, giggling like a maniac. He grunted out a complaint though I felt his smile against my skin, and a moment later there was another generous helping of our delicious and expensive wedding cake being rubbed into my face and neck.

"Man, you look good enough to eat," he joked, running his lips down my neck and licking icing off my chest until I was laughing so hard I could cry.

"Tally, your dress!" Phee called out. She was smiling and laughing, too, hanging onto the moment like a thread the same way I would if it were her and Frankie. The front of my dress was covered in cake and getting more ruined by the second and I threw my hands up, too happy to care.

"We can wash it off," Mateo suggested. "I could use a bath,

too." There was mischief in his expression, a light in his pupils that only sparked that way when he was about to get himself into trouble. I recognized it and took two steps onto the sand, back out of his reach, but it was too late already. He came after me with a wicked smile dimpling his face.

I shrieked and turned, running in the opposite direction, as if I could somehow outlast him in a race, and it took no time at all for my husband's strong, tight arms to wrap around me and lift me straight off the ground and over his shoulder, headed toward the waves.

"Mateo Duran!" I cackled.

His sweet laugh filled my ears as he kicked out of his dress shoes and flung my heels off my feet. I weakly lashed against his back with my tiny fists. "Yes, wife?"

Then we were submerged in sand and saltwater, suit and dress and all. I clung to Mateo and wrapped my legs around his waist. So much for the dress, for the hair and makeup, for the cake, the perfect wedding, the drama-less bachelorette party. So much for keeping all our secrets, and walking through life unscathed. I liked this version of it much, much better.

"Full moon tonight," I pointed out.

"I wasn't going to admit it, but I told the sky guy that I wanted to give my girl the moon, and he's shown up every single time."

My fingers swept into his damp hair. "I love you."

"I love you too, Natalia Duran."

Mateo's eyelashes were wet, and the moonlight highlighted his lips and jaw so perfectly when I leaned down to kiss him. Our mouths parted and our tongues swept carefully and intentionally against each other. My senses were consumed with him, brain blank, chest heaving. I gave him all of me. It was a kiss that said, *I'm home.*

Hooting and shouting came from the beach and we parted just in time to watch our entire wedding party—Frankie and O,

Angelo, my sisters, the Swans—in all their clothed glory break the water's edge and follow us into the waves.

My cheeks hurt from laughter but I threw my head back and laughed some more. People believed in magic because of moments like this. *Love* was magic. Love was family. It was earned, found. Love was simple. It hurt, it healed, it made you crazy. Love was raw and untamed. Love was whispers in crowded rooms, broken glass, crying so hard you couldn't breathe. Love was howling at the moon.

Mateo sunk his hand into the wet hair at the nape of my neck and pressed his forehead into mine. "I think this is the second best day of my life."

"So far," I said.

"So far," he agreed.

epilogue

Mateo

3 months later

THE MOVING truck whined as I hopped down onto the street with the last box of things from my parents' house in the Bronx. Angelo had driven eighteen hours behind the wheel of a twenty-six-foot U-Haul to follow them down to their new place in Pompano and help unload and move them in. Sweat dripped from my temples and down my back beneath an old cut-off Army T-shirt, and my hands clammed up underneath the cardboard as I lugged it inside and dropped it on the long marble island next to forty other ones.

September in South Florida was consistently hot, and we'd hit a record-high heat wave just in time to take a hundred trips in and out of a box truck instead of riding it out in the comfort of an air-conditioned house. The one Mom and Dad bought was a two-story, three-bedroom with an office and a garage. Enough back-yard space to add a pool if they wanted to, and a neighbor on one side instead of two. They could take a long stroll to mine and Tally's if they felt like it, or hop in the car and be on our doorstep before a Billy Joel song played all the way through.

"Last one?" Mom was twirling around in her brand-new kitchen, stacking plates in the cupboards as she unpacked them. It was weird to see her in a place that wasn't our childhood home. The dishes were the same off-white ceramic I used to eat off of in the small confines of our breakfast nook, and the coffee mugs were the same mismatched souvenirs from vacations growing up. Now they sat in newly sawed-off, builder-grade cabinets next to a stainless steel refrigerator that didn't showcase our Little League photos or house any handmade magnets.

"That's the last of it," I told her. She opened the fridge and tossed a can of beer out of the lone box sitting in it at me, and I took it to go as I walked out the back door.

After the wedding, Tally and I went on a two-week honeymoon out of the country to the Caribbean. It was exactly the decompression we needed to reconnect on a primitive level. It was like returning to our base selves after a period of heightened stress. We barely left the hotel room for the whole first week. I was inside of her more than I was out. We woke up and fucked. Ordered room service and fucked. We fucked in the shower while we washed off the fucking from before the shower. It was hedonistic and borderline primal, but it reminded me just how much I missed her for the six months we were living under the same roof yet somehow miles away.

We even managed to livestream a few times for our subscribers on the cam page. They loved the change of scenery, and for the first time in a long time, pressing record didn't feel like a job we had to finish before time ran out.

Life had resumed to perfectly normal. I saw Dr. Brinckler at the VA bi-weekly, and our talks stayed informative and entertaining, filling in my void of insecurity with tools and techniques instead. Seeing a therapist turned from a chore into a bright spot in my schedule, and if I didn't know any better I'd have said Henry and I were friends. He regularly turned down my offer for a drink outside office hours, but chuckled when I brought him a real grocery list notepad as a gift.

TechOps was thriving, and Angelo was committed to taking night classes on the basics of cyber security, malware, coding, and computer hygiene to be ready to take on a job with me when he came down to Florida. My parents went back home after Key West and put their house on the market, and it sold for over asking price in less than a week. It took a few months to negotiate contracts and empty out the house, and that gave Angelo enough time to close out his open contracts with Duran & Son and finally pull the chain on the sign above the door. The end of an era, and the start of a new one. It had become a theme.

He was up in the air about a living situation, but had saved more than enough money having never paid rent to put his own down payment on a house somewhere around here, too.

In the backyard my brother was lying on the concrete patio helping Dad screw together the new outdoor furniture with a cigarette between his teeth. His shirt was riding up his stomach, and his boots still had dirt on them from job sites up north that he hadn't bothered to clean.

"I thought you quit." I kicked his shoe and a crumble of dried mud fell off.

"Ask me again in a month," he mumbled. "Hand me that flathead."

I sucked on my teeth and swiped the screwdriver out of an open toolbox, handing it to him. My dad was working on the legs of a table and I crouched down to hold two pieces together while he twisted at an awkward angle with an Allen key.

"So what are you going to do first, Pop? Get a boat for the marina? Join the golf league?"

My parents had paid off their home years ago, so any money they had left over from the sale of the house after buying the new one went straight into their pocket. Not to mention union pension and social security benefits that my dad earned from over forty years of labor.

Metal clattered onto the concrete beside me and Angelo mumbled out a pointed "Fuck you" to a piece of the chair.

"You can join the country club," I added.

Dad sat up with a groan of exertion. His knees cracked as he stretched them out and stood on his feet. I took over, lifting the finished table off its side and centering it beneath the backyard awning for him. "I think I'll enjoy some sunrises out here with your mom first," he said. "Maybe a bike ride."

"That's a great idea." I saw a lot of me and Tally in my parents, that unwavering love that relied on the simple things like watching the sunrise together. Feeling gratitude for life, showing up for each other. In thirty years she and I would be side by side in our porch chairs, or reading a book on a hammock swing after dinner, and that would be enough for me.

"You should get one of those tandem bikes," Ang cut in. "Or no, what about a motorcycle with a little sidecar on it? We'll get Mom a neck scarf and a little helmet with the goggles."

"Bet you regret offering him a place to stay now," I said to my father.

"Clock's ticking," he replied. "He's got a month to find something."

"You know of any good realtors around here?" Angelo asked with the faintest uptick in his voice.

"Not unless you'd like a realtor who scratches your eyeballs out with her claws if you glance at her the wrong way." If he was stupid enough to look for a real estate agent in Mia, that was what he would get. She fucking hated his guts after what happened in Vegas.

His shoulders shook and he put a hand over his chest. "*Oooh*, that gave me tingles all over the place just thinking about it. Maybe I am your brother after all."

My eyes thinned, but my phone started ringing in my pocket before I could say anything else. I fished it out and saw Tally's photo on the screen.

"Hey, baby."

"Can you come up here?"

There was a knock on a window that drew my eyes to the second floor of the house. Tally was standing in it looking down at me with her phone to her ear.

"Everything okay?" I tilted my head.

"Um..." She looked backward and put the tip of her thumb between her teeth.

I turned away from my dad and brother and spoke quietly. "Did you clog the toilet?"

"Oh my god, no. Just—hurry up, Jesus."

She was upstairs organizing the hallway bathroom, putting up curtains and stocking the closet full of towels and extra toiletries. We'd had two months to get used to the idea of Mom and Dad being back in Pompano Beach for good, but a lot had changed since then. Tally was regularly seeing her sisters and stopping by her parents' place in the Palms to check in on her dad. The concept of family in such a close physical and emotional vicinity was once foreign and uncomfortable for the both of us, but Natalia was taking it in stride. She was determined to make up for lost time and build traditions not just for us, but for everyone. She'd even offered to host Thanksgiving at our house as the first big holiday with both of our families combined.

I stepped over a plethora of half-opened boxes and linens that had exploded the second the tape was cut. She was standing in the rectangular room in my favorite cut-off shorts and a loose T-shirt with her back pressed against the vanity.

"What's wrong?"

Tally lunged forward, dragging me by my shirt inside and pushing the door closed in one fell swoop. Her breathing was ragged, and her chest rose and fell without a pattern as she locked the door. I was reading the signs and they all led to one thing.

"In my parents' brand-new bathroom?" I whispered. It wasn't going to stop me, but at least the thought proved I hadn't fully rappelled into hell yet. I took two steps forward, intending to lift her onto the sink, but she shoved something into the center of my chest instead.

I blinked down at a pregnancy test.

Every nerve ending in my body started to sizzle and my mind went completely blank. Stomach hollowing, no air in my lungs, no cohesive thoughts in my brain. I didn't know what I was looking at apart from the fact that it was a long stick with a test window and two glaringly bright pink lines.

"Are you...?"

Tears welled in her pretty brown eyes, and she bit down on her quivering lip. "Yes."

"Yes," I repeated. Then again, as if confirming it with my frontal lobe. "Yes. Holy fuck. *Holy fuck.*" My hands shot straight to her face, thumbs caressing the falling joyful tears, and I yanked her mouth to mine, kissing her over and over again. Her lips, her cheeks, her head.

"I had this feeling this morning, I can't explain it. I knew something was up because I'm always so consistent on my period but it's three days late." She stumbled over her words trying to get them out while her voice shook. "So before I came here, I stopped and picked up a pregnancy test. I wasn't going to take it until we got home later, but I couldn't stop thinking about it all day. I needed to know."

"That's okay," I rushed out. "That's fine, Tal." My eyes drifted down her body and settled on her stomach. It was flat and soft, and of course I knew there was nothing there to see or feel, and whatever cells were budding inside of her wouldn't be noticeable for weeks, if not months. But our baby was there, the baby we made, half of Tally and half of me, growing right on the other side of such a small barrier. I dropped to my knees and skated my fingertips beneath her shirt, lifting it just enough to press my lips to the spot beneath her belly button.

"That's our baby." She giggled down at me with wet eyes and rosy cheeks, tangling her fingers in my hair. "We should keep it to ourselves at least for the first twelve weeks, just to be cautious."

"Not even Pike and Ophelia?" I asked.

"They just got engaged. Let's celebrate that for a little while before we spring the news on them."

"Of course." I swallowed hard. "Anything you need. Are you feeling okay? Sick? Do you need to take a rest or—"

"Mateo, I'm perfectly fine," she assured me, smiling so big it stopped my heart for a moment. I had no idea what to expect, or how to act. This was totally new and a cave had opened in my stomach, filling with what felt like wings fluttering in circles. "I'm so happy right now."

An elated breath skittered out of me onto her skin. I kissed her stomach again, wrapping my arms around her hips and holding tighter than I ever had before. It wasn't only the two of us anymore; it was so much bigger than that. Everything had changed, and I was ready for it. It felt like I was born for it. My heart doubled in size in an instant to make room for all the love I was holding for our child already.

"Is this the new best day of our lives?"

"So far." Tally beamed.

The one thing I was sure of was that every best day of my life belonged to her.

The End.

acknowledgments

Each book takes a legion of people, and I've grown more and more appreciative of my support system the more I do this because they are truly keeping me afloat. Especially after a book like this one takes a year more than I anticipated to finish.

Firstly, my husband, the greatest man on earth, who I couldn't juggle anything without, keeps me sane, fed, reminds me to shower, sits down and reads my stories and tells me wonderful, uplifting things about them. Joe you are everything to me.

My kids, I do it for you, one day your mom being a romance author will be a really cool fun fact.

My parents who check on me when I'm spreading myself thin and flaunt me around in the most embarrassingly loving way.

My in-laws, who made time in their schedules to take the kids when I needed peace and quiet, and did whatever they could to get me across this finish line of this never-ending marathon.

Kelli Mazanec, I don't know what the heck I'd do without you and your friendship. I am continuously amazed that I am lucky enough to have you.

Makenna—my magician of an editor, I am kneeling at your altar for the grace you give me and the invaluable work you do.

Finally, Anna, I know I can always count on you and I'm indebted to you forever and always for the love you've shown to me and my books.

about the author

Karissa Kinword is an international bestselling author of contemporary romance and sci-fi love stories with equal parts heat and heart. She accredits her inspiration to an early love for literature, fanatically obsessive personality, and innate fascination with the human condition. Storytelling has always been one of her life's greatest passions.

She writes and lives in the Hudson Valley of New York with her IRL book-husband and three rowdy children, experiencing the greatest happily ever after of all-time every day.

also by karissa kinword

Dirty Delta series

Christmas in Coconut Creek